BLOOD ON THE SCARECROW

Blood On The
Scarecrow

🐾 🐾 🐾 🐾 🐾 🐾 🐾 🐾

Glenn Canning

PALMETTO
PUBLISHING

Charleston, SC
www.PalmettoPublishing.com

Blood on the Scarecrow
Copyright © 2022 by Glenn Canning

All rights reserved

Hardcover ISBN: 979-8-88590-838-2
Paperback ISBN: 979-8-88590-839-9
eBook ISBN: 979-8-88590-840-5

Dedication

✹ ✹ ✹ ✹ ✹

This book is dedicated to Jan. My wife, my best friend, my world.

Acknowledgments

🐾 🐾 🐾 🐾 🐾

I would like to thank all my friends who over the years, have labored through my dreadful drafts!

Nancy Belle
John Drennan
Jim Foley
Frank Gangl
Colleen Goerlich
Brian MacDuff
Jason O'Toole
Cher Smith
Pat Wardensky

A special thanks to Palmetto Publishing:
Elizabeth P., Editor
Joseph M., Cover Illustrator
Erin M., Project Manager
Jack J., Owner

Prologue

JULY 27, 1985

BAXTER FALLS, CONNECTICUT

Sean smacked his hand on the black vinyl dashboard to kick-start the air conditioning. The scorching rays filtered through the windshield, turning the sedan into a microwave. Sean lowered the window and accelerated the car. The dog days of summer had finally arrived. A quick whiff of a farmer fertilizing his fields caused him to roll up his window promptly.

As tiny droplets collected on his bushy eyebrows, Sean said feverishly, "I'm sorry, I know I promised you, but I just can't take it any longer." His right hand slid off the steering wheel and struggled to remove his thin black tie, anchored by two silver pins adorned with F. D. He violently repositioned the rearview mirror as the vehicle veered toward the shoulder.

"Sean, please keep your eyes on the road," Blair pleaded. "I never get to see you in your uniform. You promised. How about a compromise? I'll let you take it off, but when we get to my parents' house, put it back on, at least for the ten minutes we're there, okay?"

"I thought it would be a quick picture and a birthday gift. But now it's developed into a family portrait and visiting your parents. Will this day ever end?"

"It's the chief that set up the appointment for your portrait. The Elks requested the picture for the awards ceremony. I thought it'd be nice to have a family portrait. My parents are so hard to buy for, and it would make a great Christmas present. They do so much for us and ask so little. Besides, I don't want to go. We need to go. Mom keeps asking how I'm feeling lately, and I think she suspects something. We should tell them we're expecting. And with her starting chemo soon, she needs some happy news. Dad keeps calling, asking when I will pick up the car seat. He feels so guilty for breaking the old one."

Sean pulled over to the breakdown lane and shifted the car into park. He removed the tie and unbuttoned the top collar on his white oxford shirt. "Ahh, that feels so much better," Sean sighed. He lovingly looked at his wife of six years, his kindred soul, a person who knew all his quirks and embraced rather than changed them. He studied her face and her long auburn hair, pulled back and arranged in a French braid complete with a blue ribbon. Her striking green eyes and fair Irish complexion completed the vision. He wondered where he'd be without her—Blair's innate ability to defuse any situation, whether through words or silence, spoke volumes. Today, for whatever reason, she seemed to have a special aura about herself. He couldn't put his finger on it. Blair always focused on the positives in life, and today was no exception.

Blair gently stroked his wool jacket. "I'm so proud of you," she cooed.

"I'm embarrassed by it. I do my job like everyone else at the station. Why did they single me out? What's so special about me? I'm sure your dad's behind this. The captain's excited about the publicity our station is receiving, but with your dad being the Grand Poobah or Imperial Wizard or whatever he is, it seems like nepotism."

"Listen, wiseass, my dad's not a water buffalo, nor does he socialize with Fred and Barney, and as far as an imperial wizard, he's not a member of the Klan. There's no racist bone in his body, and he'd be highly incensed if he heard your remarks. When we go over there, please do not bring this up." She glanced over at Sean and saw him biting his lower lip to conceal amusement. "It is an honor to be nominated as fireman of the year by the Elks; it's the first time they've honored somebody. The lodge event sold out, and they're very excited. Even the mayor is coming. By the way, the exalted ruler submitted your name, not my dad; he's only the leading knight. Next year it's his choice. They will let him make a speech and present you with the award. Dad's very proud of being an Elk and even prouder of you. He's going to ask you to join next year, but please don't let on that I told you. Tell him you need some time to think if you decide you don't want to join."

"How much longer till we get there?" Sean asked.

Blair replied, "About two more miles, and we'll be taking a right on Whiting Lane. It's the third house on the left, gray with burgundy shutters. Don't worry. I've already picked out the one I want. She mailed me some pictures last week. I'm so excited."

Sean readjusted the rearview mirror, checked the side mirror, and slowly pulled back onto the road.

"A penny for your thoughts," Blair said.

"Do you really want me to tell you? I'm thinking about the truck." He pushed up his sleeve and glanced at his watch. "You know Jack's going to be over in an hour, and we're not going to make it. The parts were part of a back order, and now that they're here, I'm anxious to get them installed. I've already canceled on Jack twice, and I can't do it again. He's a very busy man."

"And you're not? You have family and commitments too. Why don't you call him from my parents' house and tell him you'll be a half hour late? He'll understand. Tell him to let himself in to the garage and have a beer, and you'll be there soon. If there's one thing I know about firefighters, it's beer! Sometimes I think you love that truck more than me."

"I've had the truck longer," he quipped.

Sean glanced in the rearview mirror and saw a white vehicle approaching at a high rate of speed. He put his foot on the accelerator and sped up.

"Sean," Blair screamed as she dug her fingernails in her husband's thigh. "What are you doing? Slow down! I'm sure Jack will wait."

"It's not that; it's these idiots behind me. They keep speeding until they're right on my ass and then slow down. I don't know why they keep doing this shit."

"Then pull over to the side and let them pass. It's not worth it," Blair exclaimed. "Just let them pass, and I'll take down the license plate number and let my dad handle it."

"I can tell you the license plate; it's TRBL. Trouble! Tommy Spencer. Your dad and every other police officer know about him and his white Mustang. I think he's gonna be a senior this year."

"How do you know him?" Blair asked.

"Last year, he got caught pulling the fire alarm at the school. The chief and I went to reset the system. We talked to the principal about the kind of a person Tommy is. He remarked that he was a popular, well-mannered, smart student who underachieved and occasionally acted up. He enjoyed being the center of attention. His father treated these antics like the trial of the century, with his son always innocent. The principal rarely saw the mother and doubted Tommy ever got reprimanded. I talked to Tommy and found him friendly, polite, and overly charming reminded me of an Eddie Haskell type. He did reassure me no more alarms and understood the severity of his actions."

Sean flicked his right turn signal and pulled to the side of the road. The white car sped past them, and the front passenger pulled down his pants and mooned them.

Sean grew quiet. His jaw tightened; he wanted to say something but didn't know how to express himself. He had reached the end of his rope.

"Sean, remember, you were young once. Nobody got hurt, so let it pass."

Sean nodded and looked over at her. She was clad in a blue-and-white floral dress, and he said, "Did I tell you today you look stunning? You're the prettiest girl I know. How did I ever get so lucky? I especially like the French braid!"

"The last time I wore my hair this way, this happened." She patted her belly. "I know you love this dress. Unfortunately, I won't be wearing it after today for quite a while. I appreciate the compliment, but I'm feeling fat."

Blair gently stroked his navy-blue wool double-breasted jacket and slung it over the seat. "It's a shame you don't get to wear it more often. The only time I get to see you in this is when you march in the parade." She slumped in her seat and slowly picked up Sean's white forage cap.

"Please don't." Sean's tone changed from sweet poetry to the demeanor of a father reprimanding his daughter.

Before Sean could finish his sentence, Blair put on the hat and exclaimed, "Look at me! I feel like I should be in a parade!"

"Blair, take it off, now!" he demanded. "That's a bad omen. Nobody's supposed to wear someone else's hat."

"You're being overdramatic with all your silly superstitions. I was just trying to have a little fun and lighten your grumpy mood."

"Everybody's superstitious, whether it's a black cat or walking under a ladder. Firefighters face tragedy daily and are hypersensitive to any jinx. Superstitious or not, we never, and I repeat, never, exchange gear."

"Not even for me? I'm your wife, for God's sake," Blair said.

"I've told you a thousand times not to wear it; what are you, an idiot? Haven't you noticed I never say goodbye to you? I'll always say, see you later, or I love you."

Blair was silent. He glanced over, her body had stiffened, and her eyes squinted as she stared straight ahead. Sean thought it was as though he had hit pause on his favorite movie.

The silence continued. He grabbed the directions from between the seats. Sean realized he had lost his cool, but he couldn't back down from Blair. She had no idea how sacred these superstitions were. Not just to him but to all his fellow workers. Sean had always treated her with respect, but her cavalier attitude put him at his wit's end. Maybe he'd gone a little too far. But he believed in karma, and he never liked testing fate. She just didn't get it. Perhaps now she would.

Sean readjusted the mirror and looked in the back seat, and his face softened. Blair is my world, he thought. I need to rectify this, and I don't know how to do it. Was it childish of me to snap at her? Should I apologize? If yes, how?

He quickly pulled back onto the street. As he rounded a corner, he noticed the Shelby parked on the side of the road, its occupants watering the grass. To soothe his anger, he laid on the horn for five seconds. Sean laughed as they saluted his vehicle with their middle finger.

Sean stumbled for the exact words to express how he felt. Sure, superstition seemed childish, but it wasn't just him that believed. The whole department did. Telling Blair, he was sorry was never enough in this case, and no magic words could get him out of the situation. He needed a solution—fast. Sean knew that his father-in-law could spot tension in a heartbeat; it was just the cop in him, especially when it was his family, let alone his baby. Maybe she deserved to be chastised, Sean thought, but calling her an idiot was unforgivable.

Traffic backed up as they neared the intersection. Sean surmised the noon church service was getting out. He glanced in the rearview and spotted a white vehicle dodging through traffic like a contestant in the game *Frogger*. Sean heard horns behind him, and what started as a smattering of noise turned into a full choir. The Shelby pulled out in front of him and brake checked, which caused Sean to stop. Once again, Blair's icy stare stopped Sean from making any countermoves. To help soothe his frustration, he would deliver revenge later when no one was around. *I'm gonna teach this kid a lesson someday,* he thought.

This game of cat and mouse proceeded for the next half mile. As Sean's sedan neared an intersection, the white car slowed to a crawl. The Shelby sped up as the light turned yellow, leaving Sean stuck at the red light. Sean smacked the steering wheel several times with his right hand.

"What's wrong with you?" Blair screamed. "You're as immature as those morons. Would you please grow up and start acting like an adult? Your actions are going to put our family in danger. They will remember this car and take out their frustrations on it someday, probably when I'm driving. I know you're mad, but don't let your temper cloud your judgment. Just cut the shit and drive carefully. If you can't, then I'll drive. And lose the attitude. You've got a family—a four-year-old and one on the way. You've got to be a role model."

Sean nodded. He knew Blair had reached the end of her rope, and her use of profanity confirmed it. "I'm sorry. When we get to your parents' house, I'll call Fred and cancel. I've waited this long for the part; what's another couple of days? We'll make this a family day and spend the rest of our time with your parents."

Sean knew that Blair enjoyed surprises, not expensive gifts, or exotic travels. Still, presents that meant something took a lot of thought, even inexpensive items like reenacting their first date at the malt shop or parking at their favorite spot at the drive-in with a cold six-pack. Sean reached into the glove compartment and hid what he had pulled out with his large hand. It was a cassette that contained their favorite song. If this doesn't do the trick, he thought, nothing will. Music had been an intricate part of their lives, and certain songs had served as markers for their accomplishments. Nobody embraced music more than Blair. Similar tastes had bonded them together.

He inserted the cassette. The track rewound to start at a particular song. The hair on the back of Sean's neck stood up and goose bumps rose on his arms as he heard the opening refrains of their favorite song. It was the first they had heard after professing their love for each other. It was the first music they had danced to as a married couple. A sweet love song rarely heard on the radio. He knew it would melt the coldest heart, but most importantly, his wife could not resist the urge to sing along. Kenny Nolan opened with, "I love you so much." Sean turned to his wife and mouthed the words in her direction.

"I'm sorry, Blair. I'm the idiot. That was uncalled for." He started singing along with the music; by the third stanza, Blair joined him and grabbed his hand. "'As we travel down the road, side by side, we'll share the load. Hand in hand, we'll see each other through.'"

The harmonious duet was interrupted by the short blasts behind them, signaling the light was green. Sean started to accelerate; the car behind him blasted its horn with a sense of urgency. Blair unfastened her seat belt, kissed Sean on the cheek, and said, "I love you too. I know you didn't mean it, and I accept your apology. Yes, you are an idiot, but you're my idiot."

Wham!

A massive force T-boned the sedan as the tires screeched in resistance. The car slid sideways as the windshield exploded like a cheap piñata on its last blow. Its shards unmercifully cut anything in its path. A thunderous explosion of metal crunching metal filled the air. Smoke billowed in from every crack and crevice. Sean tried wiping the blood from his face. He noticed his wife twisted and mangled, saturated in blood, her head split open. Blair still clutched his hat. Sean took two fingers and put them on his wife's neck—a very faint pulse. "No! Blair, Blair, oh God! Talk to me! Help! Someone help us, I'm trapped!" The steering wheel repositioned tightly against his chest. Unable to move Sean was numb, his lower extremities paralyzed. Sean struggled to reach Blair. He pulled her limp body toward him and gave her a kiss. "Blair, hold on!" As his wife exhaled her last breath. A tear trickled down his cheek. He was thankful his wife's death was quick. Distraught, he tried to undo his seat belt. Sean fought to remain conscious, but the world grew darker.

He heard a tapping on the window and someone saying, "Help is on the way." Sean frantically pointed to the back seat, and the bystander looked confused. Sean barely mumbled a whisper. "My son—" Then the world went dark—forever.

Chapter 1

🐾 🐾 🐾 🐾 🐾

JULY 27, 2013

BAXTER FALLS, CONNECTICUT

Daniel's hand engulfed the knob as his right shoulder simultaneously pushed the front door—locked. How strange, he thought while inserting the key. A sweet fragrance filled the air, and Daniel couldn't place the smell.

His voice increased as each chant grew louder. "Gramps. Gramps." Daniel's voice echoed throughout the house. "If this is another one of your pranks, it's not funny."

Daniel bounded up the stairs two steps at a time, knocked once on the bedroom door, and flung the door open. The room was empty.

He retreated downstairs to look for clues as to his grandfather's whereabouts. Gramps was a creature of habit and stuck to his daily routine. An unfinished crossword puzzle—written in ink—lay dormant on his favorite recliner. Daniel scoured the kitchen in hopes of a note. Nothing. The clock read 4:13, which generally meant Gramps would be watching *Judge Judy*, but he wasn't here.

"Think, Daniel, think," he muttered as he pulled out a dining room chair and plopped down. Perplexed, he wondered how his grandfather would tackle this problem. Daniel jumped up and checked the basement door in the hallway, locked.

Slowly he climbed the stairs, his heart fully entrenched in his throat. He reached the second-floor landing and exhaled several times slowly. Where could he be? Gramps didn't have a vehicle to drive. As he walked down the hallway, he detected a smell. The smell intensified when he reached his grandfather's en suite bathroom. It was an odor Daniel referred to as the smell of death. Daniel lifted the bottle of Old Spice, saw its cap lying nearby, and inhaled the exotic aroma of nutmeg, cinnamon, and vanilla. The smell of death! The smell was from one of Daniel's earliest memories. Whenever Gramps wore it, he was adorned in a suit and going to a funeral.

Daniel quickly scurried downstairs and stared at a picture next to the front door. It was the only remnant of his past: a family portrait. His father clad in dress blues and his mom attired in a blue and white floral dress. Complete with a proud motherly smile her right hand rested upon Daniel's shoulder. He put his index and middle finger against his lips and touched the picture, a tradition he had started at an early age. Then he went over to look at the date on the crossword puzzle—July 27.

🐾 🐾 🐾

Daniel Tanner tapped the brakes, slowly turned in to the entrance, and stared at the massive iron gates. He was the type of person who looked at things from a different perspective than others. Today was no different. What was the purpose of the gates, he wondered, if someone could easily jump over the small stone wall surrounding the perimeter? He felt a cold chill run down his spine as his eyes surveyed the property. Was Gramps here? Where else could he be? All the clues pointed here. Where could he be if he wasn't here? Calling the police would be too embarrassing or, worse yet, would piss Gramps off.

These were sacred grounds. But to Daniel, a self-described born-again atheist, it meant nothing. He detested the place. His grandfather had forced Daniel to visit here in early childhood. The location held painful memories of frustration, of questions asked and vague answers given.

Daniel exited his compact pickup and pushed the heavy gate inward as the fence moaned in defiance. This place was the source of many of his nightmares. Over the years, it had become the perfect spot for teenagers who wanted to drink. It was on the outskirts of town, and teenagers gathered there many weekends. One night they toasted and christened it "the boneyard."

One memorable day Daniel had slipped up and called it the boneyard in the presence of his grandfather, resulting in an hour-long rant on respect and two weeks of being grounded. To his grandfather, it was hallowed ground—a historic cemetery centuries old, and the site of the family plot.

Daniel hopped into his vehicle and slowly navigated the dirt road. His eyes darted back and forth past rows of various-sized tombstones, many featuring names of prominent residents who had helped develop Baxter Falls. The townsfolk had honored these early visionaries by naming multiple buildings, roads, and subdivisions after them.

He proceeded up a small knoll and, on his decline, spotted a person crouched down, sitting with hands covering his face. There was his grandfather. It was the anniversary of Daniel's parents' death. Daniel paused for a second, exhaled, and prepared for the worst. Chaotic situations had prevented Daniel from driving Gramps to the cemetery today. These pilgrimages had started early in Daniel's life but slowly receded as Daniel rebelled, Gramps grew older, and memories faded.

Two car accidents separated by nearly three decades shaped Daniel's life. Both resulted in Daniel being uprooted and living with his grandfather. The first accident had tragically killed his parents, who were hit by a drunk driver just before his fourth birthday. Then, several weeks ago, Gramps had cheated death. His vehicle hit a tree, but he escaped before the car rolled down a ravine. Gramps had suffered several broken ribs, a sprained knee, and various bumps and bruises. But what concerned the doctors the most was the concussion he'd sustained. Gramps didn't remember the accident and was confused by many questions designed to determine the severity of his injury.

Gramps got argumentative and wanted to leave the hospital. The doctor gave him an ultimatum: he could go home if he had a brain scan, and if he had someone to live with him for a while to monitor his well-being. Reluctantly, his grandfather had agreed.

Before moving in with his grandfather, Daniel had had more of a long-distance relationship with Gramps. They spoke on the phone several times a week and went to dinner on special occasions. But Daniel hadn't been to the house in several years. Gramps always seemed reluctant to entertain Daniel at his home. Occasionally there would be some odd behavior or quirky conversation, but Daniel had always chalked that up to senior moments.

Upon Daniel's arrival at the house, he quickly assessed his grandfather's behavior as highly peculiar. The house was in disarray, which was highly unusual for his grandfather, a perfectionist. Several follow-up appointments later the results of the test revealed the signs of dementia. The doctor warned Daniel there would be some good and some bad days, but they could slow down the beginning of the disease with the proper medication. The appointments usually ended with Gramps storming out of the room.

Daniel coasted down the hill; Gramps oblivious to his arrival. His hands covered his face, and his back was against a stately oak tree. Daniel studied his grandfather, who was clad in a white oxford shirt, one side of the collar up, and the fabric drenched in sweat, revealing pink undertones. He wore a hastily knotted electric-blue tie, usually reserved for any formal affairs associated with the police department, and his dark blue pants. A dozen red roses at his side completed the ensemble.

"Gramps! Gramps, are you okay?" Daniel shouted. No response.

Gramps's body jumped as he started mumbling, "They stole it. They took it. Where is it?"

Daniel sat next to his grandfather and gently put his arm around his bony shoulder. Realizing how frail he was, he quietly inquired about the stolen item.

"The grave. It's not here!"

Daniel concealed a smile. "Yes, it is, Gramps. It's down this hill around the next bend. I know this place looks similar."

"But there's no tree there!" He stared out into the distance, ignoring his grandson's remarks.

"Several trees are gone. I think the hurricane last year hit this place hard. Come on, get in the truck, and I'll drive you there. It's too hot."

"No! I've already walked two miles. What're a few more yards? This date is very dear to me, and there's no excuse. You should have been here to bring me in the first place."

"Gramps, I know you don't want to hear this, but. I'm sorry. I'm truly sorry. It slipped my mind," Daniel said. "Some problems came up that needed immediate attention, and I had no choice. Please get in the truck you look exhausted."

"Sorry just doesn't cut it. And there's nothing more important than this—nothing! It's okay when things slip your mind, but it's a big deal when I forget? It's just a senior moment. Everybody has them."

"Sometimes you forget to shower or shave or take your medicine. Those are not senior moments. Come on, let's go."

Daniel got in the truck and drove to the grave site. Gramps hobbled down the hill with the suit jacket draped over one arm and the roses in his other hand. Daniel could only imagine his reaction if he told him the real reason for his tardiness—that somebody had stolen his materials. After all these years, Daniel thought, you'd think I'd be used to his stubbornness.

Daniel exited his vehicle, keeping the truck running, and turned the air conditioner on full blast. Finally, Gramps arrived at the grave site. He struggled to kneel. Daniel grabbed the roses and suit jacket and helped his grandfather.

"These flowers are beautiful. Where did you get them?" Daniel inquired as he gave the bouquet back.

"From a neighbor's backyard. I don't think they'll miss them, and if they do, I'll blame it on a senior moment," Gramps replied.

Daniel went back to the truck and deposited the suit coat. On his way back, he stood several feet away. He studied his grandfather as his mind flashed back to an earlier age when his grandfather had seemed invincible. Michael Casey stood a proud five feet nine inches. His hairstyle was a meticulous crew cut, and his demeanor matched. His Irish heritage was etched upon his face. His blue eyes were laser focused on any situation. A fellow detective had best described his grandfather as quicksand: calm and serene on the surface, but the deeper you went, the more deadly he became.

Coming back to reality, Daniel saw a man agitated with life. His trademark crew cut was now grown out, and his current style could be best described as looking like a six-year-old girl had given her favorite doll a haircut. The heat and humidity could be partially to blame for his untidy look. But most troublesome was the mental aspect of everything. The only characteristic that never changed was his stubbornness.

"Daniel, please come and kneel and say a few prayers," Gramps said.

"Thanks, but no, thanks. I feel no connection. I don't even remember them. Every person I've ever asked has detailed memories of their early childhood. But I have very few. Fragments of my dad working on his truck, my mom bathing me...but they only last a few seconds, and I don't understand why."

"Show some respect. They're still your parents."

"I've never felt their presence here, and I don't believe in the concept of heaven." Daniel remained where he was. He could be stubborn too. "I'd be a hypocrite if I did. The sun is starting to set. We need to go."

Daniel began moving toward Gramps to help him when Gramps whispered, "Daniel, stop!"

In a calm voice, Daniel inquired, "Why?"

"It's a bird." A beautiful red bird had appeared out of nowhere and landed on the headstone. He seemed to be looking at Gramps.

"So what? There are millions of birds around," Daniel said.

"But it's a cardinal. The day after your parents' death, reality set in with your grandma. While she was standing at the kitchen sink, tears were rolling. She looked outside and saw a cardinal perched on the clothesline in our backyard. The next day she saw it again. It had been showing up for a few days, and she'd never realized its significance. She researched and found out that its presence is a sign that those we have lost will live forever so long as we keep their memory in our hearts.

"When we lost Blair, I found it difficult to express words of comfort, but somehow that bird gave Grandma what she needed. Over time she grew more at peace with the world. When your grandmother found out her cancer had spread, the birds showed up again. I know Grandma sent this bird down for you and me."

After a minute or so, the bird took off into the hot July evening. "These signs happen all the time, but people never take the time to see them," Gramps said. "They're always in a rush."

Daniel helped his grandfather stand as he stumbled over to an unmarked grave and spit.

Once seated in the truck, Daniel asked, "What was that all about?"

Gramps whispered, "Just paying my respects."

Chapter 2

🐾 🐾 🐾 🐾 🐾

What was typically a seven-minute ride seemed like an eternity. Daniel and Gramps sat in the vehicle, speechless, like two adolescents playing a game of whoever talks first loses. While driving, Daniel was formulating a plan for obtaining materials on Monday. Occasionally he glanced at Gramps, who was huffing and puffing, ready to explode.

Daniel rounded the last curve in the expansive subdivision, and he noticed a familiar, yet unwanted object had appeared within the last half hour. He started to seethe inside, waiting patiently for Gramps to explain. It was not forthcoming. Silence. Dead silence.

He couldn't hold back any longer. "What's that? What's that doing here? I thought we decided. The insurance adjuster deemed the vehicle totaled. The check came in the mail the other day."

"Stop right there. You decided. I didn't. I repurchased the car for four hundred dollars. As for the check, I haven't cashed it. It's on the dining room table with the rest of the mail. Don't forget, it's my house, my driveway, and especially it's my car."

The object of discontent was a retired police department Crown Vic. This car was Gramps's last link to the career he'd loved.

"What's it about the word 'totaled' that you don't understand?" Daniel asked. "The frame's bent. I can't even imagine how much it would take

8

to fix this car. If it ever could. They're never going to allow it on the road again. Honestly, looking at that vehicle, I don't know how you survived the accident."

Gramps gave Daniel an icy stare.

"Look at what they did to the driveway," Daniel went on. "All those deep ruts—it's going to take hours to fix it. You need to call the garage and have them send someone over here."

"They towed it up here for free," Gramps snapped. "I'll fix it."

"No, you're not doing it," Daniel scolded. "It took me a half day to lay the peastone in the first place. I'll donate another Sunday; I got nothing better to do." In a softer tone, he said, "Gramps, I've told you several times I'm willing to pave it, put in concrete, whatever you want."

"What you don't understand is back when I was young, we were so poor we didn't have a driveway. We couldn't afford it. It was just the way it was, and nobody cared. When we moved here, we built the biggest house we could afford and sacrificed all the little amenities like security alarms, a dishwasher, and a paved driveway. As the girls grew older, that driveway became my best ally. When they dated, I insisted their boyfriends pull into the driveway before dropping off one of my daughters. Peastone was cheap, and it's something I could do myself. I always had the window cracked. That driveway was my alarm system. I knew about it every time one of those idiots pulled in."

"That's ingenious. I'll never bother you about it again."

Gramps gingerly walked toward the front door while Daniel retrieved the mail.

"Anything interesting?" Gramps asked as he flopped onto his green tweed recliner.

"The usual—a couple of bills, some junk mail, and this." He dropped the police newsletter in Gramps's lap. "I know you enjoy this."

"Would you mind getting my glasses?" Gramps said as he flipped on the lamp near his chair. "Before I forget, this came for you a couple of days ago. I hope you don't mind I had to sign for it."

"No problem," Daniel said as he looked at the large manila envelope. "How about a nice cold drink? Water sound good?"

"How about some lemonade."

Daniel retreated to the kitchen, and curiosity got the better of him. He ripped open the envelope to reveal a smaller envelope with the return address from a law firm called Moses, Louis, and Jerome in New Haven. Daniel grabbed a steak knife from the cutlery set and sliced open the envelope. His hands trembled as he quickly scanned the contents of the letter. The words "put a lien on your house," "freeze your bank accounts," and "Woodstock Lumber" jumped out. He felt his face redden, and his stomach started to churn.

Gramps bellowed, "Have you found them?"

"Found what?"

"My glasses. Are you okay? You sound different."

"No, I'm fine. Just for the last couple of days, all I've had is black coffee, and it's starting to take its toll. I don't see the glasses, and we're out of lemonade. You've got two choices, water, or water?"

"I'll take the first one," Gramps replied.

Daniel walked into the living room with a bottle of Aquafina and a magnifying glass. "I noticed you used this in the past. We need to get you a chain to secure your glasses around your neck, so you don't lose them anymore."

"Naw, those are for old people."

"In case you haven't noticed, you are old!"

"You didn't throw out that manila envelope, did you? This Tim guy keeps calling, and I've written down the calls and dates. He seems impatient. Do you owe him money or something?"

"No, just the opposite. He owes me money. His name is Jim, and he owns the bar where I've been working the past few months."

"Oh, you mean that place on Route 10. That bar's been in the same family for over sixty years if I remember right. I had coffee with a couple of retired detectives a few months ago, and the scuttlebutt is the owner torched his place for the insurance money. Back in the day, we used to call it Jewish lightning."

"Gramps, that's a racist remark. I'd keep that comment to yourself."

"If I remember right, the liquor board shut down his place for a few months for serving minors. He's had quite a few infractions over the years. I don't know him personally, but some officers describe him as a hippie. Every day—Woodstock! It's like a commune down there."

"Yeah, he's a little quirky. You wouldn't recognize the place. It's been completely gutted and renovated."

"I never cared for the owner of that place. Sort of a sleazy guy who walked a fine line. Does he owe you a lot of money?"

"Enough."

"Hope you have a contract. I wouldn't trust Tim."

If only Gramps knew, Daniel thought as he ascended the stairs to the second floor. His bedroom was the second door on the right, his sanctuary. He chose it for one reason only: it was his mom's room. A chance to discover the person she was. Sadly, that had never developed.

His grandfather told him he'd painted the room a dusty rose as a surprise for her thirteenth birthday—to welcome her to the teenage years.

Daniel looked at the enormous bed, and he chuckled as he fondly recalled Gramps's explanation. Dubbed a little princess, Blair reasoned royalty in waiting deserved a queen-sized bed.

In the closets were her proud possessions, including a massive record collection of 45s she'd purchased with her allowance money. He played them in hopes of getting to know her better. It was an eclectic mixture, from classic rock to bubblegum pop. He knew the songs by heart, and sometimes, to comfort himself, he played them and sang along.

Posters of teen idols covered the walls. She'd carefully ripped them from magazines. Daniel covered them with pictures he'd bought at Spencer's of his favorite bands. He was ashamed of his mother's pictures but didn't have the heart to take them down.

He shut the shades entirely, flipped on the fan, collapsed on the bed with his arms up, and intertwined his hands behind his head to help alleviate the cramping of his fingers. Daniel closed his eyes and rubbed his temples as the air circulated, hoping to avert a migraine. He felt as though his head was in a vise, and with each passing moment, it tightened.

Knowing he needed to get going but unable to muster the will, his mind wandered to the past forty-eight hours. It had started with the theft of material sometime late Thursday night or in the wee hours of Friday morning. The material consisted of mahogany and teak woods to build a lavish deck in the next two weeks. It would be next to impossible to replace them in the time frame needed. He was confused as to why Dennis from Woodstock Lumber never returned his phone calls. Maybe this attorney letter had something to do with that. While filling out the report, he had pondered using his grandfather's influence but decided it would be more of a hindrance. The police turned out to be a stone wall. They considered it a petty crime, even though the wood's monetary value was over $5,000. He wondered what other crimes were so pressing that they had dismissed his report.

His stomach hurt from all the acidity of endless cups of black coffee. He had an attorney's letter stating they were putting a lien on his house and freezing his bank account. Lastly, Gramps was mad at him. Here was a man who'd dedicated his life to raising Daniel, and this was how Daniel repaid him. Since living under his roof, he'd studied Gramps from near and far and realized there was cause for concern. His erratic behavior and various times of confusion made for an emotional roller coaster. For someone who was so analytical how could Gramps not see that in himself?

Daniel could see the sparks flying from Gramps already. How am I going to take care of him while doing my work? Daniel wondered. Should I hire a caretaker? I can't worry about this now. I'll have to address this in the next few days.

He finally sat up, turned on the light, and shut the fan off. He thought about taking a shower, but he didn't work today, he was dog tired, and he was going there to get his money and wish Jim luck on his new venture. Daniel didn't plan to stay long and decided his dress was appropriate enough.

He studied his guitar mounted on his wall over the bed. It was the gorgeous bright orange of a midsummer-night sunset, accented by a mahogany hue. Daniel fondly recalled the summer when he'd found the guitar in his parents' attic. Excited, Daniel had brought the guitar to a friend's garage. The discovery of the instrument prompted his friends to rummage through pawnshops and secondhand stores in search of musical instruments. He passed the guitar around and allowed his friends to feel as cool as he did. They each attempted to mimic the moves of the great guitarists of their generation. They dreamed of starting a band.

Gramps had warned him not to take the guitar out, as it was one of Daniel's father's cherished possessions. Daniel defied him. Later in the summer, after a day of rehearsal, Daniel left the instrument behind. When he went to the garage again to rehearse, he found the headstock cracked. No one accepted the blame, which started his natural distrust of friends and classmates. He brought the guitar home and hid it from his grandfather. One day he came home from school and found the guitar mounted in a case over his bed. The guitar remained there for years, and neither he nor his grandfather ever discussed it. The garage band fell apart. Everyone went their separate ways. Daniel, however, never forgot those summer days and nights when it seemed like anything could happen in their unbuilt lives.

The teacher he admired most, Mr. Russell, the art instructor, wrote Daniel's favorite quote in calligraphy. It was from Marilyn Monroe, and it said, "I believe that everything happens for a reason. People change so that you can learn to let go. Things go wrong so that you appreciate them when they're right, and you believe lies, so you eventually learn to trust no one but yourself. And sometimes good things fall apart so better things can fall together." He could still repeat it by heart. It became his mantra, especially the part "trust no one but yourself."

He pulled out a light flannel and threw it over his T-shirt. He needed to go to J. W. Morgan's tonight and collect his money no matter how tired he was. Jim was a customer who had constantly changed materials, upgraded projects, and appeared overbudget—another demanding customer who set Daniel's timetable rather than consulting him first. Jim was always in a rush. Somehow, Daniel found the energy to complete every task. The only obstacle remaining was the final payment. Daniel's bill not only included the work on the tavern but material for other parts of the remodel, which he was not doing himself. Daniel knew he had exceeded his credit limit substantially at the lumberyard. It was now Jim's grand reopening, and he needed to straighten out his bill. Daniel had hoped to get there early, but once again, time had slipped away. He was already three hours behind schedule. Thankfully, Jim had an office where he could discuss these issues in private.

Daniel plodded down the hallway, thinking about his grandfather. He was irritated with Gramps. But he was more irritated by his own actions. Here was a man who'd given up his career to take care of him and raise him when no one else wanted him. He was a man Daniel loved and respected, yet he'd never found the time to tell him what he meant to him. Daniel needed to correct this problem and address this issue and not abandon him as he did last time.

Daniel went down the stairs to the dining room and retrieved his truck keys.

"Daniel, we just got home, are you going out again?" Gramps asked.

"Don't you remember? I told you I have to go out and get my final payment."

"I was just testing you," Gramps chuckled.

"I'll stop at Vinny's Deli and get you your favorite on my way home. You can have it tonight, and I'm sure you'll save some for tomorrow."

Daniel returned the living room to kiss Gramps on the forehead. He tapped his back pocket to make sure the letter was still there.

"One minute before you go," Gramps said. "I need to ask you a question. You know how important this is. What was so critical that you couldn't take me to the cemetery this afternoon? Where'd you go?"

"Why so nosy? But if you gotta know, it was the police station."

"What?" Gramps yelled. "Why'd you go there?" Before Daniel could answer, Gramps continued his rant. "I already know your answer. You went to find out about the accident. You just can't let sleeping dogs lie."

"Gramps, it wasn't about that. I'm running late. We'll talk about this tomorrow morning."

"You're always going somewhere. You never have time for me."

"It's not that. I need to go before it gets busy," Daniel stated.

"Don't slam the door this time. Leave, see if I care!"

Daniel gently shut the door. Gramps's last few statements felt like a hundred paper cuts across his heart. The man forgets everything, Daniel thought. Why not that I walked out and didn't come back? It happened over ten years ago.

Chapter 3

❀ ❀ ❀ ❀ ❀

Daniel navigated his truck up and down aisles looking for a parking spot. He noticed a large white canvas banner attached to the tavern's side stating, "Grand Reopening, J. W. Morgan's," written in hunter green and gold. It had been three weeks since he was here last. Jim had had the large Victorian structure painted barn red accented by white trim. Renamed and newly remodeled, J. W. Morgan's was back in business, transformed from a local dive into a premier social gathering place.

Circling the parking lot a few times, Daniel searched for a space. He sat in his truck idling, watching for patrons leaving. After a few minutes, he found a perfect spot near the stairs by the entrance.

He flung the flannel on the seat and thought, It's just too hot for this. Daniel slowly climbed the stairs, entered the bar, and noticed a hive of activity. The dining area had been turned into a waiting room until the upstairs opened. Daniel maneuvered toward Jim's office, as the bar area was three deep. Countless patrons and waitresses crossed his path, oblivious to his presence. Music blared from speakers on the ceiling as Daniel rapped on Jim's door. He put his ear to the door to listen and could only hear the music. He tried the doorknob, locked. He thought, What the fuck? The guy called me several times, and now he's not here. He was so insistent about me showing up tonight. Damn. Sunday would have been better. Oh well. What's another day? It's not like I can deposit the check tonight.

Daniel took another look at the bar and analyzed the situation. He knew if he made his way over there and got jounced around, he'd take his anger out on someone. Standing several feet away from the crowd, he stared at Ethan, the bartender. As Ethan made his way back and forth along the bar, Daniel finally caught his attention.

Within minutes Ethan was at Daniel's side with a bottle of Budweiser. "This is crazy, isn't it?" Ethan said. "If you're looking for Jim, he told me to give you the beer and go upstairs and check out the upper level. You haven't seen it since it's finished, have you?"

Daniel nodded and said, "Thanks. Why would you leave on a night like this?"

Ethan shrugged and said with a touch of sarcasm, "You're not the only one looking for him. He seems to bring out the best in people lately."

Daniel longed for quiet, and upstairs seemed like the perfect haven. He took his index finger and notched a small tear in the label to mark his beer. He opened the pocket doors and noticed just a couple of stage lights were on. The faint strains of a guitar tuning up caught his attention. Daniel hadn't seen the finished project since he had completed his work. He could smell the fresh paint. Daniel turned right at the top of the stairs and heard a bucket of ice being emptied into a sink. He noticed an unfamiliar face.

The bartender said, "Gee, I'm sorry, sir, we're not open till 9:30."

"I'm a close friend of the owner; he wanted me to see the finished product before the crowd comes."

The bartender extended his hand and shook Daniel's. "Hi, I'm Dale."

"Daniel. Nice to meet you, Dale."

"Oh, you're the guy that built the bar and stage! You did a fantastic job."

"Thanks," Daniel said.

Behind Daniel, voices in unison yelled, "Surprise, happy birthday!"

Stunned, Daniel turned around and saw friends on the opposite side of the stairwell. His mouth agape, Daniel was at a loss for words. During high school, Daniel was never part of the inner circle, preferring to stay on the outside, as he had several part-time jobs that kept him busy. Working those jobs, he felt he was helping Gramps when he turned over his paycheck. Thus, he hadn't had much time for making friends or playing sports after school.

His old high school friend and former homeroom classmate Warren Tucker approached him and gave him a big bear hug. They were best friends throughout their freshman year. But Daniel had started working in his sophomore year, and the only time they saw each other after that was in homeroom. Now Warren said, "Hey, stranger, happy birthday. It was great seeing you last month. We missed you at the last class reunion. Jim gave me a heads-up and told me your birthday was coming soon and suggested we celebrate it here with a few friends. I spoke with a couple of guys, and they all loved the idea and wanted to see you."

Taken aback by the gesture, Daniel didn't know what to say. Since high school, he had become even more of a loner and rarely saw what friends he had. Touched by the gesture, he said, "I apologize for my appearance. I didn't know I'd be seeing anyone I knew here tonight."

The guitarist took his cue from the crowd and broke into a bluesy rendition of "Happy Birthday."

"And my birthday is still two weeks away!" Daniel said.

"That's what makes it a surprise," Brad chimed in.

They all burst into laughter. Daniel's uneasiness soon subsided as he gulped each bottle of Budweiser. His hand was never empty; everybody wanted to buy him a drink. He explained to his friends how he now took care of his grandfather due to Gramps's dementia, and his construction job took up all his time. They commiserated with him. Many of them commented on Daniel's excellent job of remodeling the unique bar. He received all the congratulations in stride. He thought it was one thing to do the work, another to get paid.

Daniel heard someone coming up the stairs and saw Jim carrying a box with a blanket over it. He put it behind the bar, hidden from view. Jim's appearance had changed drastically since Daniel last saw him. The ponytail, beard, and granny-style glasses had been replaced by designer lenses, a layered haircut, and a goatee. He looked fifteen years younger.

Jim greeted him warmly. "Hey, there's the birthday boy. About time you got here." Jim tried to hug him, but Daniel thwarted his attempt by sticking out his right hand.

Daniel put on a pleasant face, but questions swirled in his mind: Is it me? Or is he really that phony? I've been here forty-five minutes, and I don't know what he's talking about.

Jim gathered everyone around. He went back toward the bar and retrieved the blanket-veiled crate. "I decided—no, we decided—to get you a present," Jim said, beaming. "It will be a great companion for you." He lifted off the blanket to reveal a kennel, opened the door, and out bounced a shiny black puppy with a white patch that resembled a bear's paw encompassing its left eye.

Daniel could feel the color leave his face. His blanched expression was noticeable to all.

"You don't like it?" Jim said.

The last thing he needed was another mouth to feed and look after. More bills, he thought as he muttered, "I don't know what to say. I'm dumbfounded, speechless."

"How about 'thank you?'" Jim said with a forced smile.

Everybody laughed and thought it funny—except for Daniel. He bent down and picked up the animal. The puppy licked his scraggly face.

Daniel asked Jim, "Where did you get him?"

"An animal shelter. It's just a mutt—possibly a lab–terrier mix. It's a miracle the puppy is alive. The dog warden told me she got an anonymous tip. The caller said she heard strange noises, a howl of some sort from an abandoned barn. They investigated and found the puppy. It was defending its mother and other pups against a coyote, and the mother was badly injured. They tried to save the mother, but her injuries were too severe. They had to put her down. This puppy is the lone survivor."

The crowd fell silent, and some shook their heads in disbelief.

"How terrible," Daniel replied.

"The dog warden thinks it's approximately seven weeks old. It's in relatively good health. Surprisingly, it didn't sustain any injuries. The dog had been quarantined and tested for rabies, and the results came back negative. The animal shelter will need the kennel back on Monday when they reopen. I also have dog food, bowls, and a leash. The pup had his first set of shots. There's a business card there; the dog warden recommended this vet."

Daniel mused that it looked like he'd thought of everything—except Daniel's consent. He felt put on the spot and didn't want to tell everyone why he didn't want a puppy; they wouldn't understand. He put the puppy down, and it stayed by his legs while he socialized.

The house lights blinked, and Dale's voice boomed in the cavernous room. "Sorry, guys, you need to go downstairs. We'll reopen in less than an hour."

Daniel surveyed the room. "Where'd Jim go?" he asked.

"Are you talking about Ziggy?" Fred responded.

"Who?" Daniel inquired.

"He scurried down those stairs like it was last call. Ziggy—Jim. Don't you remember? I know you were with us several times. It was our hangout on weekends during our junior and senior years. We called the bartender Ziggy because he looked like the picture on the Zig-Zag papers. He always had something rolled up hanging from his lip."

They all laughed in delight, recalling fond memories of high school.

"Hey, Warren, do you mind grabbing the crate?" Daniel asked.

"Sure, no problem," Warren stated.

Fred walked over to Daniel and put his arm around his shoulder. "Looking at that stage does it ever bother you that we couldn't get our band going?"

Daniel quickly replied, "No."

Once downstairs, Ethan rushed over to Daniel frantically, talking about the upstairs room and puppy. Daniel half-heartedly listened while scanning the crowd for Jim. Daniel placed the puppy back into the kennel and joined his friends at the bar.

Ethan reiterated, "How do you like the puppy?"

Daniel answered, "He's cute, but it's not the right time for me to get a dog."

Daniel's friends sat at a table with a "reserved" sign. He placed the crate under the table. Located in the back of the tavern was Jim's office. Daniel spotted him as he neared his office. Now was his perfect opportunity. "Jim, wait a second. Can I talk to you in private?"

"I can give you a minute or two. I wanted to give you a check anyway."

They went into Jim's office. "I already have it made out," Jim said, and handed a sealed envelope to Daniel.

A feeling of uneasiness overcame him. He decided to open the envelope, something he never did in a client's presence. But something in Jim's demeanor prompted Daniel to break his golden rule. He looked at the amount twice. Jim had given him a small fraction of the total amount he owed.

Daniel's anger burst forth as he slammed his fist hard against the top of the desk. Startled, Jim jumped, and his eyes grew wide. It was a side of Daniel Jim had never seen.

"Is this a fucking joke? Are you serious?" Daniel paused to collect his thoughts while the fire inside raged. He reached into his back pocket, pulled out the envelope, and violently threw it at Jim. The letter bounced off Jim's chest and ricocheted onto the desk.

"What's this?" Jim said while pointing at the envelope.

"It's a fucking lawsuit. Open it up and read it! The attorney is freezing my checking account on Monday. They're starting proceedings to put a lien on my house. And I don't even know why! You mailed a check to Woodstock Lumber, didn't you?"

Jim opened up his ledger and put a pair of bifocals down at the bridge of his nose. He took his index finger and ran it down the page. "Here it is. I sent a check out last week."

"Why are you looking up your records? I told you to send a certified check three weeks ago. When exactly did you send it? What was the amount?" Daniel screamed.

"I sent five thousand dollars in on Monday. I postdated it, and it won't be good until this Tuesday."

Daniel slammed his fist on the desk again and screamed, "Five thousand dollars! It needed to be thirty thousand dollars! What are you, a fucking idiot? I don't know if you heard me. Their attorneys put a lien on my house. It was my parents' house. I can't lose it. I'm not fucking losing another thing!"

With a look of remorse, Jim said, "I'm sorry, Daniel, it's all I got. It's all I could give you. Right now, I'm in over my head. I had to go high end on the business, as I needed to attract a better clientele with their disposable income. If I didn't, I could lose everything."

"I'm sorry too, Jim. I stand to lose *my* business too, as well as *my* home. It's not a decision *I* made. It's a decision *you* made for me. I think you need this more than I do." He flung the check on Jim's desk.

Jim whimpered, "I'm sorry. My taste got the better of me, and I didn't keep a good handle on the costs. Come back tomorrow, and we can discuss this. I'll see how much money I can give you based on how much I make tonight. I'll pay you in cash."

Daniel paused for a second, then snapped, "Not only did you promise to send the certified check, which you never did, but you also put my credibility on the line. I use Woodstock Lumber for all my jobs. On Monday, I have to go there and talk to the president. I don't know if I'm more embarrassed by your promise to pay or my stupidity in believing you would."

Jim slumped down in his chair. "Danny, I promise to repay you with interest."

"There's only one other thing worse than liars, and that's anybody who calls me Danny. My name is not Dan or Danny; it's *Daniel*," he screamed. The mere utterance of "Danny" evoked childhood memories of his classmates when they found out his parents had died. He heard the refrains of "Little Orphan Danny, Little Orphan Danny." Daniel grabbed the attorney's letter.

While leaving, he could hear Jim saying, "Somehow, I'll make this up to you. I promise I'll make it up to you."

He spit back, "That's what I get for trusting you!" He paused for a second to compose himself. He had the original contract, but Jim had changed so many things. The revisions were numerous and always trans-acted by a handshake, not written up as a change order with the signatures of the owner and contractor. Legally, Jim could stick it to him if he wanted to. He had to calm down before facing his friends.

Too fucking late, he thought, slamming the door. Everyone was look-ing, so he quickly readjusted his attitude and returned to the bar where some friends waited. Ethan had a Bud ready for Daniel. He patiently waited for Daniel to pay. Daniel said, "Tell Jim it's on him, with inter-est. He'll understand." He guzzled the beer and felt its coolness as it streamed through his body. Daniel made up his mind: he would have a good time tonight.

As Daniel made his way back, a friend, sensing darkness in the air, asked, "Are you okay?"

Daniel collected his thoughts and said, "Yeah, I'm fine, just a mis-understanding. Good friends, cold beer…" His voice trailed off. He bent down to pick up the puppy out of the crate. Once again, with his velvety black coat and silky tail, he licked Daniel's face and adoringly looked Daniel in the eyes. As Daniel's callus-ridden hands stroked the soft fur, he looked into the puppy's eyes. They were a vibrant brown, the shade of a Hershey Kiss, with a look that could melt the heart of a miser. Not wanting to face the reality of getting rid of the pup on Monday, Daniel wandered among his friends. The animal instinctively followed. A wait-ress approached him, carrying a tray filled with shots. "These are on Jim. Where would you like them?"

Daniel pointed. "Would you mind putting them on the table over there?"

The puppy ran between the waitress's legs, which caused her to drop and spill the whole tray. Daniel quickly grabbed the puppy before he had a chance to lap up much liquid.

The waitress said, "I'm sorry, I'm sorry. Do you think it'll get sick?"

Josh's baritone voice bellowed, "Not if you give him a chaser."

His friends erupted. All the banter and amusement erased the sands of time as Daniel felt a closeness he hadn't felt in a while. A feeling he'd lost during his high school years.

23

Daniel asked the waitress, "What was in those shots, anyway?"

"Sambuca," she replied. "Stay here; I'll bring another round."

Josh remarked, "I think Ziggy remembered us! Isn't that the shit we got sick on one night?"

"Hey, why don't you call him Sambuca?" Aaron suggested. "It suits him."

"I haven't thought that far ahead yet," Daniel mumbled. He then thought, *If I name the dog, it's mine.*

The puppy sat at his feet as he stood by the bar, and Daniel felt the presence of two paws on his calf. Daniel picked him up and stroked his fur. "Hi, Sambuca. You caused a mess back there. I'll bring you somewhere nice and quiet, and you'll be safe. I'll leave a window cracked for you." He went to his truck and gently placed the puppy on his flannel shirt. The pup immediately turned around several times and settled himself. "I promise to find you a good home." He locked the door and went back inside.

Daniel strolled over to a table to talk. Joe asked, "How's Charlie and Nick working out?"

"They're a great addition. Thanks for the referral."

"Tell Alex I said hi," Joe said. "She's a terrific girl, I don't know what she sees in you!"

"Neither do I," Daniel replied softly.

The house lights flickered, an indication the band was ready to start. Daniel and his crowd headed for the stairs and a rush of other patrons. He heard somebody upstairs tap a tambourine, quickly followed by a guitar and the distinct sound of a Hammond organ. The band erupted into a rousing rendition of "Gimme Some Lovin'." The stage lights pulsated with each drumbeat. They had a five-piece band. The vocalist was short, rotund, and follicularly challenged, with hair on the sides, tightly pulled back into a ponytail. The rest of the band members seemed to be in their fifties or sixties.

As soon as the song ended, the lead singer said, "Thanks for coming out to J. W. Morgan's. Welcome to Jim's grand reopening. We are the Pony Express, made up of current and retired postal workers, playing the best of the sixties, seventies, and eighties. Tonight is special for Jim, but we also know it's someone's birthday. Is there a Daniel here?"

Daniel shied back until his friends pushed him forward. Daniel reluctantly joined the singer on stage as the band started to sing "Happy Birthday" to him loudly into the mic. The crowd quickly joined in. Heat suffused Daniel's face. Daniel was motionless as he stared at the lights. He saw Jim creep up the stairs. Daniel quietly thanked the performer and attempted to leave the stage. The lead singer put his arm around him and yelled into his ear over the crowd's din, "It's your night. Anything special you want to hear?"

He quickly blurted out his favorite '60s song. The singer hesitated. "Usually I reserve that for a special encore, but tonight's your night, and I'll do it." He addressed the crowd. "Here's our tribute to Tommy James and the Shondells." The band started clapping rhythmically, and the patrons joined in. The drummer set the tempo as Daniel jumped off the stage. His buddies quickly formed a circle and playfully pushed him around.

"Hey, Tanner, fifty bucks says you don't have the balls to sing it!" The friend held up the fifty-dollar bill. Daniel snatched the money and hopped back onto the stage.

The band leader looked at Daniel and said, "Are you ready?"

"Born ready," Daniel said with a slur.

Daniel felt so out of character, but he grabbed a mic and sang feverishly, "Here she comes now, say, 'Mony, Mony.' Well, shoot 'em down, turn around, come on, Mony." In his inebriated state, with inhibitions cast aside, he sang. The crowd clapped even harder. He saw Jim grinning as he gave Daniel a thumbs-up gesture in a corner.

Still aggravated, Daniel decided to have a little fun at Jim's expense. He held the mic with his left hand, raised his right hand, and fist pumped it with every lyric. He looked directly at Jim every time he said "Mony, Mony" and rubbed his thumb across his middle and index fingers—the universal gesture for money. The crowd quickly joined in the motion. He chuckled to himself. He knew he was saying, "Fuck you, Jim, I want my money," while the rest of the crowd innocently followed his lead.

Chapter 4

🐾 🐾 🐾 🐾 🐾

The sun filtered through the window and awakened a fully clothed Daniel. He repositioned himself away from the sun, laid his head on a pillow, swung his feet around, and noticed he still wore his work boots. Momentarily blinded by the discomfort, he put the pillow over his head. Daniel tried unsuccessfully to salivate in his dry mouth. His stomach churned, and his head was holding auditions for a drum recital—the wonderous effects of a hangover. There was a whimpering sound when he accidentally kicked something in his bed.

Startled, Daniel eyed the foot of the bed and saw the puppy inch toward him. Daniel faintly recalled naming the puppy Sambuca before the night had gone dark. Daniel pulled down the shade, and, pausing for a second as his eyes adjusted, he realized he was back at his own house, not at his grandfather's. Did the fear of losing this house drive me back here? He thought. The room spun, so he lay back down. Sambuca finally reached his face and licked him with enthusiasm.

What happened last night? He had a good time. He couldn't remember if he did anything stupid or offended anyone. He thought about the confrontation with Jim and wondered if he had gone too far. A full plate of aggressive behavior with a side dish of sarcasm might negatively affect his business. How did he ever get home? It was almost inconceivable that

26

he'd driven five miles drunk. He pulled the shade and saw his truck. A sigh of relief ensued.

He felt his mouth start to salivate and quickly ran to the bathroom. He heaved into the toilet. He heard a whimper and a thump as Sambuca jumped down from the bed and opened the bathroom door with his paws. He sat down beside Daniel and comforted him in his time of need.

Daniel staggered to his feet. The toilet began to overflow, so he pulled out a plunger and manually flushed the toilet. Daniel's eyes burned as he saw the reflection of himself in the mirror. His unshaven face and disheveled hair said it all. He cupped his hands together and splashed cold water on his face several times before gulping some down.

He was exhausted. He helped the puppy up onto the bed and collapsed upon the mattress. "Don't get too used to this. You're going back on Monday." His mind quickly focused on his grandfather, who was all alone. Maybe he did think I left again Daniel thought. I need to call him. The phone rang several times before his grandfather answered. Daniel asked, "Are you okay?"

"Daniel, where are you?"

"I'm at my house taking care of a few things. I should be back in a few hours. I'll take care of dinner. I'm bringing a guest with me."

Daniel went to shower and, on the way, spoke to Buca. "Buca, it's nothing personal. I can't keep ya. I'm sorry. I know you're all alone in the world. And boy, do I know that feeling. But tomorrow I'll take you back to the shelter. They will find someone to care for you and love you better than I can."

The puppy twisted his head from side to side while watching Daniel talk. "I can't believe I'm talking to a dog. But you seem to be listening." Daniel hopped into the shower and, after rinsing his hair, looked at the fogged shower door and saw a dark fuzzy silhouette with two paws up against the glass. Daniel chuckled.

🐾 🐾 🐾

Daniel arrived at his grandfather's house at three o'clock. He adjusted his sunglasses as he gently picked up Sambuca. "Just a Dream," by Jimmy Clanton, played on his grandfather's stereo. Gramps used to be a big Frank Sinatra fan. Early in his career, he'd moonlighted as security at a music venue. On one rare occasion, Gramps had offered his meal, a bowl of homemade jambalaya, to Jimmy Clanton. Touched by the gesture, Mr. Clanton had insisted Gramps and his bride sit in the front row. Later that evening, he gave them a signed album. A memento they cherished. His wife wore out the song "Venus in Blue Jeans," whereas Gramps preferred "Just a Dream."

Daniel knew it by heart. Gramps must feel melancholy today and miss Grandma, he thought. He did this occasionally. Maybe it was why he hadn't heard the knock. He proudly held out the puppy. "Gramps, meet our guest. His name is Sambuca. I like to call him Buca." Boy, I like the sound of that, he thought.

"I think I went to school with a Sam Buca," Gramps said.

Daniel smiled. "No, Gramps, it's Sambuca, just like the liquor. He earned the name last night."

"How did he do that? You gave him alcohol?" Gramps asked.

"No, no, some accidentally spilled on the floor, and he lapped some up before I could get to him," Daniel chuckled.

"Where did you get him?" Gramps asked as Daniel removed his sunglasses. "You look like you had a rough night!"

"Gee, thanks. What an understatement. It was Jim's grand reopening last night. Little did I know why Jim was hounding me to go. They surprised me with a party and this." He extended the puppy toward Gramps.

"What? Did I miss your birthday? Why didn't they invite me?"

"No, Gramps, relax. It's still two weeks away. We'll go out to dinner when it comes time to celebrate. I promise."

Daniel held the puppy and confessed, "Buca is starting to grow on me, but I'm not keeping him. Do you remember Peter Franklin? He was a year ahead of me in high school. He lived a few doors down. Well, his mom still lives there. Her name is Kelly, and she's widowed. Maybe you and Kelly can drop him off at the animal shelter tomorrow? You'd be doing me a big favor."

Daniel thought this couldn't have worked out any better. Kelly and Daniel had discussed her looking after Gramps. As of today, she still had not given Daniel her final answer. He'd call her after dinner and see if she'd do this tomorrow and see how they got along.

With the enthusiasm of a toddler, Gramps asked, "Can I hold the puppy? Is it a boy or girl?"

Daniel said, "I don't know." He turned Buca over and said, "It's a boy! Yes, you can hold him, but don't get too attached."

Daniel put Buca in his grandfather's lap. The puppy quickly settled his rear on Gramps with his front paws nestled on the armrest. "For dinner, I ordered Chinese," Daniel said. "It should be here within a half hour. I asked for additional fortune cookies because they skimped out last time, remember?"

Eventually, Gramps gently put Buca down on the floor, and the puppy immediately took off and began to sniff around. Daniel smiled wryly and said, "Don't get too comfortable, Buca. You're outta here tomorrow."

"You're not keeping him? He's an adorable puppy," Gramps said. "He'll do you some good; you won't be so lonely."

"You and Kelly are returning him tomorrow."

"We will, but I still think you should keep it."

I can't keep him, he thought. But he didn't want to disappoint Gramps. And Buca would be a good companion and therapy for him. Deep down, Daniel knew the reason not to keep the dog. It was guilt, pure and simple. Every time he looked at that dog, it reminded him of his parents. They had been in route to pick up a puppy for Daniel's birthday when the terrible car accident happened.

"I noticed that letter from the attorney," Gramps said. "Usually, when you must sign for it, it's for a specific reason. I can't help noticing; it's the cop in me. Are you okay? Can I do anything for you? I worry about you. I'm not trying to pry. Just remember, I'm here for you."

"You've always been there for me, Gramps, and I know you always will be. I promise, if I need something, I'll ask for your help. I'm fine—the letter was nothing I couldn't handle. It's just a misunderstanding.

"Hey, Gramps, did you see which way the puppy went?" Daniel called out, "Buca, Buca."

The dog slowly bounded from step to step, coming down the stairs. At the bottom landing, Buca dropped something from his mouth. Daniel went to pick it up. It was his old flip phone. Losing it had been a blessing in disguise, as the new smartphone could do much more. "Good boy. You found my phone. I didn't think I'd ever see it again."

"See, the dog is good for you. And he's smart."

Daniel went to his bedroom to charge the phone, with Buca one step behind. After several minutes on the charger, the phone showed fourteen missed calls. Buca scampered under the bed, which gave Daniel the idea of where the dog could have found the phone Daniel had lost near the end of the week. He'd replaced it on Saturday with a new Android.

The missed calls alternated between Dennis and Jim. Dennis's last message sounded desperate. He asked Daniel to return his call, as it was urgent. "Two weeks ago, my boss told me to shut down your account, but I know you ran into a little difficulty," Dennis said. "My boss is mad as hell at me, and I need to talk to you. I don't know why you're avoiding me."

Daniel's heart sank. Dennis had been his friend all along. Once again, Jim was the crux of his problems. He returned to the kitchen and eyed a freshly dethawed coconut cake on the counter. "Where did the cake come from?"

"I panicked when you said you were bringing a guest, so I took out the cake I was saving for your birthday," Gramps responded.

Gramps bent down and picked Buca up. The dog circled three times and then nestled in his lap with his head on Gramps's arm. Taking his opportunity, Gramps asked, "Daniel, you don't want to keep this dog? Look how cute he is."

"Don't get attached. Promise me you'll take Buca to the pound on Monday."

Gramps quickly changed the subject. "Did I ever tell you we had a dog when the kids were young? He was a retriever mix named Corkey. He looked like the dog who was the lead in *Old Yeller*. The girls loved him. One day he got out of the house and tried to follow the girls to school and got hit by a car. The girls wept for days. I tried convincing Grandma we needed to get another dog, but she wouldn't hear of it. She said she couldn't go through it again."

"I never heard that story," Daniel said.

"I haven't thought about that dog in a long time. We buried Corkey somewhere in the backyard. They constructed a wooden cross. He was sweet like him," he said, pointing to Buca. "Smart too."

"Stop it, stop it. I know what you're doing. We're not keeping him."

"It's time to move on. You can't live your life in the past. You've blamed yourself for your parents' death. It had nothing to do with you."

"It had everything to do with me. It was my birthday that caused it. They were going to get me a puppy," Daniel said.

"I suppose you're the one who served the other driver all the liquor? After the accident, I investigated the man and his family. He'd lost everything and started drinking heavily. Sooner or later, he was going to kill himself or somebody else. Unfortunately, your parents were part of that collateral damage. His wife and daughters were so humiliated. I heard they moved out of town and changed their last names. Somebody told me the driver's wife was pregnant at the time. We tried to sue, but they had nothing."

"I never knew that!"

"Sorry, but I didn't think you needed to know. Do you think your parents would enjoy seeing how it has affected you?" Gramps asked.

Daniel said in a soft voice, "No."

"Your parents couldn't wait to pick up the puppy. They knew you'd be excited. I knew your mom was looking forward to it."

"Just do as I ask tomorrow, okay?" Daniel demanded.

Chapter 5

KANSAS

Anthony Kurtis's fingers gripped the steering wheel as he maneuvered his blacked-out SUV along the Kansas interstate. It was five in the morning, and he was tired. He was here previously on a mission with no success, but today was different. Two things had changed. He had his boss's son, and he was prepared to deliver his final ultimatum. Giancarlo was lying in the seat next to him, oblivious to the world. It was time for that to end.

There was a brief yelp as the team's junior member felt the left headphone be yanked from his ear. He glared over at Anthony, holding the black cord from his earbud with a smug smile.

"Oops," Anthony said while holding part of the cord.

"What the fuck did you do?" Giancarlo said.

"Is that any way to talk to an adult?" Anthony chided. "You need to show some respect. Swearing makes you seem uncivilized, ignorant, and crude."

"Then act like an adult," Giancarlo replied as he crossed his arms. "There are better ways to wake me up. Pissing me off isn't one of them."

"You need to wake up. I'm tired and hungry. You've been sleeping."

"Well, you won't let me drive, so what else is there to do?" Giancarlo snapped. The mood turned icy in the car as Junior fumed at being stuck in a car going to Kansas. He quizzed Anthony numerous times about their assignment, but Anthony refused to answer.

Anthony paused to let his understudy's childish antics dissipate and snapped, "Now I understand why the school kicked you out. I've lost count. Was this the fourth time?"

"Fuck you. It was the fifth and final time. I graduated with honors. I'm done," Giancarlo stated proudly.

"How'd you do that? You have another year left," Anthony said.

"Everybody has a price," Giancarlo smirked. "Even the headmaster at Berkshire Prep."

Giancarlo looked out into the darkness. A crack of thunder broke the silence; lightning illuminated the countryside. For a brief second, he could see acreage upon acreage cornfields on each side of the highway. Splat! A huge raindrop christened the windshield. The skies opened. A deluge followed. He looked at Anthony as he turned on the wipers. Anthony had started to look old. His dyed jet-black hair was in sharp contrast to his crow's-feet and worry lines. He had blue eyes and stood an imposing six foot six. He always wore an Armani suit with Italian leather loafers. Anthony looked menacing for a good reason. He rarely fought and preferred to mediate a situation. Looking dangerous tended to help the mediation process.

Giancarlo Dominick Jr., the heir apparent to a powerful family, took after his mother's side in physical appearance—blond hair, fair skin. Standing at six foot one, he was still growing. He was thin and wiry, in stark contrast to his father, Giancarlo Dominick Sr., who was short and stout, with an olive complexion. Anthony had dubbed Giancarlo "Little G" at an early age. Back then, Junior had embraced the moniker. He wasn't so impressed these days, though.

Anthony fiddled with the radio. With the inclement weather, he got static. One station came in loud; it was at the end of a commercial. Then the refrains of "Rain on the Scarecrow" began. What a fitting song, Little G thought. The drive to Kansas was the first one-on-one excursion between Anthony and him. Anthony and Little G had been friends; now, they were student and teacher. But Little G was a poor student. Instead, he lived to irritate Anthony. It was part of his training to be the boss someday.

"Check the GPS for a diner," Anthony said.

"Two miles up, we take exit twenty-five on the right," Little G said. "What are we doing out here? It's a huge waste of my time."

"I've been out here once before. Your dad has a plan for a farm. He has been refused twice, and this is his last proposal. He doesn't like disappointment, and the owners don't understand that saying no to him is not an option. Our job is to 'help' them on that journey."

"Why didn't my dad talk to me about it? How come I didn't have a fucking say? It's typical of my old man, always telling me what to do and where to go with no explanations."

Anthony had listened enough. Tired of the brat's tirade, he exercised rank, snarling, "Quit your whining and just shut up! Maybe you'll learn something."

He leaned over and cupped Little G's mouth to silence his tantrum. The disgusting smell from Anthony's nicotine-stained fingers permeated Little G's senses, making him gag. He slapped the hand away, opened the window, and stuck his head out to suck in some fresh air. After a minute, he composed himself and closed the window. Little G ran a set of trembling fingers through his wet hair and snapped, "Don't you ever fucking do that to me again."

Anthony treated the threat with all the weight of a feather falling upon a scale, continuing the conversation as though Little G had never spoken.

"There's one thing I know about your dad: he keeps his cards close to his chest and never loses."

Little G contemptuously spit out a straw he had been chewing as Anthony continued, "If you want to know the details, ask your father. I know he didn't tell you, but I can't if he didn't. The one thing I know about your dad is he's calculating and doesn't make a move without doing his homework."

Anthony veered off the ramp and turned down the speed of the windshield wipers. "Oh, and by the way, pick up the straw on the floor when we get out. I don't like garbage in my car," he snapped.

"It's a straw. Get over it."

"It's a sign of disrespect. Unlike you, I didn't grow up with everything handed to me. When I tell you something from now on, you need to listen. You're in the majors now, not T-ball."

A few minutes of awkward silence ensued, broken only by Little G's staccato directions to the twenty-four-hour diner's parking lot. It was filled with semis, pickups, and SUVs. Many of the trucks even had rifles mounted inside their cabs. It looked like the set of the movie *Urban Cowboy*.

Little G quipped, "Are we gonna have to hunt for our food?"

Anthony locked up his SUV and warned his unwilling apprentice, "Watch what you say. These people work hard for their money. It's a tough life. They're not going to appreciate some wiseass, so mind your manners and shut your mouth. We don't need to call attention to ourselves. Just walking in there will do that."

Little G strutted to the diner clad in faded blue jeans, complete with two large holes at the knees, framed by the fringe, and wearing a brown T-shirt with his favorite band—Hatebreed. Anthony strolled behind with a cigarette. He took a few drags, blew the remnants into the air, coughed, doused the half-smoked cigarette in a puddle, and carefully deposited it in the receptacle by the door.

"See, this is how you dispose of garbage. It is important always to do things right."

Little G said, "I get it. Give it a rest. I fucking get it. I'll throw the straw away." He even politely held open the diner door for Anthony to enter first.

The place was boisterous with various men, mostly unshaven and many sporting baseball caps. Little G became uneasy with the prolonged stares. Anthony and Little G's entrance silenced the customers.

35

The waitress passed by with a load of plates, and in a soft Midwestern accent, she cooed, "Sit anywhere. Make yourselves comfortable, honey. I'll get you two coffees."

"I want a Monster," Little G snapped.

"A what, dearie?" she asked.

"A Monster! What are you, retarded?"

Men rose to their feet. Anthony rolled his eyes and scowled. "I'm sorry," he said, pointing at his sidekick. "He has Tourette's and hasn't taken his medication this morning. I apologize. He can't help himself. Giancarlo, say you're sorry."

Little G eyeballed Anthony and saw the unique darkness only associated with a shark's eyes. He backtracked. Quickly. Sheepishly he replied, "Tourette's…it's a curse. Gee, I'm sorry, ma'am. I meant no disrespect. I can't help myself sometimes."

As the patrons sat, Anthony said, "He'll take a coffee."

An empty corner booth cluttered with dishes caught their eye. The waitress cleared it and came back with their coffee and menus. The aroma of freshly brewed coffee, cooked bacon, and hash browns filled the air and tantalized their senses. Anthony stared at Little G's T-shirt. "I have to ask—Hatebreed? What's that, some social comment?"

"I guess you don't know everything. It's a fucking band."

Anthony rolled his eyes, took the menu, and ordered them two specials.

Little G whined, "Why'd you do that? What if I don't like the special?"

"Life's full of surprises," Anthony replied. "Deal with it. We need to be out of here fast, so I'm keeping it simple. No Monsters."

He pulled out a small notepad and pen and handed them to Little G.

"What's this for?" Little G asked.

"Note-taking. Do you remember how to write? I plan on telling you things once and only once, so jot them down."

Little G nodded slowly. "Whatever."

Anthony continued, "While you were sleeping, an exciting news story came over the radio. It seems there was a woman in Minnesota—a grandmother—"

"What's an old lady got to do with me?"

"I don't have a habit of talking to myself, and I'm not gonna start now. When I speak, you need to shut up—and listen. Until your father tells me otherwise, I will keep teaching you these lessons. Why does everything have to be about you?"

"Why does everything have to be a lesson?" Little G countered.

Anthony shook his head and rolled his eyes. The waitress delivered their meals and refilled their coffee. "One day, she was feeling ill," Anthony proceeded. With each word, Anthony's voice progressively grew softer. Little G half-heartedly took notes. Anthony continued, "And they rushed her to the hospital and found she had a cancerous tumor in her leg. With no money, no insurance, and nobody to care for her grandchildren, she didn't act as quickly as she should have. She refused treatment, even though radiation and chemo might have helped. She needed her leg amputated a few months later."

Little G was intrigued by this turn.

"Can you speak up a little? Why would somebody do that to themselves?"

Anthony's voice grew. "In the recovery room, the woman woke up and realized they had cut off the wrong leg."

"Holy shit, that's fucked up," Little G said.

"The doctors and nurses didn't care since she wasn't paying for it. They rushed her back into surgery and amputated the other leg. In the end, the woman could not sue the hospital." Anthony stared at Little G as he took it in.

"What the fuck! How come she couldn't sue?"

Anthony paused and bellowed, "She didn't have a leg to stand on."

The booth on their side had been eavesdropping and erupted in laughter. The waitress chuckled to herself as she walked by. Little G felt a warmness as blood rushed to his cheeks. He put his elbows on the table and engulfed his face with his hands. He hissed, "You're a fucking asshole. Do you like tormenting me in public?"

"Only when it's necessary. Did you learn anything?" Before Little G could respond, Anthony said, "Don't get caught up in other people's stories. Compassion and empathy should never be shown in life. They are for weak people. You, by contrast, are a general in an army. Remember, not every story is what it seems, and every action has consequences. And above all, never be swayed by sentiment, because your enemies won't. Listen with your eyes and see with your ears. Look for little tells—the inflection in their voice, their movements. Are you writing any of this down?"

Little G pulled out the notebook. "Yes, I wrote both down." Little G had scribbled, "#1. Don't be an asshole. #2. See number 1."

Chapter 6

❧ ❧ ❧ ❧ ❧

MISERY, KANSAS

The fog slowly dispersed as the sun cut through the haze. Thick clouds that resembled cotton candy hovered over the farm. The screen door slammed as Travis Wyatt emerged from the house to survey the damage from last night's violent storm. Branches lay strewn about his property. That which had survived the storm didn't look much better. The main barn and four smaller buildings were in disrepair, with weathered wood and peeling paint. Some outbuildings were beyond repair, but he refused to demolish the structures. Family history and sentimentality prevented him from doing so. Instead, he reinforced the buildings with come-a longs and thick timber. They relied on each other for their existence. Someday when they fell, it would be like a domino effect. The family used several of these buildings to house farm machinery, but Travis had only the tractor.

The year had been arid. Set squarely beside the gambrel-style main barn was the water tower, which last night's rain had partially filled. Adjacent to the water tower was the iron windmill, oxidized by time. The ladder that led up to it had several rungs broken or missing.

The silo, on the other side of the water tower, was composed of vertical oak planks. Several of its bands were missing. Trace elements of rust marked the area where straps had once existed. On its side was a faded image of the American flag, discolored by decades of the sun. The farm was still a special place for Travis, despite or perhaps because of its dilapidation. It was the location of those treasured memories of when his dad used to tell him and his brother stories. He used to love sitting on his father's lap with no care in the world. Every time he looked at the front porch, the memories seemed like yesterday. A swinging bench hung from the front porch's ceiling. They spent the time looking at the family album. Several pictures of his grandparents captured a bygone era of how beautiful the property had been and its manicured landscape. Travis longed for those days. Generations of Wyatts had cleared fields but left the trees surrounding the house intact.

One photo showed a white gazebo his father had unintentionally burned down when he was a teenager, the result of playing with fireworks. All that remained was its rock foundation. Ashlee, Travis's wife, to beautify the site, had planted flowers. Now he tried to sidestep a mud puddle, but his foot slid. A hole in one of his boots absorbed the water and mud. "Another day in paradise," he said to the chickens, rooster, and three cows, the only remaining members of a once-proud herd. They at least provided enough fresh milk and eggs for his family.

He walked over to his 1957 International Harvester, the last piece of equipment his family had purchased. Peeled red paint revealed the vehicle's age. Baling wire and duct tape had taken this piece of machinery where no tractor had gone before. He tinkered with the tractor and discovered it needed a new spark plug. It wasn't much to look at, but it still worked perfectly.

He went into one of the barns to fetch his toolbox and a black transistor radio, a relic from the 1960s. Something shiny caught his eye. It was a family heirloom, his brother's gold-plated watch. The time and date were forever stamped upon the broken glass. His eyes fixated on the calendar—July 28. A chill ran down his spine. Had it been twelve years? He grabbed his toolbox and radio, shoved the watch in his pocket, and walked outside. He heard the faint strains of a Buffalo Springfield classic on the radio. He grabbed a deep socket out of the toolbox and placed it over the spark plug. He attempted to loosen it, but it wouldn't budge. Then his sweaty hand slipped off the socket and was sliced on a sharp piece of metal, making him cry out in pain. Sweat stung the open wound. He quickly pulled his hand back and cried out, "What the…" He caught himself before saying the profanity and wiped the blood on his well-worn jeans.

His wife, wearing a yellow sundress and white Dearfoams scuffs, ran out, took her Carolina blue apron off, and fastened it to his hand. "Are you okay, Travis? That looks serious. You need to go to the hospital."

"It's only a scratch; I don't care. I'll repair it like I always do—super-glue," Travis said casually.

She grabbed his hand. "This looks serious. Let's go into the house and clean it up." He reluctantly agreed.

He asked rhetorically, "Do you know what day it is? It's July twenty-eighth."

She turned red with embarrassment. "I was hoping you wouldn't notice. I know it bothers you, but you must let it go," Ashlee pleaded.

"I try. But every time I look at TJ, I see the spitting image of his uncle. It's hard. He looks like him and acts like him. TJ is just as stubborn and pigheaded."

"I rang the bell for breakfast. Didn't you hear it?" Ashlee asked in a vain attempt to divert him.

"I guess I was preoccupied," Travis said.

"You're always preoccupied." She giggled as they went inside. She grabbed his hand and peeled back the apron. "Let me have a closer look. I think you need stitches."

After bandaging his hand, Ashlee scolded him, warning, "Please eat your food before it gets cold. We'll access your wound after breakfast." He took his first morsel, a crispy piece of bacon. The blood seeped through the bandages; he hid it from Ashlee's view.

Travis heard a sound from the front of the house and jumped out of his seat, looked out a window and, abruptly and screamed, "Where's TJ?"

"He's outside feeding the chickens and gathering eggs with Kansas. What's wrong?" Ashlee asked.

Travis bolted for the front door. As he slammed it, he yelled, "Ashlee, stay inside. I'll handle this."

"Handle what?" she asked, following him. "Travis, what's wrong?"

"Stay put."

A black SUV with tinted windows inched onto the property, dodging potholes almost with disdain, on its way toward the main house. The driver's door opened slowly, and an imposing figure eased out of the vehicle. He was tall and wore a navy-blue pinstripe suit. Sunglasses hid the driver's identity. Travis glanced down at the New York license plate. It read "Mr. K."

"Get off my property," Travis stuttered. "I'm not telling you again."

The vehicle's passenger got out and giggled under his breath and mimicked the farmer's speech pattern. The man growled, "Shut your mouth, Giancarlo." He reached into his pocket and took out a cigarette and lighter. The sun's rays bounced off the gold lighter and temporarily blinded Travis. The man smirked, satisfied with his childish antics.

To Travis, the man said, "I don't know if you remember who I am."

"I know who you are," he snapped, his arms folded, and legs spread apart.

The man continued, "Well, just in case you've forgotten, my name is Anthony Kurtis. Mr. Wyatt, we have drawn up a generous proposal that will secure your family the necessary money to sustain a fruitful life." He paused as he inhaled his cigarette. "We'll also put your son through college. He must be around eleven or twelve now? Remember, we're renting, not buying. You could still live here, and we'll fix it up better than new. If you want to work in the fields, you could. We won't get in your way, and you don't get in ours."

"I still don't know why you want to do this," Travis replied. "The soil is depleted after generations of farming. The barns are run down and dilapidated."

Anthony deliberately took a long, slow drag before he spoke next. "Our boss hasn't told us what he wants. And if we don't question him, why should you? If it's important to him, it's important to me. In the past, you haven't been very cooperative. We came here as a common courtesy. Consider this your final notice. I suggest that you sign the proposal when it arrives in the mail." As a final gesture of disrespect, Anthony flicked the cigarette butt toward Travis, and it landed just short of his boots.

Their engagement was disturbed when TJ popped off his air rifle and ran toward them. Kansas, their family dog, ran close behind. Anthony reached into his suit coat and pulled out a pistol. He pointed the gun in the direction of TJ.

"Whoa! What the fuck are you doing?" Travis shouted. "It's my son, and it's only a BB gun. Put that thing away."

TJ continued running toward his father.

"TJ, come over here and stand behind me," Travis shouted.

TJ obeyed and stood cowering behind his dad.

However, the growling dog slowly crept forward and barked several times until Travis told him, "It's okay, boy, heel."

Giancarlo raised his hands over his head with his fingers extended and yelled, "Boo," and laughed.

The sound caused the fur on the scruff of the dog's neck to stand on end as he started to inch closer to the trespassers. Travis commanded the dog to heel as his carotid artery quivered and his heart pounded.

"What a beautifully marked dog. And very protective," Anthony smirked.

Travis clenched his teeth and answered, "Yes, he is. He's extremely territorial. He doesn't like you here, and neither do I. Now get out." Travis watched his dog and saw his eyes follow Giancarlo. The young instigator took three steps forward as Kansas moved slowly toward him.

"Kansas," Travis yelled. "Sit."

The dog paused uneasily.

Travis snapped, "Lie down."

The dog instinctively followed his commands.

But when Giancarlo bent forward to tie his sneaker, Kansas did not stay. Instead, he swiftly advanced with a low growl. Anthony pointed the gun at the dog and fired. Kansas yelped and fell to the ground.

Travis jumped in front of the dog and stuttered, "What the fuck are you doing? If you're going to shoot someone, maybe you should shoot that asshole." He pointed to Giancarlo. "He's provoking my dog. Trying to kill my dog is no way to win me over. Get off my property before I call the sheriff."

TJ raced toward his wounded dog and ignored the blood. He placed the dog's head on his lap. Kansas released a small sigh and soulfully gazed at TJ.

Travis and Anthony looked squarely into each other's eyes. With a last parting shot, Anthony warned, "We haven't even started persuading yet. Wyatt, I strongly suggest you sign. Our next visit will not be as pleasant."

The car zipped off in a hiss of dust and flame, and the mocking sound of laughter came from the interior.

Chapter 7

🐾 🐾 🐾 🐾 🐾

LAFAYETTE SPRINGS, LOUISIANA

Beau sat at the maple dining room table. Suspended above was a cheesy wagon wheel chandelier with two burned-out bulbs. His four children impatiently waited for their mom to arrive. Beau placed his elbows on the table and looked at his phone. The weight of his elbows caused the table to rock. He took a pack of matches out of a kitchen drawer and deftly wedged the matchbook between the table leg and linoleum floor.

His wife, Tanis, ran in and said, "What—pizza again? I thought you told me you'd make dinner."

"No, I told you I'd get dinner. Ta da—I got dinner," he replied, scratching his scalp through his thick ebony hair. Momentarily he took his eyes off his cell phone. "What did you do to your hair?" he asked.

"You like it?"

"You look like a little boy."

"I'm sick of being treated like a beauty queen. I want people to take me seriously."

"Who doesn't take you seriously, baby?" Beau replied.

"None of my law professors," Tanis stated. "Behind my back, every-body calls me Elle Woods from the movie *Legally Blonde*. This will show them I'm serious."

Beau's attention was fading, drawn instead by his ever-trusty cell phone. It was never far from his side. His eyes reverted to the screen. Ready to pounce at the first sign of a message.

Tanis snapped, "Put that damn thing away. Dinnertime is the only time we get to spend as a family. You're not setting a good example for our children."

Beau ignored her, but he was not at ease despite the public bravado. His marriage had started to decline many years ago, but now it was in free fall. It had started with college. The early days consisted of Tanis staying home with the kids, cleaning the house, cooking meals, and doing laundry. But she always told Beau that when the kids were of a certain age, she wanted to do something meaningful. He was vague on the timing and said, "I'll let you know." He never wanted her to do it and never thought she would. The way she didn't fight back when he berated showed she lacked confidence. Then out of the blue, she defied him and enrolled in the local college.

Tanis being independent now was much too soon. In truth, it would probably have always been too soon. The gap had widened since she started law school—the erosion of their marriage combined with Beau's unhappiness with his job. She had never worked when the kids were young, yet now her career came first, he thought. As the man in the family, he felt his career should come first. For the last fifteen years, he had been the animal control officer of St. Pierre Parish. Promised the sheriff's job, he approached his job half-heartedly. He had never given it his all, but this year was different. For Beau, this was his year. As sheriff, he would see some action and be part of a team. He would get respect from the community, something he now lacked. He would shed what he considered a menial career.

"Why are you still dressed in uniform, and what's the van doing outside?" Tanis asked. "What's up with you tonight? You usually come home and take a shower and relax. You better not be going out. I told you I have to study. My bar exam is less than a month away."

"I'm on call twenty-four/seven. I don't have anything planned, but when the phone rings—"

"Well, it's not ringing tonight. Turn it off," Tanis stated.

He put the cell phone in his shirt pocket. "You happy?"

"I'm not happy until you turn it off. Damn it, Beau. I told you I have to study tonight at the library. I'm meeting some of my classmates."

"Why can't you do it here?"

"First, the kids never give me a moment's peace. Second, the house is a mess. Third, I need to do research. Do you care to hear the fourth, fifth, and sixth reasons? Or have you heard enough?"

Beau countered with, "First, I can't shut the phone off; second, my job is twenty-four/seven; third, I'm going out if it rings. Is that enough, or do you want more?"

"This is just more of your childish antics—another reason I need to study at the library," Tanis replied. "Whether you like it or not, I will be a lawyer. I've worked hard, and this is my dream job. The kids won't need me forever."

Inevitably the phone burst to life with the ringtone of "Who Let the Dogs Out." Beau's eyes lit up when he saw the caller ID. He glanced up at Tanis. It was the call he had wanted, the call he had waited for.

"Don't you dare—"

Beau took out his cell phone, and all they could hear was, "Yes, yes, okay, I know where it is. What time? That's in fifteen minutes. It's going to take me at least twenty to get there. I got it. Yes, I can put on my siren. Wait till I get there. I'm leaving now." He looked at Tanis and stared her down. His catchphrase rolled off his tongue. "Duty calls, gotta go."

"Beauregard Alain Leland, you stop right there. You can't get Drew to go on the raid?"

"It's my tip. I need to get credit for it."

"No, you need to stay here with the kids as promised," Tanis said.

"You told me you wanted me to work my way into a new job with better pay. Now is my chance. This is my time to shine. It may be the one break I need to become sheriff. You take them."

The twins began to wail. "You promised them," Tanis said.

"Why can't they go to my parents' house? Or have my parents come over here?"

"You know Tracy is deathly afraid of your father's dogs. Your parents don't care. The dogs are more precious than their grandchildren. They let them stay in the house whether the kids are there or not."

"I don't have time for this bullshit right now," he said, racing out.

Chapter 8

😺 😺 😺 😺 😺

BAXTER FALLS, CONNECTICUT

Daniel entered the tavern with the enthusiasm of a death row inmate taking his final walk, knowing what lay ahead but not knowing how to say it. His mind was in overdrive about how he would broach the subject with Jim. Had he gone too far that night? Did he jeopardize anything with his antics? What if Jim refused to pay? Right, wrong, or indifferent, he needed to solve the problem.

He headed over to the bar. Ethan greeted his arrival with an open bottle of Bud.

Daniel said, "Is Jim around?"

Ethan nodded and pointed to the office. "He's holed up in there. I think he slept there the last few nights. I haven't seen him this bad since he quit drinking."

"I need to talk to him," Daniel said.

He sharply knocked on the door and heard, "Not now, Ethan." Daniel entered the dark cavern. The only light source was the sun trying to break through the slats in the venetian blinds. Jim was at his desk, his shirt rumpled, his hair a mess. He had his head in his hands, and he stared at a bottle of Macallan scotch.

"Jim, you got a couple of minutes?" Daniel asked.

"Sure, come on in and take a seat," Jim answered in a meek tone without taking his eyes off the bottle. "I've been expecting you; I just didn't know when. I'm sorry, um, I don't know what to say...um, I fucked things up, and I ruined things for you." There was a moment's pause before Jim, who still hadn't looked Daniel in the eyes, continued. "I've made a mess of my life, my business, and now your business. I don't know what to do. I mortgaged everything to the hilt. I don't know where to turn. I've been contemplating whether to drink this bottle or sell it. It's worth a few thousand dollars and was a gift from a very dear friend. It's funny. I am now sober, and my most cherished possession is this bottle. Daniel, I've got four thousand dollars. You can have it all. I know it's just a drop in the ocean, but it's a start. I promise to make it up to you."

Startled by his friend's obvious pain, Daniel said, "If I'm ever going to get my money back, this place needs to be open. You'll need some working capital for now, so keep it."

"I don't blame you if you want to hit me," Jim said. "Hit me several times. I deserve it. I let you down, my patrons down, and myself down."

"I just wish you had been honest with me," Daniel said.

"I don't even know what to say. Sorry isn't enough, and you're right."

"My grandfather told me about this adage on several different occasions: If you hate what you see, don't blame the mirror."

Jim lifted his head and looked at him for the first time. "Huh?"

"If you're as sympathetic as you sound and it's not some phony bullshit, you'll go home, take a shower, and get some rest. Leave the piss-poor attitude there and come in here with a new attitude. Be a new man." Daniel grabbed the bottle of scotch and looked Jim directly in the eyes. "I'm taking this home as a down payment. I don't need you doing something stupid. And I, too, am keeping the bottle as a souvenir. I don't want to be a Jim, or more precisely, someone who takes advantage of others with his idle promises." Daniel left and went to the bar.

"Where's the crowd?" Daniel asked Ethan.

"On Mondays and Tuesdays, we don't open till four. How's the puppy doing?" Ethan asked. "What'd you name him?"

"He's doing okay. I call him Sambuca. He's very trainable. He already knows to sit by the door when he needs to go outside. Gramps gets a big kick out of him. But Gramps and a friend are bringing him back to the pound today. It's just the wrong timing for me, and I can't keep him. He's already had a rough life, and I can't spend the time with him he needs. He needs to be adopted by a family."

"Jim told me the back story of the puppy, and he reminds me so much of you," Ethan said.

"How so?"

"He's a survivor. He fended off coyotes to protect his family. You're a survivor too. You lost your parents. I can't imagine what toll it's taken on you. Sambuca is also a fighter—he beat the odds. And that's you, Daniel. You never give up. Jim piled so much work on you, and you never complained. You forged ahead without a whimper. Daniel? Are you listening? Did you even hear a word I said? Daniel?"

"Huh? I'm sorry, what time's it?" Daniel asked while sipping his beer.

"It's somewhere around one thirty. Why?"

"Just hold that thought." Daniel frantically dialed Gramps, and when he answered, Daniel asked, "Gramps, have you run your errands yet?"

Chapter 9

🐾 🐾 🐾 🐾 🐾

MISERY, KANSAS

In the dwindling darkness, Travis sat at the kitchen table and heard his wife sneeze with her trademark three short bursts. His eyes strained to read the clock. It was 4:13 a.m. For the last few months, Travis had had trouble falling asleep. Getting up in the morning was never a problem. He was an early riser. It was his favorite time of the day. Dawn breaking, a cup of coffee, and the serenity of a quiet house—three of life's simplest pleasures, he thought. In truth, he couldn't afford many others. He took the time to reflect upon the day's activities without interruptions. He impatiently tapped his fingers on the table with a few days' mail stacked up before him. Travis knew he couldn't pay these bills. Opening them was acknowledging that they needed to be paid.

The kitchen was straight out of the 1950s: water-stained wallpaper, warped cabinet doors, and a few chips out of a cast-iron sink laden with dishes from last night's meal. Kansas lay on a pile of blankets in the corner, occasionally whimpering as he struggled to get comfortable. The boards creaking in the night or the wind blowing through the trees set him on edge, and he sometimes growled in his sleep. The trespassers a few weeks ago had heightened Kansas's protectiveness.

Travis said, "It's okay, Kansas, we're going to the vet's today" in a barely audible voice. Ashlee gently patted Kansas on the head as she entered the kitchen and asked him, "Are you hungry, boy?" Kansas thumped his tail. Her white slippers floated across the linoleum.

She flipped on the microwave light and looked at her husband. He was paler than porcelain. She asked, "Did you get any sleep?"

"A little."

"Travis, you're putting too much pressure on yourself. Things will be okay." Ashlee grabbed his arm and gently rubbed it.

He kissed her forehead. "I wish I could be as optimistic as you. This is becoming the most difficult time of my life." Then, in a rare burst of emotion, he whispered with a bleak intensity, "Thanks for being here."

She said, "This is exactly where I'm supposed to be. Right by your side."

He was blessed to have Ashlee. She looked as beautiful as when they'd met in college. He had never believed in love at first sight, but when they met…

They both arrived on the campus of the University of Missouri in the same year. Ashlee had been born and raised in Missouri. Her mom, a single parent, had worked several jobs and was never home. Ashlee was a high-honors student at a private school and went to Mizzou on scholarship with dreams. Everything seemed possible during those trying years, filled as they were with her can-do attitude.

Travis was a three-sport athlete in high school and an average student. He dreamed of playing ball professionally and finally accepted a full ride to the university via his high school records as a quarterback. A small fish in a big pond, he had leaned on Ashlee as his rock. Her unexpected pregnancy forced them to drop out of college after their freshman years. All that seemed so long ago now as they sat there, waiting for the sun to rise.

"I missed cuddling with you this morning," Ashlee said.

"I'm sorry, hon, I couldn't sleep. I rolled back and forth. I was afraid I'd wake you," he said.

"Aren't you going to open the letter?" Ashlee asked.

"What's the difference? We can't afford the vet bill anyway. Or that one, or that one, or that one." Each time he pointed at a different envelope.

"No, this one." She handed him an envelope postmarked a couple of days ago. "Mr. Dominick's proposal came in the mail three days ago. Aren't you curious?" Ashlee inquired.

"No," Travis said.

Travis shrugged and mumbled, "These a-holes come on our property and act like they own the place. They shot our dog, disrespected us, and almost shot TJ. I don't need to open it. If Dominick wanted the farm this bad, why didn't he come out here personally instead of sending his flunkies?" He stood, kicked the chair, and proceeded to pace. "What do they want with this place? Why can't they do it back in New York? What's so special about our place? The buildings are in disrepair. They said I could still plant the fields. Exactly what part of the farm are they using? I have an obligation. How about the neighbors who rent some of our property—the Russells, the Wards, the Daltons. Are they still allowed to farm? These families have rented our land for generations. What are they going to do? I gave them my word. I can't kick them off. These people aren't just our neighbors; they're our friends. Have you asked yourself, are these bullies putting them and us in any danger? Think about that while I go to the bathroom."

When he returned, the kitchen light was on, coffee was brewing, and Ashlee was reading a letter with a small piece of paper in her left hand.

"What are ya doing?" Travis shouted.

"I'm reading your letter."

"I told you I'd think about it. I didn't tell you to open it," Travis said.

"I'm sorry. Is there any harm in looking?" Ashlee asked.

"No, but I thought we'd make a family decision."

"I'm not deciding. I was just curious about what Mr. Dominick was offering. Look, he sent a check for our vet bills."

He snapped, "It's one check. Do you think they're going to make things any better? Their intentions are bad. I sense it. Anything from them will be tainted."

Ashlee, however, had had enough of grandiose speeches and unpaid bills. She retorted, "You say they won't make it any better. Can it worsen? Our dog is in pain with a bullet wound, and we can't even pay the vet." Then, stung herself by the truth of her query, she backpedaled. "I'm sorry. I shouldn't have said that."

"No. You're right," he said. "On all fronts. I apologize too. I shouldn't have gotten this mad. See, they're already splitting us apart as a family by making us argue."

"Let's keep an open mind. You realize the thugs are gonna return," Ashlee said. "They've come twice. They've shot Kansas. What's to prevent them from killing any of us?"

He crossed his arms. "I've got guns. I'll defend this property to my last breath," he said. "After they shot Kansas, I went the proper route and filed a report at the sheriff's office, called several times, and left messages, and that lazy fuck Clint still hasn't gotten back. I don't know how he ever got elected sheriff. He's an embarrassment to our community. I'm sorry, Ash, I shouldn't have used that word. I'm beyond frustrated."

"I know you've got a lot on your mind." She got up and rubbed his neck, and he slowly felt the tension begin to ease.

"I need to go outside to do my chores."

An hour later, he returned.

Ashlee had not moved. She sat frozen at the table—a letter and contract in front of her.

He was going to start shouting, but where had that gotten them?

"Read it out loud," Travis said.

"Dear Mr. and Mrs. Wyatt,

Enclosed is a check to pay your vet bill and all necessary future appointments.

It was an unfortunate incident.

I talked to your vet, who assured me this would cover all expenses.

I am glad nobody in your family got seriously hurt.

Sometimes my men get too aggressive.

Please note that I'm submitting a very generous proposal as to the main issue at hand.

I plan on restoring all buildings to their original condition, which would make your father and grandfather very proud.

I need an answer by August 21.

Please note that if I do not get an answer, the next visit may not be so cordial.

Sincerely,
Mr. Dominick
P.S. I heard the vet did a great job stitching up your hand."

"I can't believe it. After reading the paperwork, I can't believe it," Ashlee said. "Do you know how much they're willing to pay us?" Without letting Travis get a word in, she blurted out, "Ten thousand a month! Do you know what we could do with that? We could get all new farm machinery, livestock, fertilizer, everything we need to have a productive farm again. TJ could finally get his operation to correct his hearing. He also needs a phone—he's the only one in his class without one."

"Whoa, whoa, slow down," Travis shouted. "What do they want with this worthless piece of property? Why so much money?"

Ashlee hugged him. "They're not trying to buy the property; they're leasing. You're too hard on yourself. Calm down. Maybe it's our way out."

He shouted, "Our way out of what? Our responsibilities, our heritage, our family name?"

"You've never asked for this. It's your family's legacy, and it's become your albatross. I mean our albatross. Occasionally, Travis, you have to swallow your pride. You have to look at life differently than your grand-parents and great-grandparents did. Times change. You must be your own man."

"As bad as things have been, I have many great memories of my grand-father and father. My core values have stayed the same. I'm not a sellout."

"You haven't been happy in years. You don't even go on the property where your father had a heart attack—where your brother died."

"Ashlee, I've had my reasons," Travis said. He drew himself up, saying, "It's not how a man falls; it's how quickly he gets up that is the measure of a man." He pointed to his chest. "I get up. I always get up."

"Sometimes, though, a man needs help to get up. Your mom stuck by your dad through thick and thin, no matter what. Didn't she always say things happen for a reason?" she asked.

"You know she did."

"Well—maybe *this* is our reason. I know you're a proud man. Sometimes it pays to step back and reevaluate a situation. Maybe now is not a time for pride."

He got up and went outside, and Ashlee followed. The sky was awak-ening with vibrant hues of orange and yellow. Travis looked for Ashlee's hand and kissed it. "This is what I love every morning. It doesn't exist anywhere else in the world. I want TJ to be able to see this every day."

"Maybe we need to talk to Mr. Dominick and ask him his inten-tions," Ashlee said.

"Right now, we need to get TJ up and go to the vet's," Travis said. "We'll discuss it later."

Chapter 10

🐾 🐾 🐾 🐾 🐾

ONE YEAR LATER, 2014

BAXTER FALLS, CONNECTICUT

Daniel pulled out a ladder-back chair, plopped himself down, and set his Budweiser on a coaster. He watched the patrons at J. W. Morgan's from afar. He reached into his pocket, pulled out his phone, and laid it on the table. Unconsciously, he nicked the label with his right thumb to distinguish his beer from others. Gramps hates when I'm late, he thought.

"Hey, Daniel, thanks for stopping by. Sorry I didn't give you more notice," Jim said.

Daniel put his foot on a chair in a friendly gesture and slowly moved it out. "Take a load off."

Jim sat and proclaimed, "Hey, can you believe it's been a year?"

Daniel raised his bottle to toast Jim, and Jim guzzled the last two mouthfuls of his drink.

"Let me get you another. What're ya having?"

"Thanks, but no thanks," Jim said, "There's only so much tonic I can take. It's been six and a half years since I drank. Ironic, isn't it? Owning a bar and not drinking?"

"I give you credit. It must've been hard to do," Daniel said.

"To be honest with you, there are days I miss it. But I don't miss the late nights, stupid conversations, cotton mouth, and hangovers—especially hangovers. Watching my customers' antics has given me a sobering effect."

"So, Jim, what can I do for you?"

"I called you here for a reason. I know I've apologized a thousand times."

Daniel shook his head in disbelief. He'd had this conversation on numerous occasions. 'You didn't call me down here to apologize again, did ya? I'm tired of this shit. Get over it—I did."

"Please, just let me finish. As I was saying, I'm genuinely sorry for treating you the way I did. I didn't mean to cause all your financial hardships. I had a chance to take this business where it's never been. I knew I was over budget; I shouldn't have been spending the money I did. I couldn't help myself. I was out of control. It didn't hit me until opening night when you stormed into my office. The look in your eyes…I wouldn't have blamed you if you had hit me that night. I would have deserved it. Even if you had beaten me up, it wouldn't have matched the pain inside. You were the last person I wanted to hurt. You were there for me from day one. It was your idea for upstairs. How stupid was it of me to try and appease you with a dog? A couple of days later, I heard you weren't keeping him. It tore me up inside.

"I called you down here to thank you. I appreciate all the little things you do around here fixing a door, painting. I don't notice half the stuff you do until after it's already done, and usually Ethan lets me know. And I realize I'm not billed for most of it."

Jim smiled. "So today, I'm giving you three envelopes. The first is a check to show you my appreciation for all your work. On opening night last year, I promised to pay you with interest. This brings me to the second envelope, which contains a document you need to sign. I'm giving you five percent of my business."

"Wow, thank you, you didn't have to do that, but—"

"No buts you've earned it. And the third envelope is a dividend check paid to all the shareholders. We had a great year."

"I don't know what to say to you. I'm speechless."

"Well, you deserve it."

"I want to thank you too, Jim. After that incident, I had to reevaluate my life. Last year I had so much anger and hatred inside. It was eating me up—you, the bar, and the world. I decided to take all the negativity and use it as a tool for motivation. It took me a while to find it. But I did."

"What a great attitude."

"I straightened out all the bills with Gramps's help," Daniel explained.

"How's Mickey doing these days? Haven't seen him in a while."

"Every day is an adventure. He has his good and bad days. Unfortunately, the bad far outweigh the good now."

"Sorry to hear, Daniel. If there's anything I can do, let me know."

"We have a lady watching him. Kelly is an angel. How she puts up with him, I don't know. She's been a godsend. She's taken a huge burden off me, and I've been able to refocus on my business. I've gotten quite a few leads from the bar. Thanks to your generosity, I'll be able to start an addition on my house—an oversized garage with an office upstairs."

Daniel looked at his phone. "I hope you don't mind. I gotta get going." He extended his right hand, and Jim shook it.

"It's the least I can do," Jim said.

"Why, were you considering ten percent?" Daniel chuckled.

"Thanks for being a true friend. I don't know where I'd be without you," Jim said.

Daniel answered with a sly smile, "A true friend and business partner. One last thing. Happy anniversary." Daniel put a box beautifully gift wrapped in beige paper with a hunter-green bow on the table.

"I appreciate this, but you didn't have to do it," Jim said. He hurriedly unwrapped the box and appeared speechless. His eyes fixated on the present. His eyes watered.

"Normally I don't believe in regifting, but this is where it belongs," Daniel stated. "I know what this means to you."

Jim picked up his prize memento, his bottle of scotch. "I don't know what to say. I'm at a loss for words," Jim said.

"How about…thank you?" Daniel offered.

🐾 🐾 🐾

Daniel parked his vehicle and saw Gramps wave to him from the front porch.

"Do you need any help?" Gramps asked.

"No, I got it." Daniel took the pizza from the truck and brought it into the kitchen while Gramps shuffled to his chair. Daniel grabbed three plates, put pizza on them, and brought them to the living room, where Gramps was sitting in his recliner. The unmistakable aroma of a freshly baked pie filled the air. "Kelly, want a piece?"

"Sure, but would you mind if I take it to go? I'll see you boys tomorrow," Kelly said.

"Mumm, that smells delicious," Gramps said.

"It's a Gramps special. Do you mind holding my plate for a minute?" Gramps nodded as he extended both his arms.

Daniel went to the front door and scanned the yard. He whistled, and Buca bolted into the house and settled next to the recliner with his head perched on the armrest. "Buca, go to your spot." The dog reluctantly obeyed, with its tail between its legs.

Buca had matured into a robust, fifty-five-pound, shorthaired dog with a silky coat, broad skull, powerful jaws, and muscular, stocky body. He had remained all black with a white paw print encompassing his left eye. His ears drooped down a little but always perked up when he heard something.

Gramps handed Daniel his plate and asked, "Where have you been? I expected you earlier. I thought you told me you'd call me if you're running late."

"You're right, Gramps. I'm sorry. Time got away from me. But I've got some great news." Daniel reached into his pocket and proudly pulled out the three envelopes. "I got a bonus check, a check for the property maintenance, and lastly"—Daniel broke into a big smile—"I'm now a minority owner of the bar. This check allows me to put the addition on my house."

"Well, he wouldn't have the place if it wasn't for you, Daniel. You earned it. You better cash it quickly before it bounces."

"Gramps, I know you don't like him, but I've come to trust him. He's changed. Everybody deserves a second chance. He noticed Gramps hadn't eaten all his pizza. "Gramps, what's wrong with the crust?"

"Nothing, just full." Gramps put the plate on the side table and placed the napkin on top. "I'm excited for you to be able to build your garage. Does it mean you won't be sleeping here anymore?"

"No, I'll be here most of the time. When I'm gonna be late, I'll call for Kelly to stay until I get home."

"Do you have a couple of minutes to talk?" Gramps asked.

"Sure, Gramps, what's on your mind?"

"Kelly is…for somebody who cooks and cleans, she's not very good at her job. She does vacuum, but she doesn't like to dust, and she's a horrible cook. To avoid the work, Kelly takes me for a lot of rides. She sits down and does crossword puzzles and watches her soap operas. I can't believe I pay her for that. I wrote everything down in case we need to fire her."

"What are you talking about? Fire her? We've discussed this many times. Kelly is here to be your companion first, and any cleaning she does is a bonus. She's the mother of a friend. She could use the extra income. She's lonely, and we thought you two could become friends."

Gramps was unconvinced. "She hounds me until I take my medicine—she's pushy. Occasionally, she crosses the line and asks personal questions. I find it annoying and rude. It's almost like being married without the benefits. At my age, there aren't too many benefits."

Daniel grinned and stood to take their plates.

"I'll just keep my napkin," Gramps said. He kept the crusts hidden.

"Okay, Buca, you can get up," Daniel said on his way to the kitchen.

Buca jogged over to Gramps, jumped onto his lap, and put his head on the chair's armrest. Daniel watched intently. Gramps petted Buca, broke one of the crusts in half, and carefully balanced a piece on Buca's nose. Buca looked cross eyed at the crust and waited patiently for a command. "Okay, Buca," Gramps said. Buca reared his head up, flipped the crust piece into the air, and caught it in his mouth.

Daniel came back in as Buca caught the crust. "You spoil him."

"The smartest dog I've ever seen. Aren't you glad you kept Buca now?"

"Gramps, he adopted me. He's more than a dog—other than you, he's my best friend."

Chapter 11

😺 😺 😺 😺 😺

THREE WEEKS LATER

"Where's Leslie?" Gramps whined. "I'm hungry, and it's too damn cold in here. The only thing missing is my toe tag." Gramps sat rigidly in the booth, attired in a burgundy polo shirt. He started to shake.

"Gramps, shh, lower your voice, calm down. Let me close the duct above your head. The waitress is very busy. When she looks this way, I'll get her attention."

Gramps looked at the unfamiliar surroundings, seemingly confused.

"It's been a while since you've been here, huh, Gramps?"

"Years and years," he said, surveying the busy tavern. "The last time I was here, it was much smaller."

Gramps fidgeted with the menu and opened it up. "Doesn't Tim pay the electric bill? It seems awfully dark in here."

"It's Jim. And it's called atmosphere."

Gramps rocked back and forth.

"Now what's the matter?"

"It's the medication. It binds me up. I haven't sat on the throne for a couple of days."

"You should be telling Kelly these things. There's medication you can take to alleviate the problem. Where's your glasses?"

"I don't know. I lost 'em a couple of days ago. I think Kelly hid 'em."

"Gramps, stop. Why would you say that?"

"So, I can't keep an eye on her anymore. She got mad at me. I keep writing things down. Maybe if she cleaned, she'd find them."

Jim sneaked up on Daniel and made him jump. "Jim, you remember my grandfather. His friends call him Mickey."

"Long time no see. You look good. How ya doing?"

"Hi, Tim, I'm cold."

Daniel's eyes rolled as he shook his head in disbelief.

"What brings you out tonight?" Jim asked.

"It's Daniel's birthday," Gramps stated triumphantly.

"Well, Daniel, happy birthday," Jim said.

"Shh, not so loud. It's just another day. Thank you, Jim. I thought Gramps could use a night out. Jim, when you see Leslie, please tell her we'll have the specials," Daniel said.

"I'll get the order in right away then," Jim said.

Gramps hesitated, then asked, "Is everything okay, Daniel? You seem a little down."

Daniel reflected a minute. "This is a tough year for me. I've lived longer than my dad. I often wonder how different life would have been if they were alive."

Gramps shushed him.

"Your parents would have been so proud of you. You're like your father—he always worried about things he had no control over. Your mother was the opposite, and that's why they made a great pair. Your luck seems to have changed. You're busy. The addition you wanted has begun."

"Yeah, but I often wondered how my life would have been different if my parents had survived. Maybe I'd have a brother or sister, or both." His voice trailed off.

"Enough about the past. Tell me about your addition."

After the meal, Jim came by with a couple of pieces of German chocolate cake. "Your day isn't complete without a piece of cake and a birthday wish."

"Thanks, looks yummy," Gramps said with a gleam in his eye.

Daniel said, "Hey, Gramps, you look like you are still cold. How about a nice hot cup of coffee with a shot of Sambuca?"

"That sounds great."

Daniel asked Jim to scoot over so he could get the drinks.

"Let the waitress take care of it," Jim said.

"No, I want to go. My legs are starting to stiffen up. Can I get you anything while I'm up there?"

"My usual," Jim said. "With plenty of ice."

As Daniel neared the bar, he noticed Ethan with what appeared to be stubble on his upper lip. "I know. It's my attempt to look older," Ethan said. "Did you come here to break my balls, or do you need something?"

Daniel grinned. "Both. I'll take a shot of Sambuca, a Budweiser, and Jim's usual, extra ice."

"This time, use a tray," a low, seductive voice said with a laugh. Daniel turned around and saw a tall, sultry redhead. He looked at her quizzically and felt a rush of blood overcome his face. She responded, "You don't remember, do you? Last year at the grand reopening, you spilled a drink on my suede purse and ruined it."

Daniel responded, "I'm sorry. I was a little under the weather."

"You were a *little* under the weather? That's like calling a hurricane a gust of wind."

"I don't remember much from that night. But I remember the night you had problems with some guys, and Ethan threw them out. If he didn't, I was going to."

"Thanks, but I can handle myself."

"I noticed. What do I owe you for the purse?" Daniel asked.

"Nothing. It was old, and it gave me a reason to buy a new one. I love purses."

"Well, let me buy you a drink," he said.

"Umm—I'm getting ready to leave. I'll take a raincheck. Is that the same puppy from a year ago?" She pointed to a secluded part of the bar.

"Yes. I was ready to give him away that night. Now I wouldn't sell him for a million dollars."

"I know that feeling. I also have a dog. What's his name?"

"Buca—I mean Sambuca."

"Interesting. A dog that hangs out in a bar should be called Sambuca." He held out his hand. "My name is Daniel."

The redhead stood and took his hand. "Yes, I remember. You don't. I'm Lindsey. Nice to meet ya." She looked over at Buca again.

"Is he friendly? Would you mind if I went over to him?"

Daniel said, "Sure, no problem, he's very friendly."

Jim, Daniel, and Lindsey arrived at the table simultaneously. Jim had a bowl of food for Buca. "Mind if I give this to him?" he asked Daniel.

"Sure, go ahead."

Jim put the bowl down.

Buca looked away.

"I can't believe he won't touch that. It's New York prime," Jim said.

"That's because he needs permission. It's okay, Buca."

Buca wolfed down his dinner.

Lindsey dropped a flyer on the table. "I think this is something you might be interested in."

"Leslie, you got the check. I'm paying," Gramps said.

"No, Gramps, this is Lindsey. Lindsey, my grandfather, Mickey."

"Nice to meet you, Mickey," Lindsey said.

Gramps scooted over and patted the cushion. "Please sit down." Gramps poured the Sambuca into his coffee and stirred. He took a sip and said, "Just what the doctor ordered."

Lindsey quipped, "That sounds like my type of doctor." She picked up the pamphlet. "Here, take a look. I need it back, though. It's the only one I have."

Gramps shifted his weight from one cheek to the other as Daniel perused the pamphlet.

Lindsey inquired, "Mickey, is there something wrong?"

"I'm backed up farther than the Long Island Expressway on a holiday weekend!"

"Gramps!"

"No, that's okay. I find him charming. He reminds me of my grand-father," Lindsey said.

"Please, don't encourage him," Daniel replied.

Daniel took the leaflet and began reading. "It's a no sanctioned dog show put on by the Every Dog Club," Lindsey said.

"My dog's not a purebred."

"He doesn't have to be. It includes all dogs."

"You got a second? I'll go into Jim's office and make a copy. It's very intriguing. I'll be right back."

Minutes later, Daniel returned with the flyer. Lindsey showed Gramps pictures of her dog on her phone. "This is my baby, Starr. She's a keeshond; it's a Dutch breed."

"What a beautiful dog," Gramps said.

To his surprise, Daniel felt faintly disappointed when Lindsey said, "Sorry, I have to go." She got up and offered Gramps her hand. "It was a pleasure to meet you, Mickey. I hope you have a good night."

Mickey inquired, "One quick question. Do you clean houses?"

"Gramps, stop!" Daniel said. "You're embarrassing me. I'm sure Lindsey has a job."

"Yes, real estate. What's Mickey mean?" Lindsey asked Daniel.

"Oh, nothing important. I'm sorry," Daniel said.

After Lindsey's departure, Jim said, "Enjoy the rest of your evening."

Gramps handed Daniel an envelope. "I knew this would be a tough birthday for you, and I wanted to do something special."

Daniel opened the envelope, and his eyes grew wide. "Gramps, I don't mean to be rude, but you forgot to fill in the amount."

"I did it on purpose. I want to pay for the bathroom, and I don't know the cost."

"I budgeted for a bathroom," Daniel protested.

"I know. But you only do it once, so do it right. The check is something I want to do for you. Please let me do it."

Daniel tried to suppress his emotion, but his eyes became misty. "Thank you, Gramps. You're the best." He got up and hugged his grandfather. Daniel asked for the check, but the server informed them his dinner was on Jim. He left her a generous tip. "Time to go. It's getting late," Daniel said. "C'mon Buca, it's time to go home."

Chapter 12

🐾 🐾 🐾 🐾 🐾

MISERY, KANSAS

"Boo," Ashlee said in a low baritone voice.

Travis leaped out of the kitchen chair, banging his right leg. He rubbed his kneecap.

"Why'd you do that?"

"I'm sorry," she uttered in an unapologetic tone while trying to stifle her laughter.

"Doesn't sound like you're sorry."

"I am." She kissed his cheek.

He complained, "I hate this kitchen. You would never have been able to sneak up on me on our old floor like that. I used to hear every creak, every sound, every movement."

"Oh, no! It's beautiful, Travis; it's my dream kitchen. Oak cabinets, tile floor, granite countertops, and stainless-steel appliances." It was straight out of a *Country Living* magazine. "How can you not like this?" Ashlee asked.

"I don't know how to explain it. It's like a gift. I can't appreciate it. And we certainly didn't earn it." He saw her look out the garden window above the sink. "Whattaya looking at?"

Like a crow curious about a shiny object, Ashlee stared at the cupola. She was mesmerized by the sun's rays on the copper roof as light beams danced throughout the yard and a gentle autumn breeze whispered through the silhouette of a tractor weathervane. Travis noticed her infatuation. "Pinch me; I must be dreaming. This isn't the farm I remember. It's beautiful. Aren't you excited?"

"I don't know. Yes and no," Travis said.

"What do you mean?"

"We're flaunting this place now. Most of our neighbors are struggling. A few have even lost their farms. And here we are, putting all this money into our farm. I can't even imagine what they're saying about us other than we sold out."

"Who cares what they think? Travis, this is our dream, what we envisioned."

"I care, and so should you. They're our neighbors. I didn't envision this shit. I always thought me, and TJ would be doing this—someday. Much in the same way my ancestors did. The only way to explain it is like a kid getting a new toy and not wanting to open the box and ruin the moment. This farm is just a shiny new toy, and it's not what I want—nor do I want to play with it."

"But they rebuilt everything. It's better than new," Ashlee said.

"I enjoyed all the minor imperfections done by my ancestors. It added character. At least they felt accomplishment and pride when they finished a project. I never had a say in what these guys did. They never passed anything by me. I have several albums of Wyatt history. Dominick rebuilt this place how he wanted, not how we wanted. What bothers me the most is they don't own this damn farm—we do. Yet they do as they please. I don't know if my family would have been proud of these changes."

"Taylor would have loved this!"

Travis had to concede. "He would. He was a perfectionist. Even when tilling the fields, they had to be in a straight line. He would even lay his clothes out the night before. He was an early riser and never needed the alarm. He got up so damn early that he beat Dad, and boy, did that piss him off." Travis gazed off in the distance and looked skyward as he watched the clouds drift. He still found it hard to believe Taylor was not around whenever they talked about his twin.

When Travis and Ashlee married and had returned to the farm, the Wyatts embraced her as their own. Several months later, upon Travis and Ashlee's return from an obstetric visit, Travis ran to the back fields to inform his brother of their exciting news. Taylor was riding the tractor. He rushed to proclaim, "Ashlee wanted me to tell you at dinner, but I can't wait. It's a boy. We're having a boy!"

Taylor continued plowing the land as he gave his brother a thumbs-up. "Taylor, slow down. I want to talk."

"I got to finish first," Taylor yelled.

"Would you be the godfather?" Travis shouted over the hum of the motor.

"I'm going to be a godfather!" Taylor leaped gleefully out of his seat and pounded the air with his fist. The tractor landed smack in the middle of a woodchuck hole, which caused its front tire to dip and threw Taylor off. In a split second, everything changed. Travis watched in horror as the tractor fell on top of Taylor. Travis moved swiftly, shut off the engine, and attempted to lift the tractor off his brother. He saw Taylor's foot had been sliced off and his right arm nearly severed. Travis ripped off his belt, put a tourniquet high on his brother's arm, tore off his T-shirt, and tied his brother's leg midcalf.

Taylor watched Travis, not once crying out in pain. He was in shock. "Stay awake, Taylor, keep your eyes open," Travis said. "Everything's gonna be all right. Talk to me. Hang on while I get help." Travis ran to the adjacent field and yelled to his father, "Call an ambulance—there's been an accident. It's Taylor. The tractor fell on him. Dad, I need the truck. Run to the house, and make sure Mom stays inside. She doesn't need to see this. Tell Ashlee to wait in the driveway for the paramedics." Travis hopped in the 4x4 and sped to the adjoining field. He attached several chains to the bumper and pulled the tractor off his brother.

"Taylor, we have an ambulance coming."

"What happened?" Taylor asked.

"The tractor fell on you. You're going to be fine. The ambulance is on its way."

Minutes felt like hours as Travis waited and clutched his brother's hand. He saw his father running toward them from the house and then abruptly stopped ten feet away. He looked at the bloody carnage, grabbed his chest, and fell to the earth.

Travis felt several nails dig into his bicep. He heard several refrains of "Travis, Travis, you're doing it again. You've got to stop reliving the past. You did everything you could."

A big part of him had died that day. "Taylor wouldn't believe the transformation." He brushed a tear from his eye.

"I think so too," Ashlee said while she hugged Travis.

"There isn't a day that I don't think about him. There are some days I feel him right beside me."

"I only knew him for a short time, but I miss him too," Ashlee said. "But you can't live in the past. There are too many ghosts here. What's done is done. Accept that the farm's improved. Come on, let's take a ride and go to the store. I have some items to get. We should be back in an hour."

"Let me whistle for TJ."

"No, he'll be fine. There are lots of people around, and he has Kansas. He needs to have some responsibility."

🐾 🐾 🐾

After returning home, Travis asked Ashlee, "Where's TJ?"

"I don't know. I haven't seen him since we returned. I've heard Kansas barking out back, so I'm sure he's nearby," she replied.

"What time is dinner?"

"In about a half hour."

"He better not be bothering the workers. Kansas isn't too happy with all this activity." Travis heard a commotion and went out the back door, letting the screen door slam behind him. He heard a familiar voice as he walked to the front of the house. As Travis neared, the voice intensified. It was TJ yelling, "Ándale—ándale!"

Travis shouted, "Who you talking to?"

TJ pointed toward the roof. "Them."

"You better not be bothering the workers," Travis stated.

"I'm not. I'm working."

"Whattaya talking about?"

TJ strutted around with the cockiness of a rooster. "I'm the new boss. Little G told me ándale means 'good job' in Spanish, so I keep serenading the workers."

"That's not what it means. It means hurry up!"

"Dad, they have been working faster."

"If I were working, I'd be extremely insulted. I told you to stay away."

"What time is it, Dad?"

"It's almost four thirty. Why?"

"Little G said I could get paid. They stop at five. I only have a little longer."

"Your days done, and so is your job. Go get paid," Travis said. "After you're done, go in the house and wash up. Supper's almost ready."

TJ ran off toward the barns. Travis reentered the house and sat at the kitchen table. Within ten minutes, TJ entered with a red face. Travis said, "Don't let the door—" But it was too late—the door slammed. "Don't you ever listen to me?"

The only response Travis got was TJ scurrying up the stairs. "Goddammit," Travis yelled. His feet violently pushed the chair backward. He slammed both palms on the table and shot out of his seat. He shuffled to the bottom of the stairs. "TJ, TJ!" he screamed. Silence. "Get the fuck down here now. I know you can hear me. Every month I'm paying the hospital bills for your surgery, which tells me you can hear. Don't make me come upstairs."

TJ, with shoulders slumped, eyes cast downward, descended. Travis pursed his lips. He took a second to compose himself. He thought, Don't treat TJ as your parents treated you. TJ's very emotional. "Have you been crying?"

"No. Wyatts don't cry," TJ said as he wiped his face with his dirty hand.

"What's the matter?" Travis asked.

"Nothing."

"C'mon, what's the matter?"

"Little G paid me with this." He extended his arm, holding out a purple Nintendo Gameboy Advance. "It's a piece of shit. It doesn't work."

Sharply Travis said, "Watch your language. Come over here and let me look at it." After close examination, Travis hid a smile. "TJ, this is why it doesn't work. There are no games in it."

"When I went over to get it, Little G smirked and said, 'Kid, you crack me up.' He only gave me this. Why is he always picking on me?"

Paternal instincts kicked in. "Let me take care of it. I'll go and find that asshole. You stay here," Travis stammered. He took the Gameboy and, enraged, went out without regard to the door. Travis had reached his end of his rope and was a man on a mission. Tired of having TJ be the brunt of these wiseasses' jokes, he took long strides toward a barn. A bulkier, darker figure replaced him. Travis caught a glimpse of Little G as he fled. A light trail of laughter filled the air.

"Mr. Wyatt, what's the matter?" Anthony asked.

"What's the matter?" he stuttered.

"What can I do for you?"

"That punk keeps taunting my son and making him the brunt of his jokes. I'm tired of it. I don't find it funny, and neither does my son."

"What'd he do this time?" Anthony sighed.

Travis explained the situation.

Anthony put a hand to his mouth to hide his smile. "I'm sorry, sir, it is funny."

"Maybe to you, but they didn't appreciate it, and neither did I. I raised him better than that." Travis reached into his pocket. "This is how he paid him, and there's no game with it. It's useless. Much like him."

"Okay, okay, I apologize. Let me go, and I'll get TJ something he can use," Anthony said.

"What he can use is a lot less of that asshole and the relentless taunting."

"I'll take care of it. It's Little G," Anthony stated.

"It's Little G what?"

"That's his name, not 'some asshole' or 'kid.' It's Little G. I require a little respect too. I'll be back within a half hour and take care of the situation. I promise your son will be happy."

Anthony returned shortly and laid on the horn. The Wyatts came out of the kitchen door and stared at the truck. A brand-new red-and-white Honda CRF 250 dirt bike was in the bed. Anthony proudly stated, "TJ, this is for you."

"Wow, this is mine?" TJ asked. "Thank you, Mr. Kurtis."

"Yes, you earned it. I'll go get Little G; he can teach you how to ride." He returned with a reluctant Little G in tow.

"What's this, Anthony?" Travis asked.

"What's it look like? It's a dirt bike."

"He's way too young," Travis said.

"He needs to grow up. Learning to use the dirt bike will help," Anthony said. He looked intently at Little G. "Teach him. Show TJ how to ride, and make sure he wears this." He gave Little G a helmet. To Travis, Anthony said, "Maybe it will stop his taunting, and Little G and TJ could bond."

Little G got the dirt bike out of the bed of the truck. With defiance, he threw the helmet on the ground, kick-started the Honda, and revved the engine. He released the brake and left a trail of dust behind him as he popped a wheelie. A high pitch resounded through the property.

TJ's jaw dropped. "Dad, he's not wearing the helmet."

"Don't get any ideas. You're going to wear it when on the bike or not ride it at all," Travis said. "That kid doesn't need it; he's already brain dead." Travis could see Anthony wasn't too pleased with the comment, as his forehead furrowed. Tough, he thought. Softly Travis said, "Ándale!"

Chapter 13

🐾 🐾 🐾 🐾 🐾

LAFAYETTE SPRINGS, LOUISIANA

Beau, clad in his khaki work clothes, was reading the newspaper at the kitchen table. He heard the click-clack of high heels outside the screen door. His lips puckered as he hastily gulped the last remnants of shine from the mason jar.

"C'mon, Beau, reservations are at six p.m. We'll be late. Where's Stacey?"

"I sent her home. I'm not going out," he said, returning to his paper.

"What do you mean you're not going out? Tonight, is our date night, and you promised not to drink. I don't mind a couple of beers, but not this moonshine. When did you become a redneck?"

"Leave me alone; I'm not in the mood."

"What about what the marriage counselor said? Didn't he say we're supposed to compromise even if we don't feel like it? Don't you want this marriage to work?"

"I said I'm not in the fucking mood. Drop it."

"But I am. I've got some exciting news."

Beau lifted his eyes from the newspaper. "Well, go out and celebrate. I'm not stopping you."

Beau himself stopped, looked again, and asked, "You wore *that* to work today?"

"It's my power suit," Tanis said. "It distracts people, especially men. When they're on the stand, they stammer and can't concentrate—they're so damn busy visually undressing me. This suit clouds their judgment. Men are idiots, such pigs; it's so easy to fool them. They only have one thing on their mind—sex. So, I give them a little taste of what they want, and they unwittingly give me what I want—information. They're just too dumb to realize it."

The suit was a navy-blue pinstripe complete with a sexy slit on the side of the skirt, tailored to accentuate her every curve. Several pieces of gold jewelry adorned the outfit. Her hair, which used to be short, was now shoulder length, and she wore very little makeup.

Privately Beau thought she looked stunning. Trapped by habit, Public Beau snarled, "You look like a hooker. You're changing clothes; you're not going out in that."

She stared at Beau with flared nostrils. Tanis slowly composed herself and let rip in full prosecutorial style. "If I'm going out, I'll wear what I want, when I want, and go where I want. And if you are not part of it, so be it. You're getting more and more like your father every day. Don't take it out on me if you're having a bad day. What's your problem?"

"I'm quitting my job. I've had it. I put in countless hours, and I've done everything they've asked of me. And more. I don't even get thanks. They gave the sheriff's position to someone straight out of the academy. He's not even from Louisiana. He's a snot-nosed loud-mouth Yankee. This is the fucking good old boys' network at its finest."

"Beau, I'm sorry. I don't know what to say. I know how badly you wanted that position. You were so dedicated to your job, and you'd make a great sheriff."

The compliment softened Beau, who said, "I'm sorry about the comment. I shouldn't have taken my frustrations out on you. I don't ever get to see you like this. You look beautiful. But—I just can't take it anymore."

Tanis murmured, "I'm questioning whether or not to tell you."

"Tell me what?" Beau asked.

"It's something I heard secondhand, and I can't prove it. I've left it bottled up inside me for the last couple of days. But you need to know—"

"Tell me what?" He pounded his fist on the table.

"You're going to be mad."

"I'm already mad. What the fuck's the difference," Beau yelled.

"You probably won't believe it. This news is going to change the family forever."

"Tanis, quit fucking playing games. I'm not in the mood. Just spit it out."

"I heard it from an unnamed source whom a few deputies overheard. It seems your father came down to the station and was bad-mouthing you. He didn't want you to be sheriff. I hate to be the one to tell you."

"My father would never do that! He knew how much I wanted it."

"Are you sure he wouldn't do it?"

"I'll get him over here right now." Before finishing his sentence, Beau started dialing his parents' home number.

"I don't want him over here," Tanis said.

"I need to hear it from him and no one else. You're a big-shot lawyer. Don't you need to hear both sides of the story? I still don't believe a word you said. My father wouldn't do that."

"Fine. It'd give me great pleasure to see your dad squirm. My source was credible." Tanis crossed her arms.

Beau finished dialing and spoke with his father. "He'll be over here in a couple of minutes."

"Don't you even want to hear my news?"

Consumed with his woes, he shot her down at first. Finally, he relented. "I guess I have to."

"You're an inconsiderate bastard. Everything's always about you."

He felt a sudden rush of guilt. Still filled with rage, Beau found it hard to concentrate, but Tanis was right; he was inconsiderate. But who wouldn't be in his position?

"I'm one of two candidates for the position of assistant DA. I have one month to prove I'm worthy," Tanis said.

"I thought you were working for attorney Jeb Truman. Aren't you happy there?"

"Very happy. But this is a once-in-a-lifetime position with a great starting salary. I'll be making more than you, Beau."

Tanis realized it might not have been the wisest point as Beau winced. But it was too late now. Everything, including saving her stupid husband from himself, was too late. She plowed on. "It seems Jeb is good friends with the DA, and he owed him a favor. I'm the favor."

"So, you're sleeping your way to the top?" Beau asked.

Tanis went to slap him, and he grabbed her hand. "It's bad enough you look like a hooker—now you're acting like one!"

"You're an asshole, Beau Leland. You can't be happy for someone other than yourself. You have to turn it and make it sordid."

"All I know is I haven't gotten anything in a month. Somebody must be getting it," Beau said bitterly.

Virgil entered with a stub of an unlit cigar clenched between his yellow teeth. He looked at Beau and sneered at Tanis. In a deep Southern drawl, he said, "Whattaya need, a judge or an audience? Either way, I'm enjoying the show. Do continue."

"Ask him. You know he's gonna lie."

Virgil snarled, "Shut up, bitch." He looked at Beau. "What's up?"

Tanis directed the question to Beau. "You're gonna let him talk to me this way?"

Beau hesitated. "I don't know. With all these allegations, maybe you deserve it."

"What are you talking about, boy?" Virgil asked. He was an imposing six foot three with what was left of his shoulder-length gray hair pulled back and held with an elastic band. He had a grizzled, unkempt look as he continued to chew on the cigar. He wore fatigue pants and a green T-shirt complete with holes and food stains. Virgil had served in the military during the Vietnam War and was part of special ops. His temper and rude demeanor had earned him an early discharge. Characteristics that still existed. "Hey, Toots, make yourself useful, get me a beer."

"Only if you take it to go," Tanis countered.

Beau said, "Why don't you tell him. You're the one with all the information."

Sharply Virgil interrupted, "Somebody tell me."

Tanis reveled in the moment. "I heard from a reliable source you've been bad-mouthing Beau. You told the chief not to promote your son. This is lower than I ever thought you capable of. But I'm not surprised. It sounds like something you'd do."

"Fuck you," Virgil stated. He turned to Beau and put a hand on his shoulder. "Son, it's true. But it's not for the reasons you think. You'd make a great sheriff. But I have bigger and better plans for us."

"What the fuck are you talking about, *us*? He's got nothing to do with you," Tanis said.

"It's got everything to do with me. I'm his father."

Beau turned his head from side to side as he watched the verbal tennis match with an open mouth.

"I'm his wife. Get the fuck out of my house, you low-life scum."

"What? Your house? It's my fucking house, you ungrateful bitch, and don't forget it. You're just renting the place; you don't own it. You poisoned my son. Get the fuck off my property." Spittle drizzled down the sides of his mouth onto his scruffy chin.

Tanis looked at Beau for support. "Aren't you going to say something?"

Beau looked at her.

He did.

He mumbled, "Bye."

Chapter 14

🐾 🐾 🐾 🐾 🐾

BAXTER FALLS, CONNECTICUT

Thump, thump, thump. Daniel's nailing gun playfully kept time with the beat of the radio. Sambuca rolled around on the floor, shook his head, and erupted with a gigantic sneeze. His nostrils were full of sawdust. Daniel laughed. "You okay, boy? You're one crazy dog, Buca."

It was an Indian summer type of day, hot with little wind. He picked up the bottom of his shirt and rubbed the sweat from his face. The trees were beginning to change colors. "Hey, Buca, bring me a two-by-four."

Buca headed to the pile and dragged one toward him. Then he stopped in his tracks, dropped the wood, and let out a low growl. Wondering what was going on, Daniel walked toward the front-end gable of the garage. He peered out the rough-framed opening and saw a familiar sight—Kelly's red Toyota RAV4 inching up the driveway toward the structure.

"It's okay, boy. It's Gramps." The growling stopped immediately and was replaced by a thumping tail. Daniel raced down the stairs with Buca hot on his heels. He stood patiently by the passenger-side door with its tinted windows and waited forever for his grandfather to get out. Buca's tail lightly rapped against the vehicle. The car door squeaked as it opened, and Gramps slowly exited, donning a pair of aviators. "Gramps! Kelly! What a pleasant surprise."

"We thought we'd head over here for a while because Kelly has an appointment," Gramps said.

Gramps reached back in the car and retrieved a brown bag. He proudly held it up. "Lunch from Vinny's." he said. "You're his best customer. He's threatening to name a sub after you!"

"See you later," Daniel said as he waved goodbye to Kelly.

Gramps took off his shades and replaced them with his bifocals. He surveyed the garage with fascination. "Wow, this is great. It seems a lot bigger than a two-car garage."

"It's oversized. I needed extra space for my workshop."

"Oh yeah, I forgot about that." Gramps held out the bag to Daniel. "Lunch for us and a treat for Buca," he said with a big smile.

"Let me go put this inside. I can't wait to show you the progress I've made. It's been ages since you've been here," Daniel said.

"Well, show me around."

Daniel pointed to the front gable. "The opening up there—I'm putting in a bay window complete with bench seat because Buca loves to lie in the sun. Do you see the square hole cut on the side of the garage?"

"Sure do."

"I'm putting in a doggie door. When I'm not home, he likes being outside. The door gives him an option." He gently led his grandfather around the corner toward a massive staircase. "Let me show you my office upstairs." They slowly ascended the stairs, Buca in front while Gramps and Daniel brought up the rear.

Gramps's eyes grew wide as he gawked at the office. "This is huge."

"It appears to be large now, but when I put my walls up, it'll shrink." Daniel showed Gramps various plans for the office, which were outlined in blue chalk. They headed toward the rear of the structure.

"Let's head downstairs and eat lunch. I'm famished." Once downstairs, Daniel retrieved the brown bag and handed it to Gramps. He reached inside and proudly took out a rawhide bone. Buca grabbed it and dashed off to his favorite spot underneath a sprawling oak tree in the front yard.

Daniel's cell phone rang. He looked at the number and said to Gramps, "Give me a second. I need to take this." He turned away. "What's up, Dennis?"

"It's Robbie, Mr. Tanner. I'm calling in regard to your window order."

"What's the problem?"

"Dennis is out today, and I can't read his writing on one of the estimates. I want to verify it before shipping it out. We have several bay windows here, and I need to double-check the number."

"I have the book upstairs; I'll go get it." He raced up the stairs two at a time, grabbed the Andersen book of windows, flipped through to find the dog-eared page, and quickly confirmed the number. "Is Dennis, okay? Is he sick?"

Robbie chuckled. "No, he's on his way to the home show. This is one of my new responsibilities. I'm moving up the chain."

"Congratulations, Robbie. I plan to see Dennis on Friday and take him out to dinner on Saturday. I'll tell him what a great job you're doing." He hung up and went downstairs. Gramps was nowhere to be found. The brown paper bag sat on his workbench, untouched. "Where's Gramps?" Buca's ears perked up. Daniel scanned the garage and surveyed the property, but there was no sign. He began to call his name frantically, but the birds chirping in the background were all he could hear.

In a full-blown panic, he yelled, "Buca, find Gramps. Where is he?"

Daniel had fond memories of a similar game when Buca was a puppy and Gramps would hide.

Finding Gramps was real, though, and he depended on the dog.

Buca was curiously alert as though sensing the reality of the danger. He sniffed the ground with purpose and went toward the house. Zigzagged around with his nose to the ground as he headed toward the thick vegetation off to the side yard. Daniel yelled out for his grandfather. Buca spooked some squirrels in his wake.

Daniel struggled to catch his breath. After a couple of hundred feet, he spotted Gramps in a small clearing, petting Buca. "Gramps, are you okay?"

"I'm all right. Why?"

"Why'd you wander off? I thought we were going to eat."

"Well, you were on the phone, and I didn't want to interrupt your call. I wanted to see if it was still here."

"What are you talking about? What's still here?" Daniel asked.

"I wanted to find a tree, that birch tree." Gramps shuffled over to a tree. "This." He pointed to a particular spot.

Daniel walked over and looked. Though they were aged with time, you could still see the initials "BT and ST."

"Shortly after moving into the house," Gramps explained, "your parents carved their initials in the tree. Your dad used to call it his sanctuary, a place to escape. They liked being alone. Now it's all overgrown. It took me a while to find it."

Gramps pointed to an impression in the earth and said, "This is where your dad used to light a fire. They'd spend hours out here. They found it spiritual, or at least that's what your dad called it. On several occasions, we'd come out here and knock on the door, but we couldn't find them, even though their car was here. After we got no answer at the door, we saw smoke coming into the area one evening. I thought there was a fire. I ran through the woods, yelling, 'Fire, fire! Call the fire department!' Then I ran back here and saw your parents howling in delight."

"How come you never told me that story before?"

"I don't know. I guess being here brought up some memories." Gramps hesitated. "There's something else I should have told you a long time ago. Your parents aren't buried at the cemetery, Daniel. I apologize."

Daniel's knees buckled. "What do you mean, Gramps?"

"Your parents were cremated. It was more of your dad's wish than your mom's, but she went along with it. They were free spirits, into all the ecology bullshit. Being buried was a waste of good earth, your dad often remarked. Your grandmother refused to have their ashes in the house. It was too much of a tragic reminder of their death. Here was the one place on earth where they felt secure. We came out one night and scattered the ashes. When we looked up, we saw a shooting star. At that moment, we knew we'd made the right decision."

"Why didn't you tell me?"

"All your life, you've had a hard time coping with your parents' death. I didn't want to add to it. By going to the cemetery, you had some closure. Something solid."

"It was a lie, Gramps. You lied to me."

Gramps looked at the ground. "I'm sorry—you deserved the truth. It was a white lie; I didn't intend to harm anybody. I only did it to spare your feelings."

"While we're talking about the cemetery, who was Henry Gale?"

Gramps's face turned white. "Where'd you hear that name from?"

"Gramps, cut the bullshit. Who is Henry Gale?"

"That's the name of the man who killed your parents. I kept his name out of the papers. So, who told you his name?"

"The caretaker of the cemetery. It took several visits, but I finally wore him down. Well, you probably don't remember, but you spit on an unmarked grave last year when we were at the cemetery. I can't believe their family buried him three plots away. I can only imagine your disdain when you walk past that site."

"As for the unmarked grave it was a family plot. And wasn't always that way. About a month after your parent's death, I went to the cemetery at night with a sledgehammer and took out some of my frustrations. Several days later the police chief called me into his office. He confronted me about the vandalism, and I denied it. But he saw right through me. I was never charged and every time they erected a new stone, somebody destroyed it. They finally erected the gravestone unmarked.

"You've been hounding me for the details of your parents' death. This is the only time I will talk about it."

"So why now Gramps?" Daniel asked.

"You deserve to know the truth and you're mature enough to handle it.

"I personally never knew him. Your aunts went to school with Henry Gale. Quiet, hardworking family guy. Something happened on that day, and I could never quite figure it out. I investigated that accident from every angle, the case consumed me every waking moment. The only person who truly knows what happened is six feet under and I'll have to wait till I die to find out those answers. A couple weeks after the accident

I found out his blood alcohol level was four times over the legal limit. That's when I lost my cool and destroyed his headstone. I know this isn't everything you want to know, but that's it. That's all I know. Please don't ever bring this up again. One piece of advice don't let it destroy your life like it's destroyed mine."

"But Gramps…"

"No more questions."

"Thanks," Daniel said as he wrapped his arm around his grandfathers' shoulder.

As they walked out of the woods, Daniel patted Buca and said, "Good boy. You found Gramps." He could feel his jaw tighten. He said to his grandfather, "You have to let me know where you're going. You can't wander off like that. You had me in a panic."

"Don't worry about me. I'm not a little kid. I can take care of myself. Why is everybody always bossing me around, telling me where I can go and what I can do?"

"It's because we care. I realize you didn't tell me about my parents for the same reason."

"I get you care about me, Daniel, but—don't smother me. Please."

Daniel was thankful Kelly had dropped Gramps off. He was having one of his good days, and Daniel and Buca were enjoying him. He only wished Gramps had more days like this.

Chapter 15

🐾 🐾 🐾 🐾 🐾

"Yeow," Daniel yelled as he rolled off the couch onto the floor. As he extended his right arm to cushion his fall, he knocked over several empty beer bottles. Buca jumped to attention. Daniel limped around the living room to ease the pain. "Sorry, boy. I'm all right." When the leg muscle cramp mercifully subsided, he massaged his neck, stiff from sleeping on the couch. He focused his attention on the cable box. It read 8:43 a.m. "Damn!" he cried out. "I did it again!"

He shook his head and ran his hand through his tangled hair, which was filled with sawdust. He had worked late into the night to finish framing the interior walls. Having promised himself a reward of a few beers before heading home, he had more than delivered on the pledge.

In his quest for coffee, Daniel walked toward the kitchen. He eyed the table strewn with lists of construction costs and architectural drawings. Buca was hot on his heels. "C'mon, Buca. You need to go out."

Last night, Daniel had told himself he was only resting his eyes until the eleven o'clock weather came on. He never saw the forecast. The soft, monotonous sound of the TV had lulled him to sleep.

Daniel let Buca back in. "Boy, are we in trouble. I promised Gramps, we'd make him a big breakfast today." Daniel rushed into the kitchen to retrieve two bottles of water from the fridge. He used one in the coffeepot and most of the other in Buca's dish. The rest of the water he splashed on his face. Daniel ran into his bedroom to change clothes. Atop the bureau was his cell phone, fully charged. He noticed three missed calls—all from Kelly. Daniel quickly hit redial, but it went directly to voice mail. He repeated this several times with the same result.

He listened to the messages and heard, "Daniel, I just arrived at your grandfather's house. Something's wrong. He's standing in the doorway with his robe open, and he's only wearing his underwear. He seems a little disoriented. I'm gonna try and calm him down. I don't know what to do. Please give me a call." Beep. Oh shit, thought Daniel, here we go.

Message two: "Daniel, he's getting confrontational, very argumentative. I'm going to try and get him in my car and go to the hospital. Please call." Beep. Why didn't I hear these phone calls? he thought.

Message three: "Daniel, I'm sorry, but I've called an ambulance. He refused to listen to me. He's very agitated, and I can't get him to budge. He'll be at Veterans Memorial Hospital."

Poor Kelly, Daniel thought. Gramps must have been a handful. In the background of the message, Daniel heard faint knocking at the door. Kelly followed up by saying, "They're here; gotta go."

Daniel changed quickly and raced out the front door, along with Buca hot on his heels. "Sorry boy, I can't take ya, be a good boy." He saw a yellow Post-it attached to the dashboard above the glove box. Scrawled upon the note was just the letter X. He jumped out of the vehicle, ran into the garage, grabbed the can of fluorescent orange paint, and sprayed an X on the ground to mark the drop spot for materials.

As he headed east to Veterans Memorial Hospital, Daniel pulled the truck off to the side of the road. His body lurched forward, and his eyes stared at the morning sun. His eyes started to water. Pulling out his phone, he kept hitting redial, but the phone went directly to voice mail. "C'mon, Kelly, pick up. Please pick up." He slammed his fist on the seat in frustration. He shifted the truck into drive and sped off to the hospital, where Kelly met him at the door. They hugged each other. "Kelly, I'm so sorry. How's he doing? Tell me again. How did it start? What room's he in?"

"Slow down, Daniel." Kelly grabbed his right hand and gently rubbed it. "I haven't talked to the doctor yet. As far as I know, he's still in the ER. They won't release any information unless your family."

"Tell me what happened. Start from the beginning, okay? I tried to call you back, but it went straight to voice mail."

"Hospital rules—no cell phones allowed. You need to shut yours off."

Daniel put his phone on vibrate.

Kelly continued, "When I got to your grandfather's today, he was standing in the front doorway in his bathrobe, underwear, and undershirt. He didn't recognize me at first and wouldn't let me in. Finally, I convinced him and tried reasoning with him in the living room. He started to swear. I tried to get Mickey to come with me to my car. That's when he got destructive and started throwing things around the house. I didn't know what to do. My gut instinct was to call an ambulance. They had difficulty getting him to calm down when they arrived and gave him a sedative. I followed in my car, as they wouldn't let me accompany them. He was already in a room when I arrived. That's all I know right now."

Daniel slumped in a chair; he knew he had done wrong. The guilt ate away at him. "Kelly, I should have been there. I can't lose him."

"You're not going to lose him. He's in the best possible place. He's done some minor odd stuff before, but nothing to this degree." She sat down next to him and said, "Daniel, are you okay? You look horrible."

"I guess I've been burning the candle at both ends."

"You need to slow down. You can't take care of your grandfather if you're not taking care of yourself."

"It's not that easy. I'm running a business, and my employees and their families depend on me. The addition I'm doing is important to me, but it's also vital to Gramps. He paid for the entire bathroom. I want him to see it finished."

"But at what price?" Kelly asked. "You're running yourself ragged. You're pushing yourself way too hard. Sooner or later, something's going to happen. When's the last time you had a good sleep?"

Daniel hung his head. "I don't know."

"Are you still having nightmares?"

"Huh? What are you talking about?" Daniel asked.

"Your grandfather hears you cry out at night. He's very concerned. He didn't know who to talk to, so he confided in me. Mickey knows a lot more than he lets on. I've noticed that about him. He's very complex—sly as a fox one minute, stubborn as a mule the next."

"That's Gramps," Daniel said.

"Maybe you should talk to someone about your nightmares. There's a lot of medications that can help you sleep."

"I can't do that. I need to be able to hear Gramps during the night if he needs me," Daniel explained. He excused himself and went to the men's room to splash some water on his face. When he returned, Kelly had two coffees and a plain toasted bagel.

"When's the last time you ate?"

"The bagel and coffee sound great—I didn't eat supper last night. I don't know how you do it. I can't imagine how he is with you."

"It's my job. I've grown quite attached to Mickey. Did you ever consider how he feels? He's very independent. Being self-reliant is a core value. If he is getting rebellious, I don't blame him. He hasn't said it yet, but I think he knows something's wrong. Today was so out of character, between what he had on and how he handled himself. That's not Mickey."

"I won't need you tonight, tomorrow, or Sunday," Daniel said. "I'm not going to the home show. I'm still going to pay you for your time, and I won't take no for an answer. Consider it a bonus. You've earned it."

Kelly mouthed, "Thank you."

Daniel sipped his coffee as he scanned the emergency room. The speakers were announcing various doctors. Daniel stared at the doors and was at the edge of his seat every time one swung open.

Finally, a young physician approached. "Hi, I'm Dr. Bailey. Are you the daughter?" he asked Kelly.

"No, I'm his caretaker, and this is his grandson, Daniel Tanner."

Daniel shook the doctor's hand. "I want to thank you. How's my grandfather doing?"

The doctor spoke with a faint air of disapproval, asking, "Did he take his medicine last night and this morning? He appears to have a loss of memory."

Kelly said, "I think Mickey hid his medication box, because I haven't seen it in a day and a half." She turned to Daniel. "I'm sorry, Daniel, I should have told you. I had other things on my mind, but it's no excuse. He's doesn't like taking his meds, and I constantly hound him. I think he resents me now."

The doctor continued, "Some of the tests came back a little abnormal. Daniel, can you get me a list of medications? Please include the dosage."

Embarrassingly for Daniel, Kelly opened her pocketbook and handed over an envelope. It was common practice for her to keep an updated list of all Mickey's meds. This was the latest list of all his medications from the insurance company.

The doctor carefully read each one. "Daniel, some of these shouldn't be used in conjunction with each other."

"Well, he has several doctors, and he recently got a new cardiologist," Daniel said.

The doctor was in full disapproval mode as he warned, "His dementia has progressed, and his episodes will increase. He needs to take his meds. I will make some personal recommendations to counteract the dementia. There are several new medications out. To further evaluate his condition, we need to run some more tests. He was argumentative. I had to sedate him. We'll move him up to the third floor in the next hour. I'll have the nurse let you know when he's settled. On a positive note, however, we ran a battery of tests, and he knows his name. He's a little fuzzy on the date, but he knows who's president."

"Do you know how long he'll be here, Doctor?" Daniel asked.

"It'll be at least a few days."

"Thank you, Dr. Bailey, for all you've done," Daniel said as the doctor walked away.

Daniel reached into his pocket and pulled out his phone as he exited the structure. There was a missed call from the plumber. He listened to his voice mail. "Daniel, this is Wayne from Hometown Septic. You were supposed to meet me at your house at around ten. I got the part, but your dog won't let me out of the truck. Call me as soon as you can." In the background, Daniel heard Buca barking.

He hit redial and talked to his plumber. They chatted for a few minutes, and Daniel explained the situation. "I have an idea, Wayne. Why don't you hold the phone out the window, put it on speaker, and I'll see if I can get Buca to leave you alone. If you feel uncomfortable, we can always do it another day." Wayne did as Daniel suggested, and Daniel yelled into his phone for Buca to go lie down. After a minute or two, Buca followed his orders.

"I'll stay and keep an eye out for your dog. If I have any problems, I'll text you. Good luck with your grandfather."

Daniel thanked Wayne and proceeded back to the emergency room.

When Daniel reentered, he checked in at the desk. He flopped into a seat in the lobby and closed his eyes. People came and went, babies screamed, and a TV set echoed in the distance. Daniel slowly lost consciousness amid the chaos of the ER.

He felt a tug on his flannel shirt. "Mr. Tanner?"

He straightened in his seat. A nurse said, "Your grandfather is now in room six two nine. I just want to prepare you, he may be out of it, but he's resting comfortably."

It was a two-patient room, but the first bed was empty. The room had an antiseptic smell, which made Daniel gag several times. So intense. A curtain was entirely drawn around the second bed. Daniel moved it gently aside. Gramps looked peaceful—too peaceful, Daniel thought. Here lay a decorated veteran and a respected pillar of the police department. But mostly, he was Daniel's hero. Now he was frail. Gramps was lying in bed in a fetal position, looking so helpless and fragile. Where had the time gone? In the background, machines beeped, monitoring all his vitals.

Daniel stood over his grandfather, took his hand, and rubbed it. "Gramps, I'm sorry I wasn't there for you. You've always been there for me. But I'm here now; I won't leave. I love you. I need you. We're gonna get through this thing together, as we always have."

Daniel took a chair, put it right next to the bed, and waited for him to wake up. He kissed his grandfather's hand. The rhythmic beating of the machines slowly lulled Daniel back to sleep.

A buzz in Daniel's pocket startled him. He lifted his head off the bed. For a brief second, he forgot where he was. Daniel pulled out his phone. "Hi, Wayne."

"Hey, Daniel, how's your grandfather doing?"

"Resting comfortably."

"Just wanted to let you know I finished the job. All you need to do is turn the water main back on. I'll leave the bill in your back door."

"Thanks again. It'll be nice going in the house again. Tell your brother-in-law he can pick up the Porta-Potty. I'll see you soon," Daniel said.

His grandfather's eyes opened. Had Daniel's conversation woken him? He brushed his grandfather's hair back, caressed his head, and said, "Gramps, are you okay? You had me worried."

"Where am I?" Gramps said in a soft tone.

"In the hospital. It's late afternoon. Kelly said you were incoherent this morning. Your appearance and behavior concerned her, and she called the ambulance."

"I don't remember. I don't remember anything," Gramps said.

"Have you been taking your medicine?" Daniel asked. Gramps shrugged. "You need to take your medicine. See what happens when you don't?"

Gramps asked, "When am I getting outta here?"

"I don't know. You've been through quite an ordeal. Please don't give the nurses any problems. The doctor needed to run some more tests, so it will take a few more days before they discuss discharge." He took out a business card and put it on the table near the bed.

"I know your number."

"The card is not for you. It's for the nurses and doctors. I'll be back first thing in the morning. Is there anything special you need?"

"If I'm going to be stuck here for a few days, you can bring the newspaper and my readers."

"Are you hungry?" Daniel asked. "They left some food on a tray."

"No, I'm tired," he whispered.

Daniel bent down, kissed his grandfather's forehead, and said, "I love you. Remember, no problems."

Gramps mumbled something, but the only thing Daniel could make out was, "Love you too." Gramps closed his eyes and went back to sleep.

Chapter 16

😾 😾 😾 😾 😾

The crunch of the tires on the gravel reverberated inside the truck. At the top of the knoll, Daniel stopped and flicked on his high beams. He looked at the massive outline of the garage, which dwarfed the ranch-style house. Buca ran over to the truck and wagged his tail. Daniel opened the door to let him in. Once settled, he started to lick Daniel's face. "Calm down, boy, calm down. I'm glad to see you too."

The sky was ablaze with vibrant red, orange, and yellow tones, rivaling any Thomas Kincaid painting. Daniel veered the truck around the construction site, the materials delivered today to inspect that everything was there. Then he drove toward the back of the house. He pulled his vehicle behind the garage and flicked on his high beams to view Wayne's work on his septic. Thrilled, Daniel shut the truck door after letting Buca out. He took Wayne's bill from the back door, inserted the key in the lock, and turned the kitchen lights on.

Upon returning from the basement, he stood at the kitchen sink, letting the water run to cleanse the system. Daniel reached into the cabinet, grabbed a can of Purina ONE, and filled Buca's bowl. Laying the bowl on the floor, he said to Buca, "Sit." As his dog obeyed his command he paused and said, "Okay Buca, eat..." Buca remained where he was. "I know today was a long day. I'm sorry. On the bright side, you don't have

96

to go to a kennel this weekend. I'll be home." He chuckled to himself for talking to the dog. It was something he never thought he would do. But Buca was more than a dog. He was Daniel's kindred spirit, someone who was loyal, obedient, and loving.

Daniel pulled out his phone and started texting an apology note to Dennis. He felt a cold nose nuzzle his hand. "Buca, please, I need to let Dennis know I'm not coming this weekend." His dog retreated to the living room and returned with something in his mouth. He dropped a tennis ball at his feet. "I know, boy. You want to go out and play. Let me get a few beers, and we'll be on our way."

He put on a navy-blue hoodie, grabbed a couple of beers and a tennis ball, and headed out to the backyard with Buca. The sun had fully set, the sky had darkened, and his yard was beautifully illuminated by the harvest moon. He placed the beers on the deck rail and headed out, ball in hand. He threw the tennis ball and said, "Go get it, boy."

Daniel walked back to the deck and grabbed the beers. Cracking open another beer, he savored the first gulp. After a time, Buca didn't retrieve the ball but instead sat there and looked at his master to let him know he had enough. Daniel whistled for Buca, who followed him into the woods. They navigated their way through the thick underbrush and found the spot Daniel's parents used to visit. Daniel sat cross legged beneath their particular birch tree. Dreamily, he leaned back against it. His dog lay next to him and put his head on Daniel's lap. "Buca, I like this spot, don't you? Finally, I feel their presence."

He thought about Gramps lying helplessly in the hospital bed. It seemed Gramps was never going to get any better. He knew this day was coming but hadn't envisioned it arriving this quickly. Kelly was the one who spent the days with him, whereas Daniel spent the nights. He could only imagine the toll it had taken on Kelly. She handled the majority of Gramps's care. Gramps's refusal to let Kelly make dinner forced Daniel to cook. He came home so tired most nights that he just said yes and nodded in approval when Gramps talked. And then, two hours after, Gramps went to bed. So, Daniel didn't see much of him. The signs of deterioration had been right before his eyes, yet he'd refused to see.

Gramps seemed disinterested in life, from filling his crossword puzzle with made-up words to not watching some of his favorite shows.

Now, faced with finding the perfect spot for his grandfather, Daniel thought about assisted living or a nursing home. He had started broaching the idea several months ago. Gramps would agree to it on his good days, but he had a look of bewilderment and betrayal on his bad days. Gramps's placement could easily be out of Daniel's hands if the doctors decided and took control of the situation, though.

Buca lifted his head off Daniel's leg as his ears perked up and he emitted a long, low growl. "Calm down, boy. It's only a barn owl." Again, a long low growl emanated. "I heard it this time. C'mon, Buca, let's go."

He reached into his pocket for his phone. Then he remembered it was on the kitchen table. In the distance, he heard the roar of a 4x4 pickup truck speeding into his driveway. The noise resounded in the autumn night air. He crept out of the woods, and Buca followed closely behind. They exited the thick vegetation and sneaked around the back using the forest's outer edge as cover. Sporadically, the silence of the evening was broken by a crackle of a branch underfoot.

The headlights of a truck dimmed as they reached the summit. The truck turned around in position for a quick getaway. The purr of its engine knifed through the night. Three distinct voices spoke, and one sounded familiar.

Daniel felt his pulse quicken as the hair stood up on his arms. He squinted in vain to identify his intruders.

"There's a light on in the house," a nervous-sounding voice stated.

"There's no vehicle. He's not here, I told you," said the familiar voice.

Daniel darted behind the garage, inched along a bit, and peered around the corner. His heart pounded. He felt his blood pressure rise. Two shadowy figures were putting his materials into the bed of their truck.

"Make sure you get all the windows. Don't forget the cupola—it's worth a lot of money."

Buca let out a low growl, and the ghostly figures jumped. Their presence was compromised.

"Sic 'em, boy."

Buca chased one of them and sank his teeth into the man's jeans. The guy howled in agony and whipped his leg around to disengage the dog, which caused a significant rip in his pant leg and some missing skin. The dog somersaulted as he tried not to let go. In the end, the ripped jeans were the only thing in Buca's mouth.

One of the two men ran to the Porta-Potty for haven and closed the door, with Buca in relentless pursuit.

Daniel got a running start, locked his arms around the third person, and tackled him. The thief hit the ground and lost his breath, with Daniel on top of him. He tried to roll the person over, but he was too heavy. Daniel sensed a presence hovering over him.

An intense pain radiated through his rib cage. The crushing blow sent Daniel flying onto the ground on his back. The thief stood over Daniel; his face concealed by a black ski mask. Daniel grabbed his side.

The thief violently swung again. Daniel raised his left arm to deflect the impact. Nails pierced the back of Daniel's hand, and he heard the crack of his bones snapping. The intruder lifted the two-by-four again. Daniel, stunned, was in a vulnerable position. Then, Buca leaped and sank his teeth into the man's arm. The man cried out in pain as he dropped the two-by-four. The other assailant regained his breath and violently kicked Buca in the head. The brave dog lay motionless on the ground for a few seconds. Buca, dazed, merely watched as the thieves hopped into their truck and sped away.

Daniel stumbled to his feet, but the pain stopped him in his tracks. He stood there in disbelief. Fuck! he thought as he replayed the scene in his mind. Who the fuck were these assholes? He saw the taillights disappear into the night. Some of his materials fell out of the back. They seemed to know him. Who knew he was supposed to be away?

He called Buca, who limped his way. "Are you okay? Good boy, you saved my life. You did a great job." Daniel stroked his head. His hand gently petted his dog, checking for injury. When he reached his right side, Buca whimpered. Daniel rubbed the area again, looking for a broken rib. Buca whimpered. The pain seemed to be in his hip. The dog growled a little.

"What's the matter, boy?"

The dog headed over to the Porta-Potty, and his growling increased. Daniel attempted to open the door, with no luck. He pounded it with his right hand and rocked the Porta-Potty several times. The only sound Daniel heard was the water swooshing. Finally, he yelled, "If that's what you want, stay in there, you son of a bitch. If you come out, I'll let my dog rip you apart, you fucking coward. Stay there. It's safer than being out here." He commanded Buca to sit and watch.

He staggered toward the house to get his phone and alert the authorities. His ribs throbbed; he used his right hand to apply pressure. The Porta-Potty door creaked open, and Buca instinctively growled. "Hold your ground! Don't let him out!" Daniel shouted.

Entering the kitchen, he felt woozy. Gingerly he sat down, aching all over. He dialed 911 on his cell phone and put it on speaker. He told the police his address and described what had transpired. He closed the conversation with, "Take your time. He's not going anywhere." He grabbed a large ziplock bag and retrieved a plastic tray of ice cubes from the freezer. His left hand quivered as he attempted to pop the cubes out. Frustrated, Daniel tossed the whole tray into the bag and put it on his left hand. He went into his bedroom and from the top bureau drawer grabbed an M-80 and went back to where Buca was still on guard.

"You low-life piece of shit. The police are on the way." Daniel burnished the M-80 and made several attempts to light it while his left-hand shook. Finally getting it lit, he threw the M-80 down the vent pipe of the Porta-Potty. Boom!

Chapter 17

🐾 🐾 🐾 🐾 🐾

ONE MONTH LATER

Daniel stealthily glided into the dark tavern. The only light came from behind the bar as Jim feather dusted the bottles. Daniel, clad in a polo shirt, khakis, and soft-soled shoes, reveled in the moment of surprise. "Is this a dry county?" he asked.

Jim swiveled, dropping his duster. "How long have you been standing there?"

Daniel replied, "Long enough to see you missed five bottles. It looks like it's hard to get good help these days."

"What would you know about working? You've been retired for a month now."

"Two more weeks and I'll be getting rid of this." He pointed to the cast on his left hand. "I'm tired of doing paperwork."

"What brings you in here? The early-bird special doesn't start until four thirty. Where ya been, at the senior center hustling the old folk?"

"That's tomorrow night. I just got back from court. Today was the final sentencing of the thieves who stole my materials. The assholes were also responsible for stealing about eight grand of decking on another one of my jobs. Because of the brutality of the crime, they got charged with third-degree grand larceny, assault, and criminal trespass. They were sentenced to two years in prison, suspended, and put on probation for five years, with five hundred hours of community service. If it weren't for Sambuca, I wouldn't be here. I still have a hard time believing it was Robbie from Woodstock Lumber."

"You're never going to get compensated. Scum like them filter through the system all the time."

"They sounded very remorseful in court. They didn't appear to be awful kids. They got hooked on opiates. It's incredible how addiction can ruin someone."

"Ain't that the truth. What did Dennis say to you?" Jim asked.

"He has apologized numerous times for Robbie's behavior in this mess. He oversaw deliveries and was the mastermind behind the theft ring. I saw Dennis in court today. Dennis felt embarrassed over this whole situation. The lumberyard replaced the damaged materials. He saw a lot of himself in Robbie. I can't thank Detective Howard enough. He gave me an envelope with all his notes to give to my attorney when I file a civil suit. Before I drop this off, there's one picture you need to see." Daniel handed the picture to Jim facedown. "I don't understand why, but the detective said not to show this to anyone, so please keep it under your hat."

Upon receiving it, Jim flipped the image over and burst out laughing. It was a picture of Robbie outside the Porta-Potty, slathered in the contents, including pieces of human feces and a luminous blue dye. Jim grabbed his side. He tried to say something, but each time he couldn't. He held his hand up and said, "Talk about having a shitty day!"

"Down in the dumps? Feeling blue?" Daniel joked.

They both doubled over in laughter, each holding their sides.

"Thanks, Daniel. I was starting to drag. This has invigorated me."

"Think I can get a beer now?" Daniel asked.

"You've earned it." Jim walked over to the cooler and grabbed a Budweiser. "Served the way you like it: ice cold and personalized." He dug his nail into the label.

Daniel took a swig of beer and heard a familiar voice behind him. Lindsey touched his shoulder as she sat on a stool next to him.

"What's so funny? I could hear you guys out in the parking lot."

Daniel turned and saw Lindsey. "It's an inside joke."

"Technically, it's bathroom humor," Jim said.

"Well, I'm an adult," Lindsey shot back. "Why can't you tell me?"

"Sorry, it's a little blue," Daniel said.

"That's pretty shitty," Lindsey remarked.

They laughed again.

"You guys can be such assholes sometimes," Lindsey stated as she playfully punched Daniel on his right arm. "Is this a bar? Or a daycare center?"

Now composed, Daniel said, "Lindsey, I'm sorry. If you want to know, I'll show you."

Lindsey shook her head.

"This whole conversation has been a *waste* of time." Daniel motioned for Jim to get Lindsey a drink and pointed to his pile of money.

"How are you feeling, Daniel?" Lindsey asked.

"My ribs are still tender; the cast should come off in two weeks. What's up with you? You busy?"

"It's been slow. One of my customers wants to have an open house this weekend. Nothing doing. Starr has her groomer's appointment early Saturday morning."

"Where's your dedication? I own the place, and I work every day," Jim said.

"Saturday is the dog show," Lindsey said. She turned to Daniel. "Are you still doing the dog trials?"

"Yes, I wouldn't miss it. The only good thing about my injury is it's given me more time to practice. Sambuca masters every trick I give him."

"How's Mickey doing?" Lindsey asked.

"He's hit a couple of rough spots, but they've changed his prescriptions, and it seems to be helping. Sometimes he's back to being his old self, a stubborn Irishman. I can't thank Kelly enough. She monitors his meds, and it's made a world of difference. Thanks for asking."

"He's such a sweet man. Tell him I said hi," Lindsey said.

"Hey, how's the truck going, Daniel?" Jim asked.

"I ordered the last two parts from a guy in New Mexico. They were shipped four days ago."

"What truck is this?" Lindsey asked.

"It's an old nineteen forty Chevy pickup I inherited from my father. I'm slowly, and I repeat slowly, restoring the vehicle."

Daniel discretely placed a twenty under his coaster, even though Jim never charged him. Jim went back to cleaning the bottles. "Well, I gotta get going and see if my parts came in," Daniel said. "I'll see you Saturday, Lindsey, and good luck. Jim, thanks for the drinks."

Chapter 18

❧ ❧ ❧ ❧ ❧

Daniel lowered the passenger-side window. Sambuca placed his front paws on the base of the window and stuck his head out. His jowls vibrated in the crisp autumn air. His nostrils flared, picking up the scent of the other contestants. Daniel pulled into the parking lot south of the armory. He stared at the massive brick building, which had been built in the early 1920s in honor of World War I veterans.

He reviewed the pamphlet and mentally went over the routine. Before exiting the truck, he took out Buca's new royal-blue nylon collar, complete with owner tags. He noticed the tags listed his house phone number, not his cell phone. "Damn, why didn't I notice this sooner?" He prided himself on his attention to detail, and this minor flaw bothered him.

He slipped the collar over Buca's neck for the first time and secured it with his left hand. He grabbed a box of props with his right and headed toward the armory. The "Every Dog Show" was the only competition that featured mixed breeds. Dogs of various sizes and colors paraded by them. He slowly inhaled the cold air to calm his nerves. He had no idea what to expect when he got inside. He was impressed with how Buca seemed unfazed.

Casually they made their way to the massive double doors, which allowed the early arrivals to register. Daniel followed when the doors opened. Up ahead was a registration booth with five people behind the table. The woman who waited on him looked familiar—Mrs. Parker, he remembered, and her name tag confirmed it. She had been his high school teacher. When he got up to her table, she recognized him and hugged him.

She said, "Hi, Daniel, so nice to see you. Is your dog vicious? He's a pit bull, right?"

Startled, Daniel replied, "No, he's a lab terrier mix and extremely friendly."

She gave him a card with a number to determine his place in line as she wished him well. He handed her his paperwork.

The Elks color guard and a few local politicians gathered in a corner, waiting for the opening ceremonies. Daniel placed his box down and watched participants' practice. Curiosity got the better of him as he saw the mayor giving several interviews. He inched closer.

After the interview, the mayor strolled in Daniel's direction and bent down to pet Buca. Daniel introduced himself and remarked how prosperous the town was under the mayor's leadership. Daniel stumbled over how to address him. "Mr. Spencer—I mean Mr. Mayor—I—"

"Please call me Thomas."

"Gee, do you still have your white Shelby? It's a gorgeous classic," Daniel said. "My grandfather remarked that you were hell on wheels when you were younger, and he and the police had trouble catching up to you."

"Funny you should say trouble—TRBL was my license plate. I re-registered the vehicle several years ago. That plate is on the wall in my garage. Who is your grandfather?"

"Mickey Casey," Daniel replied.

"I remember him. In those days, I guess all the police knew who I was. Yes, I'll never sell it. My father bought it for me on my sixteenth birthday. It took me several years to restore it, and next year, I plan to use it in the Memorial Day parade."

"I just want to say my grandfather and I always vote for you."

"Thanks for your loyalty." They shook hands, and then the mayor moved on.

After the random chat with the mayor, Daniel moved to a more secluded spot near a banner of the show's corporate sponsor, Nestlé Purina.

He saw Gramps and Kelly enter the armory and select a bottom-row seat on the bleachers. At Kelly's side was a huge bag. She had covered some of the town's events as a freelance reporter. He made his way over to them and sat next to Gramps with Buca in front of him.

The Elks stood at attention on a raised dais, holding several flags, and the town's high school band started with the national anthem. Everybody stood and put their hands over their hearts. Next in the program was the promoter. Leonard Scott stood stoically; his face draped in fear as two fingers tapped the mic. The crowd grew silent. After a minute of silence, he meekly said, "Thank you, Baxter Falls, for hosting this event. My name is Leonard Scott." The diminutive man pushed his blond hair back out of his eyes. With each new line, his voice grew louder. "My family is from this beautiful area, and it's nice to see it finally. Before I start, let's give a round of applause to all the volunteers, the Elks Club, the high school band, the judges, and the registration people. And most of all to the mayor, the honorable Thomas Spencer." He now had the audience in his hand with the skill of a preacher at a revival.

While the crowd clapped, Daniel noticed how the promoter seemed uneasy. He kept tugging at the top of his shirt as if it were too tight. He sweated profusely.

"Welcome to the Every Dog Show, a contest for all breeds, mixed and purebreds. Today's program consists of three segments. The first will be the agility performance, then the obstacle course, followed by the best in the show. For the first time in political history, you'll be able to stuff the ballot boxes. Each vote will cost a quarter, and proceeds go to the local animal shelter. After judging, your votes are counted, and prizes are awarded. How about a round of applause for our corporate sponsor, Nestlé Purina. Let the games begin."

Daniel looked at his number. "I'll be the seventh contestant. I better get going," he said to Gramps and Kelly.

Daniel and Buca waited as patiently as they could for the first six contestants to complete their demonstrations. At long last, it was his and

Buca's turn. Daniel brought his box of props to the middle of the ring. "Let's go, Buca. Showtime." He took out a small wooden pole attached to a rubber base, commanded his dog to stay, walked fifteen yards away, and placed the stake. He walked backed to Buca and removed his leash. He spoke to the panel of judges about the importance of having a good partner when playing horseshoes. Then Daniel took a rubber horseshoe out of the box and threw it toward the wooden pole. He held up two fingers. Sambuca picked up the horseshoe from the Astroturf and placed it over the bar. Daniel held up one finger, indicating a leaner. Once again, he threw it near the pole. Buca retrieved the horseshoe and gently placed it against the stake. The audience applauded.

Daniel walked to the seesaw with Frisbee in hand and commanded his dog to walk up the seesaw. Buca scampered onto the apparatus and deftly balanced himself. Gingerly he walked down as the board descended. Daniel retrieved a chair as a prop. He told Buca, "Sit." He then released a Frisbee into the air, and his dog jumped over the chair and caught the disc in midflight. Most of the audience stood and clapped. He was pleased and tried to suppress a smile, but he couldn't. His dog had performed so well. Daniel threw it again, and Buca caught it.

Then something changed. Without warning, Buca dropped the Frisbee, ran to the edge of the ring, and stalked someone. It was a mysterious figure in a black hoodie. Buca stayed on the field's perimeter, never entering the crowd, growling low. He bared his teeth. "Buca. Come," Daniel said. But his dog did something he had never done before: he defied his commands. Buca's fur stood up, and he snarled as the person weaved through the crowd. Daniel was perplexed; it was so out of character. He ran to Buca and hurriedly put the leash on him. The person stopped, looked around at Daniel, and pulled back his hood. It was Robbie, one of the three men who'd stolen Daniel's property.

"I've been warned not to have any contact with you. But can I talk to you, Daniel?" Robbie said. "I'm leaving for rehab on Monday, and I need to apologize."

Buca growled. "Sambuca, sit, heel," Daniel said.

"I am truly sorry," Robbie went on. "I have a substance-abuse problem, and it got the best of me. I've made quite a few mistakes, and now is the time to atone and make them right. I'm ashamed of my actions. Stealing from you was nothing personal, just what I thought was easy money. I'm sorry I ruined your performance. I didn't mean to. I just needed to come by and apologize in person."

"You took a big step in the right direction. I accept your apology. Best of luck in your future," Daniel said. "I'm sure it wasn't easy coming to this event. You're still young enough to change your life. Good luck to you."

Daniel walked back to the ring and realized his time was up. He heard the next person being introduced. The show didn't end as Daniel had wanted it to. He kept rehashing the conversation in his mind. Then he let out a small chuckle, realizing that he'd sounded like his grandfather in an attempt to counsel Robbie.

Chapter 19

❀ ❀ ❀ ❀ ❀

Daniel opened the door and noticed his grandfather was fast asleep. As he gently tried to close the door, a gust of wind slammed it shut. The loud noise woke his grandfather from his nap.

"Sorry—did I wake you?" Daniel asked.

"I wasn't asleep. I was resting my eyes," Gramps said as he pulled the afghan up higher. "What's the temperature in here? I'm cold."

"It's at sixty-eight, Gramps. A little too cold for you. Let me turn it up."

"No, don't. Have you looked at the price of oil these days? It will soon be over three dollars a gallon. Those damn foreigners are bilking us so much for oil, while our government rewards their efforts with foreign assistance. This shit needs to stop! I refuse to turn the thermostat up."

"Gramps, you're shivering. Let me get you a better blanket."

"No! Your grandma knitted this for me as a sweater for St. Patrick's Day, and it morphed into a Christmas present." The afghan had variegated shades of green and now sported a few holes from decades of use. "No work?" Gramps asked.

"Don't you remember? Today was my last day of physical therapy. Tomorrow I'm back to the daily grind."

"Congratulations. Let's celebrate. I'll take you to lunch. Where's your sidekick?"

"I'll go get him. He's out fertilizing the lawn."

Daniel opened the door, and the dog ran straight to Gramps for his usual hug. "Smartest dog I've ever seen. I love this guy," he said, hugging Buca.

Daniel started flexing his left hand and realized Gramps was watching him. "Before you ask, it's fine. I'm looking forward to going back to work. My bank account has slowly evaporated. Between not working and the insurance deductible, I need the money."

"How about those bastards that robbed you? Can't you sue them?"

"A civil suit is years away. The hospital wants its money now."

"Where did Kelly go? She was just here," Gramps said.

"When I drove up, she was out in the yard having a cigarette. I told her she could go."

"What? Another break?"

"Gramps, stop it. As I've told you a million times, I hired Kelly to assist you, not as a housekeeper. She's not here to wait on you hand and foot and do all the household chores."

Daniel cleared his throat as he prepared to talk to Gramps about his living situation. For the past year, he'd rehearsed this speech in his head. Now, at the time for discussion, he was hesitant. He knew Gramps would go on a tirade. But it needed to be said. "Gramps, maybe it's time to take the next step and consider moving. The house has outgrown you, and it's too much for you, especially when I'm not here all day."

Gramps looked as though an invisible shovel had hit him in the face. But there was enough of Gramps still left for defiance. Daniel now launched into making an adult decision on living conditions, choices he would be against himself. But today was a special day for Gramps. Daniel felt it was the right time to talk about his options while Gramps was coherent and alert.

Gramps said, "Daniel, we had nothing when I came back from the war. Me and your grandma lived in a small apartment. We scrimped and saved and were finally able to buy a house—this house, our home. It's filled with memories. I'm not going to one of those damn nursing homes. Those homes are prisons—no, better yet, waiting rooms for the cemetery!"

"Gramps, there are a lot of other options. There are group homes, assisted living, and—how about a compromise, you live with me? My house is smaller, and we could save money."

"No, I can't move in with you. I would never do that. I don't want to be a burden. I appreciate the offer."

"You were there for me. Now I want to be there for you. I don't need your answer today. Let me get some brochures, and we'll discuss this next weekend," Daniel said.

"Now, are you hungry?" Gramps asked.

"Gramps, I know what you're doing: changing the subject. The answer is yes, as I haven't eaten lunch. And this is not a dead issue. We need to discuss what to do with you."

Gramps rolled his eyes.

"What place did you have in mind?" Daniel inquired.

"How about Morgan's? I like their food."

"Grab your coat and give me five. I want to watch the weather."

Daniel always silenced his phone during physical therapy, and he restarted it now. There were five missed calls with voice mails. Lindsey, sounding frantic but barely audible, said something about a dog. The following message was much the same, ending with, "I don't know how she can fend for herself. Please call me."

"Gramps, sit down for a few seconds. I need to make a phone call." Daniel called Lindsey, and she picked up on the first ring. "Lindsey, I just got your messages. What's wrong? What's the matter?"

He could hear her sobbing. "Starr's missing; she's gone. I don't know what to do."

"Calm down, Lindsey. Me and Gramps are heading over to Morgan's for lunch. Why don't you join us? We'll formulate a plan. Gramps has been through situations like this; he's very insightful."

He hung up. Gramps asked, "What's going on?"

"Let's get in the car, and I'll fill you in," Daniel said.

Upon arrival at Morgan's, they observed Lindsey in her car, staring down. Daniel walked over to the car, knocked on her window, and startled her.

Lindsey jumped out and hugged him. He felt her tremors. Lindsey's face was blotchy, and her eyes were red and swollen. He tightened his hug. She started, "Daniel—"

"Not out here. It's too cold."

They headed into Morgan's and went to a back booth. Gramps said, "What exactly happened, Lindsey?"

"Around nine a.m. this morning, my phone rang. I was going outside with Starr. When I answered, it was a man asking for a two-bedroom rental. I had to go into the house to look up the information. He asked about the neighborhood, school system, anything, and everything, which kept me inside while Starr was out. He ended the conversation abruptly and remarked he had enough information. When I went outside, Starr was gone.

"I walked through the whole neighborhood and called until my voice became hoarse. I don't understand. My backyard is fenced in and is too high for her to jump over."

"I think the first thing you need to do is have some posters made up and post them around," Daniel suggested.

"You should offer a reward. It's amazing what people will do for money," Gramps said.

"I was looking through the pictures when you knocked on my window. They know me well, so I'm going to Staples to have them made up."

"Well, I know the police won't do anything; they never get involved with animals," Gramps said. "Did she have a collar on?"

"No collar. It mats Starr's fur. I don't know how she got out. My backyard's fenced, and the gate was still locked."

The waitress came by. "Hi, Daniel. Is it six o'clock already?"

"No, I had to run a few errands today, and we decided to treat ourselves."

The waitress put down a few menus. "The specials today are—"

"I'm sorry, Jamie, can you get us some water for now? It'll be a little while before we're ready to order. I'll let you know."

"Sure, no problem. Take your time."

Gramps continued, "Most dogs get picked up by animal control or come home when they get hungry. Maybe they saw something, or they'll see her in the future. I've got a bunch of suggestions for you. Call the Humane Society, and contact the route carriers for the post office, FedEx, and UPS. Tell all your neighbors and especially their kids. I know it may sound morbid but contact the public works department. When dogs get hit on the side of the road and don't have a collar, they get dumped in the landfill."

Daniel looked at Lindsey and saw her eyes had welled up. "Gramps," he scolded, "that's very insensitive of you."

"You need to cover all bases. That's the cop in me. Sorry, I didn't mean to be rude or disrespectful, just realistic. Where's my food? I feel hungry."

"Gramps, we haven't ordered yet. I'll get Jamie's attention."

Lindsey said, "Daniel, I'm sorry, I'm not hungry. Maybe Starr's waiting for me at home." She gave Daniel and Mickey each a kiss and stood to leave.

"Lindsey, I'm here for you. If you want to talk or need some help, don't hesitate to call," Daniel said.

Chapter 20

Daniel sat at the kitchen table, going over quotes. He balled up the paper for the fourth time and threw the form so Buca could play with it. His left hand tapped on the table. When Daniel was under extreme stress, he found himself talking out loud. "Think. You need to concentrate. We need to get these quotes done," he said.

The cell phone rang, showing an unknown number. Daniel declined the call.

Within a few seconds, his phone rang again. He declined.

Less than a minute later, his phone indicated someone had texted him. He read the message. "I'm feeling down. Do you need a drink? You game? Lindsey."

Kelly had graciously offered to take care of Gramps tonight, take him to the movies, and stay over so Daniel could do his work. Daniel contemplated for a few minutes before replying. His concentration wasn't there. Then he thought, why not? Maybe a few drinks would help. Worst-case scenario, Sunday was still available.

He texted, "Meet you at Morgan's at eight."

Lindsey replied with smiling emojis.

Daniel pored over the quotes for the next hour. He rubbed his hand through his hair, finally snapped a pencil in half, and chucked it toward the kitchen garbage can. "Arr, that's it. I've had enough."

Startled, Buca picked his head up, and his ears went back. "I'm sorry, boy; I didn't mean to scare ya." Daniel looked at his watch and decided to quit for the night. *I'll just get there early,* he thought. *That's not a bad thing.*

🐾 🐾 🐾

Daniel stationed himself at a table near the entrance and slowly sipped on a Budweiser. He should have finished that paperwork. But he realized he was going out for all the right reasons. Lindsey was in distress, and he needed to support her. Even if it meant his work went by the wayside. Daniel sensed Lindsey wanted to deepen their friendship, and he wasn't ready. He cared for her, but he wasn't sure he could manage a close relationship with anyone other than Gramps right now. He was attracted to her, but he didn't want to lead her on. Now was not the time.

Daniel saw her coming into the building and went over to greet her. Snowflakes were glistening on Lindsey's dark red hair, and Daniel brushed a couple of them off her shoulder. As he closed in to hug her, he could smell the intoxicating aroma of jasmine. She turned to kiss him on the lips. He instinctively moved his head sideways, and her lips grazed his cheek. An awkward silence ensued.

"I just heard they upgraded this dusting to a possible three to four inches on the weather forecast," Lindsey said. "Looks like I'm not having the open house tomorrow."

"Those idiots never seem to get anything right."

She took off her coat, and Daniel saw a different side of Lindsey. Gone was the business casual, replaced by form-fitting jeans, a tight green sweater that accentuated every curve, and knee-high leather boots. "You look nice tonight," Daniel remarked.

"Thanks, you look nice too. I appreciate you coming out on a night like this. Ever since Starr disappeared, I can't hang around my house. It's lonely."

"I understand. What can I get you?"

"How about a seven and seven," Lindsey said.

"Go get comfortable. I'll be right back."

Over the speakers, "Happy Xmas" by John Lennon played. Morgan's had gotten into the festive spirit. A small spruce decorated with white lights was tucked away in the corner. After Daniel arrived with Lindsey's drink, they toasted, and she nervously inquired, "I hope you don't mind me asking, and there's no tactful way to say it, but whose voice is on your answering machine?"

"She used to be my girlfriend. I don't have the heart to change the recording," he finally said. "How did you get the landline number? I usually don't give it out. My cell phone has become my lifeline. I can't tell you why I still have a house phone. I rarely check it. I guess I just left it there for the recording."

"Somebody in the office had the number. I find it intriguing. Is there a story behind it?" Lindsey asked.

"Let me start from the beginning. Maybe it'll help you understand because I sure as hell don't. When I was in my early twenties, I was rebellious. I resented life. Hell, I hated life. I don't know why I had a mean streak. At the time, my only friend was alcohol, or so I thought. Gramps never knew when I was coming home, and neither did I. The only difference being he cared. That's when we got into an argument over a trivial matter. As to what it was, I don't even remember.

He continued, "In a moment of immaturity, I moved into my parents' house, which had been vacant for decades. I was ill prepared to make a move. I did it out of spite. I didn't like who I had become. My grandfather stayed away from me for months. I struggled with life and how to apologize to someone I respected and loved.

"It was during one of those months I first noticed Alex. I didn't realize it at the time, but she was always around. One night I was getting sick outside a bar when she came over and comforted me. I didn't know why she did it. I didn't know it then, but she was my angel, my savior. She became my world."

He looked out, seeking a break, uneasy with the emotions he felt. Outside the window, snow fell. He felt like that snow. Distant, cold, falling into a dark abyss. With a start, he turned back to Lindsey. She was watching with a strange intensity. He rubbed her arm and said, "I'm sorry. Did I say something wrong?"

"No, I'm caught up in your story."

"Anyway," he said, "Alex and I started seeing a lot of each other. I gave her a key, and one day when I came home, she had moved in.

"She had a big heart, was always willing to help someone in need. She was a social worker dedicated to inner-city youths. I warned her to be careful, as she was going into dangerous places. Alex used to take my old blankets and put them in her trunk to give to the less fortunate."

His eyes were soft now as he recalled, "I rarely spent holidays with her, as she always volunteered on Thanksgiving and Christmas Day at the homeless shelter. She was so naive. She would give a stranger her last ten dollars and think nothing about it. I often warned her the world would eat her up if she stayed that way. Oddly enough, I found this character flaw made her more attractive."

"That's not a character flaw. More people should be that way. The world could use more Alex's." Lindsey said.

"Yes, but she was just a little too naive. Most took advantage of her. I know it bothered her to separate the good from the bad in those situations. She was always giving people second and third chances. Infatuation quickly grew into love for me, and I proposed several times. She turned me down. It wasn't because she didn't love me. She wasn't ready for the commitment.

"Alex was instrumental in getting my grandfather and me back together again. Gramps loved her enthusiasm and passion for life. She was the type of girl musicians would write songs about." Daniel pulled out a necklace from underneath his sweater. Attached was a gold chain with a medallion. "She gave this to me. Imagine an atheist wearing a religious medal. I've always beaten myself up over the stupidest things and questioned my judgments. On several occasions, I'd tell her I was a lost soul. She gave me this, and I've never taken it off.

"One day, I came home from work, and she acted cold. It was out of character. On several occasions, I asked her what was wrong, and she said nothing. That hurt. I felt helpless. Something was bothering her, but I could never figure it out. She wasn't willing to share it with me. She spent more time at work and less time at home. I barely saw her. Alex was like this for almost a month. Toward the end, it was affecting her sleep. I'd find her sitting in the living room staring into the darkness at two a.m., huddled up with a blanket.

"One day, I came home, and she had moved out. She disappeared without a trace, and she ghosted me. I called her cell phone, and she'd had the number disconnected. I called her office. They said she had given her two weeks' notice, and they didn't know where she was. I never found out where she went, why she went, or what caused this. I became numb and isolated myself. I didn't mind her leaving. She could have left anytime she wanted. The puzzling question was why. It still haunts me." He brushed his eyelid. "All my life, I've had lots of questions without finding answers. This was just another.

"Once again, I started drinking, and every time I began to drink, I would get flashbacks of her when she told me I didn't need to drink. I was better than that. I finally pulled myself out and threw myself into work. I'm a better person today because of her.

"I know this sounds hokey, but I keep a can of Alex's favorite hairspray in my bathroom. I spray it on my pillow in troubling times to comfort me. Please, Lindsey, don't ever tell anyone about this. You're the only one I've told. Saying it out loud sounds foolish. Since then, I've been hesitant to get close. That's why I pulled back when you kissed me. It was instinct. I feel embarrassed."

Lindsey had a sorrowful look in her eyes. "Don't feel bad. I fully understand—no offense taken. You were hurt, and it takes a while to get over something like this."

"It was a few years ago; it still torments me."

"You had no closure. I can't imagine what you went through. She left without any explanation," Lindsey soothed.

"Other than Gramps, I didn't think I could love anyone again. Then Buca entered my life. God, to think I never wanted that dog. When I received him that Saturday night, I was ready to ship him out on Monday."

"He was such a cute puppy. Why would you want to do that?" Lindsey asked.

"It's not that I didn't want him. I just didn't want any dog—ever."

"Why?" Lindsey continued.

"Guilt," Daniel stated. "When I was four years old, my parents were killed in a car accident. They were on their way to get me a puppy for my birthday. I've carried this guilt for almost thirty years that I'm responsible for my parents' death. I thought the presence of any dog would be a constant reminder that I was responsible."

"That's crazy. Why would you put that burden on yourself and at such an early age?" Lindsey asked.

"Buca has helped heal the pain, not cause it. Buca came at the right time in my life. The dog was a distraction, something to take my mind off caring for Gramps. I believe he was destined for me. Jim told me that a coyote killed the other puppies and Buca's mom. He was an orphan, much like me. As stupid as it sounds, we're kindred spirits." Daniel gulped down his fifth beer. "Little did I know that Buca adopted me, not the other way around."

With a smile, she lightened the subject. "Hey, I thought we were going out to forget about life's problems. Let's go upstairs and listen to the band."

Daniel started to reach into his pocket, but Lindsey stopped him. "You've been buying all night; this round is on me. How about a shot? When I come back, we'll go upstairs."

"Thanks, but no thanks, Bud's fine."

Lindsey seemed to be gone for a long time. Daniel sat with his elbows on the table and chin cradled in his palm, puzzled, and confused over why he had bared his soul. Was it the liquor? Or did he have feelings for her? Impatient at the wait, he headed to the bar and walked straight into trouble. A man had grabbed Lindsey's beer and smirked, "Nice of you to buy me a beer. This makes up for the other time the bartender took mine away. Don't you remember that episode, bitch?"

"I do," she replied.

"It's *my* beer," Daniel said as he grabbed it from the man. "But if you want it that bad—"

He poured the beer on the guy's head.

The man's eyes opened wide, and his mouth was agape. Daniel blocked his wild punch as the bottle flew out of his hand.

Ethan yelled, "Cut the shit; take this outside."

Patrons started to crowd around and cheered, which enraged the man more. His round face turned crimson, and his pug nose snorted. He pushed Daniel, who took a backward step and promptly snarled, "Hey, stupid, outside now." Two burly bouncers quickly escorted the two combatants to the door.

Lindsey grabbed Daniel's arm and said, "Please don't go outside."

"This has been brewing for a long time. He needs to learn a lesson," Daniel hissed. So they trudged through the thick snow to a secluded part of the parking lot. A crowd circled them as they took turns mouthing off at each other. Daniel bent down, took off his sneakers and socks, and put them on the ground near Lindsey.

"Oh, Daniel, don't do this. He's just an asshole. Don't lower yourself to his level," Lindsey said.

The other guy's eyes, however, widened in disbelief. A comical look of panic was etched on his face as he watched Daniel's bare feet.

The two adversaries circled each other in the snow, but the obnoxious loudmouth grew quieter. Daniel circled his opponent as he motioned him to throw the first punch. "What's the matter, asshole?" Daniel said. "You were such a hothead in the bar. Did the beer finally cool you off?"

The crowd clamored. The man blinked uncontrollably and breathed heavily. Trace elements of vapor emanated from his nostrils. He kept looking down at Daniel's feet. "The bitch isn't even worth it, and neither are you," he said and began to push people aside as he headed for his vehicle. "Fuck you and fuck this place!" He peeled out of the parking lot. As he accelerated on the newly fallen snow, the car fishtailed and narrowly missed several parked vehicles. The crowd applauded as Daniel bent down and carefully put on his socks and sneakers. The mob disbanded, which left him and Lindsey behind.

"Wow, that was great," Lindsey said. "It was unexpected. Why fight in bare feet?"

"I'll let you in on a little secret: I didn't even know I would do that until I got outside. It was my idea of psychological warfare. To be honest, I didn't feel like fighting. My hand is still a little sore." He absentmindedly rubbed the scar. "I didn't know if it would work, but I had nothing to lose. He's been asking for it for a long time. What I did to him was far more humiliating than if I'd beat him up. Hopefully he'll leave you alone now. I own a stake in the restaurant, and Jim wouldn't have been happy with me fighting someone in the parking lot. Not to mention all the possible lawsuits."

Her soft Southern drawl was warm as summer as she whispered, "Let's go inside before your shining suit of armor gets rusted, hero."

Chapter 21

❖ ❖ ❖ ❖ ❖

The first snowfall of the year, and Daniel was ill prepared. Mother Nature had deposited five inches. He stared at his truck clock, and the neon blue light read 1:08 a.m. "Damn, why'd I stay out so late?" Daniel lamented. He felt guilty for having left Buca alone for so long. But when he left, the ever-loyal dog had refused to go in the house. And there was a doggie door. He shifted his truck into four-wheel drive as he navigated the unplowed roads, the sky a canvas of black littered with twinkling stars. He floored the vehicle going up to his driveway, and the rear end swayed. Reaching the summit, he pressed the garage door opener.

"Buca, I'm sorry," he shouted out the window. "Come on, let's go." He yelled Buca's name several times and then put his hands together and whistled. But there was no sign of his pet. He grabbed a flashlight from the garage and searched some more but found no trace. He scratched his head when he realized that were no dog tracks in the snow. Odd! he thought. If Buca had taken off, he did it before the snow started. He remembered Lindsey's hair had had snow on it earlier. Which meant Buca had been gone four or five hours. He panicked. His heart raced. He felt queasy.

Daniel hurried into the house and eagerly listened to the answering machine. There were just a couple of business calls. Guilt gnawed at his soul. Damn! he thought. Why was I gone so long? Why didn't I keep him in the house? He returned to the truck, put it in reverse, and slowly navigated down the slick driveway. The vehicle slid several times. Slowly he scouted the neighborhood.

He called out Buca's name every fifteen seconds for what seemed like an eternity and eventually pulled over to the shoulder of the road and emitted a loud whistle. It echoed in the cold, quiet night, and a few dogs howled in the distance. He started to shake uncontrollably. He rolled up the window. Where could Buca be? I trained him much better, he thought. If he were anywhere around, he would come. Dejected, Daniel headed home, hoping Buca had returned in his absence. After pulling into the garage, he yelled Buca's name several more times and whistled before entering. In the garage, a pile of blankets awaited his arrival.

He upped the thermostat, plopped down in a living room chair, turned on the TV, and covered himself with a blanket to ward off his chill. His grandfather's voice replayed in his head—the older man's sage advice to Lindsey. The words repeated over and over and over. For the first time in a long time, Daniel felt alone. He went into his bedroom, grabbed the can of hairspray, lightly sprayed his blanket, and retreated to the living room. Eventually, the liquor and late evening took their toll. He closed his eyes while his mind still raced.

His cell phone awakened him. His grandfather said, "When are you coming to pick me up? You're late for breakfast."

"Isn't Kelly still there?"

"Kelly and I got into an argument."

"Is she still there?" Daniel repeated.

"How do I know? Let me peek out the window. Yes, she hasn't left. She's in her car. She refused to talk to me."

"What did you do this time?" Daniel asked.

"Nothing. Why am I always getting blamed? She stormed out and slammed the door."

"Stay inside. Don't make matters worse. I'll handle it when I get there." He hung up and dialed Kelly's phone.

"Hi, Daniel," she said. "Your grandfather is—"

Daniel interrupted, "I know, he's impossible. Can you please wait there until I arrive? I have something for you."

"No, I'm sorry. I've got to get out of here before saying something I'll regret."

"Please, just stay there in your car. I promise you you'll be happy. It's important."

In record time, Daniel reached his grandfather's and pulled up behind her car to block her from escaping. He quickly made his way to the passenger door of her car. Once inside, he noticed Kelly had been crying.

"Kelly, I'm so sorry. I know you're going through a lot. I think Gramps is getting worse because he knows he's going downhill and there's nothing he can do. You know he's fond of you, and I appreciate you more than you realize. I've been thinking about options, and events like today help make my decision easier."

"Oh, Daniel, today was just a bad day for me. I'm sorry I was so sensitive. I've tried."

"I know you tried. I don't know what to do with Gramps. This situation has been the hardest decision I've ever had to make. Whatever I do, I know I will question my decision. My head tells me he needs to go to a nursing home; my heart tells me I should take him home with me and just look after him. I know I'm asking a lot of you, but could you please stay on another month or two while I do all the necessary research on nursing homes? I don't need the decision right now. Take a few days and think about it."

"I will, but I need to go. I've got an appointment," Kelly said.

As Daniel exited the car, he gave Kelly a lilac-colored envelope. It contained a gift card for a three-day getaway at the Spa at Norwich Inn.

Daniel walked back to his truck to move it for Kelly, all the while shaking his head in disbelief at the childish antics of his grandfather.

He went into the house to confront his grandfather. "Gramps, you are going to have to stop this. She's there to help you. You are getting old and need assistance."

"Need assistance with what? Don't you dare mention nursing homes. I can go to the bathroom on my own."

"Gramps, you are not the same as you used to be. You are fighting a lot, and your memory is fading. You forget to take your medicine. You don't know what day it is sometimes. If you can't accept the truth, we need to do something drastic."

"Yeah, I forget occasionally, but not always. Who doesn't? Aren't I entitled to forget things sometimes? Ever hear of senior moments?" Gramps said.

"If it was only sometimes. But it's more often than that. You're a handful. I've offered for you to live with me, and you don't want to. You're leaving me no alternatives. I know you don't want to be in a retirement home, and I don't blame you. But we are going to have to do something. There is a group home the next town over. I talked to a lady, and she said quite a few residents are veterans. There's a pool table in the game room, and every Wednesday, they go out bowling. They have a lot of activities. You'll have your own room. I'm not sure if they have any openings, but let's check it out. We'll still keep your house."

Gramps's eyes narrowed with dark suspicion. "Why are you doing this to me? Do you think you're going to take over my house?"

"Gramps, I have my own house. I don't need yours. I love you. I would never do anything to hurt you."

"You say you're not going to hurt me. Well, this is hurting me. You also said you'd always be there for me."

"You taught me right from wrong and always did the right thing. As much as it pains me, this is the right thing," Daniel said.

"The right thing for who? You?"

Daniel evaded the question with the suggestion, "Let's go out for some breakfast and then check out the place. You don't have to stay there—you can come home with me. You've condemned the idea before you even know what it's all about. Why don't you give it a chance?"

Gramps looked out the window. He looked frazzled and defeated. Daniel, by contrast, though flushed, felt relieved. He had finally confronted his grandfather about the reality of assisted living. Even though he still wondered if he had done it the right way—and even if he had, whether Gramps would talk to him anymore—he knew it was right.

Daniel was quiet on the way to the diner, and his grandfather asked why. "I have a lot on my mind," Daniel said. "I have two more quotes to get out, and I'm tired."

"Tired? I thought you stayed in last night," Gramps said.

"No, I went out," Daniel said sheepishly.

"You missed the turn back there. Poppy's isn't this way."

"Let's try somewhere different today."

"No, I like going there, and I like his food. What do you have in mind?"

"A restaurant by the interstate. It opened last year. It's called Omelet It Be.'"

"What a dumb name for a restaurant."

"Gramps, it's a pun. It's a play on words. It's like having breakfast with the Beatles. It's full of memorabilia. You'll like it."

They reached the diner, and two massive orange public works department vehicles with plows caught Daniel's attention. Most of the vehicles were pickup trucks with plows. He pulled in to one of the few empty parking spaces and gently guided his grandfather over the slippery sidewalk. Daniel then led Gramps to a red vinyl-clad booth.

"Be right back. Gotta go to the men's room," Daniel said. On his way to the bathroom, he stopped at the tables where the municipal workers sat. He showed them pictures of his dog and asked if they had seen him. All replied negatively.

On Daniel's return, Gramps had a frown on his face.

"I thought you had to go to the bathroom," Gramps said. "What's up? What's the matter?"

"It was out of order."

"You've always been a horrible liar. I saw someone come out a few seconds ago."

"Okay, okay. You're right. Buca didn't come home last night, and I asked a few guys if they had seen him. Unfortunately, they hadn't."

Daniel's cell phone rang after the waitress cleared the table and took their order. It was Lindsey. "Gramps, I need to take it. I'll be right back." He got up and walked outside to talk.

127

"Did I wake you?" Lindsey asked.

"No, I've had a couple of hours sleep. I'm at breakfast with my grandfather."

"Are you okay? You don't sound quite right."

"I'm tired," he said.

"I called to thank you for a lovely evening. You don't sound the same. What's wrong?"

"Buca is gone, and I've been looking for him for hours."

"Is there anything I can do?"

"I don't even know what to do. It's not like Buca. He's a one-person dog. I don't know what he would do if someone strange approached him."

"Can I do anything for you? Do you want me to go to Staples? If you send me a picture, I can go there for you and make a flyer. I feel helpless. Please let me do something."

"I'm not sure what I want on the poster yet. I've got to get going. I don't like leaving Gramps inside alone for too long. I'll call you later."

"Please do. I'm worried about you."

Daniel returned to the table and sat lost in thought.

Chapter 22

❧ ❧ ❧ ❧ ❧

Daniel sat up in bed, his frame rigid, his throat dry. Living with Gramps had caused him to be a defensive sleeper. A sound had awakened him. Was it from the dream? Mystified, he stayed motionless, listening, hoping against hope it was Buca coming home. He glanced at the night table; the luminous clock read 3:15 a.m. The tangled blankets and bedsheets were around his legs, his pillow on the floor. He yanked the sheets and blanket free, fluffed up the pillow, and reflected upon his vision. This one had been different. It wasn't a nightmare about his parents' death, something he relived countless nights. Instead, it was about Buca. He was alive but in jeopardy. Helpless. The details were foggy. Daniel struggled to fall back asleep, hoping to recapture that magic moment. It never occurred.

Haunted by Sambuca's disappearance, Daniel's nightly excursions into various neighborhoods heightened his frustration. His heart told him Sambuca would come home if he were this close. Daniel waited for Gramps to retire before he began his quest, which inevitably ended up at Morgan's. Generally, at the last call. The only difference about this night was that he had gone out earlier than usual. He needed to escape because everything around the house reminded him of his beloved pet, even the unopened Christmas presents to his new bed waiting for him to get home.

The only positive thing that had happened in the past week was that the relationship between Kelly and Gramps had become harmonious. Gramps was finally accepting Kelly as a companion. She was staying with Gramps tonight.

The fragrant aroma of burning oak filled the tavern. The crowd was sparse, as Daniel had hoped. He retreated to his usual corner, a dimly lit alcove, his escape from reality. He plopped down a Budweiser and began his ritual with the label. A feeling of desperation surrounded him. Where else can I look? What else can I do? I need to find him, he thought. His search for Buca consumed his life and clouded every judgment. It was beyond obsession. His physical appearance had deteriorated. He had lost interest in everything, and the sleepless nights were now the norm. It had been a few weeks since Buca disappeared, and he couldn't reconcile himself to his loss.

Daniel stared aimlessly at the wood ceiling; his eyes darted from one wood grain pattern to the next. He rubbed the scar on his left hand. It was a permanent reminder of how Buca had saved his life. His mind slowly recalled the eventful night, as it had every night after he daydreamed his way through five beers.

Daniel was getting ready to leave when he heard the sound of a bottle hitting the table. Jim had sneaked upon him. "Hey, buddy, you got a few minutes. I'd like to talk to you," Jim said.

"It's your bar, do whatever you want."

Jim looked Daniel square in the eyes. "It's none of my business, but I'm worried about you. As an alcoholic, I know the telltale signs of someone going down the slippery slope. I've been in your shoes before; I've walked that road. I'm very concerned about you. Excuse my French, but you look like shit. I can tell from the bags under your eyes that you haven't been sleeping. I appreciate your business, just not under these conditions. I'm here for you anytime you want to talk."

"Nobody understands what I'm going through," Daniel sighed.

"I know. I know how close you were with your dog. But in reality, Daniel, it's just a dog."

Daniel raised his voice. "Why does everybody always say that to me? It's not just a dog. He's a part of me. He saved my life. I owe it to him. But it's more complex than that. All my life, things have been left unanswered. I need answers to those questions. And that starts now!" He slammed his fist on the table. "My parents died when I was young. I never got to say goodbye. I had a girlfriend I loved. And poof! She vanished. I should have pursued it, but I didn't. Now, my grandfather is slipping away. Every day I say goodbye. On most days, he wakes up and never remembers. I need him to remember. He's slowly erasing memories of me.

"Then along came this dog I never wanted. I was going to get rid of Buca. But something inside of me told me no. I was goddamn lucky I didn't. Now he disappears with no explanation. If somebody had found his body, I could accept that he was dead. But until someone does, I still believe he's out there somewhere, waiting for me. I feel his presence."

"Daniel, I'm so sorry. I wish I could do something for you. I don't know what to do," Jim said.

"Neither do I, Jim. Neither do I."

🐾 🐾 🐾

As Daniel approached Gramps's front door, strains of a familiar tune filtered through the door. "Hi, Gramps. Hi, Kelly," he said. They were so engrossed in a scrapbook that they both jumped at the sound of his voice.

Kelly recovered first. "Hi, Daniel. Any luck tonight?"

"None," Daniel said.

"I can't believe nobody has seen him. He has such distinct markings," she said.

As Daniel slumped into a chair, Kelly tried to cheer him up. "Daniel, sit next to me, and we'll show you what Mickey and I have been working on. They're pictures from your grandparents' early years."

"Thank you," Daniel replied. "Where did you get all these scrapbooks?"

"It was thanks to your suggestion about finding some common ground. Mickey and I have put our time to good use. We created these albums from all the pictures he had lying around. He's been a delight."

"What a great idea. I've never seen some of these photos before." Daniel sat on the couch with them and noticed they had not gotten far into this particular scrapbook. In each picture, Gramps told a story. They came across a photo of Gramps and Grandma at an exotic locale. "Where was that picture taken?"

"Florida. Your grandmother had never left the state, and I wanted to bring her somewhere special. I got a rubber alligator at the gift shop and scared her. It took her a while to get over my prank. It was the loneliest honeymoon a man ever spent. She was livid," he chuckled.

For a moment, as Gramps's white hair bounced up and down, he was happy. It was as though time had reversed, and Gramps was in the moment. A solitary tear caressed the outside of Daniel's eye. He flicked it away.

But Kelly had seen. "Daniel are you okay?" she asked.

"I don't know. I really don't know," he replied.

Chapter 23

🐾 🐾 🐾 🐾 🐾

SOMEWHERE IN THE FOOT-HILLS OF THE APPALACHIAN MOUNTAINS, NORTH CAROLINA

The voice from his cell phone GPS repeated several times, "You have reached your destination." Little G pressed the button, and the tinted windows rolled down. An early morning breeze greeted his face as he squinted his eyes to survey his surroundings. He didn't see anything but a long gravel driveway. Feeling impatient, he gunned the engine up the steep incline. Rocks spewed everywhere. A house camouflaged by nature sat at the summit, surrounded by tall pine trees.

Little G saw a painfully thin man with long gray hair and a ruddy complexion, clad in bib overalls and a faded yellow sweatshirt. He was holding what appeared to be a shotgun. Little G assumed that this must be the man he would meet. He had heard a lot about him. Billy Ray was a legend in these parts. But it couldn't be Billy Ray—could it? Little G had seen more impressive scarecrows. He had envisioned him as much more menacing, more imposing, more authoritative, more polished, with a sprawling estate and a fenced yard. More everything, really. This location was straight out of *Deliverance*.

Little G stopped the car by the man who strolled toward him. "Do you live here?" Little G asked.

"Yup," the man replied with a thick Southern drawl.

"You own the place?"

"Yup."

"I'm Agent Vick. Michael Vick from the Humane Society. We've had numerous complaints of animal cruelty."

Startled, the man jumped back. Without missing a beat, he slowly raised his rifle.

"Whoa." Little G reveled in the moment, then laughed. "I'm just fucking with ya. You can relax."

Billy Ray scowled as a mature-looking Giancarlo exited the car. Little G had grown several inches, and his once wiry frame now bore twenty additional pounds of muscle. He confidently strutted toward Billy Ray. He wore a dark pinstripe suit with an open-collared Gucci shirt and Italian shoes. The pair of Armani sunglasses framing his face gave him an ominous look. Little G snapped, "I am here to buy a pup. My father has set it up."

Billy Ray said, "Sorry 'bout the gun. Me and Shelby don't take kindly to strangers. I 'spected someone older."

"What the fuck, you didn't know I was coming? What did you want me to do? Send up a flare?" Little G asked.

"I don't mean any disrespect, sir—I 'spected someone older. You caught me off guard."

"Enough of this bullshit. Where are the pups?" Little G demanded.

"We got quite a few. But there's this one. A real mean son of a bitch."

Little G took off his sunglasses and slowly eyed Billy Ray head to toe. Silent intimidation was something Anthony had taught him and taught him well. It certainly worked, as Billy Ray shrank back. Little G enjoyed the moment before he insolently drawled, "I'll be the judge of that. Now where's that Southern hospitality I've heard so much about?"

"Huh? What do you mean?" the man mumbled.

"Where are your manners? You didn't even introduce yourself."

"I'm sorry. My name is Billy Ray," he said awkwardly. He took off his baseball cap and wiped his hand on his overalls, then extended his right arm. "Nice to meet you, sir."

Little G ignored the gesture. "My name is Giancarlo; my friends call me Little G. You can call me Mr. Dominick."

Stung, Billy Ray said, "Mr. Dominick it is. Would you care to come into the house? We've got fried chicken and gravy, grits, cornbread, and sweet tea."

"It's ten o'clock. I'm not eating lunch. But I'll take a coffee if you have any." He paused for a second. "Black."

Billy Ray frantically shouted to his wife, "Sandy—Sandy, get Mr. Dominick a black coffee." He turned to Little G. "Would you like to see the dawg?"

"I'd rather have a tour of the place and look at your setup first."

Sandy brought out the coffee. Little G snatched the mug without comment. Billy Ray brought him into the big barn, which housed all the males.

As the door opened, a rancid odor of animal waste greeted them. Little G took out a handkerchief from his pocket and put it over his nose and mouth. He started to gag. "Don't you clean this place? It smells like a sewer!" He took off his sunglasses as his eyes began to water.

Billy Ray said, "I love the smell. I'm used to it." Little G saw ten stalls with their doors closed. A dog with a massive thick chain around its neck was in the first stall. The dog lunged at Little G as he stood at the gate.

"Careful, boy, he'll eat you for breakfast," Billy Ray said.

The dog was predominantly brown, with a smattering of white. "This particular dawg is in training," Billy Ray stated. They then went about visiting each subsequent stall one by one. "Each dawg has a name that begins with Dixie."

"Why Dixie?" Little G asked.

"That's the name of our kennel." When they reached the last stall, Billy Ray said, "That's the daddy of the one I got picked out for you. Best of the bunch."

"Is this it? That's all you have?"

Billy Ray's face turned red. "Yes. It's about quality, not quantity. This ain't no puppy mill. We breed for all the right reasons. The next barn I will take you to is where the bitches and puppies are."

"How long have you been doing this?" Little G asked.

"All my life. All my family's life. We started during the war."

"The first world war?" Little G asked.

"No, the real war—the Civil War. My great-great-grandpappy started the business. He sold the dawgs to chase those yeller-bellied cowards back up north where they belong. Between battles, the guards let the dawgs fight for money. When the war ended, they brought 'em home. That's how this all started."

A disinterested Little G yawned, sighing, "Somehow I thought this place would be bigger."

Billy Ray ignored the comment and continued, "After the war, our name spread. Many people came to us for dawgs. They heard we were the best." Billy Ray puffed out his chest. "We've been doing this for over a hundred and fifty years. With each puppy, our reputation lives on."

The next space looked like something out of hell. Little G started to look interested as Billy Ray said, "Over thar is where we train the dawgs. It's the keep. Thar are metal dawghouses out back. Each dawg has a different temperament. Some dawgs need to bake in the hot sun to toughen them up. On others we use water torture. It gets 'em real mean. Our dawgs are battle tested."

Billy Ray pointed out an area. "See those ropes and tire swings? It's where we toughen their jaws and give 'em grit. And see that machine over thar? We harness a dawg, and he goes in circles tryin' to get the bait. It could be another dawg, a cat, or even a rabbit. After twenty minutes, we put the critter in an arena and let the dawg at 'em. It gives them a taste of blood." A deep rut underneath the apparatus indicated generations of use.

"Where do you hold the dogfights?" Little G asked.

"I don't have a pit. We don't do that shit. We have too much to lose. But in honor of you coming today, I have a surprise."

"Surprise? I hate surprises," Little G said.

They cautiously approached another stall. Billy Ray carefully picked a puppy out of a litter, and despite its tininess, the pup snarled. "This," he said proudly, "is the one which showed the most promise. The dawg will be worth much more after his father becomes grand champion."

The puppy growled again. "This puppy has 'gameness,'" Billy Ray stated.

"What does that mean?" Little G asked.

"It means he's got a mean streak in him. He ain't 'fraid."

Little G carefully studied the puppy. It was robust and much larger than its siblings, brindle in color. He started to horse around with the puppy, who grabbed hold of his fingers. Little G winced.

"After weaning, the puppy will be ready in three weeks," Billy Ray said. "Now, to whet your appetite, we have a little show. Let's go to the temporary pit." He leered. "Have I got a treat for you at the training site. I've been waiting for this moment. One of my best dawgs will go against a bait dawg we got in. I hate that dawg!"

Billy Ray's son, shuffled toward the pit. He looked as though he had been the unwanted beneficiary of the worst of his father's genes. As he struggled with a crate inside, a dog snarled throatily and attempted to bite him. Billy Ray commanded his son, "Mason, go get the duct tape."

"What's the duct tape for?" Little G inquired.

"We tape his muzzle. That's how we always do bait fights."

"If your dog is so fucking good, why the duct tape?"

"Fuck it, you're right. We don't need no tape." To Mason, Billy Ray said, "Go get Thor."

Thor was dark brown with white spots on his feet. The dog appeared to weigh between seventy and seventy-five pounds and had several scars on his nose. He was a grizzled veteran.

Billy Ray held Thor back while Mason opened the other cage. Mason picked up the back end to forcibly eject its inhabitant.

The dog emerged from it all matted and caked with mud. He looked emaciated. And despite the ferocity of his growls, his big soft eyes had a look of bewilderment, as though this was not a natural space for him.

"I don't know how much fight the dawg will be able to put up, as he has eaten very little in the last few days," Billy Ray said. "You would think he was in mourning or something. I put him in one of the metal dawghouses out back. I tried toughening him up. He wanted no part of it. On the bright side, at least you'll get an idea of what my dawg will do. No matter the size, Thor ain't 'fraid. He'll viciously attack any dawg, healthy or in distress."

Billy Ray immediately released Thor. The other dog appeared to hear the aggressor's growls and entered the pit cautiously. Thor charged, full of pride and certainty. It was almost as though he instinctively knew this was just another bait dog. But seconds later, it became dangerously clear to Thor as the dogs reared up and locked jaws that this was no ordinary bait dog. The other dog eluded Thor in a split second, latched on to his throat, and violently shook him back and forth. Blood spurted out as the dog savagely ripped at Thor's neck.

Billy Ray grabbed the cattle prod and hit the bait dog several times. Alarmed, he yelled to Mason, "Get the mace. Quick, boy, get the mace."

But even the few seconds it took meant it was too late. By the time Mason returned, the dog stood listlessly over Thor's dying body. It did not seem enthused by victory. Its tail was curled determinedly between its legs as it turned around to face whatever enemy would come next. Though it had won the contest, it looked like an animal waiting for death. Not beaten but aware life only had cruelty to offer. Yet its back was straight. This dog would not give its enemies the satisfaction of an easy submission. The mongrel slowly turned and stalked toward Billy Ray, who, with slightly trembling hands, doused him with mace. He especially made sure to spray his eyes. The dog yelped and tried to clear his eyes with his paw—a futile effort. Billy Ray pulled Thor's lifeless body by his hind legs to the outside of the pit. He cursed as a second, more vicious dog, entered the arena. Billy Ray struggled to hold on to the snarling form until he closed in and let him go. "Rebel go get the bastard," he shouted. "Rip him apart. Send him to hell!"

The clamor of paws on clay filled the air. Rebel had his sights set on the cur. Little G watched with fascinated eyes. The bait dog couldn't possibly see him. How unfair was this fight? But as Rebel lunged, the other dog dropped down on all fours, and Rebel flew over him and landed on the other side, head over heels. Rebel quickly regained his poise and charged. This time the bait dog put his rear in the way, seemingly to protect his face. Rebel bit his hindquarters, and the dog yelped. But the bait dog held to the plan, maneuvering backward until he had Rebel in a corner. He rapidly reversed his stance, and the dogs locked jaws. Each viciously bit the other and fought for an advantage. Both dogs snarled and grunted from their endeavor. The duet of death went on for several minutes. The arena filled with the rank competing smells of fear and blood—and impending death.

Billy Ray yelled, "Damn, quick, get me the cattle prod. I need to defang Rebel." He zapped each combatant with the prod, and they separated. Billy Ray released the tooth caught in Rebel's lip. This moment of hesitation had allowed the mangy mutt to clear his eyes with his paw. Little G watched in delight. The dog lay, taut and coiled, close to the ground. Rebel charged. But the dog jumped sideways, the shimmy causing Rebel to flip and land on his back. The bait dog moved in for the kill and grabbed Rebel's testicles. There was a shrill howl.

Billy Ray yelled, "Damnit, Mason, fetch my gun. That dawg's no good to me without balls." To the dog, he exclaimed, "You son of a bitch." He tried to zap him with the cattle prod. "You cost me money. You are the work of the devil. You're fucking possessed. I should have killed you when I had the chance." Billy Ray zapped the dog repeatedly, and he released Rebel from his jaws. "I'm going to send you straight to hell. Right where you belong." He readied to fire.

"Stop!" Little G bellowed. He pushed the gun up as Billy Ray pulled the trigger. It fired harmlessly into the air. "Get your dog out of there and leave this dog to me. I want this dog."

"This dawg ain't for sale," Billy Ray screamed. "He's mine. I'm going to kill this son of a bitch."

"If you shoot, you'll never be doing business with us again. If you didn't hear me, I said, *I want this dog!*"

"All right, take the bastard. Get him outta here. Crate and all. He's untrainable."

Little G threw a thousand dollars at Billy Ray, who promptly scooped up the money and began counting. "Thanks for the money. I would have given you the dawg for free."

The dog headed for a corner and shook intensely. A gash on his hindquarters dripped blood. His coat was covered with blood, saliva, and matted fur. He softly growled as he headed to the crate. This plastic crate was the only safe place in his world.

A red-faced Billy Ray said, "I need to get my dawg to the vet. I have to go. You can see yourself out."

Little G could not resist a parting snipe. "Thanks for putting on a great show. I really enjoyed it. Remember I told you I hate surprises? Well, I lied. I love surprises, especially this one."

After Billy Ray had left, Little G had Mason help him clean up the dog. He closed the door to the kennel. Mason got a hose, and they rinsed off the animal. Little G was pleased with this beautiful dog with shiny black hair and a white paw mark encompassing his left eye. Even he knew this dog was unique in a peculiar way. What was it Billy Ray said? Oh yes—gameness.

Chapter 24

2015

LAFAYETTE SPRINGS, LOUISIANA

"We need to talk," a familiar voice shouted on the phone. "And I'm not taking no for an answer."

Before Beau could get a word in, the phone went dead.

Beau awaited the visitation with some dread. In Tanis's world, there was no "just talk." It was a one-sided affair. She talked—he listened. Beau wished he could live like his father, who treated his mother as a servant and always dictated what she could and could not do. Although Beau never saw his father hit his mother, he occasionally noticed telltale signs of physical abuse. Beau swore he would never do that. But a man had needs and rights.

He reluctantly let her into the kitchen, admiring against his will the new and improved Tanis. She had allowed her blond hair to grow out and had pulled it back into a ponytail. Light makeup and large hoop earrings framed her face, and she looked sharp in a tweed business suit. She usually looked great, but today was an exception.

"Would you like to have something to drink?" he offered.

"No, thank you," she said. "This isn't a social visit."

"It never is. Take a seat. You look nice," Beau said.

"Don't try flattering me. I look horrible, and I know it. I'm at my wits' end. I'm not able to sleep, and you're the reason."

Beau stopped and stared. Her tirade didn't affect him; they had become hollow words. He was immune to her verbal punishment. Upon closer inspection, he noticed bags under her eyes and that her hair was not perfect, but his attention was more out of habit than concern.

"Beau, are you even listening to me? I don't think you heard a word I said."

"You were talking about how the kids are doing, right?"

"No," she screamed.

"It must be about the money. It's always about the money. I know I'm a few weeks behind in child support," Beau stated.

She sat at the table with eyes blazing. "A few weeks! You're almost two months behind, and what's today, Thursday? Yeah, tomorrow makes eight weeks. When am I going to get my money? Or do I have to go to court?"

"When I have the fucking money is when. With you, it's always about money."

"That's not so," she said.

"How are the kids?" Beau asked.

"Since you asked, they miss you. I don't know why; you're never there."

"I called the other night," he replied defensively.

"You need to see them. Not just talk to the kids on the phone."

"You know I'm busy and on call twenty-four/seven. I don't have much spare time. Why are you *really* here? You couldn't call like you usually do?"

"This is personal. Beau, I know what you and your dad are doing. The DA assigned me some tasks to look into regarding shady dealings, and you and your father are at the top of that list."

"I don't know what you're talking about," Beau said.

"Shady dealings," she repeated.

"No shady dealings. Everything is on the up and up."

"Yeah. What about those dogs that keep disappearing from the pound?"

"What?" he stuttered.

"Don't you play stupid with me. I know how stupid you really are."

"I found them homes. Some of the dogs go missing in the middle of the night. I think some owners are stealing them back."

"If that's true, why don't you spend the night at the center?"

"Not in my job description," Beau stated.

"Well, you could let the police know it's happening."

"I've talked to them in the past, and they don't care. Why should I? You didn't care when you lived here, as long as the money kept rolling in. Anyway, why suddenly are you getting into my business? Why the sudden interest in my life?"

"The money rolling in," she snorted. "What money? I don't ever see any. But that's not the only reason I am here. They know you and your father are involved in dogfighting, and there's an ongoing investigation."

He pounded his fist on the table. "I wouldn't be in a hurry there if I were you, baby. Do you think money grows on trees? Well, it doesn't. How'd you think we got the money to put you through law school? All the little extras you bought without my permission. The clothes, the books, the hair, the nails. Where do you think all the money came from? Sitting on my ass?"

She got up and pointed her finger at his face. "Don't blame this on me, and especially my law school. You wanted me to go as much as I did."

He smacked her finger away. "Don't ever point your finger in my face again. How come the DA thinks something's going on? Where's your evidence?"

She hesitated. "The vet, Dr. Bradley, has been under scrutiny for quite some time. He takes care of animals, specifically dogs that have been in a fight and dogs that have come from you."

Tanis continued her verbal assault, rapidly firing questions, not giving Beau a chance to respond as she snapped, "Why is it that some dogs suspiciously disappear after you bring them back? Why is it that dogs are disappearing all the time? Why does Virgil live so high on the hog on an army vet's pension? Lots of questions. No explanations."

143

"You're not giving me a chance to answer. Nobody ever comes to claim them. It's like nobody cares." Beau was on what he thought was a roll, snapping, "You came here tonight looking for money, put down what I do for a job, and accuse me of crimes? You don't deserve the money. You got a job. You couldn't wait to tell me how much you make and bragged you make more than me. You can take care of yourself."

Tanis, however, hit him with a straightener, snarling, "It's not alimony it's child support! If you want it changed, take me to court. You agreed to it. Oh, and your county cell phone? They're investigating your calls. Incoming and outgoing. They found quite a lot to a particular number. They're going to find out sooner or later, probably sooner."

"I only agreed to all your demands to keep the peace. My business wasn't one of your demands. Stay the fuck out. Now you're 'investigating' me, the deal's off."

He raised a quivering hand.

"What are you going to do now? Hit me like your father hits your mother? Don't think I don't know. I've seen the bruises. I know the signs of a battered woman."

He lowered his hand.

"Don't forget your father in all this. Virgil controls you and pulls your strings. You're his puppet. Don't you see he's putting your job in jeopardy? Your career. Your pension. The kids' benefits if you get fired and put in jail. If your father cared about you that much, he wouldn't put your family in such peril. He only cares about himself."

She took a chair beside him and took one of his hands in hers. "Virgil is fully retired, with benefits. You, on the other hand, have everything to lose. I was the one who brought the papers over to have the judge sign the warrant. The judge made a sarcastic remark— 'I guess divorcing him wasn't enough.' At that point, I realized what was in those papers. Soon we'll raid the doctor's office. Consider this visit a courtesy call. Next time someone comes knocking on your door, it'll be with a pair of handcuffs. I'm trying to give you a heads-up and save you embarrassment. Either stop or get out of it before it's too late."

He pulled his hand away. "Save embarrassment for me, the kids, or you?"

"Oh, Beau, it's like you—always twisting the truth and turning it on somebody else."

"You think you have a lot of evidence. You don't. You don't know shit, Miss High-and-Mighty Assistant DA. How come the cops aren't here now if you know so much?"

"They will be—and sooner than you think. As far as the investigation is concerned, I'm trying to give you a heads-up. I don't understand why you do this. I thought you became an animal control officer because you loved animals. As for the money, I want my fucking money, and I want it *now*. I'll tell the kids you gave them your best, whatever that is."

She slammed the door as she left. It was uncharacteristic of Tanis to show her temper. Maybe she'd turned into a scorned woman. She peeled out of the driveway. Beau felt his heart race. He sat down to collect his thoughts and calm himself. He phoned his dad. "Dad, they're on to us—" Beau heard the line go dead. He redialed, and the line was busy. He went across the street.

Virgil screamed at him, "What the fuck are you doing?" He reached into his army fatigues, pulled a lighter, and relit his cigar.

Beau raised his eyebrows in question.

"Don't you know our fucking phone lines could be tapped?" Virgil continued. He poked Beau's temple repeatedly. "Don't you ever think, boy? I should rent out the space between your ears. You don't use it. You have to think, boy, think!" Virgil exhaled, blowing a cloud of smoke into Beau's face.

Beau coughed. "I'm sorry, I'm sorry. You're right—I wasn't thinking."

"What are you talking about, anyway?"

"Tanis stopped by and told me they are serving the vet a warrant soon, and they have some dirt on us."

"Dr. Bradley is too smart to get caught. We pay him well enough; he won't rat."

"He'd better not, because I got a lot to lose," Beau said.

"And I don't?"

"That bitch is taking me to court."

"I got something planned where we'll make good money. You can square up with that bitch and finally get her off your back." Virgil leered. "You just have to be patient."

Chapter 25

🐾 🐾 🐾 🐾 🐾

BAXTER FALLS, CONNECTICUT

Daniel trudged up the concrete stairs of his grandfather's house. He'd been out looking for Buca and putting up more flyers, with no results. Daniel's very existence now appeared to be split in half: life with Buca and life without him.

He walked into the living room and heard Gramps's belly laugh. He spotted Kelly on the couch. "Is anything wrong, Kelly? Where's your car?"

Gramps looked in the direction of his grandson. "Why are you home so early? Finally figured out Buca won't show up at Morgan's?" he said with a sly smile.

Daniel sighed inwardly with relief. Gramps was having a good day.

"I'm glad you're home early. I have a surprise for you," Kelly said. She smacked her open palm on the couch. "Come, sit here. I hemmed and hawed as to whether to give it to you. If you don't like it, I'll understand. I felt like it was your decision." She picked up a box wrapped in a blue ribbon. Her hand trembled as she gave it to him.

"What is it?" he asked.

"I won't be disappointed if you don't like it. The decision is ultimately yours."

Daniel slowly opened the package as he sat on the couch. It was a black scrapbook. On its spine was written in gold leaf "Sambuca." As he opened the cover to the first page, he saw pictures of Buca as a puppy. "I took them several days after you decided to keep him," Kelly said.

Daniel's green eyes went wet.

"You don't like it?" she asked.

"No, I love it. When did you start the album? When did you find the time?"

"Ever since I started here, I've been taking pictures. There were pictures of Buca from the first moment when I met him. I know how much he meant to you."

"What do you mean, meant? How much he means to me. He's still alive. He's out there somewhere."

"I apologize, Daniel. It came out wrong."

"Sorry, no, I'm wrong, Kelly. I didn't mean to jump down your throat. I'm a little on edge. I shouldn't take it out on you. Kelly, Buca and I bonded. We're kindred spirits. I know he's out there waiting for me. Somewhere. He's a survivor..." His voice trailed off.

He stopped. Daniel wasn't going to let his guard down, least of all in front of Kelly. "The album is beautiful."

He started looking at the pictures again from the beginning. He was amazed at how small Buca had been. Daniel liked the photo of Buca with a huge bone. He wiped away more tears. There were pictures of Buca playing in the leaves at Halloween, as he frolicked in his first snowfall, at Christmastime covered with bows. There were various pictures of Daniel wrestling with Buca. "This is great. I can't thank you enough." He turned the page and saw photographs of his garage in various stages. There was his dog as he dragged a two-by-four, and another of him covered with sawdust.

"Smartest dog I've ever seen," Gramps said, not for the first time.

There was even one of Buca as he hung his head out of Daniel's truck with his paws on the window. Daniel hugged Kelly and choked back his emotions. "I love this so much. You can't imagine what it means to me."

"After seeing how thrilled Mickey was with his scrapbooks, I started putting this together. Nothing but the best for my boys."

Daniel flipped over the page and saw a lovely picture of Buca at the dog show, catching a Frisbee in midair. "I thought these pictures didn't come out," Daniel said.

"I said that because I wanted to surprise you," Kelly said.

"You certainly did," he responded.

"I didn't know she was doing this either," Gramps said.

"You never told me why Buca suddenly stopped that day. What caused him to get out of the ring? I was afraid to ask you, as you seemed preoccupied," Kelly asked.

"It was one of the thieves who stole my property. He worked at the lumberyard; he was the mastermind. He came there that day to apologize before serving his punishment."

A ribbon and the show program were in the back of the book. "How did I get a ribbon?"

"The show wasn't a competition. The judges handed out first-, second-, and third-place show ribbons. Later, after you left, I went up to the table. Buca, although disqualified, was awarded the people's choice ribbon. They loved his performance. Even the judges remarked on his routine when I took the ribbon. And I got one more present for you."

It was a thin, sizable gift. He quickly unwrapped the package. It was a framed eight-by-ten of him and Buca standing in front of the corporate sponsor banner, Nestlé Purina.

It was Gramps, of all people, who made the critical intervention. With a rare glint in his eye, he suddenly said, "Maybe it's the Irish cop in me, but I find it strange the kid who stole your material showed up. Do you think he had anything to do with Buca's disappearance? Or that maybe he knows something?"

Daniel was speechless. Deep down, he thought it couldn't be Robbie. He dismissed the thought. But later that evening, in his bedroom, Daniel stared at the scrapbook and allowed his mind to wander. Would Robbie steal Buca? And why? He was perplexed. Struggling with his thoughts, he tried to relive his brief encounter with Robbie at the dog show. He ran a hand through his hair. It was one thing to have a drug habit. It was another to steal a dog. What would Robbie even be able to do with him? Buca hated him. But Daniel couldn't get Robbie out of his head.

Was this an act of revenge? He'd seemed apologetic and polite, so humbled. Daniel couldn't imagine how hard it was for him. On the other hand, Daniel thought, he had the nerve to steal my construction materials. What's to stop him from stealing a dog? Revenge is a prime motive in a lot of crimes.

Daniel's inner conflict gnawed away, and he felt compelled to call Dennis, the manager from Woodstock Lumber. There was no answer, so Daniel left a message on his home voice mail. A short time later, Dennis called back. "Daniel, what is the emergency? You sounded desperate."

"Sorry, it's not an emergency, Dennis. I've got a couple of questions haunting me, and you're the only one who can help."

"What can I do for you?"

"Do you know where Robbie is? Have you seen him?"

"As far as I know, he's still in rehab. I've had no contact with him."

"I need to find out if he took my dog or had anything to do with his disappearance."

"The owner of my company informed me to stay clear of Robbie. It's been a major embarrassment to our business. I know he was doing drugs, but stealing your dog? It doesn't sound like him. He loves animals."

"What about revenge? Is he spiteful?" Daniel asked.

There was a moment of hesitation, then a whisper of "Daniel, you're not alone. A couple of my customers have lost their dogs."

After hanging up, Daniel went to the computer and looked up the Baxter Falls newspaper's lost and found. There were an unusual number of ads for missing dogs, Lindsey's and his among them. Daniel researched earlier editions and found that there appeared to be a smattering of missing-dog ads. He further observed how new ones seemed to pop up each week. Daniel finally reached a part where the lost-and-found section contained no ads. He took note of the date, retrieved Kelly's scrapbook, and looked at the dog show program. He noticed the disappearances had started a few days after the competition. Was that a sheer coincidence? He doubted it.

He squinted as he read excerpts from the *Hartford Courant* and *New Haven Register*. The timelines remained the same. Weariness started to set in, and his eyes burned. He struggled to focus—a strange circumstance. All clues led to the dog show. But why?

Studying the program, he remembered the name of the show was "Every Dog Show." They had a number printed. He dialed the number and heard, "Our office hours are between eight and four, Monday through Friday. Please call back during regular business hours. We thank you. See you at the next show." It sounded legit, he surmised.

He dialed a number from one of the missing-dog ads. A groggy voice said, "Hello?"

"I'm calling in regard to your—"

Daniel looked at the computer screen. Click. The line went dead. The time read 11:03 p.m. He slapped his forehead with his hand and said, "Oops!"

Chapter 26

✿ ✿ ✿ ✿ ✿

Daniel raced to the emergency room, dodging several employees, children, and parents, and found Lindsey slumped in a chair. She immediately got up, and he hugged her and said, "How's he doing? Have you heard anything yet?"

"I'm sorry, they won't tell me anything because I'm not family."

"I can't thank you enough for coming here when I was unavailable." Daniel excused himself and returned in a couple of minutes.

"What did they say?" asked Lindsey.

"Lindsey, how about we go to the cafeteria? I'll buy you lunch."

"How will the doctor find you there?"

"I gave the nurses my cell phone and put it on vibrate. They will call when the doctor is ready to see us."

Daniel was silent for a couple of minutes at the table to compose himself. He was looking at Lindsey in a whole new light. Gone were the makeup and fancy clothes; she had her hair in a french braid, and she was clad in a powder-blue sweatsuit. He thought she was a natural beauty.

"I'm sorry I'm such a mess. I was in the middle of my aerobics class."

"You look great," Daniel said. "Now, what exactly did Kelly say?"

"When I first got here, she was crying hysterically. She kept repeating, 'It's my fault, it's my fault.' I tried to calm her down. After I got her a cup of tea, she described what had happened. Mickey had decided to take a midmorning bath while Kelly was cooking breakfast. Mickey got out of the tub, dressed, and proceeded down the stairs in stocking feet without his slippers. She thinks he fell four or five steps. She grabbed the portable phone on the way to comfort him and dialed 911. He was awake and alert but very sore. Kelly was worried you'd be mad at her for this. I reassured her it was just an accident and that accidents happen and not worry about it. I've been here for about four hours. She couldn't stop thanking me for coming."

"She's a saint—most people would have quit by now. Gramps is such a handful. And with all she has been going through, I don't know how she does it."

"Kelly adores you and Mickey," Lindsey said.

"We love her too! Though my grandfather denies it, he's really attached to her."

Daniel's phone vibrated, and they went to the ER, where the doctor waited. He called Daniel into a side room where he could have a private consultation. Daniel looked at his name tag and noticed it was the same doctor who had treated Gramps last time.

The doctor wore a frown, and he looked directly at Daniel. "I'm not pulling any punches. I'd put him in a nursing home if it were my grandfather. Immediately. I'm not talking in a few weeks. He's a danger to himself. You're taking a big chance, between his dementia and living in a house with stairs. Luckily, his hip is only bruised, not broken. I'm more concerned about the contusion on your grandfather's head."

"What if he came and lived with me? I have a single-story house," Daniel said.

"I've read your grandfather's history. In my professional opinion, I recommend a nursing home. I know it's not an easy decision."

"But some days he seems so normal," Daniel stated. "He's got a great memory."

"Most people with dementia live in the past. They remember everything. It's the present that becomes frustrating. For somebody his age, your grandfather is in good health physically, but mentally…I am sorry to be blunt, but he is a car crash waiting to happen."

"Well, for now if I can keep him at my house, we have Kelly. She watches him when I'm not around."

"What happened today then?" the doctor asked.

"He's so damn stubborn. He refuses anybody's assistance, even mine."

"Nursing homes have changed a lot in the past years. Studies have shown that a patient's transition is smoother when they can comprehend. I've seen patients leave their homes in the middle of the night and wander the streets, not knowing where they are. One of the benefits of a nursing home is alarmed doors and twenty-four-hour care. It's not only for the patient's safety but for their family's peace of mind."

"Well, Doctor, is it okay if he comes home now? Will you explain this to him about the nursing home? He's not going to listen to me."

"Yes, I'll talk to him before discharge."

"Thank you, Doctor. When I talk to him, it falls on deaf ears," Daniel said.

"You can take him home. Pay careful attention to the bump. We did a CT scan on him. I don't believe he has a concussion. But if he starts vomiting, get him in here right away." As the doctor was leaving, he said, "Any questions? If not, I have to talk to several other patients."

"No, no more questions," Daniel said. "Thanks for everything."

Daniel went back to where Lindsey waited and relayed the information.

"Kelly wanted me to ask you if you knew about Mickey's plan to sell his house," Lindsey said.

Daniel shook his head. He relived past conversations with Gramps about what this house meant to him. All the memories. But maybe, hopefully, Gramps had finally accepted the fact something had to change.

Lindsey said, "Daniel, you look exhausted. Did you get any sleep?"

"Yeah, but it was a long trip to Baltimore. There was an accident on Ninety-Five, and I got home late. I'm fine."

"Tell me about your trip. What'd you find out?"

"Before going, I spoke to Mr. Wilson, and he agreed to meet me. But once there, he pawned me off on his assistant. She also had an agenda and had very little time with me. I explained the dog show in Connecticut, and she kept insisting there was never a show in Baxter Falls. I had to keep telling myself to calm down. Luckily, I'd brought down the scrapbook and showed her pictures. She said that anybody could make up a banner and that it wasn't theirs.

"I showed her a picture of the promoter, Leonard Scott, and she remarked that he looked familiar but couldn't place him. She told me she remembered a quirky guy with long brown hair and a scruffy beard, a real odd duck. He only wanted to work registration, and she told him that the people had to be bonded in this sensitive area, complete with background checks. He started swearing at her and stormed off. When I showed her the picture of Buca and me with the Nestlé Purina logo in the background, her jaw dropped. She pointed out that all four corners of the logo were supposed to be red. These were white. She surmised Nestlé Purina would never have authorized the use of that banner, as they took pride in their trademark. She repeated the last thing. I believe he conned everyone. She quickly excused herself."

"I don't know what to say. I'm flabbergasted. Why would somebody do something like that?" Lindsey asked.

At this point, an attendant wheeled Gramps to Daniel. Gramps looked so innocent and frail, his pink skin the color of a newborn now covered in bruises and scrapes. Gramps looked at Daniel and said tearfully, "Daniel, Daniel—"

"I know, Gramps, I know. You're coming home with me."

🐾 🐾 🐾

Daniel gently guided Gramps into his house. On the way, he saw a package on his stoop, and he nudged it aside as he led Gramps to a chair. He had beer bottles scattered around and an empty pizza box on the kitchen table. Daniel apologized for the mess. "Gramps, are you hungry? Is there anything I can get you? Do you want the television on?"

"I'm sorry, I'm exhausted and would just like to lie down."

"Gramps, tomorrow we'll go to your house and pick up some of your clothes, your recliner, and your afghan. We'll stop at the grocery store and get some of your favorites." Daniel led him into the room he had had as a young boy and settled Gramps into his old bed, surrounded by all the toys from his youth.

Daniel cleaned the house absentmindedly, intermittently jotting down notes of items they needed from the store. While doing these mundane chores, this one question baffled Daniel: Who the fuck was Leonard Scott? Overwhelmed with curiosity, Daniel went to his bedroom, sat down at the foot of the bed, and turned on his Mac. An eerie glow filled the room as he impatiently waited for it to boot. He googled "Leonard Scott." Several results appeared, but none matched his description and age. He looked the name up on Facebook, with the same result. Could it be an alias?

Daniel opened the scrapbook and looked at the Every Dog Show program. He pulled up their website and compared it to the program from the show he'd gone to in Baltimore. The only difference was the mailing address—the Baxter Falls entry had a PO box in New Haven, Connecticut.

Daniel looked at the promoter again and said aloud. "What if he's not the person? Should I go to the New Haven post office? Is this another dead end? Leonard Scott must know something. How am I ever going to find him?"

Chapter 27

🐾 🐾 🐾 🐾 🐾

Daniel shifted from side to side in bed, unable to get comfortable, and kept looking at the clock. Since he couldn't sleep while his mind was in overdrive, he decided to get some coffee.

Sitting at the kitchen table, Daniel replayed the events of the last several days, from his grandfather's accident to the conversation he'd had in Maryland. The most frustrating part was, who the hell was Leonard Scott? Did he have anything to do with this? Why would he want Buca, and what could he do with him? What was his endgame?

Daniel got a second cup of coffee and remembered there was a package on the front porch. He hadn't ordered anything. What was the box doing here? He opened the door as dawn was breaking, retrieved the package, and brought it to the kitchen table. It had no return address. He shook it. Daniel went to get a pair of scissors and cut the tape on the box. He dumped the contents onto the kitchen table. Thud! A note and something enclosed in bubble packaging fell out. He grabbed the scissors to cut away the wrap and carefully unfolded it. Shaken, he picked up Buca's royal-blue nylon collar, complete with dog tags.

Daniel unfolded the note carefully. It included a home address in Plattsburgh, New York, and a telephone number. It read: "I found this on the side of the road. I've left several messages, so I decided to mail them to you. Cody Ward."

Daniel's jaw dropped. Could Buca be only a state away? So near, yet so far? How had he gotten there? Why upstate New York of all places? Why had Cody found just the collar? Was Buca dead? Stop it, he chided himself. I can't think like that.

Daniel's glimmer of hope became a raging inferno. He always knew Buca was out there, and the collar reaffirmed his instinct. All the insecurities and burden of guilt he felt about Buca melted away. He studied the tags and remembered they bore his home number and address. Since moving back into his house, he hadn't checked any landline messages.

He went into his bedroom and looked at the answering machine. The indicator light had burned out. He pressed play and listened as a woman said, "Mr. Tanner, Cody Ward. I recently found your dog's collar on the side of the road. I want to return it to you. Please call me back. My number is…" Daniel went through the other messages; they were all similar. He never thought about his landline. He only kept it because his old business cards had that number and Alex's recorded message. He didn't want to lose that.

He headed toward his computer with a sense of urgency and frantically googled the address. It was only five hours away. He impatiently waited until nine o'clock before he called Cody, but there was no answer. He left a message. He couldn't wait to talk to her. He had always believed Buca was out there somewhere, and now he had proof.

Daniel dialed Cody's number so often that he had it memorized as days went by. It used to ring out, but now it went straight to voice mail. Was this some cruel joke? But how could anybody be so sick? It couldn't be a hoax. It was definitely Buca's collar.

Three days passed since he started calling Cody, and he called again. This time it picked up on the second ring.

"Hello, is this Cody?" Daniel asked.

"Yes," she said hesitantly.

"I'm Daniel Tanner, the person you sent the dog collar to."

The demeanor in her voice quickly changed. "Oh, yes. I'm sorry I didn't get back to you sooner. I listened to your messages. I'm a nurse, and many nurses got stranded at home with the recent blizzard. I worked double shifts and stayed at the hospital."

"Where did you find the collar?" he asked, excitement heavy in his voice.

"I found it on the side of the road near a dumpster. Or should I say my dog found it. He's always finding things. Because of the snow, you couldn't even see it. Were you up here recently?"

"No, that's the mystery. I've never been there. I live in Connecticut, and my dog went missing over a month ago. The collar is the first positive proof I've had he's out there. Would you mind if I came up? I need to see where you found it."

"Of course, I wouldn't mind. When would you like to come?"

"As soon as possible. It's at least a five-hour drive." Daniel struggled as he talked to contain his excitement.

"How's Saturday sound?" Cody asked.

Daniel agreed, thanked her, and they finalized the plan. Daniel celebrated with a beer before calling Lindsey.

"I finally got a hold of the person who found the collar. I'm going up there on Saturday," Daniel said.

"Oh, that's great news. What did this person have to say?" Lindsey asked.

"Not much more than what was in the note. I'm relieved it wasn't a hoax."

As soon as Daniel got off the phone, a great sadness overcame him. He hadn't considered Lindsey's feelings. She'd suffered through the same ordeal. Was it wrong of him to call her?

Daniel called out to Gramps, "How does a road trip on Saturday sound to you?"

"Where are we going?"

"To Plattsburgh, New York, to talk to the woman who found the collar."

"What are you talking about?" Gramps asked.

"The collar. Buca's blue collar," Daniel said.

"Oh, you finally reached them?"

"Yes, I just got off the line with her," he said.

Gramps's eyes glowed. "I know the area. You want an old man in your truck for five hours?"

"You'd be doing me a favor. Since you know the place, you can earn your keep."

"I'm not a cheap date. It's gonna cost you."

"What? Another early-bird special? I think I can afford it. Let's be on the safe side and pack an overnight bag."

Chapter 28

🐾 🐾 🐾 🐾 🐾

PLATTSBURGH, NEW YORK

Daniel eased into Cody's driveway at 11:45 a.m. A little vortex of snow playfully danced across her front yard as the wind blew. It was deep in places, but the driveway and sidewalk were clear. Daniel's hands perspired despite the fourteen-degree temperature. He and Gramps got out of the truck and gingerly walked toward the front door with arms entwined.

Her house was tucked away in the northeast corner of the community. The neighborhood was secluded. The ranch-style house had sidewall shakes painted charcoal, accented with white trim and black shutters. An American flag attached to the home whipped in the wind. A deep growl emanated from the house when Daniel knocked.

The front door opened an inch or two, restrained by a chain lock. A young-looking woman peered through the opening. "Hi, Daniel," she said, smiling. "Give me a minute; I'll put Shiloh away."

Daniel looked at his grandfather, who was shivering. "Are you cold?" He extended his hands on his Gramps's arms and rubbed them up and down.

"I'm fine." His grandfather blew on his hands to warm them.

"Where are your gloves?" Daniel asked.

"I don't know; I forgot where I put 'em."

"Well, put your hands in your coat pockets," Daniel suggested.

"Leave me alone. Stop doting on me."

Once inside, Daniel surveyed the room. Modest colonial furniture was scattered around. On the mantel was a photo of a man in military uniform, a dog standing at attention by his side.

"Sorry about the holdup—I needed to put our dog in the kennel," Cody said. She was an attractive, thirtyish woman with light brown frosted hair in a pixie cut. A beauty mark adorned her right cheek. "Not that Shiloh isn't friendly. He's cautious around strangers."

She extended her hand. "Hi, I'm Cody."

"I hope you don't mind. I brought my grandfather along. Michael Casey."

Gramps chimed in, "My friends call me Mickey."

She shook his hand. "Well, Mickey it is. Come on into the kitchen," Cody said warmly. "Would you like some coffee, tea, or hot chocolate? Here, let me take your coats. Please take a seat."

"Coffee for me," Daniel said. "How about you, Gramps?"

"Coffee sounds great," Gramps said.

"I just brewed a fresh pot."

The kitchen was as cozy as the living room. The circular table was covered with a seasonal tablecloth, the curtains matched, and a sweet aroma filled the air.

"Is that oatmeal raisin cookies I smell?" Gramps asked.

"Yes, I just finished baking them. They're cooling down. Would you like to have some with your coffee?"

"I'd love some," Gramps replied with a twinkle.

"Did you have a nice drive here?" she asked.

"Time went by fast," Daniel said. "It was a very scenic drive."

Daniel got down to brass tacks once they had their coffee and cookies. "Cody, I need to thank you for sending me the collar. Most people would have thrown it away. Can you explain again how you found it? My dog has been gone for over a month. For it to be up here over three hundred miles away is puzzling. It's a starting point, but where could he be? And why? I just don't get it. I really need to see that place you found it."

"About two weeks ago, I was out running with Shiloh, something we do every night. It's much more challenging during the wintertime. It gets dark a lot earlier and is so cold. We weren't too far into our run when he began digging at the snow on the side of the road. I imagine he picked up your dog's scent. He was insistent upon uncovering the spot. So, I let him continue. He discovered something shiny, and I picked it up. It turned out to be Sambuca's collar and tags. My first thought was to call the owner as soon as possible. I returned home and called and left a message. When I didn't hear back, I called and left another message. I was starting to think you had moved or something, so I decided to mail it to you.

"We have a veterinarian about a half mile down the road from where I was. I thought maybe it might have come from there and that you had visited him. I checked several times, and no one was there."

Daniel said, "I had been staying at my grandfather's and didn't get the messages. You've given me new hope. I've had people calling me saying they saw Buca around Connecticut. None of the leads ever panned out. What you sent me is my first piece of concrete evidence. Buca is smart. If there were some way he could come home, he would." Daniel pulled out his cell phone. "Here's a picture of him. Have you seen him?"

She studied the picture intently. "That's a very distinct-looking dog. I've seen bear prints in the snow that look like one over Sambuca's eye. I'd remember seeing him. We're so far out in the sticks, we rarely see any other dogs."

"What kind of dog do you have, Cody?" Gramps asked.

"He's a Belgian shepherd. My husband is in the special ops, the bomb detection unit. He mostly guards the embassy and is not at the forefront of the war. He's overseas now. Shiloh was his first dog. He retired after several tours. He has another who'd been with him for a tour and a half. I imagine when my husband retires, we'll have a house full of dogs!" She went into the living room and brought back the picture from the mantel. "Here is my husband, James, and his dog, Dakota." James was wearing his dress blues, and he looked about six foot three. Dakota was brown and tan and stood at attention. In the background was the American flag.

"Beautiful picture," Daniel said. "I would expect him to get attached to them. They are saving the lives of Americans. The next time you talk to him, please thank him for his service, and thank *you*."

"I didn't do anything."

"Yes, you did. James has your support." Gramps said.

Daniel said, "We've taken up enough of your time. Do you mind showing us exactly where you found the collar? I can follow you in my truck."

"No, I don't mind at all. I can only imagine what you're going through. Now that I have Shiloh, it's not so lonely at home. Give me a minute to bundle up." She handed them their coats.

Daniel and Gramps followed her to the spot, and Daniel got out. "Gramps, you stay in here. It's too cold. I'll leave the truck running."

"This is where we found it," Cody said as she pointed to an isolated spot on the side of the road. "I don't know how much good it will do you, but I hope it helps."

"You said there's a veterinarian down the road?" he asked. "How far away is it?"

"From here, about a half mile on the right. It's located in a strip mall. Directly across the street is a Dunkin' Donuts. The vet isn't there most of the time and works odd hours. It's why I don't bring Shiloh there. He's peculiar. I don't ever see cars there during the day. He seems busy late at night."

"Well, it wouldn't hurt to talk to the vet, just in case." He hugged her and said, "Thank you so much for your hospitality and for sending the collar to me. I can't thank you enough. I don't know what I'll find, but at least it's a start."

"Keep me posted," Cody said, concerned. "You have my number, and you can call anytime. Goodbye, Daniel, and good luck." Before leaving, she stopped by the truck's passenger door and said something to Gramps. Then she drove away.

Daniel retrieved the hammer from his toolbox. He viciously swung the claw into the snow until he hit the pavement. He looked for blood or fur or any telltale sign of distress, but there was nothing, and he felt relieved. After five minutes, he gave up and got back into the warm truck.

"What were you doing?" Gramps asked.

"Looking for evidence. Cody did say there's a vet about a half mile down the road who may or may not be open. I think it's worth checking to see if they saw Buca."

Daniel followed Cody's advice and headed toward the strip mall. He soon spotted Dunkin' Donuts and located the veterinarian's office. But there were no cars.

"Do you mind stopping in Dunkin' Donuts? I need to use the bathroom," Gramps asked.

"Sure, let's get some coffee."

Gramps nodded.

Daniel waited for Gramps to return and found a good seat to view the strip mall.

"What do you think you'll find out at the vets?" Gramps asked as his shoulders shook.

"You okay?"

"Yes, I'm fine, just a chill. Old age, ya know?"

"Hopefully this vet will show up soon. I need to ask him a couple of questions." Daniel moved around in his seat, trying to get comfortable. "I don't know how you did this, staying in one place during stakeouts."

"Most officers hated them. I loved it, especially when we caught them in the act. The looks on their faces—the element of surprise—it gave me such a rewarding feeling. It made it all worthwhile."

Time passed, but there was no sign of life in the parking lot across the street. Daniel noticed Gramps was starting to look very pale.

He asked, "Gramps, how are you holding up? Are you tired? This trip has been quite an ordeal." Daniel didn't even wait for any answers; he quickly summarized his thoughts with, "What if we stay here another hour, and if there's no action, we go find a hotel. We can come back early tomorrow."

"Look, there's a car pulling up to the vet's over there," Gramps said.

Daniel turned his head and saw a black Mercedes park near the office. An older man got out and ran into the building. "Let's go. We don't want to miss him."

When he and Gramps were back in the truck, Daniel quickly maneuvered into the parking lot. A second car, a white sedan with tinted windows, pulled into the vet's office and parked right next to the other vehicle. A man got out and walked briskly into the office. Daniel caught a glimpse of him. Though the man looked strangely familiar, Daniel couldn't place him.

"What did you see?" Gramps asked.

"I'm not sure. The man was too far away. I didn't get a good look at him. He was all bundled up."

"Did either one have a pet with them?"

"No," Daniel replied.

"Don't you find that strange?"

"Maybe they're picking up their pet," Daniel said.

"Park behind both of them. Two men without pets going into a vet's office seems shady. I can't tell you what it is. It just doesn't add up."

"Why park behind them?"

"So, they can't get out. Doesn't it seem odd to you? It's Saturday afternoon; the place should be jammin'. No cars? No customers? What vet isn't busy on a Saturday? Think about the last time you had to wait an hour because the vet was busy. Not having cars is highly unusual. I have an uneasy feeling about the place, the situation."

"Quit it, Gramps. You're starting to spook me. Either way, I need to talk to the vet. I want answers," Daniel said.

He maneuvered his truck laterally behind both vehicles so neither could leave. Gramps opened his overnight bag and took something out. "I brought this along in case we ran into trouble. I want you to bring it in there with you." He handed his grandson a silver-plated Smith & Wesson pistol with walnut handgrips.

"Where did you get this?" Daniel asked.

"I've had it for a while. It was a retirement gift. I've never used it. Now seems like the time."

"No, I'm not taking that. You watch too many movies."

"You're better off having it than not. It's there if you need it," Gramps stated.

"Isn't that extreme?"

"The hair is standing up on the nape of my neck. I always trust my instincts. I want you to be safe. You want me to go in with you, and I'll carry it?"

"No, I need you to stay out here if anyone else comes. Here's my cell phone. I'll dial 911. If it gets out of control, you can call the authorities. If anything happens to me, hit the send button, and the call will automatically go through."

Daniel went to the door. The sign read Dr. Phillip Cole, DVM. He tried to open the door—locked. He pressed his ear against the entryway—silence. He knocked on the door, and when there was no answer, he shouted, "I know you're in there. I'm not leaving." He banged on the door incessantly.

From inside, a voice said, "Hold on. I'm coming. I'm sorry, we're closed."

"This will only take a minute," Daniel replied.

The door opened a crack, and an older man who appeared to be in his early sixties, with white hair and a mustache, apprehensively peeped out at him. "I'm swamped. I don't have time."

"I've lost my dog." Daniel started to pull out his phone, then remembered it was with Gramps. He started describing Buca.

"No," the man replied without even listening. "Now get out of here."

"Have you seen him? Somebody found this collar a half mile up the road," Daniel said. "You sure you never treated him?"

"Positive. So, what does that have to do with me?" the vet asked.

"Maybe the other vet knows. Where's the other person? I want to talk to him," Daniel demanded.

"I don't have any partners. I work alone," Dr. Cole said.

"What about the other person I saw come in here?"

"There is no other person. There's nobody in here. We're not open for business," Dr. Cole stated indignantly.

"I saw somebody come in here." Irritated at the stonewalling, Daniel pushed the door, which Dr. Cole had his foot wedged against.

"What're you doing?" the vet asked.

"I know there's somebody else in here," Daniel shouted.

"I thought you were looking for your dog. What do you want with the other person? What, do you think I'm a liar? I'm calling the police. You're trespassing."

"Sure, go ahead and call them. I know there's someone else in here with you."

Grudgingly the man said, "Okay, come in and see yourself."

Daniel cautiously went into the reception area and ran into the hallway, passing several examination rooms. And as he turned the corner, he heard a metal door slam. Illuminated above the door was a sign that read EMERGENCY EXIT. He darted toward the door, and in one swift move, he slammed the panic bar, and the door flung open. "Stop. I want to talk to you," Daniel yelled. He rounded the building and found himself back in the parking lot near his truck.

He frantically motioned to Gramps to wind down the window and shouted, "Which way did he go?"

Gramps pointed with his right arm. "He went out the driveway and down that way," he said. "Who is he?"

"I don't know. But something tells me this man has answers."

Daniel noticed a figure in a quick retreat. He jumped in the driver's seat, gunned the engine, and took off after him. The man stood on the side of the road with his thumb out as he desperately tried to hitch a ride. In a last-ditch effort, he jumped in front of an oncoming car, forcing traffic to skid to a halt. The man climbed into the back seat of a vehicle.

Daniel swerved in front of the motorcade and blocked someone in during this commotion. Horns blared as he exited the truck.

Daniel heard a voice cry out, "Get me out of here! Get me out of here!" He saw the man push money toward the driver. "There's another two hundred if you get me out of here."

Daniel heard the driver yell, "Whattaya doing? Get the fuck out of my car. Out."

The hijacker locked the doors as Daniel neared. He brandished a knife from his pocket and waved it at him through the window.

Daniel returned to the truck, took Gramps's gun, returned to the car, and pointed it at the man.

The driver again yelled, "Get out, get out!" All the while, he kept hitting the unlock button.

Daniel kept pulling on the door. Finally, the door opened, and he pulled the hijacker out. Daniel gasped.

It was a face from the past. Leonard Scott.

Chapter 29

🐾 🐾 🐾 🐾 🐾

Daniel examined the jackknife and saw a Boy Scouts emblem on the handle. "I hope you stole this, because I have a hard time believing the Scouts would let you join. You're not Scout material," Daniel said. "Gimme your knife before you hurt yourself."

He violently threw Leonard into a snowbank, picked him back up, and said, "Get the fuck over there," and pushed him toward his truck.

"Somebody call the cops. They're kidnapping me," Leonard yelled.

"No one cares now. Just shut the fuck up and get in the back," Daniel said, pointing to his truck. "We're taking you back to your car." With a twist of the steering wheel, the vehicle did a U-turn. Daniel's eyes kept shifting from road to rearview mirror. Daniel's adrenaline pumped. He was finally going to get some answers.

Back in the parking lot, Daniel yanked Leonard out of the back of the truck and demanded, "Let me have your wallet and keys."

Leonard uttered, "No fucking way" with a look of bewilderment.

Daniel extended his right hand, grabbed him by the throat, and squeezed Leonard's Adam's apple while lifting him. "Give me your fucking wallet and keys."

Leonard reached into his pocket and reluctantly turned over his possessions. He stood there in silence with his eyes shifting from side to side when Daniel let go.

"I want some answers," Daniel said. "Just shut the fuck up and let me talk. In my estimation, we have about fifteen minutes before the police arrive. I'm sure somebody called them. I'm not sure if it was the vet or the people who saw me pull the gun. Either way, they'll be here soon."

"Good. I want to make a complaint," Leonard said.

"About what? That I took your wallet and car keys?" Daniel asked. "I'm pretty sure the police will be anxious to talk to the man in the blue Ford Edge. It sure looked like a carjacking to me. All I did was save him. And made a citizen's arrest."

"Whoa, slow down. What do you want to know?" Leonard stammered, visibly shaken.

"My dog. I want some answers about my dog," Daniel said.

"What are you talking about? I don't know what you mean. What dog?" Leonard said defiantly as his eyes continued to dart back and forth.

"I hope that you're not thinking about running. The last time I checked, a person can't outrun a bullet. I'm tired of playing games. Where's my dog?"

"What dog? Can you be a little more specific?"

"You don't remember me? You were the promoter of the Every Dog Show we had in our town in Baxter Falls. After you left, a lot of dogs disappeared, mine included." Daniel pulled out the gun. "Maybe this will jog your memory."

"Whoa, whoa, slow down." Leonard backed off.

Gramps had been standing in the background. "Wait, I got a better way to make him talk, and much more satisfying." He put down the tailgate, then went to the toolbox and pulled out a hammer. "Are you right-handed or left?"

Leonard stood tongue tied.

Gramps gave his grandson the hammer and said, "Your decision, Daniel. Let's break some fingers."

"You're fucking crazy, man," Leonard said.

171

Daniel showed him the picture on his cell phone. Leonard looked down at the ground and shook. Daniel could tell he wanted to say something but didn't know how. He knew whatever came out of his mouth would be a lie. But that was going to change with some persuasion.

"I don't know the dog. I've never seen him," Leonard stammered as he stamped his feet for warmth. "It's too damn cold out here. I can't think."

"Okay, let's start with some easy questions. What's your name, and what were you doing at the vet's office?" Daniel asked.

"I'm Scott Leonard."

"That's funny. In Connecticut, your name was Leonard Scott. And both of you, for all intents and purposes, seem to be the same fellow."

Daniel pulled out many IDs from Leonard's wallet, all of which contained different names with the same picture. "Looks like you got an identity crisis going on. Remember, the clock is ticking, and we're down to about ten minutes. I suggest you start talking."

"I've got nothing to say."

Gramps looked at the various IDs. "Guys like these never tell the truth unless you hurt them."

"I've had enough of this," Daniel said as he grabbed Leonard and brought him over to the truck's bed.

"No, let me see the picture again." Leonard's face went ashen, and he blinked uncontrollably, not looking Daniel in the eye. "If I tell you the truth, you'll let me go?"

Daniel said, "Maybe."

It was enough.

Leonard said, "I remember that dog. He's one mean son of a bitch. I shipped him somewhere down south—I think it was North Carolina. From there, I don't know where he went. I don't have the address. He was a new client."

"What do you mean, a new client?"

"I'm a dog broker. I get in orders, and I fill them. I hold dog shows in various states. People are so dumb; I get all the information I need at registration. I send out a couple of guys who pick up the dogs and bring them to me."

Daniel screamed, "Who the fuck are you to steal my dog? How can you do that? How'd you even get him?"

"It wasn't easy. We had to tranquilize."

"You better find out where he is, and for your sake, you better hope he's alive."

"You're gonna get me killed," Leonard pleaded.

"It's either by them or by me. Make your choice. I want answers."

He turned to Gramps and said, "First, Gramps, give me the keys to his car."

Gramps threw the keys to his grandson. "Get the registration. That's where he lives."

Daniel dragged Scott by the scruff of the neck to the passenger door, opened the glove compartment, and pulled out his registration.

"There's nothing else in there. Gimme back my keys," Leonard whined as he pulled out a pack of Niagara cigarettes in a green-and-white box. He took out the last one, crushed the empty box with trembling hands, and tossed it, narrowly missing Daniel.

"Go fucking pick that up, you litterbug."

Leonard retrieved the box and put it in his pocket.

"Are you responsible for all the missing dogs in Connecticut?" Daniel asked.

"No. So far, I've only taken ten to twelve dogs from that show."

"You're one sick bastard. I will give you forty-eight hours to find out where my dog is. If you don't, I will finish the job I started."

"Okay, you got the registration. Now give me my wallet and keys," Leonard said.

"Wait a second, Daniel. He's hiding something," Gramps said.

"There's nothing in there of any interest to you. Give me the keys," Leonard begged.

Daniel looked in the window. "Doesn't seem to be anything else inside here."

"Check the trunk," Gramps suggested.

Inside the trunk, Daniel found a cardboard box full of forms underneath a pile of blankets. Below it lay the multiple banners and papers from dog show entry forms—some filled out, others blank—to a list of clients and their various addresses.

Gramps said, "Let's turn over the evidence to the police."

"You do that and you'll never see your dog again," Leonard screamed. He screamed even louder when Daniel took direct action and lashed the hammer into Scott's hand.

As Leonard began to yelp, Daniel icily calmed the situation by putting his hand over the thief's mouth.

"Shhh," he hissed. "There is a way that doesn't involve much blood and pain. Yours." Daniel gave Leonard his business card, along with the keys. "You have forty-eight hours, and I mean *forty-eight hours*, not a minute later, to tell me precisely where my dog is. If I don't hear from you by Monday at four o'clock, I'll track you down and kill you. It's not a threat. It's a promise. Frankly, I don't believe anybody's gonna miss you, so you better pray that my dog is still alive. Your life depends upon it. Just remember, I know where you live. One final question—what happened to the keeshond you took?"

"What's a keeshond?"

Daniel gave a brief description of Lindsey's dog.

"That dog is no longer with us. A chemical company purchased it."

"I wish Buca were here—I'd let him rip you apart. Since he's not..." Daniel turned to walk away, stopped, pivoted, and swung and hit Leonard squarely on his jawline with such force that Leonard fell to the ground. "Ow, that looks like it hurts. I suggest you get going. The police should be here any minute now."

Daniel lifted the box and put it on the front seat between him and Gramps. They got back in the truck to drive home.

About a half mile down the road, Gramps took out the clip, studied the gun, and put them in the glove compartment. "Add these in there too." Daniel reached into his pocket and emerged with Leonard Scott's fake IDs.

As Gramps closed the glove compartment, he said, "Next time you use a gun, make sure the safety's off," he chuckled.

"Oh, Jesus!"

Against the mocking laughter of his grandfather, Daniel said, "I want to thank you, Gramps, for your help."

"No, thank you, Daniel."

"Whattaya mean?"

"It's the first time I've felt useful in quite a few years. Alive. No confusion."

"You were awesome. It's a side of you I've never seen."

"I know my memory is slipping and I'm a burden. Today felt so natural. So normal." His eyes sparkled, just like in the old days.

"So, what are we gonna do? Are we gonna turn over this evidence?"

"No, I can't. Scott was right. I'll never see my dog if he gets locked up," Daniel explained. "This evidence is my bargaining chip. I want to think I might be saving some dogs' lives by having these papers. I have to remain patient."

"Yeah, forty-eight hours," Gramps chimed in.

Daniel felt renewed hope that maybe Gramps would have more days like today. He pondered the events of the last thirty minutes. Daniel didn't have a clue as to where the safety was on the gun. He'd put his life and Gramps's in danger and didn't realize it. His stomach churned. Daniel drove for another minute down the road, pulled to the side, opened the door, and vomited.

Daniel's eyes burned as he strained to read the highway sign: Baxter Falls, 50 miles. His phone rang, and the screen read Restricted Caller. He turned to look at his passenger. Gramps was asleep and snoring lightly.

On the phone, Leonard began, "I have the information you requested—some good and bad news. First, you never heard it from me. I located your dog, but it's not in North Carolina anymore. My client sold it. It's a miracle he's still alive."

"What do you mean it's a miracle he's still alive? What did the buyer use him for?"

"He's a breeder of pit bulls, and he used your dog as bait. Your dog essentially became a sacrificial lamb used in training. But this lamb turned. So, the guy sold your dog to a very influential family who is powerful and well connected. The dog is no longer a bait dog but rather a dog in training. They aren't going to give him up. I would count your blessings and let the dog go."

"It's not your fucking dog. Just tell me where Sambuca is."

"That's the problem—I don't have the information, at least not now. I'll know more in a few months, sometime during the summer. Just have some patience. The people who have him think highly of him. They're not giving him up."

"I expect you to give me the address as soon as you have it."

"It's a suicide mission. I found out what you wanted. Now give me back my stuff," Leonard said.

"You're not gonna get it back until I know where my dog is," Daniel said.

"If you go looking for your dog, you're not coming back."

"It's the chance I'll take. If I were you, I'd only worry about getting me the address. Just remember, I know where you live. You're only four hours and fifty-three minutes away."

Chapter 30

❖ ❖ ❖ ❖ ❖

MISERY, KANSAS

The red and white cotton oaks shimmied in the wind at the Wyatt farm in a wild, playful dance. The dogwoods and redbuds were in full bloom. Nature was slowly stripping away the chill of winter and replacing it with pink and white foliage. Spring was here.

Ashlee's body shivered as she sat on the cold cedar slats of the gazebo. Travis quickly jumped up, removed his faded denim jacket, and placed it on her shoulders. "C'mon, let's go inside," Travis gently coaxed her.

"No, I'm fine," Ashlee said as she pushed the jacket away. Ashlee had a look of awe as she surveyed the surroundings. She murmured, "I'm beginning to see what the generations of Wyatts saw in this property. It's like the farm's transported to a golden age of simplicity. I love sitting out here. Have you seen the daffodils and crocus pushing up through the mulch? In another week, everything will be in full bloom."

Travis did not bristle as usual. Wealth was starting to improve his attitude. Instead, he admitted, "Yes, Mr. Dominick has done a lot for us, but I don't understand those gates at the driveway's end. I don't know why they were installed. Our farm is becoming a fortress. They're slowly isolating us from our neighbors," Travis said. "It's hard to justify renting out the back acreage and not welcome them through the front gates."

"Anthony said we're getting our remotes so we can do what we want."

"And the cobblestone driveway? What's up with that? It's just not functional," he asked.

"Why are you always being so negative? I think it's beautiful. It enhances the property."

"It's not practical. Gravel or peastone or even concrete would have made more sense. My farm equipment will eat up those pavers," Travis said.

"You haven't been on your farm equipment in almost a year."

Travis hesitated and decided it was better to ignore his wife's comment. But it stung. What did she mean? Was she happy or mad that he wasn't farming?

Still, it was hard not to like the new veranda with its wooden swing, or the flowerbeds and saplings that had replaced the former weeds and bare spots. And it was definitely hard not to like the smell of money.

Suddenly, however, that which was all too easy to dislike, an ongoing dark shadow, moved into distant view, heading toward the estate. As the black Hummer reached the gate, Ashlee and Travis headed inside, exiles in their own home.

Little G leaned on the horn. He got out of the driver's side and walked around to the back of the vehicle. He hit the key fob, lifted the window, and put down the tailgate. The barn door swung open, and the vet ran out.

"Good afternoon, sir. I hope you had a pleasant trip?"

"Cut the formalities. I need some help. Be careful where you put your fingers—this dog is vicious. I want you to do a complete checkup. And I mean a complete checkup."

Doc came over as a throaty growl came from the cage. "Hey, where'd you get the dog?" he asked. "I thought you were getting a puppy."

"Plans changed. Just do as I say."

"What about your father?"

"Fuck him. I'm my own man. Besides, he already knows. I had the dog at our home for a while."

"Where do you want the cage?" Doc asked.

"Put him in barn three, stable two."

"What's his name?"

"He doesn't have one yet. I'm struggling to find the perfect name—something that sounds menacing. The person I got him from hated him. He thought he was from hell," Little G said.

"Why don't you call him Satan?"

"Too cliché. I think I'm gonna call the dog Drake."

"What's that got to do with the devil?" doc asked.

"Drake is the name of the company that makes Devil Dogs," Little G said smugly.

"I like it, good name. Let's move him."

They slid the cage toward the front of the tailgate. They grabbed it and carefully kept hands and faces away from the opening. The dog softly growled. His weight shifted in the cage as he backed away from the vet, snarling. Slowly, they brought the dog to his new home.

"Back out of the stall, Doc. I don't want to spook him," Little G said. He looked down at the dog and murmured, "It's okay, Drake. Settle down, boy. Welcome to your new home. I got a nice meal for you. It's okay, Drake."

Dr. Winston stood by with a long pole with a noose attached in case of an emergency.

After a few minutes, the snarl subsided. Little G sensed Drake calm down as he talked to him. He mumbled words that meant nothing to Drake so he could get used to the tone of Little G's voice again. Eventually Little G moved forward and opened the cage door. Surprisingly, Drake stayed inside. He slowly backed out of the stall, cautiously kept both eyes on the crate, and opened the gate. Little G thought he had made some strides with Drake at his home. Maybe the long cross-country trip or the strange surroundings had made Drake's progress regress. He had a long way to go to train the dog in a short amount of time.

Little G's phone rang, and it was a number he didn't recognize. With hesitation in his voice, he said, "Hello?"

"Mr. Dominick, it's Billy Ray. Do you remember me?"

Little G said, "Yeah, I remember you, hayseed. You're the man with all the surprises. What do you want?"

"Mr. Dominick, someone's out to get your dog."

"What! Who? How do you know?" Little G snapped.

"The person who sold him to me called. He told me the former owner roughed him up for information. He is hell bent on getting his dog back. The person who took the dog is a loose cannon. He'd sell his grandmother for a quarter. The only person he's loyal to is himself. What do you want me to do? How do you want me to handle this?"

Little G collected his thoughts before replying, "Here's what I want you to do."

Chapter 31

😺 😺 😺 😺 😺

BAXTER FALLS, CONNECTICUT

Daniel carefully cut a hole in the Sheetrock that stretched from mid-stud to midstud. He measured and took a new piece, screwed in the section, and applied compound and tape. He shook his head in disbelief. There were two more spots where someone had punched holes in the wall. When he finished, Daniel headed toward the bar, where a Budweiser waited.

"You okay, Daniel?" Ethan asked.

"Yeah, just a bit tired. It's been hectic. I've got a lot on my plate."

"Sorry, I didn't mean to add to it, especially on a holiday weekend."

"That's okay, Ethan. Do you have any idea who did this?"

"Wish we did know. We'd make 'em pay. It was a busy Saturday night. Jim hired a group called Johnny Ratchet and the Memphis Mechanics. They're a rockabilly band who brought in a rowdy group of followers. Boy—that crowd could drink. We ran out of Pabst Blue Ribbon."

"Gramps used to drink that stuff. I didn't think they still made it," Daniel said.

"We had a Memorial Day special, and Jim ordered a lot of it. Then he found the mess this morning when he went to clean. He wasn't too happy. Thanks for coming so quickly. I know he appreciates your promptness."

"Maybe Jim should think about upping his security. It doesn't take long to ruin your reputation. The bathroom should be ready for paint in a couple of days. Speaking of Jim, where is he?"

"He's in his office. He should be out shortly. Hold on a second. I'll go get him."

As Ethan walked away, Daniel's phone rang with a restricted number. His heart pounded, and his palms turned clammy. Could this be the call he'd been waiting for? It had been months. Daniel went out to the deck, where it was private.

"I got the information on your dog," the caller said. "He's still alive and will be in Misery, Kansas, on the Fourth of July."

"Leonard?"

"There's something big going down. I just don't know the details, at least not yet. I received an invitation, so I'll be going. Are you going to show up there?"

"Why wouldn't I?"

"You're bringing all my shit with you, right?"

"Yeah, I'll be there with your stuff. Anything new you can tell me about the people who have my dog?"

"Not much. It's a family you don't want to fuck with."

"What are you talking about, fuck with? I just want my dog back. That's all."

"Well, they ain't giving him up." The line went dead.

Buca was out there! And Daniel had a chance to get him back. His only regret was not hitting Leonard Scott harder when he'd had the opportunity. "Yes," he yelled in triumph. A couple of patrons walking up the steps gave him a strange look. Daniel went back to the bar with newfound energy. Now he had renewed hope; a calmness came too. At last, he had a date and a destination.

Jim was at the bar when Daniel reappeared. "Hey, where'd you go?" Jim asked.

"Outside. I had to take a phone call. I've got some good news. I've got a line on my dog."

"Aw, that's great. Where?" Jim asked.

"Somewhere in the Midwest. The details are still sketchy."

"Can't the police get him?"

"Fat chance. I need to go. I've got to meet somebody out there and return his property."

"How do you know it's not a setup?" Jim asked.

"I don't. I don't even know if I can trust the guy, but it's the only lead I have. I need to believe in something, and this is the closest I've gotten to Buca's whereabouts in a long, long time."

"Where's there? Where do you have to go? Do you know who's got him?"

"I don't know who has him. Supposedly he'll be somewhere in Kansas in early July. That's all I know. I hope he still recognizes me," Daniel finished softly, wishing he had never told Jim. I can't let people into my business, he thought. Now Jim will ask every day if I know anything else, driving me crazy.

"Why wouldn't he recognize you?"

"Because it's been a while, and he may have been through a lot."

"What's he doing out in Kansas?" Jim asked.

"It's a long story, and I don't have the time. It's complicated. We'll discuss it later."

"That's great news about Buca. Let's celebrate. I'll buy you a beer," Jim said.

"Thanks. I can only stay for one. Gramps needs me, and I've got a lot to do."

"So, how is Mickey?"

"Same as usual, cantankerous, and demanding," Daniel said. "Every year, Gramps demands I iron his uniform for Memorial Day, and every year on the morning of the parade, he changes his mind. Then we must get there early because he has a certain spot where he sits. He's afraid someone's going to take it. He's very particular."

"That sounds like Mickey. I don't know how you do it," Jim said.

"What choice do I have?" Daniel asked.

"None, I guess. By the way, thanks for coming on such short notice. I don't mean to rush you, but when do you think the bathroom will be complete?"

"In a couple of days. Be careful when you go in there. The tape's still wet."

Memorial Day was the summer kick-off to barbecuing. Few people were at the tavern as Daniel applied a second coat of tape in the men's room. In the afternoon, he sat in a booth, relishing the last sip of his beer. Impatiently he waited for Jim and Lindsey. Daniel hadn't eaten and started to get a buzz from his fourth beer. He gently rubbed his itchy eyes. He had always been private about his life and had never asked for any help with personal matters. Today was going to be different, so he was unsure how to proceed with Jim and Lindsey.

Jim slid into the booth opposite Daniel. "Hi, Daniel."

"Hey, Jim, thanks for coming. If you don't mind waiting, Lindsey should be here shortly."

"That's fine. How was the parade? Did Mickey march?"

"No. Once again, I got up at five o'clock in the morning and ironed his uniform. Like a deleted scene from *Groundhog Day*, he decides he doesn't want to march. On top of that, the parade only lasted twenty minutes. It's been a long day, and it's only two thirty."

"Can I buy you a drink?" Jim asked.

"Sure, I'll take one. Thanks."

Jim returned with a Bud and a club soda for himself. After a few minutes, Lindsey arrived, wearing a yellow sundress and sandals. She got herself a drink and came to their table. "I'm sorry I'm late. Did I miss anything?"

"What a nice outfit. The color looks good on you," Jim remarked.

"Thanks, I had an open house. Why they schedule these on Memorial Day is beyond me. Only two families showed up."

"You're probably wondering why I asked you here," Daniel said. "I could use your opinions and your assistance on some things.

"Yesterday, I received a notice from one of the nursing homes. Gramps is next on their list, and they expect him there by tomorrow, or the room will go to someone else. Going to this place is gonna kill him, and the timing is horrible. I don't know how to tell him. I've always known the day was coming. And now that it's here, I don't know what to do. Is it too soon? The doctor said to put him in the nursing home while he still has some faculties, that he'll acclimatize better."

"Doing the proper thing is never an easy choice," Lindsey said. "And Daniel, you're doing the right thing."

"I just don't want to do the wrong thing. I don't even know if Gramps knows what's going on. That's the hard part. Some days he's a joy to be around, and other days are pure hell. I don't know what Gramps I'll be talking to today. His mood often changes. Once he's in the facility, he's not coming home. He gave up his entire life and career to raise me. I feel guilty. Now I'm the parent. Please tell me I'm doing the right thing. Am I selfish?"

"Daniel, it's a matter of what's best for Mickey," Lindsey said. "During his more lucid moments, he knew this was coming. He was preparing for the inevitable by wanting to sell his house."

"He still has some good days, but they are few and far between. He needs to go somewhere with twenty-four-hour care, a nursing home. We checked out the two he was on the waiting list for, and they seemed pretty good."

Jim said, "If Mickey were in the right frame of mind, he wouldn't want you to struggle with this."

"But he's not, and I do. I need to make this decision today. I need to sell his house. I don't have the funds to take care of him in a nursing home. Most of the time, he's not in the right frame of mind. But he has his moments, which makes it hard. That's why you guys are here—to reassure me I'm making the right decision."

"Do you have any other options?" Jim asked.

"Well, there's Kelly, but she's about to quit. I doubt if I could find another caregiver like her. She's a trooper and knows how to handle him.

185

He needs somebody twenty-four hours a day." Daniel lowered his head. "I just physically can't do it."

Lindsey grabbed Daniel's hand. "As painful as it is, you're doing the right thing," she said, looking in his eyes.

"Am I doing this because I have the chance to find Buca?"

Lindsey's mouth dropped open. "What are you talking about?"

"I just found out yesterday where Buca will be in early July. Sorry I didn't tell you. I've just been so busy and preoccupied. But it means I have to go there and take him."

"What do you mean you have to take him? He's your dog! Can't you call the police? Isn't there something you can do?" Lindsey asked.

"It's complicated. These are the kind of people where you can't do that. I'm going to have to go there and physically take him."

"Sounds dangerous to me," she replied.

"What's your plan?" Jim asked.

Daniel resumed, "I don't know yet how I'm going to do it. I don't even know what I'm going to do. I haven't formulated a plan. I don't want to do anything at the expense of my grandfather. The only person who hasn't left me is Gramps. Now I'm leaving him. I promised him I'd never leave him."

"But you're not leaving him. You'll only be gone for a short while," Lindsey said.

Daniel's voice cracked. "I was under the impression Buca left me too. Now I know he had no choice. He put his life on the line to save mine. I owe it to him. I have to decide what to do, and time is my enemy. When I leave to go get Buca, Gramps will be alone."

"No, I'll visit him," Lindsey said.

"I will too, as much as I'm able," Jim said. "Give the nursing home my name as a person they can update when you're not around. I'll keep tabs on him too."

"Thank you both for your help. I know it won't be easy for you," Daniel said.

Jim finally said, "You must do what your heart's telling you to do. It's great to be there for your grandfather. Frankly, there's nothing you can do.

Mickey needs the special care that only they can give him. He's proud. He'd feel devasted if you ruined your life taking care of him when you could have gotten Buca back. He raised you with his values. He would want you to get your dog if you had the chance. He knows what Buca means to ya."

"Lindsey, has there been any action on the house since you put it on the market?" Daniel asked.

"It's still a soft market, but I'm confident it will sell. It may take a little time. I've had some showings. You need to clean out the personal items, especially the closets. Then they'll appear more spacious. Remove some furniture so that it won't look cluttered."

"Lindsey, I apologize. Could you give me a couple of minutes alone with Jim?"

"Sure, I'll be at the bar."

"Just get yourself a drink and put it on my tab. I'll be up there in minutes," Daniel said. Lindsey nodded and left the booth.

"What can I do for you?" Jim asked.

"Jim, it's no reflection on you, but would you mind buying me out as a minority owner?"

"What are you talking about?"

"I know it's something I'll regret doing down the road, but I have to get Buca back. I may have to pay someone, and I don't have much cash. I've agonized over this decision. I have little choice."

"You have one other option: I'll loan you the money. You helped me out when I was in need. Doing this is the least I can do for you. You can decide if you still want to sell your portion when you get back. Your decision is based on emotion right now."

"I've got to ask you another favor. I have a box at home. Would you mind storing it in your safe? I don't mean to be cryptic, but if I don't return, give the box to the authorities. They'll know what to do."

"This sounds dangerous. What are you getting yourself into?"

"I don't know. I just don't know."

Chapter 32

🐾 🐾 🐾 🐾 🐾

Gramps's room was the last and most challenging room to declutter and pack. Daniel entered, took all the family photographs off the wall, and carefully placed them face down on the bedspread. Ashamed by what he was doing to Gramps, he couldn't bear to look at the portraits. He stared intently at the closet door, still haunted by yesterday's conversation. It was worse than he could ever have imagined. It left an indelible mark. He rubbed his bloodshot eyes. Making this move wasn't supposed to be like this. He had envisioned a smoother transition, with it being a good day for his grandfather. But it turned out to be one of his bad days, one of the worst.

His memory flashed back to yesterday, replaying the conversation repeatedly, wondering if he could have done anything differently. Yesterday morning he had started packing Gramps's suitcase. He fought back the tears, as he knew he had to be strong for Gramps's sake. He told himself he was doing it for all the right reasons. The ER doctor had highly recommended this facility. Daniel hoped Gramps liked it there and made friends. But what Gramps would Daniel be bringing to the nursing home? The one who knew he was going? Or the one who fought every step of the way? Would he isolate himself when he got there?

From the start, it had gone wrong.

"What are you doing in my room?" Gramps yelled out. "I don't keep any money in here. What do you want with my clothes?"

"Gramps, please calm down. Sit on the bed. Today's the day you'll be going to the nursing home. Don't you remember? We already talked about this."

"I don't. I'd never agree to that," Gramps screamed. "The only thing I remember is you saying you'd always be there for me. What, now you're trying to get rid of me?"

"I love you. I'm not trying to get rid of you. I'm trying to give you a happier life. Surrounded by people your age."

"Happier life? Why would I be happier? A nursing home is a waiting room for the cemetery."

"Please don't make this any harder than it is. You may not remember, but we did talk about this. I just can't give you the care you need and deserve."

"I know what you want. You want to lock me away to get all the money from my house."

"Gramps, you know we both decided this was the best thing for you. Why not give it a chance? If you don't like it, we'll go somewhere else."

"Is this another idle promise?" Gramps asked.

Daniel hesitated, not knowing the right words to tell him. How could Daniel tell him he wasn't coming home ever again? Gramps would see right through that lie. "None of my promises are idle. I'm sorry you're taking it this way. You may not believe it, but this is harder for me than for you. I love you."

As they wheeled him away, the look on Gramps's face said it all. He refused to look at Daniel. His face was in a fierce frown, a child's scowl, with his eyes closed, defiant to the very last moment. His grandfather would not forget this day. Daniel hoped it wouldn't be his last memory of his grandson.

Now he sat on his grandfather's bed, surrounded by boxes. Daniel knew he needed to concentrate on the task, not dwell on his past decisions. He feverishly attacked the boxes with a renewed feeling that he had done the right thing. He planned to put all Gramps's belongings safely in climate-controlled storage.

As he slid the closet door open, the fragrance of Old Spice emanated. He carefully folded up Gramps's clothes and placed them in a box. He gathered his police and military uniforms and inserted them in a garment bag.

There were several boxes in the closet piled neatly on top of each other. The two top boxes had Daniel's name on them. The first was all his report cards, trophies, and ribbons. He didn't realize Gramps had kept all of them. On top was his high school diploma. Beneath the certificate were his report cards in reverse order. As he studied his grades, he wished he'd applied himself more. Daniel now planned for the future. Gone were his days of sleepwalking through life.

He rushed through his early report cards and stopped at his kindergarten progress report. He vividly remembered being six years old and looking at the comments section. He couldn't read them then because they were written in cursive, so he'd asked the bus driver what it said. The driver said, "It says you are doing well in kindergarten." Now that he could read the comments himself, he was stung by the stark reality of his teacher's assessment. The report said, "Very bright boy, knows his numbers and alphabet, very creative. Socially awkward, doesn't play well with others. Seems happiest when performing tasks alone. He needs to work on communication skills, i.e., talk about his feelings more." That pretty much summed up his life.

The second box was full of pictures and included images of his parents when they were dating, at their wedding, and a funny one of his father as he lifted his mother's shirt to show her big belly when she was pregnant. Then he found a ziplock bag full of letters tucked away in the box, all yellowed by time. He had written these in his formative years with his grandfather. Several were to Santa Claus, numerous ones to God. He vaguely remembered writing all these letters. He opened the first one carefully and read, "Dear God: My grandfather tells me you are everywhere. Today is a special day. Could you please wish my daddy a happy

Father's Day for me? Tell him I love him and miss him a lot. Thank you for doing this. Daniel."

Daniel took a second to compose himself as his eyes began to tear up. He softly repeated, "Stay strong." Growing up with Gramps, Daniel had never learned a mother's compassion—and empathy. His tragic past had caused him to become a man much sooner than nature had intended. The other letters were in the same vein—some asked God why he took his parents away from him. Daniel would write on holidays and their birthdays. He and Gramps would compose these letters at night and put them in an envelope in the morning. Daniel and Gramps would go to the cemetery with a helium balloon the following day. Gramps would attach the envelope to the balloon. Daniel never realized Gramps had kept all of these. Some of the letters showed wet spots. Gramps had never shown much emotion during those times. Now Daniel knew better. As Daniel continued to read, a tear fell. God, he thought, take care of Gramps. I can't lose him too, or I will be alone in the world. Daniel realized how sad he had been when he wrote these letters, hoping for a response that never came. The same feeling overcame him now.

The bottom box contained evidence of all Gramps's accomplishments in life. There were various commendations, including an officer of the year award from his policing career, medals awarded during the Korean War, and several awards for marksmanship. Highly decorated, Gramps never talked about the war or his honors. He was a private person—it was never about him. This was a side of Gramps Daniel never knew. He felt he needed to learn more about him than ever. With Gramps's memory rapidly declining, it would be harder to get any information from him.

He knew Gramps was a hero, for real heroes do not brag about their accomplishments. Inside one of Gramps's boxes was a letter from his grandmother to his grandfather. In the envelope was a photograph of the whole family. It jogged Daniel's memory. In it, she explained how much she loved her husband, and near the end, she said she wanted to go to a hospice and not die in front of her grandson. She asserted that her husband would grant her final request if he truly loved her. By now,

Daniel was tearing uncontrollably. He wiped his eyes and tried to calm himself by taking deep breaths.

He got back to packing and labeling boxes. Tucked away was the case for the gun they had taken to New York. Daniel lifted the lid and found the container empty except for a handwritten note that included numerous signatures. The message read: *Dear Mickey. We fondly remembered your first day on the job when you accidentally discharged your sidearm, barely missing your foot. We affectionately dubbed you "Sure Shot." Your talent on the range quickly made a mockery of the nickname. This gun is an appropriate gift that may someday save your life or someone else's. It's been a pleasure and honor serving with you. May your aim always be true. Enjoy your retirement! We'll miss you, and don't be a stranger.*

Gramps used to tell him stories of pranks the officers played on each other. He always said, "It was an inside joke." They did it to release stress. The morbid sense of humor seemed to help them cope with the tragedies at hand. Daniel had heard some of the stories several times over, and Gramps had a certain twinkle in his eye when he recounted the tales. Daniel pondered whether to tell Gramps's fellow officers he was in a nursing home. What effect would it have on his grandfather? I'll decide when I get back, Daniel thought.

When the living room was full of boxes, Jim and Ethan showed up with a sandwich and beer. Daniel gratefully took it and thanked them. Outside in the driveway stood a U-Haul truck. He had hoped to make everything in one load, and he would. It was strange, he thought, an entire life fitted into a few suitcases and a truck. Those meager possessions didn't even begin to represent Gramps's legacy.

After eating, Jim and Ethan helped Daniel decide which furniture to take and what to leave for staging. He handed the final boxes to Jim and Ethan as they finished packing the truck and closed the door.

He looked around a final time. Sadness embraced his soul. So many cherished memories, but this home was now just another house since it had lost its heart. Gramps. The last object Daniel took before exiting the final time was the only family photo of his father, clad in a fireman's suit, with his mom and Daniel. He realized it was time to go, to close the Chapter, and to write a new one where he would be his grandfather's legacy.

Chapter 33

🐾 🐾 🐾 🐾 🐾

THREE WEEKS LATER

Daniel walked into the nursing home, and the receptionist immediately greeted him with, "Good afternoon, Daniel. How are you?"

"Do I know you?"

"No, I'm new here. The nurse said you come almost every day around this time. Someone described you." The receptionist had brown hair and glasses and wore a printed frock with white pants.

"How's my grandfather doing today?" Daniel asked.

"He's having a tough day," she replied. "He's more confused and demanding than usual. I overheard a group of nurses remarking that the rare occasions you don't show up seem to be his most difficult days."

"I'm sorry," he said.

"Stop right there. We understand. You don't have to apologize."

"But does he?" Daniel asked. "Can I go in and see him?"

"You're welcome anytime, day or night. Just a warning before you go in there, we sedated your grandfather, so he may be sleeping right now."

"Is this common practice?"

"Only in extreme circumstances. Today was one of those days."

With a heavy heart, Daniel slowly walked down the long hallway. Gramps had been here almost a month, but his attitude hadn't changed. The nurses said it usually took about two weeks for the patient to get acclimated.

Gramps lay in bed covered by a sheet. The bedspread stopped halfway up. After all his grandfather had accomplished, he was now a shell of his former self. His escalating lack of mental capacity had robbed Gramps of his freedom and even his dignity. Daniel moved the blanket to cover him fully.

He grabbed his grandfather's hand and gave it a slight squeeze. "I'm so sorry I had to put you in here. I'm not even sure I did the right thing. I hope you're not mad at me and pray you understand. I appreciate everything you've done." Silently, alone, he broke down and wept, caressing his grandfather's hand,

"Gramps, I'm sorry. I have to go away for a little while. I don't want to. It is something I need to do. I hope I'm doing the right thing for you. I never told you enough how much I appreciated all your sacrifices and everything you did for me. You'll never know how much I love you. You're my hero. You rescued me when nobody else wanted me.

"I also didn't say I have a chance to find Buca and bring him home. I'm not even sure if I'm going to be able to get him back. But it's something I need to do. While I'm gone, I have Jim and Lindsey checking in on you, and I'll get daily reports. I know you always liked Lindsey and loved her smile. I hope you remember her. Please don't give the nurses a hard time."

Daniel sat in a chair, bent forward with his elbows on his knees. He rubbed his face and wiped the tears away. Daniel said a silent prayer to God to take care of his grandfather. He felt like a hypocrite praying when he didn't believe. But this was for Gramps.

He got up and gently kissed his grandfather. Gramps muttered something to him, but Daniel was unsure what he said or if he was even coherent. Gramps repeated a little stronger and louder, "Bring Buca home."

Daniel paused for a second. Did Gramps just say what Daniel thought he did? Or was it just something Daniel needed to hear from him? No, he did say it. Inside, Daniel finally felt a feeling of renewed hope. Gramps had not only acknowledged his presence but gave him his blessing to find his dog. A final tear rolled down Daniel's cheek, a tear of joy. Daniel sighed and repeated softly, "Bring Buca home."

Daniel's Mac came to life. He plopped down in his black leather chair and impatiently waited for the computer to boot while tapping his fingers on his desk.

His phone vibrated. He noticed it was Lindsey. "Hey, Lindsey, I'm sorry I haven't called you. You're on my list. I've got a lot to do and don't have much time, but I'm glad you called."

"Daniel, are you okay? You don't sound like yourself. What's going on?"

"I just got back from visiting Gramps, and I feel depressed over the situation. Every time I go to visit him, his eyes are closed. I don't know if he's sleeping or ignoring me. The staff at the nursing home told me it takes up to two weeks for new residents to reconcile themselves. Gramps has been there almost a month."

"Don't take it personally, Daniel. I'm sure he's struggling with his new surroundings and what's going on mentally. He's a proud man. I went to see him yesterday. He did the same thing to me."

"Every time I go, I tell him how much I miss him and love him. I apologize for not being able to take care of him. I thank him for all the sacrifices he made. I'm sorry for this whole situation."

"Stay positive. Let him know what's going on in your life. Give him a reason to live. You need to stop apologizing. After a while, those words become hollow," Lindsey said.

"I can't," Daniel replied. "I'm leaving tomorrow."

"How long are you gonna be gone? And just exactly when were you going to tell me?" Lindsey demanded.

"Probably tonight or while en route. I don't know when I'll be back. All my life, I've questioned my decisions. Now I've come to the point where I'd rather live with failure than regret."

Silence lingered. Daniel didn't know what to tell her. "Please don't make this harder than it already is. You're one of the last people I'd want to hurt." He couldn't tell her what it will take to get Buca back because he didn't know. "Lindsey, would you be able to pick up my mail? I have a hold at the post office, but sometimes mail sneaks through."

"I don't mind getting your mail. I have some junk mail from Mickey's. I'll just put it all at your house. On a positive note, I've had a couple of inquiries regarding the house. It shows much better with limited furniture."

"Thanks for being there. It's been a very long time since I've trusted anyone. You are very special to me."

"Daniel, I lov—I mean, I will miss you. Good luck on your trip."

"I'll miss you too. Bye, Lindsey."

He googled Misery, Kansas. He found the name and number of the one hotel in downtown Misery and dialed it.

While Daniel was making reservations from June twenty-fourth to July fifth, he heard a beep on his phone. It was a restricted caller. After a few seconds, he listened to a second beep. "I'm sorry, I have to take this call," he said, and he hung up, not waiting for her reply. He clicked on his phone to answer the call. "Hello? Hello?" The line went dead. "Shit." He heard a noise he associated with a missed call. Was it Leonard? Whoever it was, if it was important, he hoped they'd call back. As he tried to convince himself otherwise, deep down, he felt he'd missed an urgent call, which troubled him.

Who else could it be with a restricted number if it wasn't Leonard Scott? It had to be him. Why was he calling? What did he want? Had his plans changed? Was he backing out? Dozens of questions swirled through Daniel's head. He finally surmised that if it was crucial, Leonard would call back. He'd better call back.

He slumped down into the chair and started to crack his knuckles. Damn.

He googled Kansas to refresh his memory. Kansas, nicknamed the sunflower state, was approximately twenty-five hours away. Misery was in the northwest corner of Kansas, located in Thomas County.

Misery had been settled in the early 1800s as part of the Kansas Territory. It was founded by German immigrants and initially called Hannover Valley. In 1861, the town officially changed its name to Misery in hopes of preventing more people from settling. Its rich, fertile soil made it ideal for growing wheat, corn, sorghum, and soybeans. It remained a thriving farming community until the 1930s, when the Dust Bowl decimated the area. The town now lived up to its name.

He scanned the government section and read that the mayor/sheriff was Clint Grayson. The sheriff was the first person he needed to talk to when he arrived. He looked up Clint Grayson on Facebook and studied the picture of him long enough to burn an image in his mind. A chill ran through his body. Researching was something Gramps would have done—doing all the homework before. He was still reaping the benefits of Gramps's wisdom.

Daniel looked at various websites on pit-bull fighting. He studied the terminology and slang, such as campaign, champion, and gameness. The one term he kept staring at in disbelief was *bait dog*, which made him queasy. He familiarized himself with the regulations and printed out Cajun rules, a code of ethics strictly adhered to by each dog's handler. He stored the information in his suitcase. Sick stuff.

Before he turned off the computer, Daniel reviewed several dogfighting videos. Though it was morbid, he couldn't take his eyes off the screen. It sickened him to think his beloved pet was part of this travesty. He twirled the chair around, reliving happier moments with Sambuca. In one corner was where he'd backed Sambuca to teach him how to defend himself. Another spot was where he'd rolled in sawdust, and below the bay window was where Buca used to lie.

Chapter 34

✹ ✹ ✹ ✹ ✹

MISERY, KANSAS
WEDNESDAY, JUNE 24, 2015

Nothing but crops filled the countryside. Daniel spied a sign that said "Welcome to Misery, Kansas" inside a landscaped meridian filled with sunflowers. He stopped the truck and got out and stretched. His body ached while his stomach growled, yet Daniel wasn't hungry. He'd driven nonstop for over twenty-four hours. Daniel didn't want to call Lindsey just then, so he snapped a picture and texted it to her to let her know he had arrived safely. Daniel jumped back in the vehicle and scanned the radio. A DJ was ending a weather forecast. He heard, "You're listening to KKCI, home of classic rock. Here's Boston with 'Don't Look Back.' Daniel wondered if it was a sign.

The road didn't liven up much until he reached the city limits. He found a parking space, grabbed his overnight bag, and quickly got one of Leonard's IDs. The hotel building was an early twentieth-century brick structure nestled in Misery's historic district. Several boutiques and a bar surrounded it. He went up to the reservation desk.

The clerk said, "Good afternoon. Welcome to Hannover Suites. How may I help?"

"Hi, my name's Daniel Tanner. I have a reservation."

The clerk checked his computer. "No Daniel Tanner here. What's your confirmation number?"

"I don't have one. Nobody gave me one. I talked to a woman this past Monday. She reserved it for me. I gave her my credit card number."

"We give everybody a confirmation number. I'm sorry, sir, there's no reservation."

"Well, I talked to some lady."

"Do you remember her name?"

"No, I don't. Can't you check with the manager?"

"I am the manager," he said gruffly.

"Well, how about you just give me any room?"

"I'm sorry, we're booked solid for a few weeks."

"What women do you have working the reservations?" Daniel asked.

"How about a Corey?"

"Yeah, that sounds familiar," Daniel said quickly in hopes of securing a room, although deep down, he knew he had never gotten a name or confirmation number.

"We don't have a Corey working here. We also don't have any rooms available. Nice try."

"Do you have a Leonard Scott staying here?"

The manager sighed. "State law stipulates I'm not allowed to divulge our guests' names."

Daniel showed Leonard's ID and said, "This man, he's, my brother-in-law. He must be staying here."

The manager looked at the picture. "No, he doesn't look familiar."

"Can I see your register? He may be using an alias," Daniel said.

"No, I can't let you look at the register," he replied. impatiently. "I don't have time for this. I have to take care of customers who made *reservations*. This sounds like a missing-person case. Take it up with the sheriff's office."

"You don't understand," Daniel pleaded.

The manager motioned to the couple standing behind Daniel to come forward.

"Whoa, I'm not through yet," Daniel said.

"Well, I am. Get out of here, or I'm calling the police. There's a flea-bag motel on the outskirts of town. Why don't you try there? Good day."

All the frustration and the woes of the previous weeks and months came to a head. Daniel flipped. With the intensity of a spoiled brat, he swiped everything off the counter onto the floor. The papers strewn everywhere.

"Get outta here. Security!" the manager yelled.

"Don't bother. I'm leaving. Thanks for all your help," Daniel said sarcastically.

Back out in his truck, he googled Misery motel. He punched it in his GPS and headed to the edge of town, a mile from I-70. Its giant neon sign read Tradewinds Motel in blue and No Vacancy in red. He parked in its lot, hurried in, and said, "Good afternoon. I'm supposed to meet up with my brother-in-law, but I can't find him." He took out Leonard's ID and said, "Have you seen this man?"

"I don't mean to be rude, but I've seen many people come through here in the past few days," the clerk said. The motel's phone rang as Daniel stood there, and the clerk answered it. "Tradewinds, how may I help you? I'm sorry to hear that," he said. "I hope she feels better. No, sir, you won't have to pay. It'll be ready for you tomorrow. I'll take care of it right away."

Daniel hesitantly said, "Can I have a room?"

"Don't you know how to read? The sign out front says No Vacancy. It means no rooms."

"Wasn't that phone call a cancellation?" Daniel asked.

The clerk became flustered and reluctantly agreed. "Yes, but only for tonight. I guess you can have the room." As he filled out the paperwork, the clerk asked him, "What brings you way out here?"

"This man I showed you on the ID is my brother-in-law. He got into a fight with my sister. When he left, he wasn't in the right frame of mind. We're concerned about him. I traced his phone to this area. I need to know if he's okay. He's not answering his cell. Please just take a moment of your time. Study the photograph."

"Look, I'm swamped, and we're understaffed. Do you want the room or not?"

"Yes, I want the room," Daniel replied.

"Here's your key. Your room is on the back side of the motel, the second story."

"Is there any chance of getting some extra pillows?"

"Look, I told you we're swamped. I'll see what I can do. No promises."

"If you see him, please let me know." Daniel gave the clerk his business card.

The phone rang again. "I'm swamped. I get your point."

As Daniel walked away, he heard the unmistakable sound of paper ripping. He assumed it was his business card.

He moved his vehicle to the back of the motel and trudged up the stairs. The erratic hum of the air conditioner vibrated softly in the room's background. The welcome cool effect outweighed the noise. He tossed his suitcase on the floor, too tired to unpack. His body collapsed on the mattress.

At his door came a soft knock. He lifted his head off the pillow. He heard another soft knock. "Housekeeping," a female voice called out. Daniel opened the door. A teenage girl with dark hair held pillows. "Are you the one who ordered the extra pillows?"

"Yes, I did, thank you. Hey, can you tell me if you have seen this person?" He held out Leonard Scott's ID, covering the name and address with his thumb.

"Yes, he's staying in room one fifteen. He arrived yesterday."

Daniel could feel his heart pounding. "Are you sure?"

"Positive. Anybody who gives me a big tip, I remember."

"How would you like to make twenty bucks?" Daniel asked.

"What do I have to do?"

"Unlock the room for me. I promise to lock it when I'm through."

"No, I can't do that. I could get fired. Besides, my uncle owns the motel."

"Listen, he's my brother-in-law, and he could be suicidal. He had a bad argument with my sister and stormed out. He has two small children at home. I need to find out if he's okay. I fear for his safety. I don't want my nephew and niece growing up without a dad."

Daniel saw the girl's face softened with kindness, which he suspected was a rare sight in Misery. She said, "Well, okay. I'll do it. The room is one floor below."

He handed the girl a twenty, threw the pillows on the bed, and waited a couple of minutes before leaving his room.

He rushed down the rest of the stairs, looked around to see if anyone watched, and entered the room cautiously. The room was dark, and Daniel switched on the light. There was a large suitcase on the queen-size bed. He tried to open it, but Leonard must have locked it. He looked around the room for any clue as to his whereabouts. He checked the bureau drawers—empty. He looked in the trash and saw a crushed pack of cigarettes. He picked it up; it was a green-and-white Niagara box, just as Daniel remembered. He knew he was in the right place. He left the room and locked the door.

Back in his room, Daniel dozed. The long trip had gotten the better part of him. He lay down with his boots still on. Suddenly a loud pounding on his door startled him. Was he dreaming? Or was someone trying to break in? The noise persisted. It was nonstop, like a woodpecker on steroids. Disoriented, he tried to wake up.

"Open up. I know you're in there," a deep voice bellowed.

"Hold on, hold on, I'm coming."

Outside was a big black man about six foot three and weighing a hefty 290 pounds, Daniel estimated. His badge revealed him to be an officer of the law. "I'm Deputy Sheriff Ken Malcolm of the Misery Police Department," the man said. "We're following up on a report that someone saw a person illegally entering a room."

"Nobody's entered this room. Nobody's been up here," Daniel said.

"Let me be a little more specific. Someone saw you entering another room—one that was not your room, that is to say. The manager said you acted suspicious, cautiously looking around," the deputy said. "Identification, please."

"Why do you need that?" Daniel said as he rubbed his eyes.

"I ask the questions, not you."

Daniel reluctantly took out his license from his back pocket and showed it.

"Mr. Tanner. A little far away from home, aren't we?"

"I took a left when I shoulda taken a right."

"Quit being a wiseass. Do you want to do this the easy way or the hard way?"

"What do you mean?" Daniel asked.

"You ain't on no getaway. Nobody comes to Misery for the view. We know you were in that room. Now, what were you doing in there?" the deputy asked.

"What room was I accused of being in?"

"Don't play dumb with me. I ask the questions, and you answer. Again, what were you doing in that room?"

"Well, it's my brother-in-law—"

"What makes you think he's in that room?"

Daniel hesitated. "When I talked to him last, he mentioned he was in room one fifteen. That was two days ago."

"I don't know how he could do that; this occupant checked in yesterday."

"Look, it's been a long drive out here. Maybe I got my days mixed up. I need to find him. I'm worried," Daniel said.

"Worried enough to break into the room? What's he look like?"

Daniel took out the picture of Leonard, holding his thumb over the address.

The deputy grabbed the license.

"Your brother-in-law lives in upstate New York?"

"The family recently relocated to Connecticut. I guess he hadn't updated his driver's license yet."

"This photo matches the description. But that's not the name."

"He probably registered under an alias," Daniel said.

"If he didn't want to talk, why did he accept your phone call?"

"I blew up his phone with messages and filled up his voice mail. Maybe I wore him down."

"What are you doing with his license anyway?"

"I don't know. I found it in my truck. He probably dropped it when I helped him move. It's an old one," Daniel uttered.

"Do you have any proof he's your brother-in-law? You entered a room illegally. The manager saw you from inside. We don't take kindly to people like you."

"What do you mean, people like me?" Daniel asked.

"Liars and thieves."

"I didn't take anything."

"So, you admit to going into the room. How did you get in anyway? I checked the door. There were no signs of forced entry."

"I found the door unlocked."

The deputy had had enough. He squinted suspiciously and said, "I am a busy man, and this is a busy town. Do yourself a favor and get out of town tomorrow. I may reconsider B and E charges against you if you don't. Catch my drift? I also received a phone call from the hotel about a disturbance. It seems somebody threw things around the lobby. You match that description."

"Listen, Deputy, you got me all wrong."

"Wrong or right, it doesn't matter. The sheriff wants you out of here by tomorrow. We won't press charges if you leave."

"What time does the welcome wagon arrive?" Daniel asked.

"If you keep being a wiseass, you can leave now. Check-out time is at eleven a.m. I strongly suggest you adhere to it."

Before Daniel fell asleep, he called Lindsey to see how Gramps was doing.

"Resting comfortably. Although yesterday Mickey seemed very confused," she said. "How is everything going out there?"

"Not a friendly town. The deputy sheriff has already visited me. They want me out of here."

"Oh no, what did you do?"

"Nothing, it was a misunderstanding. I'm so tired; I can't think straight. I'll call you tomorrow. Tell Gramps I love him."

He hung up. Daniel was not sure if he was in the right place, but he felt this was the closest he'd been to Buca in a long, long time. A shiver went down his spine.

Chapter 35

🐾 🐾 🐾 🐾 🐾

TJ and Kansas sprinted across the backyard, dodging and pausing, hiding behind barns, hoping no one would see them. Travis followed clandestinely. Whenever Travis asked his son where he went, he never got a straight answer, which caused him to resort to drastic measures. To Travis, this trip was critical at last Travis would have some answers to his lingering questions. TJ and Kansas made their way to the building that housed the veterinarian clinic. TJ and Kansas went inside.

Travis watched through a partially opened door. He could hear and see what was going on inside. He saw a dog on a table from his vantage point, evidently asleep.

"TJ, how's Kansas been doing lately?" Dr. Winston asked.

"He's running better and doesn't seem to be in as much pain. He usually only limps when he gets tired."

"The hydrotherapy—"

"The what?" TJ inquired.

"The underwater treadmill seems to be working. I can put Kansas in it for a while if you've got some time."

"Where are Mr. K and Little G?"

"They won't be back for a bit. Don't worry about it."

"I have to worry—I can't get caught. My dad warned me to stay out of here. If only my dad knew how much it helped Kansas, I don't think he'd mind, but you can't tell. Okay, let's put Kansas in the tank and give him a little workout."

"Stay clear of the black dog over there. He's vicious."

"No, he's not," TJ said.

"How do you know?" Doc asked.

"I sneak out sometimes and feed him. He growls a little, but he's getting better."

"I wouldn't recommend you ever do it again. That dog will rip you apart. Besides, he belongs to Little G, and he's very possessive of his dog."

"What are you doing to the dog? Why is he asleep?"

"Drake? I had to sedate him. He had some minor surgery—an abscessed tooth," Doc said.

TJ and Kansas walked over to Drake. TJ tentatively put a hand out to pet him. Travis felt his pulse quicken when TJ walked over to the dog. He was at a crossroads as to whether to interrupt or let him continue. TJ continually disobeyed. This was another act of defiance. Travis struggled with his decision. TJ, though, was doing it for the benefit of Kansas. Travis believed the vet had given TJ the incentive to want to be a vet when he grew up. For now, Travis decided it was in everybody's best interest to let TJ be.

Kansas followed TJ and licked Drake's forehead several times. There seemed to be a bond between these two dogs. He didn't know what Drake had gone through. Shot and crippled while he defended his territory—that was Kansas's fate. Maybe the other dog had a similar tale?

"Have you been giving Kansas his medication?" Doc asked.

"I have, every day," TJ said.

"It's a new form of steroid that helps battle arthritis, which I believe Kansas has. Arthritis will get worse as he gets older."

"Can we put him in now?"

"Sure." He motioned for Kansas to come over. "Think you can get him in the tank?"

"Don't I always? Come on, boy, in."

Doc slowly filled the tub with warm water while Kansas walked the treadmill. "TJ, see if you can get him to run a little."

TJ ran in place next to Kansas beside the treadmill. The dog followed his lead. After a time, Doc lowered the pace of the machine. Once twenty minutes had elapsed, he stopped it and emptied the water. When Kansas came out, Travis could see he was exhausted.

Dr. Winston led them to a table and picked Kansas up. He went to a microwave apparatus, took out some towels, and rubbed Kansas's hindquarters. Suddenly there was a brief commotion. Travis slipped away, a prisoner on his own farm. Startled by the noise outside the barn, TJ and Kansas went out the back door. Little G started yelling, "TJ? TJ? Where are you?" He continued yelling.

Travis heard the muffled reply. "Hold on, I'm coming."

"Hey, how would you like to make a quick twenty bucks?"

"How about a quick fifty bucks?" TJ countered.

"You're a little hustler, huh? You remind me of somebody."

"Who?"

"Me. I like your style, kid. Okay, fifty it is. Here's what I need you to do. Tomorrow morning, I want you to go around and see if you can find this truck. It's got a Connecticut license plate. It's a white Toyota Tundra with racks on it."

"What do you want me to do?"

"Take notice of where it is and let me know right away."

"I can't go tomorrow; I have something to do. Can I do it the following day?" TJ asked.

"Sure, sure, do it the following day. But make sure you do it."

"Who am I looking for?"

"You're not looking for anybody, just the truck," Little G said. "It belongs to an old friend."

"Why don't you call him?" TJ asked.

"I'd much rather surprise him," he said with a grin.

"Do you want me to show him how to get here?"

"No, it's okay. I'll handle that. You ask too many questions. Do you want the job or not? Keep this to yourself. Don't even tell your parents."

"I'll do it. Do I get half the money up front?" TJ asked.

"What for? You haven't done anything yet."

As he extended his right hand out, palm upward, he said, "Gas."

Chapter 36

🐾 🐾 🐾 🐾 🐾

The morning sun peeked through the shades. Daniel woke up in a cold sweat and remembered he'd had several nightmares, one in which his grandfather was dying, and Daniel wasn't there to save him. Daniel couldn't believe he'd slept all through yesterday and last night. Lying around was not doing much to save Buca. It was 9:47 a.m., and he had to be out of the motel by eleven. He took a shower, shaved, dressed, and packed in a hurry. Before he left, he knocked on room 115—no answer. He cruised the parking lot, looking for Leonard's vehicle. He saw license plates from many states but none from New York.

Daniel turned down the radio and made several calls from his vehicle as he drove. First up was to check on the condition of his grandfather. They told him to call back at three. "Regardless of when I call, it's never the right time," he said, his voice heavily laced with frustration. "I'm out of state and don't have much time. I need someone from your facility to call me." He ran his hand through his hair.

"I'm sorry, Mr. Tanner. Lately, things have been chaotic. We're short staffed. The doctor on call hasn't picked up his messages. I notice you've called several times, and I apologize. I will personally hand the note to the doctor when he arrives. I am sorry for any inconvenience this has caused."

"That's what the last person said," he replied. "For what I pay, there's no excuse not to have help."

"Mr. Tanner. Once again, I apologize, and I will personally hand this to Dr. Reed. Your grandfather has had some bad days and didn't recognize where he was. It's easy to find help; it's difficult to find good help. He's sometimes combative, and we have occasionally sedated him. He's resting comfortably. His vital signs are good. Doctor rounds begin at two."

"Thank you."

He dialed his home phone and listened to incoming messages, but there was nothing significant that couldn't wait.

Daniel parked on a side street in downtown Misery, which he thought was quaint. The light poles were hung with baskets of cascading flowers, the cobblestone sidewalks inviting visitors for a stroll. American flags of various sizes blew in the breeze. He studied the charm of the marketplace. It evoked memories of what Baxter Falls would have looked like in the 1920s. A slice of Americana. A community so picturesque it belonged on the cover of the *Saturday Evening Post*. He was startled by something above him blowing in the wind. He looked up and saw a white canvas banner stretched across Main Street. Surrounded by a patriotic motif, the words read Misery Loves Company—The State's Largest 4th of July Fireworks.

He strolled down Main Street, and the irresistible fragrance of barbecued chicken roasted over a pecan-wood fire made his stomach growl. He pulled up a chair at the sidewalk café and ordered the restaurant's signature dish, a sampling of chicken, pork, and beef with a side of slaw.

Daniel studied the crowd. Could any of these people be involved? How did he separate the townsfolk from the tourists and the dog handlers? Nobody looked suspicious, especially those with families.

He felt a hand on his shoulder and turned around. It was the deputy sheriff. A booming voice said, "Do you mind if I sit?"

Daniel looked up. "Do I have any choice?"

"Not really. For someone who just got here, you're already under the skin of some influential people. I checked up on your hometown and talked to a fellow detective. He said he knows your family and that they are decent people. But you don't have any brothers or sisters. So, tell me really, who is this guy you're looking for? I checked the motel, his room. It's as he left it, and he probably never used it."

"He stole my dog. I'm here to get him back."

"A dog. All this shit's over a dog? What's he doing with it?"

"It's a long story."

"I came to talk to you about what I found. The person registered, the person on the driver's license, and the registration all have different names. When I put them in the database, it seemed like the same person, yet I couldn't tell by the pictures. I put an APB out on the license plate, but technically he's done nothing wrong. I gathered that he's a petty criminal with a checkered past. Whoever he is, he probably heard you were here and left."

"No, he wouldn't leave. I have something Mr. Scott desperately wants."

"Well, I suggest the best thing you can do to find him is go in Mr. Scott's same direction. Out of town."

"Point me in that direction—I'd gladly leave."

"Don't get wise with me. I'm telling you for your own good. Get out of town."

"What are you going to do if I don't?"

"For starters, we have a vagrancy law, and I'll put you in jail. Plus, you entered someone else's room without permission. Remember I warned you about that yesterday. There's the incident at the hotel. That's another couple of charges. Look, I'm nice, I'm trying."

"Help me find my dog, and I'll be out of here," Daniel said.

The deputy took his sunglasses off. "Do I look like animal control? What makes you think your dog is here?"

"It's why I need to meet Mr. Scott. He has contacts with a dogfighting ring."

That piqued the deputy sheriff's interest. He exploded, "A what!"

Daniel, with some satisfaction, followed up. "Dogfighting. In your town. He was supposed to tell me where I could find my dog and who's got him. I followed up with a lead. He said he'd be out here."

The cop sighed. "Do you have a picture of your dog?"

Daniel pulled up a picture of Buca on his cell phone.

"It's a beautiful-looking dog," the deputy said. "He has some unique markings. I haven't seen any dog like this around. Again, what makes you think he's here?"

"The only person who knows Sambuca's whereabouts is missing. He has all my answers," Daniel replied.

"Nobody's filed a missing-person report, so he could have gone back home for all we know."

"Not without his suitcase. It looked like he planned to be here for a while," Daniel said.

"Do you have a contact number I can call if either he or your dog shows up?"

Daniel pulled out a business card and gave it to him.

"The next few weeks will be busy," the deputy said. "I love dogs and can sympathize with you, but I can't be having troublemakers in my town either."

Daniel felt a flash of anger at the unfairness of it all. He snapped, "Who the fuck are you calling a troublemaker?"

The sheriff bristled at the disrespect and snarled, "Watch your language. Show some respect for the law."

"When I get some respect, I'll show some respect," Daniel said. "Until then—"

"If I see you around here, I'm gonna lock you up." He got up and said, "Have a nice drive back."

Daniel drove around all day looking for Leonard's car, the deputy's car, and Buca. But if this town had a mystery, it wouldn't give it up easily. He grabbed a grinder at Subway and stopped to get a six-pack of beer and some ice as twilight set in. He drove through the main thoroughfare, which exited Misery, and kept driving until he passed a sign: "Now leaving Misery, the heART of Kansas." He went several hundred feet and noticed a dirt road ahead. He backed his truck into a private easement between two fields of corn and turned the ignition off, then turned the key back one notch so he could listen to the radio.

Daniel unwrapped the ham-and-cheese grinder and slumped down in the seat. He adjusted the rearview mirror. Fast sunset, he thought. He took a bite of his sandwich and turned up the radio. Over the airwaves, the Five Man Electrical Band played their signature song. The deputy wanted me out of town, he said to himself. Technically, I'm out.

Chapter 37

🐾 🐾 🐾 🐾 🐾

FRIDAY, JUNE 26, 2015

Daniel dug out the discharge from the corner of his eyes as he struggled to sit up. His body ached from the cramped space, so he opened the door and stretched. A water bottle served as a shower as he dumped the lukewarm contents on his hair. As the water ran down, he scrubbed his face, feeling the effects of being unshaven. Putting on deodorant and slipping on a faded green T-shirt made him feel more comfortable. He got back in the truck, slumped in the seat, and stared, mesmerized by the heat radiating from the hood of his vehicle—an early warning sign of another hot, humid Kansas summer day. Daniel was amazed at the size of the corn stalks. He got out of the truck and plucked an ear, googled it, and realized it was cow corn. Planted more for feeding livestock than human consumption and had a shorter growing season. Must have been a mild winter, he thought. Fields grew on either side of the meandering road.

He thought about Leonard Scott. He couldn't understand why Leonard didn't want to meet him. Daniel had some of his paperwork. It was odd to leave all your belongings behind. In their last conversation, Leonard had said it was vital for him to recoup his items. So, where did he go? Why did he go? Did he have a choice? He said he had an invite out here, and his voice sounded excited. He seemed to be looking forward to the visit. Now there was no trace of him being here except for his luggage. It was, to put it mildly, suspicious.

Out in the fields, Daniel spotted a tornado of dirt rapidly approaching. The noise stopped as suddenly as it started. It seemed kind of far away. He got out of his truck and studied the landscape carefully, looking around for the source of the high-pitched whine. He sipped his water, and his stomach growled. Then it stopped again. He felt as if somebody was taunting him. He got back into the truck. Had he heard this? Or was it a hallucination?

Eventually, the roar came close enough for him to see it was a dirt bike. It appeared to be a teenager under the helmet and goggles. Daniel felt nervous and edgy. If the sheriff finds me on private property, he thought, this could be another charge. Daniel got out of the truck again as the rider made his way toward him. He came close, forcing Daniel to dive back into his vehicle. The rider kicked up dirt and gravel, spraying Daniel's truck. Undaunted, the rider circled the Toyota several times, making debris ping noisily off the body, infuriating Daniel.

He got out of the truck again to confront the kid. He even thought about knocking him off the bike. As suddenly as he'd arrived, the rider was gone. The cloud of dust dissipated gradually. Daniel inspected the damage and noticed dents, scratches, and a rear taillight destroyed. He yelled, "Fuck!"

Incensed, Daniel hopped back in and revved the engine, but he jammed on his brakes when he saw a shadowy figure cross his path. It was a German shepherd who appeared to be in distress. It limped toward his truck, fell about five feet away, and licked its hindquarters. Exhausted, the dog panted heavily. Daniel turned the engine off, got out, and tried to coax the dog toward him. The dog growled and attempted to limp away, whimpering in pain. "It's okay, boy," Daniel said in a hushed tone. "I'm not going to hurt you."

He crouched down and approached the dog with an open palm to let the dog sniff him. Daniel slowly inched closer. The dog was only three feet away. The growls became less pronounced. He got the cooler, took off the lid, and poured some water into the cover. He slowly pushed it toward the dog. The dog momentarily stared at Daniel and then limped cautiously over and began to drink.

"What a beautiful dog you are. What are you doing way out here?"

Was the dog hungry? Daniel got the leftovers of last night's supper from the truck. He took the meat out, cautiously approached the dog, and handed it to him. The animal sniffed it first and then gingerly took it from his hand. Daniel noticed he had a tagged collar. Finally, he got close enough to pet the dog and spoke in a soothing voice. "What's the matter, boy?" He was amazed the dog didn't growl at him. Maybe he realized he had found a new friend.

Daniel threw his backpack into the truck bed and coaxed his new friend into the cab. Once inside, the dog sniffed around. Daniel looked at the collar, which had the name "Kansas" and an address. He realized it was just down the road. He put the passenger's side window down so the dog could hang his head out, just like Buca.

He passed several farms and came to a fenced area with big gates in front. He honked several times. Some people in the back turned and looked at him but didn't budge. Out came a man from a Victorian farm-house. Daniel got out and said to the man, "Is this your dog?"

"Yes. Where'd you find Kansas?"

"A couple of miles down the road. It appears he was with some kid who was on a dirt bike. Does your son own a red-and-white dirt bike?"

"Yes."

"He damaged my truck."

The man crossed his arms. "Well, there's a lot of red-and-white dirt bikes in the area."

"Can I talk to him?" Daniel asked.

"He's in bed, sleeping. Can I ask what it's about?"

"Somebody broke my taillight," Daniel said.

"And how did he manage that? Where did this happen?"

"In a cornfield about two miles down the road."

"That's my property. What the hell were you doing on my property?"

218

"I'd been driving all night, and I pulled over for a nap. I didn't damage any of your crops."

"Well, you're still on my property. I'm not saying it was my son. But if it was, maybe he was protecting our land."

"By doing this?" Daniel pointed to his vehicle. "That's not protecting; it's vandalizing."

"Not if you're trespassing. What makes you think it's my son?"

"For starters, your dog was with him."

"What's that prove?"

"You know what? I'm going to go to the sheriff and file a complaint. I got better things to do," Daniel said.

"Whatever. You do what you have to do."

"Here, take your dog. He appears injured."

The man took the dog out of the truck. As he lifted Kansas out of the vehicle, Daniel vehemently pointed out the damage. But the man ignored his tirade and carried Kansas back toward his house.

As the man left, Daniel said, "You're welcome."

🐾 🐾 🐾

With each step heavier than the last, Travis took long strides, punishing the earth with anger. His pace quickened, and his muscles tightened. The conversation stuck in his head. As he neared the backyard, he spotted the dirt bike. He had repeatedly told his son that the bike must be stored in the barn when not in use. This was another act of defiance. Travis needed an immediate resolution. This situation had gone on long enough. TJ's irresponsibility, carelessness, and defiance had grown in the last few months. Furious, he walked over to the bike, put his hand on the engine, and noted it was still warm.

"Goddammit," he yelled.

Outraged, Travis swung open the back door. "TJ, TJ," he shouted. "Taylor Joseph Wyatt, where the fuck are you?"

Ashlee rushed into the kitchen. "What's the matter?" she asked.

"What's the matter? Where's TJ?" he asked as he started to rub his temples. "A couple of minutes ago, a stranger pulled up and returned Kansas. He said our son damaged his truck. And what did I do? I defended him. The guy described TJ's dirt bike perfectly. It had to be him. And I when I checked his bike, the engine was still warm. What's he doing up so early? He's too lazy to do chores."

"I guess it's my fault; he told me to wake him up early because he said he had something to do. I assumed it was chores. Just sit down and relax. Let me get you a cup of coffee."

Travis walked from room to room. No sign of TJ.

Ashlee gave Travis his coffee and gently rubbed his shoulders.

"Sit down with me," he stuttered. "We need to have a family discussion right now." He took her hand in his, looked her straight in the eyes, and asked, "Ash, are you happy? What have we done?"

"What do you mean, hon?"

"What have we become? What have we turned into, Ashlee? I'm sure generations of Wyatts are turning over in their graves. If my dad were still alive, he'd take me to the back shed and punish me over what I let this farm become. Maybe that's what TJ needs—a little discipline." He got up again and started to pace the floor.

"You're mad; you're not thinking clearly. Beating our son half to death wouldn't change a thing." Ashlee's eyes fixed on Travis, and she watched his every move. "He's irresponsible, spoiled, and thinks he's entitled to the world. We gave him everything, and he greedily took it all. Before we punish him, we should be punishing ourselves."

In a moment of remorse, Travis stared at the kitchen floor, knowing he had created his problem. "What we gave him, in the beginning, was stuff we always wanted as a kid and couldn't afford. But look at what I've become—I'm fat and lazy." He grabbed a handful of his flab. "I can't remember when I did an honest day's work."

She got up and went to him. "Don't blame yourself. The deal we made on the farm was essential to our existence. Did we have a choice? We were drowning in debt."

"I hate what I am and who I've become. We've grown apart as a family."

"What can we do about it?" she asked.

"I wish things could go back to the way they were. It was much simpler. We have sold our soul to the devil," he said. "The Wyatts have always had a proud legacy. Overnight I've become Judas—gave up our rights for a couple of pieces of silver. I don't want to be the one who tarnishes our heritage."

"You didn't have any choice. You had to take over the farm when Taylor died."

"Do you know what they're doing out there?" he snorted. "These dogs are being bred for pit-bull fighting. On the Fourth of July, we will be hosting a pit-bull fight."

Her face paled, and her knees weakened as she held onto the table for support. "How horrible. Oh my God! I thought they were just raising dogs."

"Horrible for the dogs. You know what's awful? It's our farm, and we're allowing this shit to go on. I confronted Anthony one day. He told me to mind my own business. It's not even his fucking farm, and he's telling me to mind my own business."

Ashlee put her hand on his arm, but Travis would not be deterred. He was a man on the brink of exploding.

"It's nothing more than blood money," Travis said. "Survival used to be the only reason blood was spilled on our farm. Not for sport. Anthony told me, 'You have such a comfortable life now. I don't see why you're complaining. You could still farm. You're just too damn lazy.'"

"Quit beating yourself up," she said as she sat down again.

"This farm even smells of death. I get a sick feeling every time I pull into the driveway. Have you gone out in the back field?" He pointed out the window. "Have you smelled it? The stench. That's where they bury their dead dogs. They have blood on their hands, and so do we. Our whole farm's tainted in blood. There's blood everywhere—blood on our barns, blood on the soil, and even blood on the scarecrow. And we allowed it."

221

He sat again and started to tap his foot. His distress intensified as each second passed.

"How do you know all this?" she asked.

"I'm not blind. I see what's going on around here. So does TJ—that's why he's the way he is, from hanging around that punk. I hear little bits and pieces. I go into the barns sometimes when no one is around. Those dogs are vicious."

Ashlee took a second to regain her composure before she said, "What's going to happen if the sheriff finds out? Could we lose our farm?"

"The sheriff." He laughed. "The sheriff's on Anthony's payroll, and I imagine his whole department is too. I talked to an attorney a week ago. He has yet to get back to me. Every time I call him, I leave a message, but he never returns my call. I think Anthony paid him off. Anthony's paid a lot of people off. I heard Mr. Dominick is coming. We need to sit down and talk. This isn't what I envisioned."

"We had no choice. It wasn't a deal. We got strong armed."

He looked straight into her blue eyes. "Nonetheless, we still signed the paperwork," he said.

Chapter 38

❧ ❧ ❧ ❧ ❧

Incensed by the early morning theatrics, Daniel headed toward town. He dialed the police station and heard a recorded message: "Office hours eight to twelve and one to five. If this is an emergency, please dial nine-one-one." What the fuck, he thought, am I in Mayberry? He hung up and noticed a flashing red picture of a battery. His phone was at 9 percent.

His mind reverted to his search for his beloved pet. Was he being ghosted? Where was that promoter? He must be here. Leonard wanted all his incriminating files. I'll wait until tonight to stake out the motel, he thought. How could a town that looks like this be hosting something so evil, especially during the Fourth of July, and trying to remain inconspicuous?

Daniel surmised the Misery Police Department was now looking for two vehicles, his and Leonard Scott's. Both had red flags—their license plates. He needed to go to the police department to file a vandalism report. Would the deputy be there? Would he allow Daniel to submit his paperwork or just arrest him?

He cruised Main Street several times and settled upon a bar called Rogue's Gallery, a few blocks from the police station. Space was open in front.

The bar was U-shaped, surrounded by stools. Art pieces hung on the walls with price tags. Daniel saw a billiard table in the back and decided to kill some time shooting pool, a game he'd once enjoyed with Gramps.

"Hey, what can I get you?" the bartender asked him. She was a petite brunette with an infectious smile and a face that lit up the room.

"Do you serve lunch?" Daniel asked.

She nodded.

"What do you suggest?"

"Our burgers are the best in town," she said.

"I'll take a cheeseburger, hold the pickle and tomato. I'll also take fries if you have them." Daniel put a ten on the bar and said, "I'd like the change in quarters, please. I'd love a Coke. Can I pay now?"

"No, I'll run a tab. My name's Randi. Nice to meet you. I'll get you some quarters."

"Daniel," he said. "Would you mind if I plugged in my phone?"

"No problem. Give it to me, I'll charge it behind the bar. That way no one will steal it. What brings you to our fair city? Are you here for the show?" Randi inquired.

"What show?" He shrugged.

She chuckled. "The fireworks show, silly. The Fourth of July?"

He nodded half-heartedly. Three other patrons sat on the other side of the bar.

With a huge smile, she said, "You never answered me. Are you staying for the fireworks?"

"I don't know. I don't have a room."

"Sorry to hear that. Um—I live in a boardinghouse; I could ask my landlord if he has a room to rent?"

She went to the kitchen to place the order and returned with the information. "My landlord has a room. It's a small one but has a full-size bed and a bureau. I don't know how long the room is available. Someone should have been in it by now. He's willing to rent it on a day-by-day basis."

"Give him a call and tell him I'll take it. I'll head over there to pay him and drop off my luggage. I guess I'll be here for the fireworks after all."

"Okay, I'll put your meal on hold until you get back."

"Before I go, what's up with all the paintings?" Daniel said.

"In the early sixties and seventies, this became a home for artisans. The hippies invaded the town and started doing paints, sculptures, pottery, stained glass, and jewelry. Rogue's Gallery is one of the places they sell their wares. Haven't you noticed the sign 'heART of Kansas,' with the 'art' capitalized?"

"Yes, I saw one last night and didn't get the meaning," Daniel answered. "It all makes sense now."

When Daniel returned from the boardinghouse, Randi greeted him warmly. "Hi, Daniel, you're back quickly. Did everything go okay?"

"Thanks. It was perfect—just what I needed."

She handed him an open Budweiser. "This is on me."

"Thanks, Randi." Daniel quickly marked his beer. "I was going to have one later. Now I have something to celebrate. Why not?"

She held up a water glass and clinked it against his beer bottle. "Cheers."

"I'll get your order in right now," she said.

He went to the pool room. In his absence, two people had begun playing. "Mind if I play winner?" Daniel asked.

"Nope," the older one said in a thick Southern drawl. "You a hustler, boy?"

Daniel looked at him quizzically. Then he realized the sound of the ten dollars' worth of quarters in his pocket was suspicious.

Daniel placed four quarters on the rail. He walked up to shake their hands. "Hi, I'm Daniel."

"Hi, I'm Virgil, and this here is my boy, Beau." Virgil was big and overpowering. Beau seemed more reserved. Virgil's arms were replete with tattoos. Most prominent on his right forearm was an image of a pit bull.

"Boy, nice ink," Daniel said.

"Thank you," Virgil replied. "This one is my dog, Ares. I named him after the Greek god of war."

"He's a champ," Beau added proudly.

"A champ? What does that mean?" Daniel asked. His body went cold. He assumed Beau was referring to dogfighting.

"It means he won a few local dog shows," Virgil said.

Daniel studied Virgil. He saw him look at his son with the intensity of a laser. To Beau, Virgil said, "Zip it." He turned to Daniel. "I'm sorry, my son gets a little carried away when we talk about our dogs. He's so proud." Daniel zoomed in on a swastika tattoo on Virgil's left arm. "You like it, boy?" Virgil asked. "I'm a proud member of the Aryan nation."

"Where you from?" Daniel asked.

"Nola," Virgil said with a big smile on his face.

"What?"

"Naw-lins," he replied with a thick Southern drawl.

Daniel was confused about what was said yet carried on as if he understood.

"Where you from?" Virgil asked.

"Connecticut."

"What are you doing around these parts, boy? A little out of your element, huh?"

"I'm just passing through, but I plan on staying for the fireworks."

"Didn't know about them. I hope you enjoy the show," Virgil said with a smirk. "I'm going outside to have a cigar. Why don't you two play? I'll take on the winner."

Daniel thought Beau might be the one he could get some answers from. Virgil, on the other hand, was a ticking time bomb. Daniel needed to be cautious.

Virgil exited as Daniel racked the balls. He motioned for Beau to go first. Beau broke, and then his cell phone rang. He said to Daniel, "Would you mind waiting a few minutes? I have to take a call."

Just then, Randi came over with his meal. He said to Beau, "No problem. It'll give me time to eat my lunch."

He attempted to eavesdrop on Beau's one-way conversation.

Beau wandered around the pool table. "What do you want now, Tanis?" he whispered. "I don't have time for this shit...What do you mean, where am I? It's none of your business. If I wanted you to know, I would have told you...Once again, it's none of your business...Do I need your permission to leave?"

His voice gradually got louder. "I'm not married to you anymore. I can do what the fuck I want…The FBI doesn't fucking scare me. They didn't find anything the first time; what makes you think they'll find something this time? What about the dogs? No more arguing. When I get home, I'll call. Tell the kids I love them."

Beau was a whole different person when he came back. He was on fire. He went over to Daniel and asked, "You married, Daniel?" The conversation had ignited Beau's face, and he was flushed with rage.

Daniel turned his head as if he hadn't been listening. "What?"

"You married?"

"No, and I don't plan on being married anytime soon."

"Good for you. A wife—or ex-wife—is like a hemorrhoid: a constant pain in the ass that won't go away. You got to find a way to soothe it, and I'm still looking. Any suggestions?"

"How about a muzzle?" Daniel chuckled.

He analyzed the conversation he thought he overheard. The pit-bull tattoo. Not afraid of the FBI, he thought. Two rednecks. The dog was a champ. They didn't know about the fireworks show. Too coincidental.

Beau went over to the jukebox, pumped in a few quarters, and put on "Every Time I Roll the Dice." "She got a roof that don't leak when the rains are pouring down…"

"Who's it by?" Daniel asked.

"Delbert McClinton. He's one of my dad's favorites. He's a blues legend."

Daniel said, "What a great song. Hey, Beau, my cell phone is unavailable right now, and I need to make an urgent phone call. Can I borrow yours?"

"No, I'm not supposed to. It's a company phone. My dad told me never to let anyone use it," Beau said while biting his nails.

"Well, I won't tell if you don't. Virgil's right outside. I'll keep an eye out and make it quick."

Beau hemmed and hawed.

"It's only going to take a minute. My grandfather's in a nursing home. He has Alzheimer's. I need to check to see if he's okay."

This sympathetic conversation must have touched Beau, as he replied, "Oh, all right. Please hurry up." Then Beau went to break.

Daniel took Beau's phone with trembling hands and turned away. He quickly looked up recent calls, and hit delete after memorizing the number. He dialed his home number and pretended to talk and get information on his grandfather. The incoming call came from Louisiana, he thought.

"Thanks, Beau. My grandfather's condition has deteriorated; he isn't doing well."

Virgil walked in while Daniel handed Beau his phone.

"What the fuck you doing, boy?" Virgil yelled.

"What are you talking about?" Beau asked.

"Your son dropped his phone," Daniel said. "I was only handing it to him."

Virgil grabbed the phone, scanned the screen, and gave it to Beau.

"How about I buy you and your son a drink? Beau and I can finish the game," Daniel offered. "I'll give you the money if you go get them."

"That's mighty white of you," Virgil said. "What'll you have, boy?"

"I got an appointment. I can't drink right now."

Virgil took off, and Daniel whispered to Beau, "I deleted the number I called and the other number too. This way, he won't know you had a call in here either."

"Thanks, Daniel. I appreciate that. I was wondering why he wasn't yelling at me. He hates my ex-wife more than I do."

Beau and Daniel finished the match, with Daniel throwing the game. "Beau, you're too good for me. I want a rematch, but I've got an appointment. How about in a half hour?"

"I should still be here," Beau said.

"Look forward to it. I love beating Yanks," Virgil replied.

Daniel went to the bar to pay his tab. "I'll see you later, Randi." He gave her his plate and drank the final sip of his beer.

"I hope so. You know where I live. Don't forget your phone."

"Oops, I almost forgot—thanks. I should be back in a half hour or so."

He got into his truck, put the key in the ignition, took his cell phone, punched in the number he recalled, hit send, and quickly touched end. He put the truck in reverse. He looked out the rearview mirror and saw the deputy sheriff's car, with the blue lights ablaze, had boxed him in.

The officer approached Daniel's window cautiously. "I thought I told you to leave town."

"I was going over to the station to talk to you about that. I need to file a report."

"About what, your broken taillight? License and registration."

"That's why I was coming to see you. I called and got your answering machine, and it said you wouldn't be in until one."

"It's two forty-five p.m. now. Exactly when did you plan on coming? After happy hour?"

"I was having a couple of Cokes."

"Don't think I can't smell beer on your breath. Give me your license and registration—now."

Daniel took out his license and handed it to him. He reached over to the glove compartment and opened it to get the registration. There, glinting in the afternoon sun, was Gramps's gun. Its presence did not improve relations. Deputy Sheriff Malcolm drew his weapon and pointed it at Daniel. "Don't make a move." He opened Daniel's door. "Undo your seat belt slowly, no sudden moves. Get out of your vehicle and put your hands on the roof." The deputy frisked and handcuffed him.

He searched the vehicle for anything else illegal. He took out the gun and pushed the barrel forward—the chamber was empty. Turned the weapon over—no clip. The deputy rummaged through the glove compartment and found a fully loaded clip. "What are you doing with a concealed weapon? Do you have a permit?"

Daniel shook his head. "I forgot it was there. It's a long story, and you probably wouldn't believe me anyway."

"Amuse me."

"Would it make any difference? I honestly didn't know it was still in there."

The deputy ushered him into the back of his cruiser, rolled down the window, and closed the door. "It's a short ride to the station house; you won't need the AC."

He went back to the truck and confiscated Daniel's truck keys, cell phone, gun, and clip. He took out a plastic bag marked "evidence" from his trunk, put the contents in, and sealed it. He locked up the vehicle, brought everything back to the cruiser, and added the evidence bag to the trunk.

Rogue's Gallery customers watched with undisguised interest.

Suddenly Virgil said really loud, "Who gave the janitor a badge?"

The deputy sheriff walked up to Virgil and stared him down. "You got a problem with me?"

"Gee, sir, I was just wondering where you kept your mop and bucket," Virgil replied.

"It will be up your ass soon if you don't behave."

"Anytime you feelin' froggy, boy, just jump."

The scene had attracted a sizable crowd. Somebody came and put a hand on the deputy's shoulder. "Any problems, Kenny?"

"Nothin' I can't handle, Clint. Hey, everybody, let's break it up and get back inside."

Daniel recognized the person who had just arrived. He was the mayor.

But it was way too late for introductions.

Chapter 39

❧ ❧ ❧ ❧ ❧

The deputy pushed Daniel into the right side of the double doors of the jail. Once Daniel was inside, he took off Daniel's handcuffs, fingerprinted him, took a mugshot, and read him his rights. Daniel rubbed his wrists where the handcuffs had left indentations.

"This is all a misunderstanding. The gun wasn't even loaded. I want to file a report about my broken taillight," Daniel cried out.

"Take off your belt, boots, and socks. Any jewelry?"

Daniel shook his head.

The deputy called out to his subordinates, "Frisk him."

Two young men shoved Daniel. One felt the chain around his neck. "What's this? I thought you didn't have any jewelry. Take it off," he ordered.

"Leave it alone. It's not yours, and I never take it off," Daniel answered.

"Have it your way," he said smugly. Daniel pulled away.

The first officer used his left hand to clutch Daniel's clavicle, and with his right he yanked the chain off, leaving behind a welt.

"You need to follow directions. Maybe this will help," the second officer said as he jabbed him in the stomach with his nightstick.

"Guys, what are you doing? Don't rough him up," the deputy stated.

They frisked him and found all the quarters in his pockets. "Looks like we hit the jackpot!" the first guy said.

"Looks like this vagrant's been panhandling," said the other.

Daniel ignored their comments.

The first officer said, "Get the fucker in the cell. Ken, we're going out on patrol. We'll be back around six. Don't hesitate to call if he gives you any problems."

The deputy inserted a key into a door separating the cells from the front rooms, and he heard the low moan of a cell door opening. Daniel felt a hard push on his back as he stumbled into the cell. He listened to the door slam.

Inside, security cameras mounted on the wall monitored Daniel's every move. A dark shadow appeared at the cell door.

"Whenever you're ready, I'll hear your story," the deputy said.

"It's a long story," Daniel said. "Sure you got the time?"

"I may not, but you sure do. The court doesn't open until Monday."

"Can I post bail? I need to find my dog—he's here."

"Do you have a license to carry a concealed weapon?" the deputy asked again.

Daniel stood and put his hand on the bars. He replied meekly, "No."

"Then you can't post bail. You'll see the judge first thing Monday morning."

"That's too late."

"My hands are tied. There's nothing I can do about it. I talked to the sheriff." He reinspected the gun. "Okay, if it's not yours, what's it doing in your glove compartment?"

"This is all a huge misunderstanding," Daniel replied. "It's not even my gun. My grandfather put it in there, and I forgot he did. I know, a thousand guys could tell you the same answer. But it's the truth."

"Oh, now you're going to tell me the truth. Smith & Wesson—this is a very expensive weapon."

"At his retirement, his fellow officers gave it to him as a gift," Daniel said.

"Your grandfather was a cop? You should know better. Okay, how about we call your grandfather and verify it's his property. What's the number?"

"He's in a nursing home with Alzheimer's. Sedated. He wouldn't be able to give you straight answers."

"Seems to run in your family."

"What runs in my family?" Daniel snapped.

"Lame excuses," the deputy shot back. "Your grandfather is in a nursing home, and you came out here to find a dog you're not even sure is out here? It sounds like you got your priorities mixed up."

"I was initially supposed to meet the guy here who took my dog, and he was going to show me where he is. Now he's missing."

"So you know who took your dog?" the deputy asked.

"Yeah, he was the person at the motel," Daniel responded.

"You mean he's not your brother-in-law?"

"No, I made that part up."

"That's when you made your first mistake: you lied to an officer."

"You're right. I should have told you the truth. I didn't think you'd believe me."

"What else have you made up? Why suddenly are you telling the truth? What makes you think I'll believe you now?" the deputy asked.

"I ran out of options. You're the only chance I have left. I have nothing to lose. Do I get a phone call?" he asked.

"Yes, I'll let you make a phone call," the deputy said and swiveled around in his chair.

"Can I have my cell?" Daniel asked.

"No," the deputy said sharply.

"As crazy as it sounds, my phone contains the only lead I know. Those two guys at the bar—the one riding your ass—are in town for a big dogfight sometime soon."

"How do you know that?"

"I don't know; it's just a gut feeling. You don't find it strange these characters show up in your town with no respect for the law?"

"Well, you did. You lied. You broke into a room and claimed you didn't take anything. You carried a concealed weapon. It's tourist season. We see all kinds. It's my job to uphold the law, not harass the visitors."

"Well, weren't you harassing me, telling me to get out of town?" Daniel said.

"You deserved it. You're hardly a role model. You had your chances. With no permit, you'll probably be doing several years in prison." Deputy Malcolm paused to take off his hat, rested it on the desk, and wiped his brow. "Tell me about the phone call you want to make."

"I need to call the number on my phone. The son, Beau, was talking to his ex-wife, and he mentioned something about the FBI. I think they are involved, and I need to speak with her to find out what she knows."

The deputy gave him his cell phone.

"Can I get some privacy, please?"

"Nope, I'm fine right here."

He dialed Beau's ex-wife. "Hello, my name is Daniel," he said quickly. "I overheard a conversation you had with your ex-husband today."

"Who is this? How did you get my number?"

"I'm in Kansas, and—"

Click. The screen went black.

"Hung up on you, huh? It sounds like somebody else doesn't believe your story."

🐾 🐾 🐾

Deputy Malcolm opened Daniel's cell door two hours later and handed Daniel his dinner. Daniel did not eat. The thought of not being able to go out and save Buca was gnawing away. Outside, the deputy was curiously busy on his phone. There were terse muttered conversations.

Afterward, a more pleasant deputy returned. He sat on a chair, looked at Daniel quizzically in the way you would look at a slightly mad but not dangerous vagrant, and half muttered, half chuckled, "Well, boy oh boy, ain't you the most pathetic prisoner I've ever had. Say, boy, now that we have both got the time, why don't you tell me your full story?"

"What good would it do?"

The deputy raised his eyes and sighed. "Boy, don't you ever want to take the well-worn path instead of sidestepping life with your bullshit and lies? Just tell the truth."

"I'm here to get my dog," Daniel said. "I entered Sambuca in a dog show. The promoter was a fraud and used the information from the show to steal dogs. He called himself a dog broker. He was nothing more than a fucking thief. He sent my dog to North Carolina, and someone bought him. Someone from a powerful family. I tracked down the dog broker from New York, and we agreed to meet in Misery."

"Sounds like a story from the *National Enquirer*. The guy from New York—what were you supposed to do when you met him?"

Daniel got up and approached the bars. "He supposedly knew where the dogfighting was going to take place. He was willing to let me know because I have some of his possessions. They are incriminating—several fake IDs and a lot of paperwork from his numerous dog shows. The registration and IDs are in the center console of my truck. He wouldn't have gone anywhere on his own. He wanted these back."

"Give me a minute."

The deputy returned with Leonard's many IDs and the registration in his hands. "Kind of a sleazy-looking guy, huh?"

"That's him all right," Daniel said, rubbing his scar.

"Well, I went to his room while I was out, but there's still no sign of him. I guess you could say he's a missing person. How do you know it's his room?"

"Someone at the motel saw him and positively IDed him. When I entered the room, I saw a pack of crumpled-up cigarettes. He smokes a unique brand. That type was in his trash can."

"The manager told me no one has been in the room for days. We agreed he'd put the suitcase in the office. He'll have to go to the office to claim it."

"Doesn't it sound mysterious? Why would somebody make a reservation and not stay there?"

"Maybe he found some local tail and shacked up somewhere. Technically I can't do anything, as no one has filed a report. There's no car in the parking lot, either. It's almost like he disappeared. He paid for his room. Legally he's entitled to it for the duration. At least this part of your story checks out. It still doesn't mean your dog is here."

"What about that asshole at the bar? Did you see his tattoos?"

"No, I didn't. What's that got to do with it?"

"I think he's in town for a reason. I obtained a phone number from his son when his ex-wife called him, without him knowing what I did."

"Look," the deputy sheriff said, "you seem to be straight. There's nothing I can do to help you now. It's out of my hands. What's so damn special about a dog? You can get another in any pound."

"He saved my life. I owe him," Daniel said.

The sheriff conceded, "You've got a story, circumstantial evidence, but no concrete proof. Have you ever fought him? Is he a good fighter?"

"Fuck no. I would never do anything like that. Buca is my pet," Daniel said.

"The one thing I don't understand is, you're putting this dog over your grandfather? You say your grandfathers in a nursing home, and you're chasing down this dog? I never had a grandfather. I don't know what it's like. But I'll tell you one thing: he'd be more important than a dog if I did. I just don't understand it. Where are your priorities?"

"I love my grandfather. He's the world to me. But there's nothing I can do."

"How about just being there for him?"

Daniel sat on the cot and put his face in his hands. "That's the thing," he said. "Hard and all as it seems, I am doing what he would want me to do. The last coherent thing he said to me was to bring Buca back. Buca is part of his life too."

The deputy stopped, then asked, "You mentioned you wanted to make a complaint?"

"Yes. This morning I was in my truck, and someone drove around my vehicle on a dirt bike, wearing a helmet and visor, kicking up dust, stones, and rocks. He dented my truck and broke my taillight. The person took

236

off. Coming behind him was a dog who limped. I checked the collar and drove to the address, and it turned out to be a fancy farm with fencing around the perimeter and a gated driveway. I honked my horn several times. A man came out—I guess he was the father—and I told him what happened. He didn't believe me. He took the dog, though."

"That sounds like Kansas," the deputy said. "He belongs to the Wyatts. That's TJ's dog. He follows him everywhere. I know the family well. It's sad, but I can picture TJ doing that. He's become a real wiseass lately. He used to be a good kid, but he's changed. It seems the family has come into money, and they all changed. They don't even come into town much anymore. I am surprised at how Travis treated you. Maybe I'll take a ride out there later and see what I can find. Did anyone else see what happened?"

"No, it was early in the morning. No one else around," Daniel said.

"Maybe I'll find out things that he won't tell a stranger. Oh, I locked up your suitcases in your truck, and I have some money. Randi brought them by because the room is no longer available."

As he left, the deputy turned around and almost sighed sympathetically. "You know, boy, you should have heeded my advice. It seems like nobody wants you here."

Chapter 40

🐾 🐾 🐾 🐾 🐾

SATURDAY, JUNE 27, 2015

Dawn ascended into the tiny little hamlet known as Misery.
Daniel jumped up as the annoying bark of air brakes reverberated through the cell, followed by the rattling of the hydraulics of a garbage truck. He sank onto the lumpy mattress and buried his head in his hands.

The long, long journey had taken its final toll.

He lay back down on the lumpy mattress with fingers interlaced through his curly black hair. This one question returned repeatedly: How would he save his dog when he couldn't even save himself? His right index finger gently stroked the inflamed area on his neck to soothe the pain caused by an overzealous patrolman snatching his cherished gold necklace—the only jewelry he'd ever worn. It had been a gift from Alex. It wasn't the monetary value that bothered him but the sentimental. Most people looked back at their lives and measured them in milestones. Daniel considered himself the eternal pessimist, obsessing over the low points. With today being the lowest.

His mind raced with staccato, fragmented questions. Should he have left? Was it the right decision? Did the stupidity of ignoring the deputy land him in jail? In hindsight, maybe the truth would have worked. But Daniel had lived his life as a loner, seldom trusting anybody and rarely experiencing the benefits of a friend. Lying wasn't something that came naturally to the grandson of a cop.

As Daniel struggled to sit up, a dull pain emanated from his lower torso, a direct result of the violent blow by the butt end of a nightstick. He swung his bare feet onto the dusty cement floor, narrowly missing the tray of food—a bologna sandwich, warm milk, and a bag of chips from last night's supper. Unshowered and feeling grungy, Daniel dug his fingernails deep to soothe an incurable itch. Daniel slowly scratched his way to the back of his wrist, where the scars of an old wound had healed. It was an area that was always sensitive. Today, for some strange reason, the area pulsated. These scars were his inspiration, his reason for being here. Gently rubbing them, this small act gave him the strength to rise—to stand in defiance.

Daniel started to pace like a caged animal. His hands grabbed the bars as he violently shook the entrance.

He looked squarely at the camera and screamed, "Somebody get me the fuck out of here!"

A patrolman from the back room said, "Cut the shit, stop the tantrum. If you keep it up, I'll give you something to be angry about."

"I'm not angry, I'm frustrated." Daniel heard the outer door slam shut.

The deputy seemed to be an authoritative figure. Where was he? Didn't Daniel have any rights? The deputy seemed to be everywhere, haunting him. Daniel mused that he had always had respect for the law, but the law appeared tainted in this town. Where was the investigation into Daniel's claims? Why wasn't the deputy tracking down some leads? Checking out those two idiots from Louisiana and running their plates? Calling Tanis? Calling the FBI? The biggest mystery was Leonard Scott. He could have validated everything Daniel had told them. Daniel's mental approach to this problem directly resulted from his grandfather's wisdom.

Daniel lay back down, closed his eyes, and prayed to his parents for a miracle.

Click. The sound of the key in the cell door awakened Daniel from his brief slumber. The deputy put down a bowl of warm water, a white washcloth, and a bar of soap. "Thought you might want to freshen up before breakfast. It looks like you could use it," the deputy stated.

In a barely audible voice, Daniel said, "Thanks."

When he finished, he lay back down and stared at the ceiling. Daniel's mind raced. His internal cross-examination was scathing and depressing. Like a slap in the face on a cold winter day. How was he going to get out of here? Were they going to put him in prison? Lindsey was the only person who knew Daniel was here. Gramps always said, rule one, "Never lie to an officer." I've made a mess of dealing with my only possible ally, Daniel thought. If I were the deputy, I wouldn't believe what I said.

I've come all this way for what? Daniel wondered. How am I going to get out of this? And what about Gramps? How's he doing? Will I ever see him again? Are the doctors trying to call me? Should I even have made that call to Beau's ex-wife? I should have called Jim. I'd have a lawyer by now.

The deputy brought his breakfast.

Daniel sat up, poked at his food, and moved it around while drinking the strong, well-brewed coffee.

"I'm going to the front," the deputy said. "I have some paperwork to do. I'll leave the office door open in case you need anything. Just holler."

"When can I get out?" Daniel asked.

"I told you, on Monday. I don't know you well, but boy, you certainly have a problem listening."

"At least can I have my cell phone?"

The deputy ignored the comment.

Daniel nervously walked back and forth across the small cell. Soon he heard a commotion in the front foyer and the distinct voice of the deputy, but he didn't recognize the other speaker. Daniel strained to overhear the conversation as the noise grew in intensity. He realized they were coming toward him. He rushed to sit on the cot.

"Am I gonna get arrested?" a younger voice asked.

"Not up to me. It's totally up to Mr. Tanner," the deputy answered.

"Can I see him? I want to apologize."

"Go ahead in there."

The adolescent walked with his head down to Daniel's cell. "Hi, I'm TJ Wyatt. I'm here to apologize. I was the one on the dirt bike. I'm sorry for what I did to your truck." He rushed on, "I know what I did was wrong. No excuses. I didn't mean to cause you any problems. Are you locked up because of me?"

"No, this isn't because of you. I seem to cause my own problems," Daniel responded. "I don't need any help."

"I have some money for you. I gave the deputy all the money I had. It's around a hundred dollars," TJ said eagerly. "Is that enough?"

"I'm sure it's enough. It's only a work truck."

"I came here because you brought Kansas back to me. I'm willing to tell the deputy the truth."

Daniel shrugged. "I couldn't leave the dog out limping. I know what it's like to own a pet. I have a dog, and somebody took him. I'd want him back if they found him."

TJ's eyes closed for a moment. "How horrible. I don't know what I'd do if someone took Kansas. What kind of dog is it?"

"He's a mixed breed."

"Do you have a picture of him?" TJ asked.

"I do. I got a picture on my cell phone. When I get out, would you like to see it?"

TJ eagerly said, "Yes, I love dogs. I wanna become a vet."

"Would you like to press charges, Daniel?" the deputy asked.

"No. The money is fine, and he apologized. That's good enough for me."

"Are you going to tell my dad I was here?" TJ asked the deputy.

"Technically, you never committed a crime unless Mr. Tanner changes his mind. I'm proud of you, TJ. You did the right thing. It shows you're growing up," Deputy Malcolm said.

To TJ, Daniel said, "Remember, you owe me one."

Chapter 41

🐾 🐾 🐾 🐾 🐾

The following day the deputy brought Daniel a breakfast tray. "Hey, I've started my investigation. I called the number on your phone. I talked to Virgil's ex-daughter-in-law, Tanis."

Daniel bristled. "What gives you the right?"

"I don't need your permission. You told me you wanted me to investigate, so I did. Calling Tanis was the logical choice. She said Virgil wasn't somebody to mess around with. He's ex–special ops and has an extensive criminal record. He's a loose cannon with no respect for the law. Virgil was charged with felony crimes in the past and never convicted. He's a member of the KKK."

"*Proud* member," Daniel interjected.

"That explains his ignorance. But I can't question someone I can't find. I have no clue where they are. I haven't seen them around. Do you think these are the two who took your dog?"

"I don't know, but I bet they know where he is."

"The problem, Daniel, is that your story is just that—a story. No concrete evidence. On the brighter side, I have a new gun." He lovingly examined Gramps's pistol with a smile on his face.

The sudden change was all too much for Daniel. He had begun to think the deputy was someone he could trust. Now everything was up in the air again. Misery was not a town. It was a nest of vipers.

"It's against the law. You can't do that. What gives you the right?" Daniel snapped. The deputy's smirk broadened.

"Well, boy, I *am* the law. Haven't you ever heard of lost evidence? It's one of the perks."

"How do you even cash your paycheck? You're as crooked as everybody else."

Deputy Malcolm turned. The deputy's demeanor started to change, his eyes started to squint and changed from a soft brown to the darkest of black. His face void of any emotion. His lips terse as he snarled, "Who the fuck you calling crooked? You won't need the gun where you're going. It will be an antique before you get out of prison—if you do."

"I thought you believed my story."

"That's not a story. It's a fairy tale. Except this one doesn't have a happy ending."

"You're as corrupt as they come," Daniel screamed.

"Are you accusing me of being dirty? I'm not corrupt."

"You're a fucking piece of shit," Daniel said.

"Those are mighty powerful words coming from a man behind bars."

"I was always brought up to believe in the power of the law and to respect it. You are making a mockery of it."

The deputy walked into the other room, shut off the circuit breaker, and clicked off all the power in the building. His holster and gun were gone. He slipped on a signet ring with the letter M emblazoned upon it. He took off his badge. "I gave you several warnings to leave, and I gave you the opportunity. You refused to take it." The deputy flung open the door to the cell. "I'm doing this for your own good. You left me no choice. Get up!"

"What are you going to do?" Daniel stuttered. He slowly rose.

"You've been asking for this. Just a little small-town justice." The deputy was about a foot in front of him, so close Daniel could smell the coffee on his breath. Daniel sensed the deputy wanted him to throw the first punch, but he refused. Without any provocation, Malcolm punched Daniel in the stomach. Daniel bent over from the pain. He dry heaved and gasped for air. He attempted to straighten up but was too woozy. The deputy gave him a right uppercut to the left eye, and his ring cut deep into his cheek. Daniel reeled back and, while falling, hit his head on the wall. The powerful impact opened a gash on the back of his skull. He felt the warmth of blood trickle onto his neck and down his left cheek. The brutal assault caused his left eye to water. It started to swell.

"Just as I thought," the deputy said. "Stay there and lie down, boy. Come on, hero. Do or die. Here's your chance to escape."

Daniel lay confused and breathing in short little gasps like a small fish suddenly yanked out of a cool stream.

The deputy cast a final chilly look at his handiwork. He laughed icily and chuckled, "Well, boy, you ain't a hero. Heroes," he contemptuously added, "get back up."

The cell door clanged.

Everything went dark.

Chapter 42

❀ ❀ ❀ ❀ ❀

MONDAY, JUNE 29, 2015

Daniel could hear a clamor from the front room on Monday morning, making him jump. He covered his head with his wool blanket. A short time later, he listened to the cell door open.

An unfamiliar voice called out, "Are you awake?"

Daniel lay motionless under the blanket facing the wall.

"I said, are you awake?"

"Yeah, I'm awake," Daniel grunted.

"Here, I got a cup of coffee for you. I'll get some soap and water; you can clean up. It would help if you looked your best today—you'll be in front of the judge. We haven't met. I'm Sheriff Clint Grayson. After we eat, we'll go to the courtroom. Don't give me any problems, and I'll put in a few kind words for you."

As the sheriff was about to utter something else, Daniel removed the blanket from his head and attempted to stand up. He hunched over, still dizzy. Blood had dripped from the back of his head to the side of his neck and dried there. His left eye was so swollen he could barely see. He touched the gash on his cheek and felt two diagonal lines.

The sheriff's mouth dropped open. "What in God's name happened to you?"

"As if you don't know."

"No, I don't know."

"Your deputy did this to me."

Enraged, the sheriff responded, "He did what? Kenny did it?"

Daniel nodded.

"I've never seen Kenny lose his cool. You must have provoked him."

"I didn't do anything. You'll have to ask him. He said he wanted to make a lasting impression."

The sheriff passed him his coffee and ran to his office. Even from behind the barrier of a slammed door, Daniel heard what seemed to be a lot of cursing and shouting. The sheriff came back in and asked Daniel, "How come the damn assault isn't on tape? Did the power go off last night?"

"The deputy turned it off."

"Why would he do that?"

Daniel looked quizzically through his bloodied face and suggested, "No evidence."

The sheriff backed down. "I'm sorry. It's not how we operate this station. I'm going to sort this out now."

He immediately dialed a number on the landline. When there was no answer, the sheriff swore and slammed the phone down. He repeated the action several times. Each time he became more agitated.

Eventually he strode back in and snapped, "Clean up before going to court. We can't have you going in looking like you've spent the goddamn weekend in a torture chamber."

Daniel studied the sheriff from his cowboy boots to his hat. The sheriff appeared to be honest. In Daniel's judgment, he was the fairest person he had met so far. After Daniel had finished cleaning up, he lay back down, put his left arm over his forehead, and waited. It was all he could do.

The sheriff came back. "Come on," he said, "we'll get you something to eat and go meet your public defender at nine thirty a.m. Do I need to put handcuffs on you?"

"What do you think? I'm in no condition to escape."

The sheriff nodded.

Daniel shuffled to the door. He towered over the short and stocky sheriff. Outside, Daniel squinted in the sun, and his left eye immediately started to water. Daniel could barely remember what day it was anymore.

Clint ushered Daniel into the café. As they were seated, all eyes fixated on Daniel. A waitress gave them menus, and the sheriff ordered two coffees to start. Daniel stared at the menu. Nothing looked appetizing.

"Order whatever you want," the sheriff said.

"I'm not hungry."

The sheriff ordered him a bagel. "I'm sorry for what my deputy did to you," Clint said. "Maybe what we can do is have you perform your sentence in Connecticut, perhaps even community service. But if we do, you have to leave. That will mean today—not tomorrow, not Wednesday, but today."

"I don't think so," Daniel said. "I'll take my chances with the judge. Somebody needs to hear me."

Daniel's determination for justice did not appear to improve the mood of the sheriff, who swiftly found a newspaper to plant his nose in. When they finished eating in utter silence, they walked over to the courthouse, where the sheriff put him in a cell. "I'll send the public defender down."

Daniel sat in the cell, dejected, and poised to get railroaded into prison.

After a time, a man in a three-piece suit entered and said, "Are you Tanner?"

Daniel nodded without acknowledging his presence.

The man blanched at Daniel's wounded, bloodied state. Like all attorneys, though, he swiftly recovered his poise and, in an accent smooth enough to lubricate a squeaky wheel, said, "Daniel, I'm the district attorney. These are some severe charges you have lodged against you. It doesn't look too good. But obviously, we, or rather you, are not looking too good either. I do not know what happened here, and I don't want to know, but Misery does not conduct business in this manner."

Daniel looked at the sweet-talking lawyer with distaste. At least the deputy was direct. This fellow was nearly the worst of them all, he thought. He snapped, "What exactly are you trying to say here?"

The DA's smile became even greasier. "Look, son, the situation isn't looking too good for either of us. There has been a series of misunderstandings. How about a compromise? I'm sorry this happened to you. We would be willing to drop the charges against you if you drop any potential lawsuit against the town. I hope we can end it here and sign the appropriate paperwork to expunge your charges, and you can walk out of here a free man. You should consider yourself lucky."

Daniel was shocked. His mouth hung open. He thought. Can this be happening? Am I going to be free? There has got to be a catch. There was always a catch in Misery. He asked, "What about my belongings and my gun?"

"You can get all your belongings. The gun stays here. When you get back to Connecticut, you can submit the proper paperwork, and we'll send it to you."

"All right, I'll sign the papers."

"We're willing to let you go today on one condition. You must leave immediately."

Daniel and the DA went to an office, and he signed the paperwork.

Daniel walked out a free man. Daniel asked for his cell phone back at the jailhouse, and the sheriff finally found it plugged into the charger on the office wall. Daniel noticed quite a few missed calls, some from Gramps's nursing home, one from Jim, and two from Lindsey.

When Daniel got into his truck, he spotted an envelope on the driver's seat. He put his luggage in the back, climbed into the cab, started the engine, and let the air conditioning run. He looked in the rearview mirror. His eye was purple and swollen on top and bottom, and it looked like it felt. The gash on his face was in the form of a V, the partial remnants of the letter M.

He picked up the envelope and struggled to read the contents. *Daniel, as soon as you get this message, give me a call. Deputy Ken Malcolm. P.S. I left a present for you on top of your visor.* Daniel moved the visor down, and a pair of police-issued sunglasses fell on his lap.

Chapter 43

❧ ❧ ❧ ❧ ❧

Beep, beep, beep. Travis spied Little G and Anthony headed toward the vehicle outside the gate. Impatient, the driver laid on the horn. A nonstop blast erupted from the front of the retired cruiser. Travis ran outside to confront the person before they could get there. He squinted with disdain at Anthony.

"Whoa…slow down, what's the rush?" Travis asked the driver. "What's your problem?"

"Travis, you got a second?" the deputy asked.

Before he could answer, Anthony said, "What can I do for you, Deputy Malcolm?" Anthony motioned to one of his associates to open the gate as the dark blue sedan entered the compound.

"Do I know you?" the deputy inquired.

"No. But I know who you are."

"I'm at a disadvantage then. And you are?" the deputy said.

"Anthony—Anthony Kurtis."

The deputy squinted suspiciously.

"What can I do for you?" Anthony asked.

"It's got nothing to do with you. Mind your own business," the deputy said.

250

"Such dedication, and working on your day off?" Anthony said sarcastically.

"An officer of the law is never truly off duty."

"I think the sheriff is trying to get a hold of you. I suggest you call him," Anthony said.

"You know a lot more then than I know. Ain't that strange. You his secretary too?"

Anthony's lips puckered at the sarcasm, and the mood did not improve when the deputy added, "say what? I'll answer him when I have a chance. I'm busy. But first, I need to handle this private matter."

The curt dismissal over, he turned to Travis. "Can we talk privately?"

"Sure, let's go on the porch," Travis said.

The deputy stepped out of the vehicle, wearing baggy dark blue cargo shorts and a light blue polo.

They got to the veranda and took a seat.

"What can I do for you, Ken?"

"I'm following up on an investigation."

"Finally doing your job?" Travis asked. "Aren't you a couple of years too late?"

"Why so sarcastic? What do you mean?"

"Well, when Kansas got shot, you sat on your fat ass and did nothing."

"I filed the paperwork," the deputy announced. "I turned it over to Clint. He specifically ordered me to drop the case. It was your word against his. They counterclaimed and said your dog attacked them."

"You know Kansas. He stands his ground and has never attacked anyone. They provoked my dog."

"What I don't get is, what's he doing on your property? Did you two make up?"

"I'm a Christian man; I forgave him. He's one of several investors."

"Investors in what?" the deputy asked.

"He invested in my property. He loves the community and thinks the farm has excellent growth potential," Travis said.

Deputy Malcolm looked at him quizzically.

Travis could feel his face reddening. If even he didn't believe what he was saying, why would the lawman? He hid his unease with sarcasm. "Ken, it's so nice to see you care. So, what really brings you out here?"

"I'm here on another matter. I want to let you know we are not pursuing the case regarding TJ—insufficient evidence."

"Why are you telling me? I said TJ didn't do it."

"Well, he was a prime suspect, and I wanted to let you know the outcome. Also, with TJ being a minor, you need to sign off on this complaint. Now, is there anything you want to tell me?"

"What do you mean?"

"How about telling me what's going on?"

"Is this going to be another one of your investigations? If you really must know, we're having a big Fourth of July celebration and have invited many people, some of them potential investors. Now, is there anything else you want from me?"

"You mean besides the truth?"

The two men stared each other down. "The Fourth of July isn't for another five days," the deputy said.

"So let me get this straight. My dog gets shot, and nothing gets done. We have a few people over, and suddenly you want to investigate?" Travis asked. "I presume you know the way out. I have to get back to my guests."

"Sure, no problem."

"Don't let the gate hit you in the ass," Travis said.

Travis carefully watched the deputy walk away. Behind the cocky talk, though, he was uneasy. The deputy seemed to be nosing around, and he was writing something on a pad.

🐾 🐾 🐾

Daniel picked up and examined the sunglasses before slipping them on. His eye immediately stopped watering. He was thankful they were there, but wondered why? He drove around town cautiously, aware of the condition of his release. The air conditioner blasted a cool stream. Daniel shook uncontrollably as his recent ordeal played out in his mind.

Eventually he decided to leave the city limits and tour the countryside, looking for a shady spot to make phone calls. His hand trembled as he pulled out his phone.

He called the nursing home. The charge nurse explained his grandfather had been roaming more frequently, and they had to strap him into a chair when he was awake. "He tried walking out of here and is a danger to himself," she said. Daniel could only hope his grandfather wouldn't realize what had happened. Being mortified would be the least of his problems. He must feel like a prisoner of war if the nurses continually sedated and tied him. I've got to get him out of there, he thought.

He called Jim. Jim's voice showed he was very relieved to hear from Daniel. It was uncharacteristic of Daniel not to return a call. He quickly explained his predicament. When he told Jim about the deputy hitting him, he heard his sharp intake of breath. He related the morning's activities and how he got out of the charges. Jim sounded relieved.

"Would you like my company out there to help you?" Jim asked.

"I don't know what I'm getting into myself. It is dangerous, and I don't want to put you in harm's way. I'd feel better knowing you are back home and looking after my grandfather. If I don't come back, remember, you've got the evidence in your safe. Turn it over to the authorities."

He looked at his recent calls list for the number of Beau's ex-wife in Louisiana. It had disappeared—deleted. Daniel frantically tried to remember the number. He wrote some numbers on a piece of paper. None of them looked right. He cautiously rubbed the back of his head. Could he have sustained a concussion?

Before he called Lindsey, he had to steel himself. She would be emotional, and he knew not to tell her about the beating. He kept repeating, "Be strong, be strong." He dialed Lindsey's cell phone, and she picked up after the first ring. "Daniel?"

"Hi, Lindsey," he said, trying to sound casual.

"Where've you been? I've been trying to reach you. The nursing home said Mickey is getting worse and taking off. They have him on twenty-four-hour surveillance."

"I called them, and they told me. Lindsey, I was incarcerated."

"What happened?" she asked.

"Well, it's a long story. It was a little misunderstanding."

"And now you're out? Have you found Buca?"

"Yeah, I'm out. No, I haven't found Buca. I'm working on a new lead. By the way, I never saw Leonard Scott. I checked his room at the motel. His luggage was undisturbed. It's almost like he was never there. His car is missing, which is strange. He seems to have vanished without a trace."

"Daniel, those people out there sound dangerous—be careful. Maybe Leonard got what he deserved. I should feel sorry for him, but I don't."

"Before coming to the spot where I am now, I passed by the motel again to look for the car, and still no luck. Nobody even seems to care he's missing either."

"Oh, please be careful—promise me!"

"I'll be as careful as I can, but I can't promise anything. You know I'll do whatever it takes to get Buca. I haven't come this far to fail."

"I know. That's why I worry about you. Anything you can tell me over the phone?"

"I don't know much. I can't find any answers. The town seems to be hiding a secret. Oh, one last thing. Could you look at any alternative nursing homes? I'm not happy with the way they're treating Gramps."

"Sure, I'll investigate it. I'll keep you posted. Okay? Keep in touch and stay out of trouble."

"I'll try, but trouble seems to follow me lately. I appreciate you keeping an eye on my grandfather. Please tell him I'll be home soon on one of his better days. I love him, and I miss him dearly."

He put down the phone and picked up the letter again. Why would the deputy leave such a cryptic message? What could be his motive? Hadn't he tormented Daniel enough?

He braced himself and dialed the number. "It's Daniel. You wanted me to call?"

"Aren't you going to thank me?" the deputy said.

Daniel swallowed hard. "You're the one who beat the shit out of me. Why should I be thanking you?"

"It got you out of jail, didn't it?"

"What do you mean?" Daniel asked.

"The only way you would get out of jail was for me to do something drastic: police brutality."

"Well, the sheriff seemed pretty nice, and he would let me plea bargain."

"Plea bargain?" The deputy's voice reached a higher pitch. "That piece of shit would have you plea bargain for three to five years and told me to trump up the charges to a loaded concealed weapon."

"What! He seemed—he was nice."

"Son, what planet are you living on? Of course, he seems nice; that's why he got the job. I have the report he had me type out. He won't look so nice when you read that."

"But why? How can he get away with it?" Daniel asked.

"This is a small town, Danny boy. Clint only answers to one person—himself. Well, some other people, maybe. He falsified the report."

"But the gun was empty."

"You and I know that, but the judge doesn't. The judge read the charges. It's a mandatory minimum two-year sentence. When I hit you, I had to wallop you. To make it look legit. The only way the town would get out of this is to let you go due to police brutality. We don't want another Ferguson. That incident put Missouri in the national spotlight. By doing what we did, we forced their hand. Son, I am not the bad guy, and neither are you. I am starting to see this town differently, and I don't like what I see."

"Why did you erase Beau's ex-wife's number? She was the only lead I had."

"For your own good. You don't know who you're dealing with. I went out to the farm and saw some of the characters."

"What farm?"

"Maybe before the conversation goes any further, we ought to meet in person. Somewhere private. Why don't you meet me at my house? Since you have nowhere to stay, you can clean up and change clothes this way."

"Do I have any choice?"

The question lingered without the deputy answering.

"Why in private, and why your place?" Daniel was still wary. It was a little early to become best friends with the man who had left his brand on Daniel's face without an anesthetic.

"Look, son, I know you're not gonna leave. My house is just about the only place you won't be rousted. So, you might as well stay here. This way, I'll keep an eye on you. As for privacy, our conversation ain't fit for the local diner. I'll tell you when you get here. How about we meet at one p.m.? Your call, of course." The deputy gave Daniel his address.

"Okay, I'll meet you."

"Hey, for the record, you are a hero."

"What makes you say that?" Daniel asked.

"Heroes never quit."

Chapter 44

😺 😺 😺 😺 😺

Daniel rubbed his chin and felt the abrasion of four-day-old stubble. He had never grown a beard before, nor had he even considered one, but now it seemed appropriate—with facial hair, he'd more easily fit in as one of the locals. Daniel felt his skin crawl. It had been even longer since he showered. The lump on the back of his head was still sensitive to the touch—it throbbed.

Why did the deputy want to see Daniel at his house? Was Buca going to fight, and when? How was Daniel ever going to find Buca in time? Or was he too late? Was the deputy someone he could trust? He seemed honest, but Daniel just didn't know. But then again, so did the sheriff. His fears subsided a little when he saw the officer lived in a neighborhood with other houses nearby.

He pulled into the asphalt driveway and saw the deputy leaning against a car, a retired State of Kansas police cruiser. The only remnant of service was a huge spotlight affixed to the driver's side door. The officer looked more relaxed and not as menacing out of uniform. Daniel quickly scanned the property. The residence, clad in clay-colored vinyl siding, white trim, and dark brown shutters, looked inviting. A brick walkway led from the driveway to the front stoop flanked by two wrought-iron railings. The officer motioned for him to park in the back. Daniel rolled down his window, and the deputy said, "We need to get your truck out of sight. I don't want anyone to know you're here."

Daniel hesitantly drove to the backyard. The deputy showed him where to park. He got a green tarp out of the garage and said, "Get all your stuff out of the truck. Here's a screwdriver and take off your plates. They're a dead giveaway. I don't think Clint knows your truck, but I'm not taking any chances. Give me a hand."

Daniel retrieved his belongings, took off his license plates, and put them underneath his floor mats before locking his vehicle. He turned around and saw a deck on the back of the house, complete with a small circular table. It had an orange umbrella and four wrought-iron chairs. The patio furniture was in desperate need of stain.

"I'm sorry I assaulted you," the deputy said. "It was the only way to get you out of there. I had to make it look convincing."

Daniel winced and nodded. "You certainly did."

"Here, grab this end," he said as he threw the tarp to Daniel. They covered the truck, moored the tarp with bricks, and entered the quaint structure through the side door. The house was spotless and sparse.

"Who's your interior decorator?" Daniel asked half-jokingly. He hoped the comment would ease the tension.

"My ex-wife. I got divorced about ten years ago, and I told her to take what she wanted. Evidently, she wanted everything. It doesn't bother me; I'm hardly ever home." The deputy pulled out a chair. "Have a seat." Ken neatly placed his own keys on a hanging board with eye hooks by the back door. "Here, give me your keys."

"Why?"

"Because I don't want you driving," Ken said. "I don't want to give Clint any opportunity to put your ass back in jail." He placed Daniel's keys on the board. "What did you do to Clint?"

"I've never met him before this morning," Daniel said.

"He seems to have a hard-on for you. For some reason, he wants you out of town even more than I do. I've never seen him act this way before. It seems strangely suspicious. Coffee sound good?"

"I'd rather have water, hot and cold," Daniel said.

"Come again?"

"A cold drink and a hot shower. I feel grubby."

"The water bottles are in the fridge. Help yourself."

Daniel drank the water in three large gulps, then gasped for air. He hadn't realized how parched he was. "Thanks, Deputy."

"Please, call me Ken." The officer showed him where the bathroom was and gave him a large towel, soap and shampoo. Daniel took a moment to enjoy the hot, soothing spray of the shower and then washed up as quickly as he could. He didn't want to take advantage of Ken's generosity any more than he had to.

Refreshed after a shower, Daniel sat at the kitchen table. "Thanks, I needed that."

"Let me look at your eye and see how it's healing."

"Jesus, you really branded me. Now I know how cattle feel."

"You pushed all the right buttons. I detest being called dirty." Ken hesitated and said, "How about some ice? That looks nasty. It'll get the swelling down."

"No thanks, I'll be okay."

Ken got up, got Daniel another bottle of water, and looked out the kitchen window. "If you change your mind, there's an ice pack in the freezer."

"Thanks," Daniel said. "Where do you think this event is gonna take place? Or do I already know?"

"If you're thinking the Wyatts', TJ's parents, it's what I believe too. I went out there this morning and saw several RVs in the back and wrote down some license plates. They were from different parts of the country, some far away. That asshole from Louisiana was there too. Virgin, Virgil, whatever. I saw him from a distance. I'd love to meet that redneck in a dark alley—I'd teach him some manners."

"What else did you see?"

"I only talked to the father. I felt unwelcome. In all the years I've known the Wyatts, I've never seen them act so rude. When I got out of my car, it felt surreal. I've never felt that way on previous visits. I thought I heard a couple of dogs barking. I can't be sure. Wishful thinking."

Daniel was already out of his chair. He said, "Come on, let's call in the calvary and raid the property."

Ken looked at Daniel. "To do that, I need a warrant, and when you apply for one, you need probable cause. Right now, it's just a party celebrating the Fourth of July. Point number two, Clint suspended me. We're on our own." He walked toward the front of the house to look out the picture window.

"You okay?"

"Yeah, just paranoid—very uneasy. I expect Clint to show up here sometime soon. If he does, you're going to have to hide. You need to stay out of sight."

Daniel returned to an earlier comment. "What did you mean by suspended?"

"I've been relieved of my duties pending an investigation. And Clint strongly suggested I call my union rep," he replied.

Daniel got up and got an ice pack. He felt the coldness against his skin and winced as he looked at Ken with renewed interest. "Why'd you put yourself in this position?"

"There are several reasons, partly personal. First and foremost, Clint lacks the necessary training to be chief. He ran in the mayoral race and won, yet he held on to the chief's job. He now collects two paychecks. The only thing that's changed is that I have to do his work and mine. He wasn't born a local and doesn't understand the Midwestern way of life. And lastly, I think he may be on the take. Some of his methods are circumspect, especially how he handled a case about the Wyatts and their dog. And there's nothing worse in life than a dirty cop. It's his job to uphold the law, and I believe he broke it. I'd like to prove it, and I already have some evidence."

Ken sat and put his elbows on the table and engulfed his face in his hands. "I find it hard to believe that all this is happening right under our noses. I detest the thought of dogfighting. I don't want my town known for something so hideous. And I believe your story, and I pray your dog is here."

"I'm sorry your jobs in jeopardy," Daniel said.

"It doesn't have to be. If this is all true, and the sheriff gets caught, I can exonerate myself," Ken said.

"So how do we go about proving all this?"

"I've called some people to try and gather evidence. I'm waiting to find out from them what we can and can't do and when. I know this isn't what you want to hear, but we've got to be patient. We don't even know for certain your dog is there. If we can prove he is, maybe we have grounds to raid the farm. The key right now is to try and get a hold of TJ. If your dog's on the farm, he'll know. I only saw him running toward the gate when I honked. Someone told him to stop and go inside. I think they're sequestering him. If anyone knows what's going on, it will be TJ."

"Do you know if he has a cell phone?"

"I don't know; the kid seems to have everything else."

"Do you know anybody in town that's his friend and might know his number?" Daniel asked.

"School's closed right now. TJ is sort of a loner, but I'll think about who he hangs around with, and I'll check with the principal," Ken said. "Give me a little while."

Chapter 45

WEDNESDAY, JULY 1, 2015

Daniel woke up early Wednesday morning and stared at the ceiling, reliving the last thirty-six hours. He was starting to get agitated. Yesterday Ken had gone out several times, and he claimed he never found any evidence. But was that true? Or was he hiding stuff? Daniel had little reason to trust the police of Misery, particularly a soon-to-be disgraced officer. Sitting around and not accomplishing anything, he felt hopelessness rise. He needed to do something. He needed to go to the core of the cancer: the Wyatt farm.

Ken was seated at the kitchen table. The smell of coffee brewing aroused Daniel's senses. They shared some small talk. The tension between them had eased considerably.

Ken said, "Here, I picked up something for you." He tossed a plastic bag to Daniel.

"Thanks," Daniel said as he opened up the bag. He dumped the contents on the table. It was his chain and medal, intact. He quickly put it on.

"St. Jude, huh?"

"What are you talking about?" Daniel asked.

"Your medallion is St. Jude, the patron saint of lost causes."

"It's something a dear friend once gave me. Thanks for the info. How'd you know who it was?"

"My father was a minister. I know all about religion. His church was in downtown Misery, a huge congregation. Everybody knew him and loved him. He passed away a couple of years ago. There isn't a day that I don't think about him or thank him for his guidance." Ken wiped his eyes.

Daniel roamed from room to room. He had lots of questions, and he needed answers. Time was his enemy. He felt useless. Being housebound had not helped him find his dog. He needed to do something—anything.

"Stop it. You're driving me up a wall. Here, take a seat." Ken kicked out a chair.

"I can't; I'm too restless. I feel like I should be doing something. But I don't know what. So, what am I doing? Just standing here." Daniel's voice intensified as he rubbed the scar on his hand incessantly. He looked at the board of keys by the back door.

"I don't want you going out in your truck; you'd be an easy target. I don't need you getting arrested. I know you're feeling helpless. Remember, these things take time. I'm expecting several phone calls. If you really care about your dog, you won't do anything stupid. There are going to be a lot of officers around town now. They'd lock you up in a heartbeat."

"I've got to do something!"

"What are you planning to do?" Ken asked.

"I don't know."

"Neither do I. So, take a seat, and let's figure this out."

"I appreciate your hospitality and everything, but I have to say something. It's bothering me that you're withholding information. You know more than what you're telling me. If we do this together, I need to know everything you know."

"I have to do some more checking before I tell you what I know. The information is premature—nothing concrete. Give me time. I'm working on it," Ken said.

"I don't have a lot of time, and neither does Buca."

"Slow down. Nothing is happening at the farm now."

"How do you know? Can you guarantee it?" Daniel asked.

Ken sadly put his head down and muttered, "I can't be sure. I feel it's too early for the action to begin. I should be finding out some answers later today. When I do, we'll formulate a plan."

"Mind if I do my laundry?"

"That's a great idea. The machines are in the basement. Make yourself at home," Ken said.

Daniel piled his dirty clothes together and brought them downstairs. Once he got the laundry started, Daniel went into his bedroom and retrieved his sunglasses and a pair of binoculars from the nightstand. He loosened his belt, tucked the binoculars into the back of his pants, and pulled his T-shirt over them.

Ken went to his bedroom in the interim, and Daniel could hear him on the phone. Daniel went to where Ken's car keys were, took an ignition key from the ring, and left the house.

Chapter 46

🐾 🐾 🐾 🐾 🐾

Daniel drove slowly through town in Ken's old police car. The tinted windows made it almost impossible for someone to see inside. Ken had called Daniel's phone several times, but Daniel had put his phone on vibrate. Ken must be mad as hell right now, he thought.

The population of Misery had exploded within the last few days. Pedestrians carelessly ignored crosswalks. He slammed on his brakes several times to avoid an accident. Damn tourists. They were more concerned with their iPhones than their safety. He navigated the vehicle in the direction of the Wyatt farm and found an inconspicuous spot to park. Sporadically RVs and cars went into the farm and didn't come out. Several men stood guard around the entrance to the property, and they appeared to question all who entered. One vehicle that entered without interrogation was a black Hummer. Could this be who he was looking for? He spent the time using the binoculars and noted the license plate numbers from many different states. He saw people on the farm from time to time but nothing suspicious.

After a few hours, he noticed the front gate open, and a red dirt bike exited. He assumed it was TJ, and he began to follow from afar. How was Daniel going to prey on TJ's sympathies? He knew TJ's love for animals, especially Kansas, was high. Daniel needed to make him feel empathetic.

Daniel drove toward the town and met TJ at an intersection. TJ approached the car. "Hey, Deputy Malcolm, I have the paperwork you wanted."

Daniel rolled down the window.

TJ looked like someone who had just seen a ghost. "What are you doing in the deputy's car?"

"I took it out to get some fresh air. I need to talk to you in private. How about we meet in the cornfield where I parked before?"

"Sure." With that, TJ sped off.

When they met up, Daniel said, "Where's Kansas?"

"He was limping kind of bad today. I left him at home."

"How's he doing?"

"Okay. He has those days that are tough on him."

"You never told me what happened to Kansas."

"Some asshole took a shot at him. Kansas was protecting me," TJ answered.

"I can't believe someone would do that to a dog."

"It's my fault. I should have grabbed Kansas sooner. I know he's aggressive around strangers when he feels threatened, but there was no reason to shoot. He was protecting me and standing his ground."

"There's no reason for animal cruelty. Hey, if you got a second, let me show you a picture of my dog—or the dog I used to have." Daniel took out his cell phone and showed TJ the picture. "Maybe you've seen him? His name is Sambuca."

TJ's face grew ashen, and he looked down at the ground and started kicking his feet in the soil. He stammered incoherently.

"TJ, I really need you to look. Have you seen this dog?" Daniel asked.

TJ shook his head. His eyes were huge. He stared at the picture.

"You know how much you love your dog?" Daniel asked. "Well, I love my dog that much too. And much like you, I also want to protect my dog."

Daniel got out of the vehicle, took off his shades, and slowly repositioned himself directly into the sun so that his eye began to water. If any gesture could move TJ, this would be the one.

"TJ, I know it's hard for you. But if this were your dog, you would want to know too." He noticed his tear was slowly getting to TJ as his own eyes watered. "Nobody has to know you told me. It'll be our little secret," Daniel said. "I just want my dog back. Have you seen him? Is he on the farm? Remember, you owe me one."

"I've seen that dog. That's Drake. I know who has it. Boy, he's a mean dog. Little G owns him. He keeps telling me he will make a lot of money on the Fourth of July."

"I bet he likes you and Kansas."

TJ puffed out his chest. "He does. How did you know that?"

"Because it was how I could coax Kansas in the truck. He smelled Sambuca's scent." As he showed TJ his hand, Daniel said, "See this scar? I got this when Sambuca saved my life. Much in the same way Kansas saved yours. I need to pay Sambuca back. I owe it to him to save his life, and I want to take him home where he belongs. Dogs are protective for a reason, and it's inhumane to have dogfights. The loser usually ends up being shot. Can you imagine?"

"No, I can't—they don't," TJ cried.

"Can I have your cell phone number if I need to call you?" Daniel asked.

TJ reluctantly gave him the number but told him, "Only call me if it's an emergency. I could get into a lot of trouble."

"The same kind of trouble you would get into for damaging my truck?"

"No worse, much worse. Real trouble."

🐾 🐾 🐾

Daniel came back full of news. He was thrilled with today's results, and a sense of satisfaction gushed through him.

He barely managed to say, "I saw TJ today," before it became apparent Ken was not in the mood for news. The six-foot-three deputy grabbed Daniel by the shirt and picked him up off the ground. "What the fuck are you doing? You stole my fucking car; you didn't even ask. They're going to lock you up, or something worse, somebody will kill you. You have no idea who you're dealing with. Give me the fucking key, now!"

Daniel gulped for air and tossed the key on the table. "I'm sorry, I'm sorry. I just needed to feel like I was doing something. And I have. I know where Sambuca is, and I know he's still alive. He's right where you thought he was. I need to get him out of there because he will be involved in a huge fight on Saturday."

"How did you find all this out?" Ken asked.

"Well, I talked to TJ."

"Did anybody see you talking to him? You realize your selfish actions could put TJ in jeopardy."

"No, nobody saw us."

"Are you certain? Are you positive nobody saw you?" Ken asked.

"No, I'm not positive, but no one was around where we were."

"Did you get his cell phone number?" Ken asked.

Daniel threw his pad down on the table and said, "No, he wouldn't tell me." If Ken can withhold information so can I he thought. "But here are all the license plates that have entered the farm in the past four hours. I thought it might come in handy if you do checks on them."

"I thought I told you to stay away from the farm. I should have known you wouldn't listen. Did anybody see you?"

"No, I was parked in an inconspicuous spot."

"Give me a couple of minutes. I have a source. Let me run these plates. It may take an hour or two. They'll get back to me." Ken swiped his key off the table. "Just in case you have any more brilliant ideas." He put the key in his pocket, went to his bedroom, and closed the door.

More secrets.

Ken returned fifteen minutes later. He was on his cell phone. "I'll be expecting to hear something by six," he said into the phone.

Chapter 47

"Ouch!" Daniel screamed in agony, dropping the pizza on his plate. He took his index finger and scraped the roof of his mouth. He gulped several mouthfuls of cold beer, which temporarily alleviated the pain. The loud ring of Ken's phone made him jump.

Ken answered, "Hello? Hold on—would you mind if I put you on speakerphone so Daniel can hear?...No, it's just us." Ken hit the button.

Daniel heard a female voice say, "Hi, Daniel, my name is Tanis. I apologize for hanging up on you the other day. You caught me off guard—my phone's reserved for business only. Ken, I don't even know where to start. I have a lot of other news. First, let me introduce Special Agent Jessie Ryan from the FBI."

The FBI! Daniel thought. Why are they getting involved in this?

She continued, "Sounds like you got your hands full up there. One of the vehicles is of great interest to us. It's the one with the personalized license plate and the vehicle registered to a Mr. Anthony Kurtis. He's a known associate of Mr. Dominick. It's a family who's been on the FBI's radar for quite some time. We are very interested in his activities.

"The other license plates belong to minor players in the dogfighting circuit. Some were arrested in the past, due to laws in their states, but none have done any serious time."

"I saw Mr. Kurtis on the property. What else do you know about the family?" Ken asked.

"The head of the family is Mr. Giancarlo Dominick Sr., from the New York/New Jersey area. He's ruthless and what you would think of as old school. He's heavy handed, and most people are afraid to testify against him. Which is the primary reason we haven't been able to convict him. He operates several business ventures—a few bars, vending companies, gambling, and trash hauling. It's the first we are aware he was venturing into dogfighting.

"Giancarlo also has a son named after him, nicknamed Little G. He's very protective of his son. He's the only surviving heir. Mr. Dominick is not someone to fool around with; he's very dangerous."

"Does he have any outstanding warrants, something we can serve?" Ken asked.

"No, he doesn't. He's cautious. That's where Anthony comes in. He's one of the main players, and you should never underestimate him."

Ken said, "How could I be so blind?"

Tanis chimed in, "Ken, it's not your fault. Crime is like cancer. If left untreated, it spreads quickly. It doesn't take much. Besides, we haven't told you everything yet. My ex-father-in-law is dangerous. I know for a fact Virgil carries several guns, with proper permits. He's very active in the gaming business. He has several kennels spread throughout Louisiana. What do you know about the Wyatt family, Ken?"

"I've known them most of my life. The Wyatts are hard-working pillars of the community. When they were younger, the twins were a little reckless, nothing unusual. One of the twins died tragically, and the other one, Travis, took over the farm. He had trouble handling it by all accounts too. They were poor, and their property was in disrepair. Recently they seemed to have come into a massive influx of money. They restored their barns and their house and got new vehicles.

"They have a son named TJ, who has always been nice, like his parents, but then they recently became reclusive and rude. I tell you, I sure didn't feel welcome when I went there. They were cold. I find it hard to believe they'd be involved. What would make a family turn like this overnight?"

"Money," the agent said.

"In desperate times, people will do anything to survive," Tanis added.

"They led a simple life, and they have plenty of farmland," Ken said.

"Speaking of land, what do you know about their property?" Tanis asked.

"The land has been in their family for generations. That's all I know," Ken answered.

Jessie said, "Well, I can add a little to that, Ken. I've done extensive research, but keep in mind these details are sketchy. During the Civil War, Kansas was a bipartisan state. The war pitted brother against brother. In Misery, particularly at the Wyatt farm, troops from both sides pilfered whatever food and livestock they had. This caused the Wyatt farm to go into bankruptcy. Outraged, Elijah Wyatt somehow managed to have peace talks on his property with the major players, including President Abraham Lincoln, Generals Robert E. Lee and Ulysses S. Grant, and authored a declaration of surrender. In thanks for arranging the summit, President Lincoln gave them federal immunity, wiping out all back taxes and suspending future payments until Elijah Wyatt became financially sound. In doing so, President Lincoln created a sovereign nation. This all occurred six months before the final surrender. We uncovered some documents that stated Lincoln would revisit this decision down the road, but we all know how that ended."

"What do you mean by a sovereign nation?" Daniel asked.

Jessie said, "Well, there is its crux and the cause of all our problems. A sovereign nation means it is immune to the law. We have no jurisdiction there. There is a loophole. Somehow, Mr. Dominick discovered this. But it is real, and it would apparently take a presidential injunction to change it. And I don't think that's high on Barack's to-do list. The only thing that can end this status is if the Wyatts cease to farm. Should that occur, the government would buy the land at current market value, and they would create a historical landmark."

"What does this all mean when it comes to Buca?" Daniel asked.

"Essentially, it means you can't arrest anybody on the property, no matter what they are involved in or doing. It's one of them little historical quirks."

"You're kidding me, right? So, what can we do?" Ken asked.

"Nothing. The family would have to cede the property to the government and lose all entitlement to the land. This is why Mr. Dominick is so dangerous—calculating. He does his homework and finds loopholes. He didn't happen on the property by chance. Our hands are tied."

"Well, mine isn't. What about when they leave the property?" Daniel asked.

"The illegal happenings are occurring on the property," Jessie said. "Once the Dominicks leave, they are no longer participating in a criminal event. And while they are on the property, they are doing nothing illegal. It's a perfect crime. Unless there's concrete proof of what they are doing, with no witnesses, we have no evidence. The best-case scenario is stopping the vehicle while your dog is in it. We could charge them with kidnapping or theft of personal property. But then it's only a misdemeanor—and we still need a reason to stop the vehicle first. The FBI doesn't want to jeopardize our case over a stolen dog. We're looking into changing the laws on dogfighting. Unfortunately, it's going to take several years."

"I don't have several years. My dog's life is at stake. If you can't help save him, I will," Daniel yelled.

Silence.

Eventually Tanis said, "I'm sorry, Daniel. I've tried exploring every possibility but have come up with nothing. It isn't going to be easy. I'm as frustrated as you are. The thought of my ex-father-in-law participating in the event curdles my blood. There's nothing I'd like better than to see Virgil behind bars, rotting in prison. You can keep a close eye on their activities, but that is all you can do legally. That's why Mr. Dominick is so dangerous—he's always one step ahead."

Daniel slammed his fist on the table and then stammered, "Isn't there anything we can do? My dog's gonna die. I gotta save him."

"Calm down, Daniel," Tanis said.

"Don't tell me to calm down. It's not your dog!"

"We can't have you compromising our investigation," Jessie said.

Voices of reason were swirling around Daniel's head, but he wanted nothing to do with them. Instead, he shouted, "I will do whatever it takes to save my dog, and to hell with your investigation. It's not my problem. You've let this happen for so long, and now you want hands-off? You say you been investigating the Dominick family; how could you not know this is going on."

"We had an agent undercover. Unfortunately, we haven't heard from him in several months. But that's not unusual in cases like this."

"That's not my problem."

"I'm part of the United States government. I'm warning you not to get involved. It's a federal offense," the agent said.

"Fine, arrest me."

"Ken, arrest Daniel on charges of interfering with an investigation," Jessie ordered.

"Can't. I don't have the power anymore," Ken said with a half grin. "I've been suspended; my hands are tied. Besides, the sheriff is corrupt. We need to end this."

"Ken, I'm going to deputize you. Raise your right hand and repeat after me," Jessie said.

Daniel grabbed the phone and smashed it on Ken's floor.

"Deputize that," he shouted.

Ken's grin widened as he uttered, "I was due for an upgrade anyway."

Chapter 48

🐾 🐾 🐾 🐾 🐾

THURSDAY, JULY 2, 2015

A short, stocky man with a thin pencil mustache weaved through the crowd with the ease of a rock star, shaking hands and exchanging pleasantries. He wore an expensive suit, and several rings embellished his stubby fingers.

Travis reassured his even more nervous wife, "Ashlee, he can't do anything. There are too many people here."

"Shush, here he comes."

Dominick smiled, but the warmth did not travel beyond his lips.

"Mr. and Mrs. Wyatt, I'm Mr. Dominick. It's a pleasure to finally meet you," he said in a thick Brooklyn accent. "I hear you requested an audience?" He took off his sunglasses, revealing several rows of crow's feet and stone-cold ebony eyes.

"Mr. Dominick," Travis began, "we appreciate everything you've done for us within the last few years. It's not that we are ungrateful. But we don't feel comfortable with what's going on here."

"The party isn't going to last long. We'll keep the noise down."

"No, that's not what I mean," Travis said.

"What's on your mind?"

"We are uncomfortable with the thought of pit-bull fighting on our property. We can get arrested."

"No, you can't. I know what I'm doing. And to prove it, several dignitaries will be coming, including the sheriff," Mr. Dominick declared.

"When we signed the papers, we had no idea what would happen."

Mr. Dominick's jovial behavior sharply changed. "What, are you trying to extort more money from me?" he snapped as his face broke into a nasty scowl. "You waited all this time to voice your concerns?"

"No, we're bothered because of our Christian values," Ashlee said, wringing her hands.

"Christian values? You suddenly got Christian values? From what I understand, you don't even attend church," Mr. Dominick scolded.

"We don't have to go to church to have Christian values. God is everywhere," Travis said.

"Cut the bullshit, Wyatt. It's funny—all the hundreds of thousands of dollars we've invested in the place, and tonight of all nights, you come to have a theological debate and complain to me? It's a little too late to turn around now. If you don't want to be around, go on vacation." He reached into his pocket, pulled out an American Express Gold Card, and handed it to Travis. "Here, carte blanche, no questions asked. Be sure to take that brat with you."

"Who the fuck are you calling a brat?" Travis seethed. "Are you talking about parental skills? I see you've done a fine job with your wiseass son."

"My comment was uncalled for. I'm sorry. Let's calm down and talk more like adults. Accusing each other's children isn't going to correct anything. What would you like to do to rectify the situation? Closing up is not an option. It's a little crazy tonight. The party is for our clientele to show them what we can offer. We only plan on doing this four times a year. Now go. You're putting a damper on my party. Give me a little time to think about the situation."

Travis thrust the gold card into Mr. Dominick's chest. "We don't need your charity! We love animals, and it's totally against our morals," he yelled. "The thought of the dogs fighting on our property and being killed sickens us."

Mr. Dominick responded, "When I invested in the farm, you were barely making ends meet. Now look at it. Sometimes you have to sacrifice something to gain something else. If there are no dogfights here, it doesn't mean they won't be somewhere else."

"At least it won't be on our property, and we don't have to see it or hear it," Travis reasoned.

"Now isn't the time or place to discuss this. We'll sit down shortly and figure out a compromise for all parties. I'm not trying to be rude, but I'm hosting a party, and I need to get back to my guests. I appreciate your thoughtfulness in having this conversation in private. But I don't expect any problems for the rest of the weekend from you. The only two options that work for you are going to the house or somewhere else. At this moment, I consider this a dead issue."

Before the last word was out of his mouth, Mr. Dominick abruptly walked away.

🐾 🐾 🐾

Daniel lay down for an afternoon nap, rolling back and forth in his sleep. His body became rigid. His nightmares about Gramps and Buca persisted.

Bam.

Ken's fist banging on the kitchen table echoed throughout the house. He heard Ken yell, "I've had it, that's it." Daniel jumped. He came out to the kitchen and saw Ken's face, eyes closed, seemingly deep in thought.

"Are you okay?"

"Frustrated, just fucking frustrated," Ken repeated.

"What's the matter?" Daniel asked.

"I've contacted several of my fellow officers to ask for their assistance, and none will help. I know Clint's behind this, but I can't prove it. Here I am, I laid my job on the line to help some of them when they needed it, and now when I need them most, they're turning their backs. It's supposed to be a brotherhood."

Daniel, for once, played moderator, noting, "Yes, but they would be putting their jobs and pension at risk. I know you did, and I sincerely appreciate it. These officers don't know me or my situation. I'm out here to bring Buca home. It's all I want. Plain and simple."

"They are officers sworn to uphold the law. They're not doing their job. Now is my one chance to prove how dirty the sheriff is. Without their help, this will be a suicide mission," Ken insisted. "Do you have any ideas how you'll pull this off? You need to be a goddamn magician with smoke and mirrors."

Daniel paused before remarking, "Let me go there alone and get my dog. You've already done enough. I don't want you involved any more than you already are. The FBI has already warned us not to interfere. I can't put your career in any further jeopardy."

"For this to succeed, we need help," Ken stated.

"Do you have the email addresses of your fellow officers?"

"I have a lot of email addresses from a group I belong to called the Tin Star. They're an association of current and retired police officers."

"I don't know if it'll work or not but let me write to them. We've got nothing to lose."

Chapter 49

🐾 🐾 🐾 🐾 🐾

Daniel punished the steering wheel, his veins popped as he held it tight. He had an abundance of emotions, ranging from frustration and anger to the extreme other end of the spectrum, excitement—the realization that Buca could only be several hundred yards away. The place was buzzing with activity. He carefully placed the old police cruiser in a spot on the side of the road, camouflaged by bushes and trees. He had limited solutions. Still, he must find a plan of action.

Amid all this chaos, at least one thing was clear: no one was going to help him. He was alone. All he could do was think of Gramps. Past conversations with Gramps about crimes, raids, the element of surprise, and how to solve dilemmas had made planning and preparation a big part of his life. What would Gramps do in this situation? He wished Gramps were coherent enough to counsel him.

The phone rang. An unknown number from Misery popped up on Daniel's screen. Since he didn't recognize the number, he was hesitant to answer. Who had his number other than Ken? And Daniel had smashed his phone. Besides, he didn't want to speak with anyone anyway, so he shut off his phone.

He needed a plan. Where to start? He couldn't do anything right now. There were too many people, and some might have guns. Ken was right about this being a suicide mission. A well-planned event with an element of surprise was a typical ploy his grandfather had used to trick suspects into revealing their deep, dark secrets.

Daniel formulated his plan as the sun started to set and night fast approached. Step one, understand the layout of the Wyatt farm. Step two, locate Buca. Finally, an escape plan under cover of darkness.

He'd call TJ, as he knew the farm better than anybody. He knew the back ways in and out. But was Daniel putting TJ's life on the line to save his dog? Was he selfish? I'll let TJ decide, he thought. With little or no other options, he turned his phone back on, dialed TJ, and got his voice mail. His heart sank. He didn't leave a message. But within seconds, his phone rang.

"Who is this? You dialed my number?" the caller asked.

"TJ, it's me, Daniel. Are you home?"

"Yes, I'm up in my room. My parents told me I had to stay here."

"What's going on there tonight? I see a lot of people coming in. Is there a dogfight? Is Sambuca—I mean Drake—going to be fighting?"

"Mr. Dominick is throwing a party. There are a couple of matches going on. Drake is not fighting tonight."

"Well, I need your help."

"I've told you, my parents have grounded me."

"When's the last time you listened to your parents?"

"Ummm—never?"

"Why start now?" Daniel said.

"Where are you?" TJ asked.

"Just outside your property, a few hundred yards beyond the gate. Come and get me. Leave Kansas in your room. He would be a distraction."

Daniel waited for TJ. He didn't disappoint, showing up a minute later. "TJ, can you get me inside the property and point out what each barn contains?"

TJ said, "There's a latch gate about fifty feet down the road. Let's go there."

Once inside the perimeter, TJ started to point out the barns.

The party was in full swing, and the Mafia dons were well soused. They had tents set up with tables and chairs underneath. Loud music filled the air, and it was easy to wander around unobserved.

Daniel and TJ had to be careful because it was a full moon. They went by the side of the house for cover, and from here, they could hear Travis and Ashlee talking on the front porch. Their conversation appeared to be about Mr. Dominick and how much they detested him. Then TJ stepped on a branch, and the conversation stopped.

"Who's there?" Travis bellowed. He jumped up out of the swing, and Ashlee almost fell off.

"Shush, dad," TJ said.

"TJ, what are you doing out here? I told you to stay in your room," Travis whispered.

"It's all my fault," said Daniel.

"Who's that?" Travis asked.

TJ came around the side of the house with Daniel in tow. "Mom and Dad, I'd like you to meet Daniel. He had his dog stolen back where he lives, and his dog is out in our barns."

Travis said, "I know you." He paused for a moment. "I'm sorry about the other day. It was rude of me not to thank you for bringing Kansas home."

Daniel said, "Are you going to turn me in?"

"No, why would I? You're not the problem," Travis said.

"I'm amazed you're letting this happen on your property," Daniel stated.

"Whoa—keep your voice down. I'm as disgusted as you are, and I don't know how to get out of it. This was never my intention. I was coerced into this and had no idea what they were doing."

Ashlee's motherly instinct kicked in as she asked, "Why is my son with you?"

"It's my fault he's out here," Daniel said. "I asked for his help."

"You're putting my kid in grave danger," Travis said. "Let's go inside. Someone could hear our conversation out here."

Travis led them inside a dark house, turned on a dim kitchen light, and drew the curtains in the parlor. "Please, take a seat."

"Do you know when the fights are taking place?" Daniel asked.

Travis hesitated a moment., "They have some going on tonight. The big event is Saturday at nine thirty p.m. Which dog is yours?"

"Mine is the black one with the white spot over his left eye. They now call him Drake, but his real name is Sambuca."

"The dog's got nice markings, but he's one mean dog," Travis said.

"Oh, he's not mean to Kansas and me," TJ chimed in.

"I thought I told you never to go in those barns. You shouldn't see what they do there.'

"Well, Doc had been helping Kansas out with his hip. That's how it started. He told me not to tell anybody, and I kept my word."

"Daniel, what exactly are you doing here?" Ashlee asked. "I don't know what you're planning to do, but please leave our son out of it."

"I'm not sure yet. I needed TJ to show me the land layout before I formulated a plan. I'm sorry. It wasn't my intent to put your son in danger. But I'm desperate and have nowhere else to turn. I need to know what's in every barn, down to the smallest detail. Even something you may think is insignificant could be crucial. Will you help me?"

Travis did not even stop to think. He said, "It would bring us enormous satisfaction to stop that arrogant a-hole."

Travis got a paper and pencil and sketched various structures, talking as he drew. "The first series of buildings are closest to the gate. That's where I stored all my tools. They now use it to house everybody's guns and cell phones. Nobody on the property carries firearms except Anthony. The entrance is secured with a deadbolt. Anthony bragged that the state-of-the-art lock could even withstand a high-caliber bullet. The door is impenetrable. To my knowledge, there are only two keys. Anthony has one, and security has the other." Travis pointed to the drawing. "These two barns over there are mine and house my equipment. They never go in there.

"The back barns have been converted into a kennel." Travis tapped on the sketch. "This is where the veterinary clinic is. The doc lives up on the second floor. He seems to be no danger—he doesn't come out at night and keeps to himself. I imagine he'll be there when the fights occur.

"The main barn, converted to an arena, is where all the matches occur. The only way in or out is through two double doors. The last barn here is where Drake is. It's air-conditioned, and he's the only dog in there. He belongs to Mr. Dominick's son, Little G. The barn has a lock system. You can only get in with a thumbprint ID. TJ, how did you get in there?"

"I went on the computer and did some research. I also found out how to add my fingerprint," TJ answered.

"I have keys to some buildings, but not the ones where they house any of their property. How do you plan on pulling this off?" Travis asked.

"I'm open to suggestions," Daniel said. "Whatever I plan, I know it will have an element of surprise. I would suggest you stay in the house on Saturday night. Once again, I apologize for having put TJ in danger. He was my only hope of getting here tonight to try to learn the layout. What can you tell me about the people involved?"

"Not much," Travis said. "Little G has blond hair and blue eyes and is an arrogant wiseass in his early twenties. Anthony is tall with dark hair and is armed. He's extremely protective of Little G. He shadows Little G's every move. And Mr. Dominick is shorter, with a thin mustache.

"The sheriff has been out here every night this week. I imagine he wouldn't miss Saturday. The rest of the crowd, we don't know. They've been arriving in droves the last few days. Several hundred feet behind our backyard, they have set up camp. There are several RVs and tents. The rest stay in town. The only thing I can assure you is nobody has a gun except for Anthony."

"Thanks for the descriptions. Can I keep the drawing?" Daniel asked. "Yes."

"Thanks, it will come in handy. I don't know how to do it, but I will be on the property Saturday night," Daniel promised.

Travis excused himself and returned with a piece of paper, which he handed to Daniel. "You might find this interesting. It's an itinerary of what will happen on Saturday night."

Daniel looked at the paper. One thing drew his immediate attention. He stared at it in disbelief. It read: "Main event fight at 9:30 p.m. Ares vs. Drake." Daniel shook as a chill ran through him.

Travis had something else in his other hand. He gave it to Daniel. It was a well-worn white cap with a red I on top of a black H, a trademark of International Harvester. "Here," he said. "You need to look like a local. Wear this."

"Travis, that's Taylor's," Ashlee said.

"Taylor wouldn't have put up with this shit. He would have helped if he was here. He'll be here in spirit. By the way, what happened to your face?"

"It was a little misunderstanding," Daniel said. As he prepared to leave, he asked the Wyatts one last question. "Do you have any toothpicks?"

Chapter 50

🐾 🐾 🐾 🐾 🐾

SATURDAY, JULY 4, 2015

It was a typical Midwestern summer night. Temperatures had swelled into the hundreds during the day, and the humidity lingered long past sundown. The barn was overspilling with spectators who struggled to move—some even complained about it being hard to breathe. The stench of cheap cigars permeated the air.

Travis saw someone open the massive double door, and smoke billowed out. The air outside was a good ten degrees cooler. He sneaked into the barn to shadow Anthony, as Daniel had asked. He saw the fight where both dogs had a death grip on each other's necks. One finally was able to get the other's jugular and was relentless in his pursuit. They called Dr. Winston to the ring. A lot of blood was spilled. The crowd was electric. The victor was barely able to stand from exhaustion.

Two guys jumped into the pit and pulled the lifeless carcass out of the ring, and several spectators booed. Travis heard someone say it had gone longer than expected. In the distance, he listened to some disgruntled bettors aggravated by their failure to pick the winner. He saw a group of men with programs in hand discussing the next bout.

Feeling lightheaded, Travis exited the barn and started salivating. He felt like his stomach was lodged in his gullet. A shot rang out—the cost of victory, he thought. Then he vomited.

"I see you enjoyed the fight," Anthony said to Travis. A hearty belly laugh ensued.

Travis took several deep breaths while Anthony went back inside. Travis followed. They removed the bloody canvas that had been thrown outside, hosed the area, and laid a new canvas for the next match. He spied Anthony talking to Mr. Dominick as they shook hands. Anthony departed.

Mr. Dominick's voice boomed over the din. "The windows are open. Place your bets. Please enjoy the complimentary drinks at the bar in the meantime. The next match is in twenty minutes."

Travis watched in wonder as hordes of people headed toward the windows to bet. He went back outside and observed Anthony approaching the guards stationed at the gate. Travis bird-dogged Anthony, using the barns for cover, in the hope of overhearing what he had to say.

"Any problem, boys?" Anthony asked.

One of the guards answered, "No, sir, it's quiet. Not a single car has gone by."

"Why don't you guys go inside and watch the last few matches."

"Gee, Mr. Kurtis, I appreciate that. I've never seen a dogfight before, and I was hoping I'd get the chance," the huskier guard answered.

"Go make some bets, here's some money. Enjoy," Anthony said.

He reached into his pocket and took out a pack of cigarettes. Three puffs later, he deadened the cigarette on the sole of his shoe and discarded it in a receptacle. Anthony left for the barn.

Travis went to work. He took out the toothpicks and put Daniel's plan in motion.

🐾 🐾 🐾

Daniel and Ken were in the old police cruiser, parked strategically about a quarter mile down from the gate. They had spent hours between Friday and Saturday reinstalling the light bar and police siren. Daniel looked Ken square in the eye. "I don't know where to start. I guess I'd say first I'm grateful for everything you've done. Because of me, you've probably lost your job and your career."

Ken interrupted, "Daniel, I'm a police officer, and I swore to uphold the law. I was doing my job. What's transpiring on this farm is unethical. If I'm losing my job, it will be on my terms, not because of that rat bastard Clint. I should be the one apologizing. I should have noticed what was going on in my community and not turned a blind eye. Have you formulated a plan?"

"Not yet. Once I give you the signal, you know what to do. Hopefully that will cause confusion. The key to the plan is to start at the beginning of the fireworks. I'll use it to my advantage and get Buca out of there. Just keep the motor running."

"You know this is a suicide mission?" Ken said.

"I know. Worst-case scenario, if they kill me, you'll have a murder investigation and can arrest the Dominicks," Daniel said. "At least it's something the FBI will investigate."

They got out of the cruiser and gave each other a big bear hug. As Daniel was about to leave, he said, "Do you hear that?"

"Yes, what is it?" Ken asked.

"It sounds like a car engine," Daniel said.

"No, car engines!" Ken said, amazed.

Ken and Daniel stood spellbound, their eyes transfixed on the country road. The low hum was that of a convoy. Ken instinctively pushed Daniel behind him. He reached into his waistband, took out the walnut-handled revolver, and held it down at his side, hidden from view. Beads of sweat drizzled down Ken's face. They saw patrol cars approaching at a snail's pace as they looked on. Their headlights blacked out. Ken let out a heavy sigh as he tucked his weapon into his waistband at the small of his back. His face changed from a nervous smile to a huge grin, lighting up his eyes.

One patrolman left his cruiser and walked toward Ken and Daniel.

"Decided to crash the party after all?" Ken said to the first officer.

"I wouldn't miss it," the officer replied.

The patrolmen left their vehicles and came to where Ken and Daniel were standing. Some were in uniform, others in plain clothes. Daniel counted somewhere between fifteen and twenty officers.

"Gentlemen, this is Daniel. What changed your minds?" Ken asked.

"With such a heartfelt email, how could we not come? It was a tear-jerker. I don't know about the others, but I don't want the state of Kansas referred to as a hotbed for pit-bull fighting," said a deputy from a neighboring town. "Many of us have animals and can sympathize with Daniel's situation. Besides, we're a brotherhood, and we stick together."

Another one chimed in, "Never cared for Clint."

"A disgrace to our badge," Ken said.

"How do you want to handle this, Ken?" said the husky officer.

"Our prime objective is Daniel's dog. He's a pit bull. He's black with a white patch over his left eye. Under no circumstances is anyone allowed on the property. Our job tonight is to create chaos. We'll line the road with our cars, leaving about ten feet between each cruiser. It will provide cover for Daniel. When the fireworks start, everybody will hit their light bars and sirens and throw smoke bombs on the Wyatt property. This should cause enough confusion.

"The FBI has warned me not to do this. If you want to back out, now is the time, and I'll understand. I don't want to put anybody's career in jeopardy. For me, it's personal. The sheriff in this town is dirty, and it is my town."

"We all need to stop this. It's a black eye for our community, our state," said an officer in the back row. Others nodded.

"If any of you have bulletproof vests, I suggest you put them on. The people we're dealing with here are dangerous. I expect they'll have guns. Prepare for the worst."

Ken looked at his watch and said to Daniel, "Are you ready? Fifteen minutes to showtime."

Chapter 51

❧ ❧ ❧ ❧ ❧

Little G brushed Drake's silky hair. He avoided the few scars on his body, particularly a long one on his hindquarter. When Little G touched him on his posterior, Drake snapped at him. In a soft, soothing voice, he said, "You're such a good boy, Drake. You're gonna do great tonight. They don't know what they're in for. Good boy."

Anthony asked, "Are you nervous?"

"About what? Tonight? I'm not the one fighting. Did you make my bet for me?" Little G asked.

"Oh, shit, not yet. I've been a little busy. You have about another fifteen minutes until the fight goes off. We've got a great crowd. The odds are three-to-one against Drake. Your dad is so pleased with his venture. The closed-circuit broadcast has generated a lot of money."

"Do you think the odds will go up higher?"

"No, not enough time."

"I don't know what they see in the other dog. That redneck hyped his dog all week. He has no idea what he's in for. I heard a quote once, not sure who it came from, maybe Eisenhower, but tonight it never rang truer: 'It's not the size of the dog in the fight. It's the size of the fight in the dog.' Ya see, I do make note of things sometimes. Yes, make the bet now. I like the odds, and I know my dog."

"How much? Five hundred sound good?" Anthony asked.

Little G grunted, "No, that's chump change. Make it five grand."

Anthony blinked. "I'll be right back." Little G was sure growing up fast.

Little G could hear the music start for their grand entrance within minutes. The theme from *Rocky* played over the speakers.

The dogs and owners started to enter the barn from a separate stall. The entrance had all the pomp and circumstance of a heavyweight Vegas fight. The crowd began to hoot and holler, which created a rowdy atmosphere. Everybody, it seemed, was caught up in the moment, except for the dogs. The warriors, immune to the drama, cautiously entered the arena.

Virgil and Beau proudly marched to the center of the ring dressed in fatigues and matching T-shirts bearing an Ares likeness. "Lougarou Kennels" was printed on the back. Beau had a white towel slung over his shoulder. They marched to the pit.

Little G picked up Drake and put him over the four-foot-high wooden barricade. Virgil did the same with Ares, putting him in the opposite corner. Ares started to growl, while Drake remained unfazed and silent. Each dog was tethered by a leash and had a muzzle device on its snout. Ares, his ears cropped and tail docked, was a reddish-brown brindle mix. He appeared to be ten pounds heavier than Drake. He had a few scars on his face and one on his back, which were easy to spot. Virgil gave the leash a little slack as the handlers stood outside, which caused his dog to lunge forward, taunting Drake. Little G watched with an amused smile. This was amateur-hour stuff. That dog needed his energy for the ring. Drake was undaunted. In a gravelly voice, Virgil repeated, "Get him, boy, sic 'em, rip him apart." Drake seemed immune.

Little G stared Virgil down and stroked Drake to reassure him. The song approached the end of the track, and the pumped-up crowd echoed the refrain. A ref wearing thick leather gloves stood in the middle of the pit. He inspected each dog for any illegal devices and patted the dogs down to ensure nobody had tampered with them.

"Gentlemen are your dog's ready?" the ref asked.

The owners nodded, took their dogs off their leashes, and held onto them by the scruff of the neck. They each removed the muzzle from their combatants.

"Go," the ref said.

Ares charged toward Drake right away. As he approached, Drake deked right, and the other dog's momentum drove his body past Drake. Ares contorted in midair, jaws snapping like a bear trap in a futile attempt to attack. Once he regained his footing, he recharged Drake. They reared up and dug their nails into each other's chests, clawing and growling fiercely. Their mouths continually snapped at each other. Each struggled to gain an advantage among the blur of snarls and spit. They locked, rolled around, and then broke apart.

Ares secured a slight advantage and dug his teeth into Drake's face. The wounded Drake let out a deep, low moan, followed by a determined snarl. His muzzle had a deep gash pumping blood. They fought for five minutes until the evenly matched pair separated, unable to breathe a moment longer. However, the respite was brief before both dogs reared again, and Ares pushed Drake back. The other dog's superior size appeared too much for Drake to handle. Drake countered every time Ares moved, but the bigger, wilier dog appeared to be constantly one step ahead of him. Finally, after another bustle of teeth and agonized growls, Ares got Drake on the ground and stood over him to go in for the kill. Drake scratched Ares's eye with his paw as he reared and came down.

At precisely 9:30 p.m., the fireworks started, and blue strobe lights pulsated throughout the barn. Seconds later, though, came the most unexpected sound of sirens. The crowd in the barn quieted and started to panic. Then suddenly, all hell broke loose.

"Stand your ground," Mr. Dominick yelled. "Stand your ground. There is nothing they can do."

His advice fell on deaf ears. Pandemonium erupted, not helped by the first smoke bombs, and the crowd rushed to the exit with the same urgency as if someone had just yelled "fire."

"Anthony, what's going on?" Mr. Dominick shouted. "Do something."

Anthony raced for the gun shed.

❖ ❖ ❖

From his vantage point, Daniel could see Anthony at the gun shed. He tried the key in the tumbler. It wouldn't enter the lock. Anthony took out his cell phone, turned on the light, and inspected the lock; something had obstructed his key. He bent down and saw fragments of wood. He cried out in frustration, "Fucking toothpicks!" He took his revolver and fired at the lock—no change.

Mission accomplished, Daniel thought. Great job, Travis.

As Daniel watched these events unfold, he jumped the fence. He didn't make it on the first try; his body ricocheted off. Behind him, he heard, "Hop in." As Daniel turned, he saw Ken behind the wheel of his car. Daniel jumped in. "Fasten your seat belt."

"What are you doing, Ken?" Daniel asked.

"Change of plans. I ain't missing this! Sometimes the worst decisions in life make the best stories. We're going in the only way."

Ken quickly shifted gear. The engine roared, and Daniel shut his eyes as the vehicle crashed through the gate. The noise of the car against metal sent shivers down Daniel's spine. Once they were inside the compound, Daniel's heart raced. His ears were deafened by the exploding fireworks, accompanied by smoke bombs. The cavalry had arrived. The barn doors swung open as spectators frantically fled into the darkness with the sheriff in the lead.

Ken momentarily paused, then followed Daniel, sprinting to the main barn.

Inside, the two dogs were buried into each other, their elemental fight continuing, indifferent to the dramas outside.

Both dogs' fur was matted with blood and saliva. A few spectators lingered, enchanted by the battle, as Daniel fixed his eyes on Virgil and Beau. They stood in the corner of the temporary arena, barking orders to their prized combatants. Their voices echoed throughout the cavernous structure. Daniel watched in horror as his beloved pet, almost unrecognizable now, struggled in the fight of his life.

Ken motioned to Daniel. "Go take care of your dog. I'll go teach that redneck some Midwestern manners."

Moments later, a startled Virgil said to Ken, "What you doing here, boy? You have no jurisdiction over this property. Get the fuck outta here."

"Who said I do? I don't have my badge on either, and today I'm feelin' froggy."

Virgil swung wildly at Ken but missed. The deputy had once again put on his signet ring. It was time for another lasting impression.

Daniel yelled, "Buca."

The dog's ears perked up at the sound of Daniel's voice. He froze. Ares took advantage of the distraction to sink his teeth savagely into the back of his neck. Buca howled in pain. Daniel hopped into the ring and kicked the other dog in his hindquarters. Ares let out a large yelp, then slowly advanced toward Daniel, who cautiously backed away. He yelled "Sambuca" several times. He looked over and saw Sambuca—coughing desperately as he spit up blood. Then Buca sank to the ground, motionless.

Ares quickened his pace and sprang toward Daniel, who tried to defend himself with his right foot, but the pit bull sank his teeth deep into his boot. Daniel screamed louder than he had ever done before in his entire life. Ares turned his head from side to side, trying to rip apart the material. Daniel hopped backward and fell to the ground. Ares released Daniel's boot. He slowly inched his way toward Daniel. His mouth salivated. Daniel crossed his arms in front of him to protect his face.

Out of the corner of his eye, he saw something charge Ares. His pet came running at the pit bull with a savage combination of force and grace, looking almost as if he had discovered something he had been born to do. He locked his jaws underneath Ares's muzzle. Buca found Ares's jugular vein in two quick shakes, and he was dead before he even hit the canvas.

Daniel hobbled to his feet and rushed to his pet's side. He tore off his T-shirt in the hope of staunching Buca's blood loss, all the while saying, "Buca, Buca, it's me, boy." Buca turned his head. His soft brown eyes looked menacing, a look Daniel had never seen before.

Off in the distance, Daniel heard someone running toward him rapidly. This was the person he'd heard about—the person who had laid claim to his dog. Little G lunged at Daniel. He sidestepped him. With seven months of frustration built up, Daniel unleashed a roundhouse. He hit Little G in the upper lip and then broke Little G's nose with a second decisive blow. Little G dropped quicker than Times Square's New Year's Eve ball. Blood gushed. He lay on the ground, writhing in pain.

Daniel looked toward Ken and Virgil. They danced around in circles like two gladiators, waiting for the other's weakness to appear. Virgil hunched over and led with his shoulder and got a running start in an attempt to tackle Ken. Ken gave him a right uppercut on the jaw and straightened him up. Ken unleashed a flurry of left and right hooks into Virgil's midsection. A final quick left hook sent him sprawling.

"Get up, you asshole; I ain't done yet. Your lesson's not over."

Virgil stayed put.

Ken looked at Beau. "You want some of this, boy?"

"No, sir," Beau answered.

However, more trouble swiftly arrived as Anthony blindsided Daniel and yanked him over the barricade. He squeezed Daniel's neck in a chokehold with the finesse of a boa constrictor. Daniel tried to break the hold and punched him several times. The more-skilled Anthony got him down on the ground and kicked him repeatedly while he curled up in a ball. Anthony pulled out his gun and pointed it at him. Daniel closed his eyes.

Just then, a second blur arrived as Kansas raced in. If there was vengeance going on, Kansas planned on joining the party. The enraged dog sank his teeth hard into Anthony's calf, and he screamed in pain. Anthony was not so easily dropped, though. He hit Kansas in the head with the butt of the gun. The impact caused Kansas to drop. Stunned, he continued to stare and growl at Anthony. "I should have done this a long time ago," Anthony shouted, aiming the gun at Kansas.

A gunshot echoed throughout the barn. Smoke billowed from the gun as TJ stood there proudly. "I should have done *this* a long time ago," he responded. He had shot Anthony in the kneecap.

293

"You shot me, you little fucking bastard!" Anthony yelled.

He fell to the floor, and Kansas jumped on top of him, heading with great purpose for his throat.

"Call him off," Daniel said to TJ.

"Why? He deserves it," TJ answered.

"Call him off. We can't be doing this," Daniel yelled. TJ reluctantly called Kansas off. Anthony thrashed in pain on the ground. He was a beaten man.

Daniel limped his way to the arena, which was slippery with blood. Gingerly, he picked up Buca, carried him over the barricade, and gently lay him down. He examined his wounds. The blood had temporarily stopped. Buca panted heavily. A low growl emanated from him.

"It's okay, boy. It's me," he said in a reassuring tone. "I'm here for you. I love you, Buca." Daniel cautiously hugged his dog and kissed him on the forehead. Buca looked at Daniel as he cocked his head.

Chapter 52

🐾 🐾 🐾 🐾 🐾

Travis was outside—with Mr. Dominick. They sprinted into the barn to see what had transpired upon hearing the gunfire.

It was a spectral scene. A recovered Anthony had his gun in his hand and pointed it at TJ.

"What the fuck you doing?" Travis screamed.

He let go of Mr. Dominick, raised his rifle, and pointed it at Anthony. "Drop the weapon—now."

"No, Anthony, put it down," Mr. Dominick ordered.

Anthony paused. "That fuckin' kid shot me."

"No, Anthony, drop it," Mr. Dominick said. "Don't make it worse than it is. We don't do our business in public. It's over, at least for now." He turned to one of the deputies. "You have no authority to do this; you're not even on any force. Technically you're trespassing."

"They are my guests," Travis said. "I invited them here."

Out of the corner of his eye, Mr. Dominick saw Little G struggling to stand up. He was a bloody mess. A less-than-sympathetic state trooper started to serve Little G a warrant.

"You have no jurisdiction here. You have no grounds to serve my son a warrant," Mr. Dominick threatened. "You need to serve it to them—they're the trespassers." He snarled at Ken, "You're not even on the force anymore. I'm going to be talking to Clint real soon about this. You are going to be doing hard time."

"You want to talk to Clint? He'll be in jail, right alongside your ass," Ken said. "As soon as the lights went on, those cockroaches scurried into the darkness, with Clint leading the way."

"You have no idea about this place. I got a legally binding agreement; I lease this property. It's a farm. A special farm. You can't serve me here," Mr. Dominick ordered.

Ken looked at Travis and said, "Is this true? I heard you don't farm here anymore, that you ain't farmed here for more than a year."

Anthony bellowed, "That lazy fuck—"

"No, Anthony, don't say a word," Mr. Dominick said.

Anthony completed his sentence. "That lazy fuck hasn't farmed here in almost two years."

Ken paused for a second. "Well then, your immunity is gone. Court opens Monday. Arrest them all. We'll have it figured out by then."

"On what grounds are you arresting us?" Mr. Dominick asked.

"Once Travis stopped farming, this became federal property, so trespassing and dogfighting are prohibited," Ken said.

"But you have no witnesses," Mr. Dominick said. "Who's going to testify against us?"

"I will," Travis said.

"No, we will," Ashlee said.

"Wyatt, you're writing your death sentence."

"I hope you're not threatening them," a trooper said, "because that will be another charge."

"What are the other charges?" Mr. Dominick asked.

"Kidnapping in the first degree, cruelty to animals, and theft of property. That's for starters."

"Kidnapping? It's just a fucking dog. Are you arresting me for dogfighting? That's a misdemeanor. I'll be out in a few hours. Besides, they're just dogs. Nobody got hurt," Mr. Dominick said. "What's going on? This is a farm that raises livestock only to butcher them later on. What we're doing is harmless fun. You're worried about a few dogs?"

"What you're doing is cruel. Dogs are bred for companionship and obedience," Ken replied.

"Well, my dogs were doing what I wanted them to do. They were obedient—they fought," Mr. Dominick countered.

"Oh shut up, you sick fuck, save your story for the judge," Ken snapped, ending the dialogue. "Get your hands behind your back."

Ken unsnapped his leather pouch and slipped the handcuffs on Mr. Dominick's wrists. He tightened them, forcing Mr. Dominick's skin to pucker. "Get him out of here." He shoved Mr. Dominick in the back toward the cruiser.

As they walked out, Ken said to one trooper, "We'd better get a couple of ambulances and a tow truck."

🐾 🐾 🐾

Daniel approached the Wyatts and extended his hand. "I don't even know how to thank you. Without you, I never would have gotten my dog back. I'm entirely indebted to you. You put your lives in danger to help me get my dog."

"We are grateful too. Through this, our family is back together. No matter what happens now, we are independent again. We've learned blood money is bad money," Travis said.

Daniel reached into his back pocket and took out the white cap. "Here, I didn't need this tonight. Maybe it brought me luck." He handed Taylor's hat back to Travis.

"No, it's yours. Please, keep it. Your actions remind me of something my brother would have done. He would have been proud of you."

"Thank you, Travis. I'll cherish the hat."

"Besides, you need to stop dwelling on the past and start thinking about our future," Ashlee said to Travis. "The cap is one less reminder."

Daniel gave Ken a big hug. "And you. I can't even think of the words to say. I can say nothing that will be worthy of what you've done for me and the chances you took. You risked your career."

"Thank you for helping me," Ken said. "As of tonight, I will finally be the boss. That little weasel Clint is out there somewhere. I can't wait to track him down. He showed his true colors tonight." He broke into a big grin.

Daniel, Buca, and Ken walked to the Wyatts' backyard near the doctor's barn. "You know what you need to do now, right?" Ken asked.

"Go home," Daniel replied with a heavy sigh.

"You know what I'm talking about."

"No, I don't know what you're talking about."

"Deep down, you know the dog is no longer a pet. It killed another dog. Your dog is dangerous. I can't have him in town. He needs to be put down," Ken said.

"I've come all these miles to save him, and now you want me to kill him?" Daniel said with disbelief heavy in his voice. "He's not going to be in your town. I'm taking him back home."

"Well, I can't allow it. He's a trained killer."

"No, he's not. He was protecting himself."

"Daniel, I respect you. But I can't let it go on. If there were some other way, I'd let you go. But I can't. I'm acting sheriff now, and I can't overlook anything. The other sheriff ignored everything, and that's why we had a problem. If you don't have the heart, I understand. I'll do it."

"Nobody is going to touch Buca again. If anything happens, it has to be from me."

"Daniel, I'm truly sorry. I know all you've gone through and how you feel about your dog."

"If you did, you wouldn't be asking me to do this. So, no, you don't know how I feel."

"Here, take this." Ken handed him his grandfather's gun. "I know how much it means to you." Ken inserted the clip. "If you can't do it, I will."

Daniel was reluctant to take the pistol from the sheriff, knowing once it was in his hands…

Ken once again offered Daniel the gun. He forcefully grabbed Daniel's hand, opened it, and slapped the weapon in his palm.

Daniel and Buca trudged to the back of the property in the darkness. With each step, the darkness enveloped them a little more. Vapor from smoke bombs lingered in the pasture, creating an eerie scene. Daniel murmured to Buca to calm him.

Overhead, the almost forgotten fireworks finale illuminated the sky with patriotic colors. They reached a spot deep in the field where all they could see were the flashing blue lights in the distance.

Daniel told Buca to sit. Buca stood there and growled a little and cocked his head. He was not the same dog. Ken was right. Again, Daniel commanded Buca to sit. This time Buca stared at Daniel. Daniel pushed Buca to get a reaction. "Come on, you stupid dog, get aggressive. Give me a reason. Just one."

Buca looked at Daniel with sad eyes, then suddenly sat as if a new reality was clicking into place.

"Why did you sit? Why'd you listen to me? It would be easier to shoot you if you didn't listen. You remember me!"

With a heavy heart, Daniel looked skyward. He spoke softly. "Give me some guidance or an omen, Mom, Dad, God, anybody. Give me a sign. A sign what I'm doing is right. I'm not here to play judge, jury, and executioner." The final scene of *Old Yeller* flashed in his head.

He knew the sheriff was right. Logically at least. Buca had become a trained assassin. If he ever injured someone in the future, it would always be on Daniel's conscience. But could you train a dog back? His hand trembled as tears rolled down his cheeks. He choked back the emotion. "Buca, I'm sorry. I'm so sorry!" he said. He couldn't bear to look at Buca while he shot him. Daniel took the safety off, aimed, closed his eyes, and pulled the trigger. Bang. A shot rang out. When he opened his watery eyes, Buca still sat there, startled.

Daniel had to keep his eyes open or miss him again. He aimed with his still shaking hand as tears flowed. He locked his left hand on his right wrist to control the weapon and fired, bang, bang, in rapid succession. To his amazement, Buca just sat there, staring.

Suddenly, Daniel realized what the last practical joke Gramps received from his fellow officers had been. The gun clip was loaded with blanks.

He reflected on the cryptic message in the note. "This gun is an appropriate gift that may someday save your life or someone else's."

It was over. Daniel had experienced enough of Misery and Misery law. It was time for him to take his own road. As sirens blazed into the distant night, he said, "C'mon, Buca, Gramps needs us. Let's go home, boy."

At the word "home," Buca's tail wagged. He trotted on, tail held high for the first time in months.

Home. He knew what that meant.

About the Author

✻ ✻ ✻ ✻ ✻

G lenn was born and raised in Wallingford, Connecticut. His hometown pride and small-town values are reflected in his writing. Glenn enjoys spending time with family and friends. Having owned an assortment of pets, he is an avid animal lover and once bred a litter of AKC Registered Akitas. Glenn enjoys writing and challenging puzzles which are his favorite past-times.

His quirky sense of humor and razor-sharp wit is included in his debut novel *Blood on the Scarecrow*. Glenn currently resides in Myrtle Beach, South Carolina with his family.

If you would like to connect with Glenn, please visit his website www.glenncanning.com.

Ingram Content Group UK Ltd.
Milton Keynes UK
UKHW020931260423
420810UK00016B/645

9 798885 908399